PanEuro

Sprinter of the Skies

Thomas Brant

CHAPTER 1 – Chaos
Thursday 7th April 2022

Sarah Marsh was sat in the Ramsgate offices of Sprint Air, a brand-new Manston based, A320neo planned, airline which had been formed to take advantage of a recent court ruling, that RiverOak Strategic Partners and PanEuro must, on pain of judicial sanction, open up Manston Airport's facilities to rival carriers under open-access regulations. It was a ruling that sent shockwaves through PanEuro's mahogany-lined boardroom and elation through the corridors of Sprint Air's modest office suite on the northern apron. Sarah, however, wasn't celebrating just yet.

Only 12 months ago, she had been part of PanEuro as a trainee stewardess, a role that had promised glamour and retro prestige but delivered sexism, powdered noses, and the suffocating aroma of nostalgia clinging to the fuselage like damp. The final straw had been Shannon. The slap. Hargreaves. After that scandal, Sarah had walked—no, marched—out of PanEuro's PR-obsessed regime, straight into the freezing sea air of Kent's bleak spring, unsure whether she'd ever don a uniform again.

Yet here she was. Sprint Air. New airline. New rules. No powdered noses.

And not in the galley.

Instead, she was taking her first flight as a First Officer.

Over the past nine months, Sprint had been using an ACMI—an Aircraft, Crew, Maintenance and Insurance—

lease from a Romanian operator with aging A319s. A necessary evil, the directors had argued, while their own brand-new A320neo remained mired in supply chain delays and bureaucratic logjams. It was far from ideal, but it kept the route authorities happy and the slots warm. Now, at last, the first of Sprint's own aircraft was on the ramp, gleaming in the fragile April sun, its pristine Pratt & Whitney engines whispering promise.

Sarah had completed her type rating at Easyjet 6 months earlier, her former RAF training meaning that her initial ground school and sim time had passed in a blur of muscle memory and suppressed adrenaline. She had been faster than most, not because she was a prodigy, but because flying was no longer theory to her—it was instinct. The irony of being passed over at PanEuro for a cockpit spot because their management, a mixture of Lords from the House of Lords and Rothschild & Co, had wanted men in the cockpit, women in the galley, because of a romanticism with the Pan Am era of cocktail dresses, captain's caps, and First Class steak tartare, wasn't lost on her. She'd seen right through it, of course, and when she'd refused to keep quiet after Hargreaves' mid-flight assault on her friend, Hayley Northcott.

And how Sarah had helped the First Officer land the plane, as Hayley had restrained the errant Captain.

And yet, none of that mattered now.

Today, Sarah wasn't a headline. She was a pilot.

She turned her eyes to the airside tarmac beyond the tall windowpanes of Sprint's dispatch office. There it stood:

G-SPTA. The very first aircraft registered to the fledgling Sprint Air fleet. Still practically factory-fresh, the livery wasn't quite as bold as the mock-ups had promised—more restrained, with navy blue cheatlines and a crisp, white fuselage flanked by a red stylised 'S' on the tail. But it was real. Tangible.

And all economy.

Sprint was an ultra-low-cost carrier with ambition, edge, and absolutely no pretence. Its aircraft didn't serve champagne in bone china, nor did they pander to heritage. There were no curtains, no flight attendants in pencil skirts mimicking 1960s charm. There were seats, oxygen, and thrust. Sprint's mantra was direct: safety, speed, savings. No frills, no fantasies. For Sarah Marsh, that was liberation.

She adjusted her collar—navy, not PanEuro teal—and checked her watch. Thirty-seven minutes to push. She ran a fingertip along her flight plan, a modest trip to Lisbon, ironically timed to depart at 10:05, the same time, Sarah knew, as fellow PanEuro veteran and fellow female First Officer Hayley Northcott was scheduled to depart London Gatwick for the same route, easyJet flight EJU8513 to Lisbon, the same route, the same airspace, and potentially the same final approach slot at Humberto Delgado. That fact amused her. A quiet race. A silent siblinghood of sorts, forged through shared frustration and sky bound ambition. Different airlines. Same battle.

Hayley Northcott: *Hey Sarah, can't believe your first flight's today! Lisbon twins?? How long's your turnaround there?*

Sarah smiled as the message flashed up on her phone. She thumbed a quick reply, her heart warming to the idea that she wasn't entirely alone in the clouds.

Sarah Marsh: *Lisbon twins for sure. 40 mins on ground if they're punctual. Next sector is a LIS to EDI then an EDI to MSE. You?*

Hayley Northcott: *Covering a LIS-MXP and then back on my normal MXP-LGW rotation later. One of the FOs from the Lisbon bases went off sick, so I've been pulled off a Geneva.*

Sarah gave a soft laugh, thumbed a "typical!" and slipped the phone into the side pocket of her flight bag. The idea of Hayley, fierce and unflappable, being bounced around the network like a deck of shuffled cards brought back memories of their brief overlapping days at PanEuro—two women chafing against a regime that was all trim and no turbine.

"First Officer Marsh?" The voice at the door belonged to Captain Neil Costello, a tall Liverpudlian with crow's feet from years in the sun and the calm of a man who'd once landed a 737 with a failed rudder actuator in Faro and barely broke a sweat. He offered a warm, professional smile as he entered the room, flight folder under his arm. "You ready to make history?"

Sarah stood, extended a hand. "Born ready."

Costello gave a soft chuckle and nodded toward the apron. "Let's go meet the girl then."

They walked together to the BYD Dolphin parked outside the offices that were on Ramsgate seafront, the small electric car humming to life as Costello tapped the ignition. Sprint's fleet of crew cars was as modest as the rest of the operation—eco-conscious, bare-bones, and just about functional.

Sarah knew that the 15-minute drive from the town centre to Manston was both a commute and a ritual. A chance to shed ground thoughts and attune to the rhythm of the sky. As the Dolphin glided up the chalky coast road past Pegwell Bay, she could just about see the radar tower at Manston rising on the horizon like a strange, skeletal lighthouse. Costello offered little small talk—Sarah appreciated that. He sensed, perhaps, that this was a moment she wanted to sit with.

"You know that they've closed the old road now," Costello said as they reached the Lord of the Manor roundabout, nudging the Dolphin onto the bypass that skirted the old Thanet Earth glasshouses. "We can't go through the village of Manston, but the new access road."

Sarah nodded, as she remembered that, earlier in the week, Kent County Council, because of the launch of Sprint and its ULCC operations, had closed the Manston Road just past the village of Manston, making it for local residents only, with the new access being off the Sevenscore Roundabout, a dual carriageway tunnel which went under Manna Hutte, under the runway, and then surfaced south of Manston village, between the runway and village, leading to the terminal. That, and a new link road for the new shuttle bus service to the upcoming Thanet Parkway station that was due to open in 2023 meant that he airport, at long last, was feeling more like an airport and less like a relic of a Cold War airbase.

As the Dolphin emerged from the tunnel, Costello took the slip road marked "Airport Staff Only", which lead to a gated car park for aircrew, both of PanEuro, Sprint, Qatar Cargo and IAG Cargo crews that were that were now frequenting Manston in growing numbers. Though small, the once-abandoned apron had come alive with movement. Sarah could see a Qatar 777F shimmering in the haze by the cargo hangars that were at the west end of the 9,016 foot runway, sitting next to an Iberia branded A321, one of the passenger fleet of IAG that was seconded to freight capacity during the quiet post-COVID shoulder months.

On the passenger stands, however, was a mix of A320neo and A321LR/prototype A321XLR planes in the PanEuro livery, a SingAir A330 and the sole Sprint aircraft: G-SPTA. Parked proudly at Stand 5, its new paint glinting with ambition, the jet looked fresh enough to smell of sealant and polymer. It was almost out of place beside PanEuro's trio of retro-themed narrowbodies, who's painted cheatlines and nostalgia-tinted fuselages still clung to the fantasy of a golden age that had never really existed.

Sarah noticed the SingAir A330, and how it was an oddity, as they were a new airline, and normally used Heathrow as their British hub—yet here it was, on a windy apron in East Kent. She wondered fleetingly whether it was a one-off diversion or part of a long-term slot strategy. Manston was growing, shifting, shrugging off its dormant past like a decommissioned hangar door finally lifted.

Costello guided the Dolphin into the tight staff car park beside the low-rise operations building. The terminal, a clean-lined modernisation of the old RAF passenger block, stood discreetly to the east, mostly empty apart from a few suited figures from airport security and Sprint's slim commercial team in hi-vis jackets. There were no gliding escalators or terrazzo floors. Just concrete, steel, and tinted glass. Functional. Like the airline.

As Sarah stepped out into the salt-stained breeze, she could hear the distant whine of the auxiliary power unit spinning up aboard G-SPTA. The aircraft's tail, proud against the flat Kentish sky, pointed directly towards them. She drew a slow breath. This was real now. Her flight. Her left-hand seat still in the future—but her name was on the manifest. Her hands would be on the sidestick. Her voice would be on the Lisbon clearance.

"What's the 330 doing here?" she heard Costello say to Sprint's Dispatch lead at Manston, Luke Rainsford, a former easyJet dispatcher with a no-nonsense buzzcut and a clipboard that never left his hand.

Luke barely glanced up from the manifest on his tablet. "Diverted. LHR's got one of the runways shut so there's a large holding stack building. We've got Speedbirds coming in the next 20 minutes and also a VS due to arrive 3 minutes before you're off. We've also got coming in in the next few a Ryanair and a TAP, as Stanstead are running out of stand slots... oh, and your plane is being swapped."

Sarah blinked. "Swapped?" she echoed, eyes narrowing slightly. "What do you mean, swapped?"

Luke looked up at her now, his expression shifting from brusque efficiency to sheepish pragmatism. "Yeah, sorry. Some journo doing the press photos broke one of the crew jump seats standing on it for a wide shot. Maintenance say they can't release the aircraft until it's signed off, and with it being the inaugural flight, they're not taking any chances."

Sarah exhaled slowly through her nose, willing her response to remain professional. "So, we're not flying the Neo?"

"No, you are," Luke said quickly, flicking to a new screen on his tablet. "Just not that Neo. G-SPTB is on Stand J."

Sarah looked over to the remote stands, where passengers would have to walk from the terminal to a coach-boarding gate, like it was 2006 at Luton. And there it was—G-SPTB. Identical livery, same fresh glint, but not the aircraft she'd mentally rehearsed flying all week.

"Literally only happened 5 minutes ago while you pair were on your way from the office in town," Luke then nodded toward the substitute aircraft. "She's prepped, fuelled, catering's loaded—just waiting on the flight crew and ATC release. Dispatch knows the media will moan, but it's still a Sprint jet, still the inaugural flight. Out of interest, which way are you-"

The sound of a PanEuro A320neo being pushed back from a gate interrupted Luke's sentence, as the distant roar of turbofans rolling into life cut through the morning breeze. The whine crescendoed before giving way to the bark of startup, and for a fleeting second, all three of them turned to watch the movement on the apron. Sprint's rival was airborne first, but Sarah wasn't rattled. PanEuro could cling to its silk scarves and pretentious nostalgia; she had real thrust beneath her.

Luke waited for the noise to pass before finishing. "I was saying, which way are you planning to route?"

"Well, we were planning 10, right over Cliffsend, and then Sandwich, Dover, and into French airspace over Calais," Sarah answered crisply, returning her attention to the practicalities. "Standard Eurocontrol slot should keep us in the corridor across the Bay of Biscay and straight down to Lisbon. Minimum deviation. Should hit TOD just south of Porto."

Costello nodded with professional approval, folding his arms against the breeze. "Good plan. Looks like we'll be climbing above the TAP A320 out of Stansted if ATC plays ball."

Luke gave a wry smile. "Just don't let the journos know it's not the original aircraft. You know how they get— 'historic moment compromised by last-minute hiccup,' or some other clickbait." He waved the tablet lightly. "I'll ping tower to confirm the swap. Anyway, there's a last minute VIP. Jeff's on board."

Sarah knew instantly who Luke was referring to, Jeff Young, the CEO and Founder of Sprint, a former bmi and easyJet executive known equally for his brilliant operational mind and for being banned from several boardrooms for calling senior civil servants "ossified invertebrates." If Jeff was on the manifest, then this wasn't just another inaugural—this was a test.

"Jeff's onboard?" Costello asked, not bothering to mask the faint note of surprise.

Luke gave a short nod. "Boarded through a side gate. Didn't even tell the comms team. Apparently wants to fly incognito, economy seat and all. Said he wants to 'feel the cabin the way punters do'. Right, half hour until boarding, so fancy a brew in the PanEuro canteen?"

Sarah had to both chuckle and groan, as she had been a PanEuro Stewardess and was still known by half the crews as being part of the Roger Hargreaves incident, where Hayley had slapped the PanEuro Captain mid-flight after his attempted assault. Walking into that canteen was bound to raise eyebrows, especially as she was a First Officer now, not a …powder-and-pout galley girl.

Still, Sarah straightened her collar, squared her shoulders, and followed the men toward the crew entrance of the canteen with the same unflinching determination that had once carried her through RAF basic training and then back again through the ranks of civilian flight school. Her strides were measured, not hurried—each one proclaiming, I earned this uniform.

Walking into the canteen, Sarah noticed that it had barely changed since she last saw it. Same faux-leather booths, same institutional aroma of reconstituted chicken and boilerplate coffee. A handful of PanEuro flight attendants in teal blouses and vintage-style pillbox hats glanced up as Sarah entered, the recognition clicking in their eyes like cockpit switches. One nudged another. Murmurs spread faster than Wi-Fi.

There were, however, the SingAir, Qatar and Iberia crews too—new faces in a new game. SingAir's contingent, in particular, seemed unbothered by the social dynamics of the room, instead working out how long it would be before they could do a ferry flight to Heathrow so their colleagues who were due to do the returning flight to Singapore could make their check-in window. The Qatar crew, distinguishable in their maroon epaulettes, were deep in discussion over load sheets, and the Iberia pilots had already claimed the window booth, taking bets on what diverts would be arriving.

"50 € en un Delta siendo el próximo vuelo a desviar. Eso o un Aer Lingus," one of the Iberia pilots declared, eliciting a round of chuckles from his colleagues. Sarah caught the edge of their wager—fifty euros on the next inbound diversion being a Delta or Aer Lingus bird. She smiled privately. The Iberians were always betting on something.

Costello moved ahead to the hot water urn and set about fixing two teas, clearly experienced enough to avoid the oversteeped sludge in the urn's filter. Sarah, meanwhile, slipped into a quieter corner booth, careful to sit with her back to the PanEuro crowd. She felt the heat of their stares, not cruel but curious—recognition mixed with disbelief. The last time she'd been in this room, it had been in regulation heels and lipstick, not epaulettes and stripes. It was one thing to leave. It was another to return with stripes.

"Of all the gin joints in all the towns in all the world, she walks into mine," Sarah heard from behind her, and she recognised the voice instantly as Captain Powers, the Chief Pilot of PanEuro and one of the pro-equality allies she'd quietly admired during her stewardess days. Captain Adrian Powers. A man who had once dared to say, on record, that PanEuro's "heritage hiring policy" belonged in a museum, not in a cockpit.

Sarah turned, raising a brow with a half-smile. "Still quoting Casablanca, Captain?"

Powers offered a mock bow. "Some clichés are earned. Like second chances and good pilots finding better airlines." His eyes dipped to her stripes, a flicker of approval in his expression. "Heard you were flying the Sprint inaugural. Can't say I'm surprised."

She gestured to the seat across from her. "Join me, or will that get you strung up by the PanEuro charm police?"

He chuckled and sat, nodding to Costello who returned with two steaming paper cups. "You do realise," Powers said, accepting the tea, "that a good third of this room is trying to figure out why you've got FO stripes, and another third are thinking of leaving and getting jobs at Sprint and Easyjet. I hope the reference I wrote helped you."

Sarah smiled and lifted her cup in a quiet toast. "It did. Got me the interview, at least. The rest I had to fly."

Powers gave a wry grin, the kind that carried a dozen memories, not all of them pleasant. "That's the thing about this business. You can't fake your way into a cockpit. Not for long, anyway."

Suddenly the door from the airside part of the canteen opened, and a group of Midland International crew, a new mid-tier airline that had its own launch a week earlier at Birmingham, East Midlands, Manchester and Manston, walked in, much to the groans of some of the PanEuro crews. Midland's uniforms were black and gold, with cream piping and navy suit trousers that made even the most sceptical PanEuro staff quietly reassess their ideas of "prestige". One of the Midland captains—tall, West African accent, polished shoes—walked over to the small group.

"Room for a Brummie?" The Midland Captain asked, and Sarah nodded, as there was a spare seat at the table, and, unlike some of the PanEuro staff, was willing to let counterparts from other airlines join the group.

"Yeah, sit down, take a load off," Sarah said, chuckling as the Midland First Officer walked over to the Qatar crew to ask where they'd sourced their reusable coffee flasks. The air of tension in the canteen was dissipating slightly, replaced with something more vital: community.

The Midland Captain smiled appreciatively. "Appreciate it. Ibrahim Adeyemi, Captain—though I'm still getting used to saying that. Just come off the Doha. Apparently

ATC has decided to block all outbounds for the next couple of hours. We were due to be heading to Athens at 11, but we've been told by our dispatch that we're looking at a 1pm departure. What flight you got?"

Sarah extended her hand. "First Officer Sarah Marsh. Sprint Air. We're heading to Lisbon on the inaugural—well, sort of. 1005 departure. What do you mean ATC have blocked all outbounds?"

Captain Adeyemi gave a rueful shrug. "Apparently they need to concentrate on diverting flights from LHR-"

"Sarah, Neil,' Luke's voice sounded over the pocket radio Sarah had picked up on her walk to the canteen. "Your sector's been delayed. New departure 1201. ATC have put a hold on departures while Heathrow's diverts drop here. Might want to watch FlightRadar24 for a bit, as there's going to be some interesting traffic. We've got a Cathay and an Emirates coming in, and a Lufthansa that's got a fuel emergency."

Sarah sighed and set her tea down with a delicate clink, her breath fogging slightly in the chilled canteen air. She wasn't surprised by the delay—this was British aviation in springtime, after all, where unexpected congestion and controller shortages were as common as bacon baps and tepid coffee. Still, it gnawed. Months of preparation, and her moment in the left-hand seat—or rather, the right-hand seat on the left-hand side of a brand-new airline's journey—was being kicked two hours down the runway.

Costello looked over at her, expression unreadable but calm. "Delays are the universe's way of testing your briefing stamina."

Powers nodded. "Or your patience," he added dryly. "Though I suppose if ATC are prioritising fuel emergencies, that Lufthansa bird's about to land with fumes."

"I'll take fumes over fire," Adeyemi said, a look on his face that Sarah noticed. "Had a Qatar A380 engine completely go while doing a Doha to Heathrow rotation once. Flame-out, compressor stall, the works. ATC held us for twelve minutes too long over the Channel. That cockpit went from glass to medieval in seconds."

Sarah raised a brow. "What did you do?"

"Prayed. Then remembered the checklist." He grinned, sipping his tea. "Got us down at CDG and had us met by half of Paris fire brigade and a very confused Air France ramp crew. They gave us croissants and then a chewing out for delaying their turnaround. Priorities, eh?"

The laughter around the table softened the tension. Sarah leaned back slightly, her eyes drifting toward the large window that offered a slanted view across the apron. Outside, a Vueling A320 taxied past in the distance, its yellow engine cowlings flashing briefly in the sunlight before it vanished behind the edge of the cargo hangars.

Looking on Twitter, Sarah noticed that there were 3 different well known aviation vloggers already tweeting about the delay to the Sprint service. Noel Phillips, a British aviation enthusiast who, it seemed, was starting a fortnight of journeys starting off with Sprint, was one of the passengers who was in the terminal, as Sarah knew that boarding hadn't yet begun.

@**NoelPhillips**: *Classic British aviation launch: Sprint Air's first ever flight to Lisbon is on hold due to Heathrow diverts! Still, this terminal at Manston is surprisingly slick. Watching the apron bustle with A380s and A320neos is surreal. Can't wait to see how Sprint stacks up in the skies. #AvGeek #SprintAirInaugural*

Sarah exhaled a short laugh through her nose. Of course Noel was onboard. She scanned the replies—some fans jealous, others joking about the irony of an "ultra low-cost carrier" being disrupted by the behemoths of global aviation.

Showing the group her phone, she saw Powers chuckle. "I see that Sam Chui is also hanging around," he said, groaning. "Apparently he only gives airline good reviews if they pay him. He was on my flight last week from here to Boston, and because the bosses paid for a business class seat and let him film the galley, he gave us five stars and called it 'timeless elegance'. I nearly spat my coffee out."

Adeyemi barked a laugh. "Mate, I know. At least that Noel Phillips is more grounded and doesn't demand to go on the flight deck, even though he's a private pilot."

"It's vloggers like Chui that give the rest a bad name," Adeyemi finished, shaking his head with fond exasperation. "Turn up with a camera, demand a caviar canapé, then complain there's no Dom Pérignon in the crew rest. You'd think he was reviewing Emirates First, not flying out of Kent in a single aisle."

Sarah grinned, watching the flicker of jetwash distort the far edge of the apron. The moment had weight—first flight jitters tempered by banter, camaraderie, and the low hum of shared experience. This was aviation, after all. Unpredictable, infuriating, exhilarating.

****

CHAPTER 2 – More Chaos
Thursday 7th April 2022

Sarah was sitting in the flight deck of G-SPTB, her hi-vis jacket neatly folded over the jump seat behind her, headset lying across the centre pedestal. The new-aircraft smell was still clinging to the surfaces, faint glue and ozone mixed with the synthetic aroma of recycled air—less comforting than it sounded, but exhilarating, nonetheless.

The problem?

Now, Swanwick ATC was saying that departure wouldn't be possible until 1442 hours, which meant that Sprint's "grand inaugural" would not just be late; it would be the late-late show, broadcast live on Twitter by every aviation enthusiast from here to Helsinki.

What was worse was that easyJet had joined the party of planes parked, as Hayley Northcott's plane had took off from Gatwick, got as far as the Channel, and then had to declare an emergency, therefore returning back to the UK.

Of course, Gatwick was now full of Heathrow diverts, and so Hayley's flight, along with two intended for Luton and a Ryanair to Stansted had joined the Manston squatters, as it was being called on Twitter and in the Manston crew room: "the squatters' terminal", "the new Southend", or, less charitably, "the world's fanciest plane spotter layby". There were more aircraft on the ground than Manston had hosted since the day of the 2012 Olympic torch relay, and this time, no one had a clue who was actually in charge.

"Ramsgate three four two, this is Manston Tower, copy?"

Sarah looked at the radio, shocked that finally, the radio had come alive, a break in the monotonous silence broken only by the gentle hum of avionics and the low thrum of the APU somewhere behind her.

"Manston Tower, Ramsgate three four two, go ahead," Sarah replied, trying to keep her tone neutral, professional, not betraying the impatience gnawing at her.

A moment of static, then the reply, "Ramsgate three four two, you're number two for departure, behind Alpine one three bravo lima."

Alpine 13 BL, or EJU13BL, Sarah knew, was the call sign for Hayley's Lisbon flight—her friend and fellow "Lisbon twin". Looking at her mobile phone, she noticed that Hayley had texted to say that the MCO at Manston, a hangar at the Cargo end of the of the airport, had repaired the issues that her aircraft had developed—something to do with a faulty engine oil sensor—and that easyJet operations had, after some wrangling, agreed to let the flight continue from Manston rather than dragging the passengers back to Gatwick by bus. In an odd twist, both she and Sarah would now be flying the same route, from the same airport, albeit in different uniforms and, as ever, in different worlds.

"Ramsgate three four two, confirming number two for departure behind Alpine one three bravo lima," she said, repeating back to the digital tower that was at Discovery Park, a sprawling campus of white and glass on the outskirts of Sandwich. The Manston digital tower—state-of-the-art, barely a year old—was a curious thing to those who'd flown in and out of proper airports. Rather than a control tower on the field, the 'tower' was a bunker of screens and headsets piped in from a ring of cameras on poles around the apron, taxiway and runway.

It was ironic, Sarah knew, that the control tower was in a place where Pfizer, a major pharmaceutical company, had once brewed up vaccines and clinical breakthroughs, now brewing up clearances for Airbus narrowbodies and widebodies jostling for a sliver of Kentish tarmac. The digital tower's detached efficiency had its fans and its critics. Old PanEuro hands muttered that you couldn't "smell the weather through a fibre optic," but to Sarah, it felt oddly appropriate—a new way of seeing for a new kind of airline.

She glanced across at Captain Costello, who was leaning back in his seat, a study in forced serenity. He'd already made two circuits of the pre-flight paperwork, reviewed the MELs and checked the flight plan as many times as he dared without betraying nerves. The silence on the flight deck was taut, punctuated by occasional updates from Dispatch and the steady clatter of rain beginning to tap the windscreen.

"Sarah, remind me—did you ever imagine your first Sprint departure would be less flight and more 'live at the tarmac car park'?" Costello said, dry as ever, eyes still scanning the apron. Sarah noticed that parked on the remote stand next to her was a recent arrival, a Eurowings Airbus A320neo from Stuttgart, another victim of the Heathrow chaos, its passengers no doubt bewildered at finding themselves at an airport none of them had ever heard of, much less anticipated visiting. It seemed that every airline within striking distance of British airspace was converging upon Manston, turning what should have been a neat, modest inaugural into an increasingly convoluted aviation carnival.

She exhaled slowly, returning a wry glance to Costello. "Honestly, Neil, I was just hoping I wouldn't trip walking across the apron this morning. This," she gestured vaguely toward the congestion outside, "is pure bonus."

Sarah turned her attention back to her phone, quickly tapping out a reply to Hayley, whose easyJet aircraft was still parked half way down the field, as, because of the 2020 reopening, the available remote stand space had increased as part of the Development Consent Order (DCO) that had finally gone through after years of appeals. Now, every patch of tarmac was a makeshift gate, and what should have been a slick PR moment was rapidly dissolving into British farce. If you listened closely, you could almost hear the ghost of Captain Mainwaring muttering about "another fine mess" somewhere in the background.

Sarah Marsh: Finally got a call from the tower. Departing after Alpine 13BL.

Hayley Northcott: Hahaha you've got my orange tail right in front of you then. I'm off in an hour. I've been put behind my dad's Speedbird that's ferrying to LHR. Seem's they're going to run Heathrow on half the scheduled arrivals for the rest of the day and he's going to be the first one to land there once they clear the queue. We've let pax off for a bit to stretch their legs again, as we'd done boarding before they pushed our departure time back, so we've got half hour until boarding happens again.

Sarah chuckled at the absurdity of it all. There was something inherently British about being stuck on the apron of a remote airport in the South East, in a brand-new aircraft, waiting for the heavens and Heathrow to align. She glanced up at the rain-streaked windscreen—grey skies thickening, the April showers intensifying as if the weather itself was mocking the ambition of Sprint's inaugural. Out on the tarmac, a pair of ground crew, fluorescent jackets shining in the drizzle, were attempting to corral a group of bemused passengers who'd slipped out of the terminal, led by an especially determined old lady with a suitcase almost as large as herself.

Suddenly there was a buzz on the secure door, which meant that one of the flight crew—likely Luke Rainsford, the dispatch lead—was requesting entry. Costello pressed the intercom. A moment later, the door hissed open and in stepped Luke, already rain-speckled and slightly breathless, with a tablet in one hand and a stack of briefing printouts in the other.

Behind him was the CEO of Sprint, Jeff Young, and also one of the AvGeek contingent, none other than Noel Phillips, the British born yet American resident aviation vlogger, who had, earlier, asked Sarah and Costello, the latter of who had told him that he could, but later and only if they were delayed even longer than what ATC had said.

"You wouldn't believe who's just boarded," Luke said, groaning. "Nigel flipping Farage. Anyway, Ops have rang. Your EDI has been bumped. One of the Belfast birds is covering it. You're now doing the 2142 Lisbon back here when you get there."

Sarah blinked. She wasn't sure what part of that update to process first—Nigel Farage? Bumped Edinburgh? Flying the return Lisbon back at 2142 local? A dozen conflicting reactions surged up her spine, but only one made it past her lips.

"Farage?" she said, incredulous.

Luke nodded, clearly in that special state of dispatcher fatigue where even the absurd had lost the power to surprise. "Yup. Apparently, he's filming a segment about British aviation. Couldn't resist the chance to be part of a new airline's first day. Just your luck, eh? Anyway, did I mention why Ops have changed your next sector? Something about block time."

Sarah knew that the change to the next sector would bring her duty time close, if not over, as it was half past 1 in the afternoon already, and they had been meant to have departed at 1005 local time, not the new 1442 slot. With a flight time of around 2 hours 35 minutes to Lisbon, plus the requisite turnaround, she'd be pushing up against the limits of her flight duty period—unless a rest period was implemented in Lisbon or she went into augmented duty with relief crew. Neither option was ideal.

Sarah narrowed her eyes at the paperwork Luke was now handing over. "So, we're flying down to Lisbon, getting maybe an hour on the ground, and then straight back at nearly 10pm local? And who's crewing that? Me and Costello again?"

Costello leaned forward, brows raised. "That's a no-go unless Ops are extending rest, Luke. I'm not flying an unfit crew across the Bay of Biscay just so Farage can waffle about sovereignty over chicken sandwiches."

*_*_*_*

By the time the flight had managed to take off, Sarah had gone through five bottles of water, three cheese sandwiches of questionable ULCC provenance, and two full briefings from Luke, who had oscillated between apologetic humour and dispatch exasperation like a man who knew that nothing in the day would go to plan and had made his peace with it.

Now, however, they were over Lisbon, stuck in a holding pattern, as the Portuguese airport had got congested, with the EasyJet Europe flight of Hayley Northcott's also stuck in the same holding stack, making it the most ironically symbolic reunion of their careers—two women, once stewardesses at a retro-themed airline, now full-fledged pilots, orbiting Humberto Delgado like satellites waiting for orbital insertion.

Sarah gripped the sidestick gently, her mind tracking fuel levels, holding endurance, and the remaining duty clock in her head like a digital metronome. They'd entered the hold twenty minutes ago, and although air traffic control was issuing updates, nothing had moved significantly. From her perspective, the roundabout above Lisbon was more congested than the M25 on a Bank Holiday.

"Lisbon Approach, this is Ramsgate Three Four Two, request updated EAT," she transmitted calmly.

A gruff but polite voice returned. "Ramsgate Three Four Two, EAT now 1609. Expect further delay. Advise fuel state."

Costello flicked his hand toward the centre console. "We've got enough to get us to Porto or hold for 10 more."

Sarah keyed the mic again. "Ramsgate Three Four Two, holding endurance ten minutes, then requesting diversion clearance to alternate Porto if no approach allocated."

There was a pause—no doubt Lisbon ATC coordinating with traffic flow—and then the reply came back, clipped but professional. "Roger, Ramsgate Three Four Two. You are advised to alternate Porto. We've got no slot before 1653. You are advised to follow Alpine one three bravo lima, who is also diverting to Porto. Contact Porto Approach on 120 decimal 85. Sorry for inconvenience, and welcome to Portugal."

Sarah gave Costello a wry, sideways look, already hearing the collective groan of the inaugural's "special guests" from the back. "At least we'll get a good photo for the AvGeeks," she muttered, before switching frequencies and reading back the clearance.

Costello managed a half-smile. "First day, first diversion. I suppose that's us initiated. And who knows, maybe the Porto ground crew will give us a cake. Or at least a coffee that isn't ULCC sludge."

As they began the gentle left turn away from Lisbon, Sarah had to admit that at least she was up front legally, not, when she was at PanEuro, sitting up front and sneaking time when a Captain who was less bothered with the SOP of men in the cockpit and women in the galley let her shadow the landing. Now, here she was, right-hand seat, headset pressed to one ear, clearing to Porto with a hold time, a fuel calc in the back of her mind, and a sense—though frayed—that she was exactly where she was meant to be.

"Do you want to handle ATC or let pax know?" Costello grinned, glancing over at Sarah as the aircraft banked gently north. "Your call, FO Marsh. But if you do the PA, try not to mention Nigel Farage. I don't think the cabin crew have enough G&Ts to tranquilise half the passengers if he kicks off about 'EU airspace' or Portuguese bureaucracy."

Sarah smirked. "I'll keep it apolitical."

She flicked the switch and keyed the cabin mic, adopting that careful, calm register that belied the fatigue and fraying nerves in her chest.

"Ladies and gentlemen, this is First Officer Sarah Marsh from the flight deck. As many of you may be aware, today's been chaos with Heathrow deciding to divert half the northern hemisphere to Kent. Due to continued congestion at Lisbon, we've been instructed to divert to our alternate, Porto, where we expect to land in approximately 22 minutes. We apologise for the inconvenience and assure you our crew will do everything possible to minimise further delays. We'll keep you updated as we receive more information from air traffic control."

Looking at her tablet, Hayley knew that the bit of trivia she was about to give would be a pub quiz answer in the future. "A bit of a fun fact for you, in that due to the delays, despite this flight having been intended to be the first passenger flight, we are now the 16th flight of Sprint Air, as 15 flights departed Edinburgh, Birmingham, Dublin, Jersey, Lille, Nice and Liverpool and Belfast while we were stuck at Manston and another 19 flights have departed while we've been in the air. Anyway, upon arrival in Porto and in compliance with UK261 Regulations, local staff will be providing refreshments, and our ground team will assist with onward arrangements to Lisbon or your final destination. Thank you for your patience and understanding on this, our inaugural, if somewhat unconventional, service."

She put the PA handset down with a little flourish, and Costello gave a gentle clap of fingertips on the armrest, a rare sign of approval from the normally stoic captain. "You missed your calling as a BBC continuity announcer, Marsh. Very calm under fire."

Sarah rolled her eyes, but the compliment sat nicely, grounding her as the aircraft continued its steady arc towards Porto. In the rear of the aircraft, the hum of nervous chatter began to rise, a human counterpoint to the drone of the engines. She could imagine the discussions: seasoned flyers dissecting every delay, first-timers eyeing the window in anxious confusion, and at least one vlogger feverishly narrating the adventure for an audience already glued to their notifications.

As they began their approach to Porto, the weather—a thick, misty Atlantic drizzle—did nothing to brighten the mood, but the runway appeared on schedule through the haze. Costello let Sarah handle the landing, a small act of trust and, perhaps, a subtle recognition that she deserved to own this moment, however far it was from the script.

She guided the A320neo down with gentle confidence, the main wheels kissing the tarmac with only a modest thump. The usual chorus of spoilers deploying and reversers growling filled the cockpit. Costello offered a quick, "Nicely done, Marsh," as they slowed to taxi speed and exited the runway.

"Ground control's on one-two-one-eight," Sarah read aloud, switching frequencies and receiving a Portuguese-accented welcome to Porto, along with instructions to taxi to a remote stand near the terminal. There was already a conspicuous orange-and-white easyJet tail at the next stand over—Hayley's aircraft, its engines spooling down.

It was a strangely heartening sight, that twin to her own journey, their two stories so entwined and now, thanks to the whims of European ATC, brought together for a few minutes on foreign soil.

The shutdown checklist complete, Sarah peered out the window to see a the hi-vis of Sprint's local rep, Antonio, and a fuel truck, which was surprising, as she had not been told as she had not been told that they would refuel before even knowing when they could leave again. Sarah reached for the intercom to speak with the cabin crew, but paused, watching the ramp team converge like ants in an organised panic.

A few minutes later, Antonio's voice came over the radio.

"We've been instructed not to deplane," he said, and Sarah picked up the transmission, frowning as she leaned closer to listen. "Pax are to remain on board and you'll be continuing on to Lisbon at 1703 local. We'll be loading a new catering trolley for your pax, and refuelling, but no passenger disembarkation unless Lisbon gets scrubbed entirely.

Sarah exchanged a look with Costello. He raised a brow, both surprised and mildly sceptical.

"Well, that's bold," he muttered, adjusting the seat armrest as he leaned forward, tapping a few notes into his EFB. "So, we're now a mobile waiting lounge. How very modern."

Sarah keyed the response to Antonio. "Understood, but we need firm confirmation from Ops that this is legal under FTL regs. We're already pushing the limits. Crew rest and fuel planning need to be redone."

"Copy that," Antonio replied. "Ops say you'll be fine. They're sending a message now."

Sarah sighed, as she knew that things were going all over the place. There was one bright side, however, and that was because the plane was on the ground, not in the air, it mean that she could use one facility that she'd been longing for since leaving Manston—the loo.

She unclipped her seatbelt, checking briefly with Costello. "Captain, if you don't mind, I'm just going to—"

"Go, go," he said, shooing her with a wave of his hand. "If anyone deserves first dibs, it's you."

Sarah made her way down the narrow aisle, nodding politely to the cabin crew clustered at the forward galley. The atmosphere in the cabin was oddly serene: passengers were flicking through the in-flight magazine, peering curiously through rain-flecked windows at the unfamiliar airport, or just sinking into a resigned sort of patience.

She noticed that the forward lavatory, her first choice, was occupied, probably by a crew member as all the passengers were seated as the seatbelt sign was still lit, so it was off to the rear one she went.

"...all the Europeans fault for this," she heard as she passed Nigel Farage talking to Simon Calder. "That's why Brexit had to happen, so we aren't stuck with Brussels ordering our airspace be overrun with …Belgian bureaucracy and Portuguese holding patterns," Farage continued, his voice just loud enough to be unmistakable even over the soft roar of air circulation and murmurs from the cabin. He was mid-rant, gesturing with a travel-sized bottle of gin in hand, while Simon Calder, Britain's most unflappable travel journalist, looked on with an expression of polite neutrality only years of delayed Eurostar services could cultivate.

Sarah pushed past, her jaw tight. She'd dealt with minor celebrities before. At PanEuro, she once poured champagne for a Love Island finalist whose idea of inflight entertainment was making TikToks in the aisle during turbulence. But something about Farage—the posturing, the selective memory, the smugness of someone who'd never flown jump seat on a stormy approach to Cork—scraped at her nerves.

The rear galley was calmer. The junior cabin crew member, Tasha, offered Sarah a sympathetic smile.

"Sorry, forward one's jammed up. Some bloke had a crap while over the Bay and got it all over the walls. A cleaner has been assigned for wherever. Do you know if we're deplaning?"

Sarah looked out of the window and saw, taxiing, a Lithuanian registered Sprint aircraft, wearing a fleet name of Sprinter, the Eastern European arm, named so because of a Polish airline operation having blocked its registration in the EU. Sarah squinted at the aircraft's livery—a near-identical design save for a bolder 'S' on the tail and a red pinstripe running the fuselage.

Legally, Sarah knew, the Lithuanian registration was to allow cabotage, a legal workaround that allowed Sprint to serve destinations within the EU without falling foul of the usual post-Brexit restrictions. It wasn't a cheat—just another example of modern aviation's strange, bureaucratic limbo. Sprint Air might paint itself in British colours and trumpet its Ramsgate heritage, but half its aircraft were leased through Ireland and registered in Vilnius.

"Ops said no. I think it's because they wasn't sure if the Lithuanian fleet was compliant with the ground handling unions here," Sarah replied, brushing a damp strand of hair back behind her ear as she moved past the galley cart. "That, or they don't want the press snapping Farage ranting about being kicked off a British aircraft onto a European plane on European tarmac."

Tasha chuckled at that. "If he does, I'll treat him like any disruptive passengers and get the gaffer tape and cuffs, the usual restraining gear."

Sarah laughed at that—though, she thought, there was just enough of an edge in Tasha's voice to make her wonder if the cabin crew wouldn't mind a bit of high-profile restraint, if only for the Twitter likes. She finished her quick detour, splashed water on her face in the rear galley sink, and made her way forward as the aircraft reverberated with the familiar drone of refuelling and the slightly less familiar clatter of a new catering trolley being hoisted aboard by a clearly harried Portuguese ground agent.

And then suddenly.

"Good afternoon, Ladies and Gentlemen, this is your Captain speaking. We've been instructed to deplane passengers for a controlled disembarkation, as Lisbon's holding pattern has grown to such a degree that all further arrivals are suspended until at least 1800. Local authorities at Porto have decided that keeping several hundred passengers captive on aircraft is a poor look for EU hospitality, and Sprint Ops have agreed to a staggered disembarkation under ground staff supervision. Please remain seated until your row is called. Cabin crew, doors to manual and cross-check."

The words, so familiar yet so unexpected after the long morning of creeping fatigue, were met first with a collective pause, then a surge of relief-laced murmurs rippling through the cabin. The prospect of solid ground, even if only for an hour, was a tonic. Sarah caught Costello's eye as she slid back into the cockpit. He was already punching the sequence into the overhead to depower the aircraft for ground operations.

"They've finally seen sense," he said, not bothering to mask the tired triumph in his tone. "Thank goodness we're at a walkable stand. Anyway, the new plan is to deplane, do customs, and then reboard on here using a Sprinter flight number so we don't get accused of cabotage."

Sarah chuckled, as she had expected nothing less from Sprint's legal and ops teams. British ingenuity at its finest: rebrand the same aircraft mid-journey to navigate arcane EU rules that seemed designed to punish new entrants rather than help them. It was another layer in the tangled web of post-Brexit aviation, and she was right in the middle of it.

She turned her attention back to the checklist and switched to ground frequency, alert for the ramp supervisors' instructions. The passengers would be called row by row for disembarkation, shepherded under the watchful eyes of Portuguese security, and then funnelled through a makeshift customs corridor established in one of Porto's underused terminal halls.

Across the cockpit, Costello tapped his fingers on the sidestick, his usual calm now tinged with weary amusement. "So, we do the slow shuffle off the plane, get frisked by customs, and then play musical chairs to get back on the same aircraft with a different flight number. All part of the ULCC charm, I suppose."

Sarah smirked. "You could say we're pioneering a new kind of travel. The 'get off and get back on' experience. Maybe next week we can add a scavenger hunt in the terminal?"

He laughed softly. "Only if it includes vouchers for a decent coffee and a sandwich that doesn't come in a plastic bag."

The intercom crackled to life. "Cabin crew, prepare for disembarkation. Please ensure passengers remain seated until called. Forward doors to manual."

Sarah took a deep breath, aware that despite the challenges, the crew's composure was impressive. The cabin crew, though visibly tired, moved with the precision of a well-drilled team, their smiles professional, their reassurances calm.

****

CHAPTER 3 – Changes, Cons and Crewmates

Friday 8th April 2022

Sarah woke up in the Holiday Inn Express in Lisbon's Old Town, the April sun on the Portuguese tiles outside casting a warm peach glow across the ceiling. The blackout curtains were drawn half open, and for a brief moment she forgot where she was—half expecting to be back in Kent, in her flat overlooking the train line, lulled by the rumble of high-speed sets thundering between Ramsgate and Ashford.

But then the scent of foreign hotel air—bleached linen and that uniquely European mix of city dust and espresso—brought her back. Her phone buzzed, dragging her further into consciousness.

06:32

And a new schedule on the Sprint Staff app.

Looking at it, she groaned at the planned schedule and aircraft types.

First flight? 0834 from Lisbon to Cologne on a A319 that was a former Hi Fly and now owned by the Lithuanian side, still with the registration of its former Maltese owner and therefore, legally speaking, part of the EU cabotage-compliance fleet.

Sarah knew that, technically, only 3 A320neos were owned directly by Sprint, the two UK-registered birds at Manston and the Lithuanian bird, while the others, a motley collection of over 150 second or third hand A320s and A319s, with registrations all over the place, from China and South China Airways, to America, former Spirit, and even a single former Airbus demonstrator, a A321 which was still German registered and therefore used mainly on Sprint and Sprinter routes across the UK and European Union, with its second day of the two brands launching being a mix of chaos.

Looking at the app, she noticed that half of the Captains, as she was being cycled through the rota, were different each flight, a mix of Bulgarian, Polish and even a German sounding name as the airline leaned heavily on its diverse pool of crew.

She knew that she, Costello and a small selection were direct hires, on different terms and conditions to the majority, who were on the usual low-cost crew leasing contracts, all channelled through third-party agencies or crewing platforms based in Vilnius, Sofia or Dublin. It was Sprint's way of legally operating inside the European Union while still claiming to be a proud "British airline", a clever façade that let them fly freely across borders that Brexit had muddied for everyone else.

Sarah sat up, rubbing her temples and letting out a deep breath. She was exhausted, not just from yesterday's mess at Manston, the delay, the diversion, the deplaning, the replaning, and finally landing in Lisbon just before 8. The fact she had done a 10 hour duty day, yet one... sorry, two, she realised, as she counted the second sector as it was a "Margate" call signed flight, being on the Lithuanian operating licence as it was an internal European flight, technically meant she'd logged a pair of separate flights with different paperwork, a different legal operator, and—laughably—two different "uniform requirements," though her navy Sprint blouse hadn't changed in reality. The whole operation was so convoluted that she imagined one of the vlogging community might try to chart the legal structure like a conspiracy theorist with red string and pushpins.

Her phone buzzed again. Another update.

Sprint Crew App Notification: *Aircraft swap: MGT7453 LIS-CGN now operated by B-DHEW. Type now A321-100. Expected departure: 08:34. Crew call: 07:35 at Stand G9.*

Sarah looked at the notification and groaned, as B-DHEW, a former Air China A321-100, was one of the most infamous aircraft in the crewing rumour mill. Word was, it had been dumped in a scrapyard in Kazakhstan before Sprint's leasing partners snatched it up at auction, refurbished it to Easyjet standards as Jeff was a former EasyJet fleet procurement executive, and assigned nominally to the Lithuanian AOC through Sprinter Europe Ltd., but operated under the same RMS dispatch system as all Sprint flights.

"At least it's got a full refurb and not plastic seat backs and ashtrays in the lavs," Sarah muttered, dragging herself from the bed. Loading up FlightRadar24, she looked at the section where new aircraft usually were listed, and there was 4 OE, Austrian registered, aircraft, all heading from Malta to Hawarden, and all four, looking at the photographs, were former EasyJet A319-100s, all using MGT flight codes.

"That's strange," she muttered, as MGT was the Lithuanian fleet code, used primarily for intra-European rotations, not UK-EU flights. If those ex-EasyJet birds were going into storage or refurb at Hawarden, then it meant that they would join the Sprint and Sprinter fleets as part of the armada of new journeys that were, according to the internal Discord chat, being added by the hour, with competition against Ryanair and Wizz.

"Can't seem to take the boss out of the Easy mindset," she muttered, putting her phone on the side table while heading for a shower and to shave her legs. "At least the uniforms aren't girdles like PanEuro."

Sarah stepped from the shower twenty minutes later, her limbs protesting slightly as she towelled off. The hot water had done its work, loosening the ache behind her shoulders and the stiffness in her calves. She pulled on the standard-issue Sprint uniform blouse—navy, as ever— and slipped into the tailored trousers issued only to flight deck crew. A quick glance in the mirror confirmed she looked presentable, if a little pale around the edges. Lip balm, tied-back hair, a dash of mascara. Bare minimum. The tired professionalism of a ULCC pilot who knew this wasn't a glamour gig. No scarves. No rouge. No preposterous PanEuro hair inspections.

* _ * _ * _ *

The lobby area of the Holiday Inn, Sarah noticed as she walked in with her suitcase trailing behind, was full of airline crews from multiple operators—TAP, Wizz, EasyJet, and Sprint—waiting for the usual motley assortment of crew buses or Ubers that the various staff had agreed to split the cost of. Sprint and Sprinter, in their infinite wisdom, had declined to run dedicated staff transfers from the hotel to the airport. Instead, it had become an impromptu, international carpool scheme.

Sarah glanced around. There was a group of German pilots in bright yellow high-vis vests—likely Eurowings—deep in conversation about their next shift to Stuttgart. A handful of Wizz Air cabin crew, clad in those signature pink scarves and dark trousers, were huddled around a table debating the merits of the hotel breakfast. A TAP captain, crisp in the airline's traditional green blazer, was leaning against a wall scrolling through his tablet with the bored concentration of a man used to delays.

"Möchte jemand ein Uber zum Flughafen teilen?" Sarah heard, and turned around to see a, what she would describe as too good looking to be a First Officer, German-accented man in a black leather jacket and a grey Sprint Air lanyard dangling from his neck. He had the rakish stubble of someone who had slept five hours and still managed to look like an editorial shoot for Flight International.

"I'll split," Sarah replied, raising her hand. "Sarah. Sprint. G9 stand."

"Max," he said, offering a grin as he gestured toward the hotel doors. "I'm on... Sprinter to Manston. What you doing?"

"LIS to Cologne," Sarah said with a wry smirk, wheeling her case toward the door as Max held it open. "Then a Düsseldorf, a Tallinn, an Orly and a Birmingham."

Max let out a low whistle. "That's not a rotation. That's a European diplomatic tour. I've got Manston, Orly, back here then the Berlin. Good job too, as I live near Berlin, so I get to actually sleep in my own bed for once." He chuckled, his accent crisp but not over-pronounced, the sort that came from years working in multinational cockpits. "Last week I was working for LOT as one of their leased pilots on their Vilnius base. Now I'm Sprint. Next week? Who knows. Maybe flying pigs for Ryanair if they buy any more bankrupt regional carriers."

Sarah laughed, not unkindly. "You're joking, but I wouldn't be surprised if Sprint's next base is in Tirana and they tell us it's part of Greater Kent."

They both stepped out into the Lisbon morning, the air cool with the promise of heat to come, and the Uber—already idling at the curb—flashed its hazard lights as they approached. Max tapped his phone and gave a thumbs-up to the driver, an older man with sunglasses and a high-vis vest on his dashboard, a sign of being an airport regular.

"Portela?" the driver asked.

"G9 Stand," Max replied. "Airside crew entrance."

The Uber pulled away into Lisbon's tidy streets, the kind that could turn from boulevards to cobbled medieval labyrinths in the blink of an eye. Sarah watched the city go past—sleepy storefronts, commuters sipping bica on kerbs, a street cleaner with an orange cart swaying between tram tracks.

"So," Max said, buckling in, "how long have you been with Sprint? You seem... grounded."

"Well... erm... I'm kind of one of the pre-ops pilots, so I've been with them a couple of months," she said, knowing that most of the pilots had only started via agencies in the last week, and had been a mix of Easyjet, Wizz, and every other low-cost airline imaginable. The revolving door of contractors and leased pilots had become a joke within the operation, but Max didn't seem to mind, leaning back against the leather seat, eyes flicking between his phone and the passing scenery.

"A couple of months, huh?" he said, a faint smile creeping onto his face. "You've already seen more chaos than most of us have on a single sector. I heard about the inaugural mess with the delays. A plane swap, a diversion to Porto... sounds like we're living the dream here at Sprint."

Sarah sighed, half-smiling as she folded her arms across her chest. "It's not all glamour, that's for sure. Yesterday felt more like a comedy of errors than a proper flight. We had Nigel bloody Farage-"

"Ah, the Brexit man?" Max said, chuckling, as he adjusted the air vent above his seat. "Did he ask to land somewhere non-European halfway through for sovereignty reasons?"

Sarah snorted. "Worse. He was holding court in the galley with Simon Calder. I don't know how the poor man kept a straight face. We ended up diverting to Porto and doing a turnaround rebranded as a Sprinter flight just to skirt cabotage rules. Farage didn't even notice—he was too busy complaining about EU bureaucracy while sitting on one of the two only owned Sprint aircraft. What you got for your flight?"

"I have ein Airbus A321. Former Lufthansa bird that had a somewhat colourful history, let's just say. It's been repainted and spruced up, but still has that smell of "we'll get it ready in the nick of time" clinging to it. Sounds like I've got an easy day compared to yours," Max said with a grin, clearly enjoying the absurdity of the situation. He leaned back in the seat, his eyes scanning the traffic as they made their way towards the airport.

"At least you're not dealing with that fleet of second-hand planes like we are," Sarah replied, her tone dry. "It's like a game of aircraft musical chairs. Who knows which one will be in the hangar this week, and which one will be trying to fly to Cologne." She rolled her eyes, but there was a flicker of humour beneath the surface.

Max laughed, clearly amused. "I think every airline in Europe has a few 'interesting' birds in their fleet. But hey, it's part of the job, right? Some days you're the one flying the shiny new jet, and other days you're the one making sure the APU doesn't fall off before you get to your destination."

Sarah chuckled at the thought. "That's the life we've signed up for, I suppose." She glanced out the window at the scenery outside, the cobbled streets winding their way through the city. It was a strange juxtaposition, really. The ancient city on one side and the modern-day aviation circus on the other. "So LOT, eh? What was that like?"

Sarah noticed the German smile as the memory of his time with LOT came rushing back. "It was... different," he said, shifting in his seat to face Sarah. "You know, working with a carrier that's part of a bigger network like that comes with its own set of rules. Much more structure, much more paperwork. The fun part was the international stuff, flying out to places like Warsaw, and the occasional hopping over to the Middle East. A bit more glamour, but I have to say, I don't mind the chaotic freedom here at Sprint." He chuckled softly. "At least you don't have to deal with endless bureaucracy."

Sarah laughed in return, thinking about all the absurdities she'd encountered so far with Sprint Air. "I think we all love a bit of chaos, but this is taking it to new heights. Aircraft swaps, random diversions, and then a CEO on board trying to blend in as a regular passenger... It feels like a bloody circus sometimes." She leaned back against the plush leather seat of the Uber, watching as Lisbon's traffic slowly filtered by in a mixture of honking taxis and motorbikes weaving in and out.

Max's eyes twinkled with amusement. "Honestly, I think this is the true test of an airline. If you can survive the first year with half of Europe's second-hand fleet and an untested crew, you've got something solid on your hands. It's like the aviation version of Darwinism. You either thrive, or you get swallowed up."

"Right now, I think we're just about surviving," Sarah replied. "Every day feels like an adventure, though I don't know if I want to keep living like I'm on the verge of a meltdown every other day."

Max laughed, nodding in agreement. "Hey, it's what we signed up for. The industry's all about the highs and lows, right? You've just got to roll with the punches. Or, in our case, the delays, the swaps, the diversions." He paused, looking out the window as they drove past a beautiful, colourful mural on the side of a building. "But you know, I wouldn't want to be doing anything else. It's still the best job in the world."

"Best job, worst chaos," Sarah muttered under her breath.

Max chuckled, his grin widening. "Exactly. And hey, at least you're flying to Cologne. Can't say I'm not a little jealous of that. I'm stuck with a mid-afternoon departure from Lisbon to Berlin, followed by a few days off in between."

Sarah let out a breath, feeling a bit of that fatigue creep into her body again. She wasn't just talking about the scheduling chaos. She was talking about the deeper exhaustion that came with constantly managing the uncertainty. "I don't know how they think this is going to work in the long run," she muttered, half to herself. "We're operating on borrowed time. We might be a brand-new airline, but with all these patchwork solutions, it feels like we're flying on fumes."

Max raised an eyebrow, clearly amused by the bluntness of her words. "Fumes? Sounds like an understatement."

"I mean, have you seen the roster for bidding?" Sarah then said, sighing. "I mean, they've got airports that might as well be pulling rabbits out of hats to keep this thing afloat. We've only been officially live yesterday and one of the routes bidding is for is from Coventry to Ibiza, and another one for Leipzig–Altenburg to Dortmund."

"Wait, Leipzig-Altenburg to Dortmund?" Max repeated with a loud snort, shaking his head in disbelief. "That's not a route, that's a sat-nav mistake. Who on Earth is flying between two cities that close together unless it's a football team dodging traffic?"

Sarah chuckled, leaning against the window. "Exactly. And yet, it's on the Sprint portal. Probably someone in Ops clicked the wrong template and decided, sod it, launch it anyway. There again the route planning team are formerly Wizz, so it probably came bundled with a spreadsheet that said: 'low yield, low demand, but look! It fits between two bus timetables.'"

Max wheezed with laughter. "At this point I'm convinced the Sprint route network is designed by a bloke in a pub with darts and a map of Europe."

They were both laughing now, the kind of fatigued, resigned amusement that came only from those living the absurdities of startup aviation. The Uber swung past the roundabout leading to Terminal 2's crew gate, where a pair of TAP regional aircraft were trundling along the taxiway towards the far edge of the apron. The sleek, familiar shape of a Vueling A320 caught Sarah's eye, parked beside what looked like a Wizz Air bird being refuelled with ground crew swarming around it like bees.

Approaching the security hut where crew entered airside, the Uber driver stopped his car and turned to Sarah and Max.

"Saia daqui. Não tenho acesso ao aeroporto a não ser que me pague 50 euros."

Sarah blinked. The driver's Portuguese was fast and curt, but the gist was unmistakable.

"The schweinehund is trying to... how would you English describe it? Rob us?" Max said to Sarah, and she looked at him. The fact it was an Uber, and so Max had paid via the Uber app, as only card payments were accepted for this particular route, made Sarah pause. The driver had stopped far outside the designated drop-off zone for crew, and the usual hustle of airport traffic had already started to pick up, with other cars and buses swarming in like clockwork.

"Is he serious?" Sarah muttered, her hand twitching for the phone to double-check the app, but Max was already on it, firing off a few words in German. The irony wasn't lost on Sarah how a Max was showing the stereotypical German behaviour of dealing with incidents, ruthless efficiency, while the taxi driver was doing what all cabbies worldwide would probably try if they thought they could get away with it.

The next thing she knew, Max and the taxi driver were swearing at each other in their native languages, an argument escalating with increasing volume. The driver's fingers pointed to the rearview mirror, indicating that Max and Sarah had to get out of the car, while Max's hand stayed firmly on the door handle, not moving an inch.

"Does this ever happen to you in Berlin?" Sarah asked, a slight laugh escaping her lips despite the tension in the air.

Max, whose German efficiency had been overtaken by a sense of indignation, grunted in response. "It happens in Berlin, but usually with the Uber drivers who think they're the ones running the airport. Not the first time I've had a run-in, but I'll make sure it's the last time here."

The situation was about to get worse when the driver leaned over and started gesturing towards the terminal, demanding payment directly from Max's phone, all while speaking fast and furious Portuguese. Sarah didn't understand the words entirely, but the tone was clear enough. This was not a legitimate claim. They had been dropped at a perfectly acceptable place, but apparently, the driver wasn't in the mood to follow the usual rules.

Max was done. He threw his phone onto the passenger seat, clearly frustrated. "This is ridiculous," he muttered, shaking his head.

"Alright, let's just get out and walk to the gate. We'll figure it out," Sarah suggested, rolling her eyes at the absurdity of the situation. As much as she had hoped for a smooth morning after the chaos of the previous day, it seemed that this was just another opportunity for the universe to test their patience.

Max shot her a look that conveyed equal parts resignation and amusement. "I don't know why I even bother with Ubers anymore. It's either this or the driver who takes the scenic route around the city, trying to charge you for a tour of Lisbon."

Without another word, they both grabbed their bags and exited the car, ignoring the increasingly agitated driver who shouted something after them. The moment the door slammed shut, the atmosphere shifted from confrontation to casual defeat. They didn't even glance back at the driver as they walked towards the terminal.

"How much do I owe you for the Uber?" Sarah asked.

Max waved her off as they paced across the painted crew lanes towards the security gate.

"Nothing. Already paid. Uber will deal with him. Might even refund me when I report it. If not, I'll survive. You can buy me a disgraceful airport coffee if you feel guilty. You on the Sprint WhatsApp?"

Sarah nodded, as she was on both the Manston base specific one and the general Sprint pilot group chat, where the updates came through thick and fast. She knew Max was right; the inconsistencies were part of the charm and the curse of Sprint Air. Every day was a new adventure— be it an aircraft swap, a random diversion, or a rogue taxi driver trying to make an extra few quid. They'd get through it, like they always did, but the fatigue was starting to creep in. "Yeah, I'm on there. Tell you what, if you give me your phone, I'll add my number to it, and we can DM each other, maybe plan a meal or something between us?"

Max handed her his phone with a smile, "Sure, I'll send you a message later." They continued walking towards the crew entrance, the looming airport terminal ahead of them. The noise of the city seemed distant now, replaced by the constant hum of airside operations—the rumbling of baggage carts, the hum of jet engines in the distance, and the occasional shouted instructions from ground crew.

Tapping her phone number into the WhatsApp contacts list, she noticed it came up as Max Detweiler, Berlin base, and that was a little odd. Was he based in Berlin? Was this how he got so familiar with the rotating chaos of Sprint Air's European routes? Sarah couldn't quite figure it out. As she handed his phone back, Max gave her a little shrug and a knowing grin.

"It's all about rolling with it, isn't it?" Max said, as they neared the security checkpoint. He slid his crew ID badge into the scanner, and Sarah followed suit, the turnstile buzzing as she passed through.

"Yeah, well, I think I've had enough rolling for one week," Sarah replied, half-joking, half-serious. "Honestly, it feels like this airline is doing its best to break me, piece by piece."

Max laughed, the sound clear but not forced. "You're not the only one. There's a reason I've only been here for a week, and honestly, I'm already looking at my next gig. Who knows where I'll be next month. You get used to it. You either fall in or fall out."

As they walked past the duty-free stores and down the long corridors leading to the departure gates, Sarah's thoughts began to swirl. Max was right in some ways— there was a certain beauty in the chaos of Sprint Air. But there was something wearing about it too. Every day felt like a new test, a new hurdle. And right now, she was far from confident she was going to clear it.

"Lebewohl, Sarah," Max said as they approached the gate area, separating for their day ahead.

* _ * _ * _ *

Stand G9 was a sun-drenched patch of concrete at the far edge of Lisbon's outer apron, nestled between a pair of cargo containers pretending to be ops offices and a cracked yellow line painted, long before the EU had intervened in airport standardisation.

B-DHEW stood squat and brooding, an A321-100 with the sort of fuselage that looked like it had been reassembled from salvaged parts, but freshly painted in Sprint livery and glaring in the morning light with defiant pride. The aircraft bore no hint of its former life with Air China, but Sarah could feel it in the bones of the jet—the slightly aged lines, the riveted skin that held stories of Pacific thunderstorms and Siberian turbulence.

Her captain for this flight was a tall Lithuanian with a shaved head and aviators that looked like they came from a Cold War surplus bin. His name tag read Captain Justas Ziemelis, and he greeted her with a curt nod, as if pleasantries were optional this morning.

"You flew Porto last night, yes?" he asked, voice clipped and heavy with accent.

Sarah nodded. "Diversion on the inaugural. Sprint style."

Justas smirked faintly, the closest he would come to laughter.

"We had one yesterday. Orly to Bucharest. Diverted to Sofia. Wrong fuel load. Dispatcher forgot density altitude. Plane couldn't make top of climb. First Officer decided then to resign on first day."

Sarah looked at the captain with an expression of quiet disbelief, but she kept her response neutral. "Sounds like quite the day," she said, settling into the cockpit, her mind still running over the chaos that had already defined the past 24 hours. Justas didn't seem bothered by the tumult of the previous flights. To him, this was just another typical Sprint adventure.

"Indeed," he replied, his eyes already scanning the aircraft systems as he settled into his seat. "Here, we all learn to adapt. The turbulence is not always from the air, yes?"

Sarah could feel the weight of the words as they sat in the confined space of the cockpit. There was a certain resilience in the way the crews of Sprint Air—particularly the older, more seasoned pilots like Justas—carried themselves. They'd come from airlines where the usual frustrations were more mundane, more systemic. Now they were part of a patchwork airline that seemed to be constantly teetering on the brink of disarray, and yet, they persevered. They adapted.

As Sarah prepped the flight deck for departure, she couldn't help but wonder how long this chaotic, fragmented operation could hold together before the cracks became impossible to ignore. The whole operation felt as though it had been put together in a hurry—an airline borne out of ambition and a need to fill a gap in the market. The more she thought about it, the more surreal it became. There they were, flying across Europe, swapping planes mid-flight, operating under multiple legal structures, all while trying to convince passengers they were just another low-cost option on the continent.

Just like Ryanair.

Just like Wizz.

****

CHAPTER 4 – Allergens & Karens
Sunday 10th April 2022

If there were two things any former cabin crew turned First Officer hated, Sarah knew from experience, it was the infestation of the species "Karenus Privilageous", a species who were known for being middle class, white women, who often demanded to speak to the manager—preferably at 36,000 feet, mid–service, over the Bay of Biscay, as if the airline's senior management lived in the rear toilet and could be summoned with a wave of a gluten-free sandwich. The other thing was allergens. Not allergies—she had some sympathy for the genuinely afflicted—but allergens, which were less a medical reality and more a moral panic, a box-ticking ritual of modern air travel, as much about Instagram stories and performative suffering as about actual anaphylaxis.

It was on a "London" Cambridge to Paris-Beauvais journey when Sarah was walking through the cabin while boarding when the complaint arrived. Having visited the lavatory, as the 18-minute turnaround, the Airbus A320, LY-NVY, one of the Lithuanian fleet that had been brought from Avion Express and, because the service was one of those on the Lithuanian operation side, was branded Sprinter, not Sprint.

The reason?

To avoid being sued by a Polish cargo operator.

The irony that it meant all the Lithuanian and Maltese operated planes had to carry that name while the British allocated allocation kept the 'Sprint' branding was not lost on Sarah. Nor was the fact that half the passengers boarding probably didn't notice the difference between 'Sprint' and 'Sprinter', assuming it was some kind of branding stunt. The real reason was buried in legal documents and AOC arrangements that had been signed off after midnight on a rainy Tuesday by someone in a Vilnius office who'd never actually been on an Airbus.

Sarah offered her standard smile-and-nod as a woman in a pale-pink twinset, toting a handbag the size of a small dog, blocked the aisle in Row 2 and flagged her like a cab.

"I must insist," the woman began, tone already halfway between indignation and martyrdom, "that this aircraft be fully sanitised of all traces of peanuts."

Sarah groaned, as she knew that the Buy on Board service offered Peanut Butter milkshakes, satay wraps, KP nuts and even peanut brittle, as the catering offer had been onboarded earlier in the day at Birmingham, and therefore it was completely impossible to guarantee anything close to a "peanut-free environment". The galley, in fact, was practically a shrine to the groundnut, a silent testament to the race-to-the-bottom economics of low-cost aviation, where shelf life, margin and supplier freebies trumped all else.

"Madam, I'm afraid I can't guarantee—"

She was cut off before she could reach the end of the sentence.

"It is a matter of life and death!" the woman hissed, voice sharp enough to flense the gloss off the faux-leather headrest of 2C. "You are legally required to comply. The captain will wish to speak to me about this. I expect—no, I demand—that an announcement is made."

"Madam, I am the First Officer, and the Captain and I are in charge of—"

"Well, get me the Captain then," the woman snarled. "Is it a man?"

Sarah let out a sigh so imperceptible that only her inner voice noticed. Years in the job had honed her skills to a fine point—diplomacy with a side order of deadpan. Her mind cycled through the possible outcomes: confrontation, escalation, social media threats, perhaps even a cabin deplaning over "medical risk." It was barely 8:30 on a Sunday morning, and already she could feel the outlines of a headache forming behind her right eyebrow.

"Captain Adams is in the flight deck preparing for departure," she said, tone gentle but edged with professional finality. "and she is—"

"She? She? I want a male captain," the woman spat, as though the very syllables had curdled on her tongue. "A man would take this seriously. A man would make the announcement. A man would understand the risks of airborne anaphylaxis."

Sarah tilted her head slightly, the smile still fixed, professional and unreadable. "Captain Adams has over fifteen years'—"

"I don't care if she has a million years. Men are much safer at the controls of an aircraft. It's scientific fact. I read it in the Daily Mail," the woman insisted, her voice rising in pitch and volume, drawing attention from other passengers. Row 3 was now openly gawping; Row 4 was fishing out their phones, the subtle angle of their wrists betraying the fact that the circus was about to be broadcast to WhatsApp groups from here to Woking.

Sarah allowed herself the briefest flicker of an eyebrow. "Madam, the Captain and I are responsible for the safe operation of this flight. If you would like, I can relay your concerns to her, but the regulations and procedures are set by the Civil Aviation Authority, not the editorial board of the Daily Mail. You are welcome to write an official complaint, but I must inform you that our contact centre is managed by Capita and therefore—"

"WHAT! You are trying to fob me off! I know my rights. If I have a reaction, you'll be in the dock. I'll sue you personally and the airline for millions! My solicitor is on speed dial!"

Sarah maintained the smile, but her patience was wearing as thin as the seat padding. "Madam, we do take allergies seriously. However, we cannot guarantee a peanut-free aircraft. I can ask the cabin crew to commence the Buy on Board service from the rear of the aircraft, and I can tell you that the Satay wraps and milkshakes are quite popular, so they may sell out before they reach the front. May I ask, did you bring an EpiPen with you?"

The woman's expression turned instantly suspicious, as if Sarah had suggested she swallow a jar of peanut butter whole. "Are you medically qualified to ask that? Are you even trained for emergencies? I demand to see your qualifications. Your airline's so-called 'crew' are nothing but trolley dollies in polyester. I will be speaking to the press—my cousin is on BBC Radio Kent!"

Sarah's internal monologue was in freefall. She'd faced engine fires, foggy Cat III landings, and once, as a stewardess, talked down a drunken rugby team threatening to urinate in the galley sink. But this, this was the modern gauntlet: a Karen in her native habitat, ready for war. She reached for the tools of her trade—polite ambiguity, gentle deflection, and an absolute refusal to allow herself to be filmed while losing her temper.

"I assure you, Madam, all crew are trained to deal with medical emergencies. If you have a medical condition that could pose a risk during flight, Civil Aviation regulations, along with the Conditions of Carriage state—"

"I paid £119 for this ticket, I am going to Paris, and you will make the announcement!" Her voice, trembling on the cusp of hysteria, now echoed down the aisle, sending a tremor through the boarding queue. "My condition is real. I've seen people collapse on flights. I don't think you understand the gravity of this situation."

Sarah resisted the urge to say that she understood all too well—having watched countless similar pantomimes play out over years in the sky. A genuine anaphylactic case needed immediate Epi administration, oxygen, diversion planning, and ATC prioritisation. But this? This was theatre.

"I'm very sorry, Madam, but unless you're declaring a medical emergency and requesting not to travel, I'll have to ask you to take your seat. We are on a tight slot."

Sarah knew that Fernando Costas, the Head of Legal for Sprint and "Mr Loophole" when it came to the legal aspect of aviation compliance, had once dryly summarised this kind of situation in a staff newsletter as "Customer perception may be the weather. But CAA law is the climate. We obey the latter."

There again, he was formerly of Ryanair, and therefore he had survived more confrontations with disgruntled passengers, Irish regulators, and EU aviation ministers than most crew survived duty rosters. Sarah privately referred to his quotes as "Fernando's Commandments," and this one had become her guiding star when navigating the turbulent skies of passenger entitlement.

The woman in 2C, now visibly shaking with self-righteous fury, finally plonked herself down—either out of sheer indignation or the dawning realisation that she was moments away from being denied boarding altogether. Sarah gave a small nod, took two steps back, and turned toward the forward galley, where the lead cabin crew member, Kelsey Norton, a Canadian born, Romanian living, bundle of sarcastic efficiency with a blonde ponytail sharp enough to slice cheddar, was preparing this flight's Duty Free stock, a Brexit advantage due to the fact the flight crossed from the UK into France, bypassing EU domestic restrictions in the most bureaucratically convoluted way possible.

"Did I just hear someone demanding a male captain and a peanut exorcism?" Kelsey asked, not looking up from her manifest but smirking like a woman who'd read the script and was ready for Act Two.

"You did," Sarah replied, voice lower now, as she moved into the safe zone of the galley curtain. "She wants to see our qualifications, insists peanuts be purged from the aircraft, and that Captain Adams be replaced with someone possessing a penis."

Kelsey chuckled, but it was the exhausted, dry kind that came from too many early reports and not enough espresso. "Tell her we'll swap out the captain for a priest. Crosses the gender gap and can perform exorcisms."

"No, that might encourage her," Sarah said. "She seems like the kind to travel with her own rosary, just in case Boots is out of antihistamines. Look, do us a favour, just to satisfy the old bag. Start the buy on board catering from the back and have Alexis make sure the bottles of milkshake aren't anywhere near row 2."

Kelsey gave a theatrical salute, twisting the manifest closed with one hand while reaching for the intercom handset with the other. "Right. Operation Groundnut Concealment underway. I'll get Alexis to stash the milkshakes behind the last row with the vodka minis and broken seatbelts."

Sarah gave a grateful nod, stepped back into the aisle, and resumed her walk toward the flight deck. As she passed Row 4, one man gave her a sympathetic smile and a slow clap. She rolled her eyes, just enough for him to catch it, and the man gave a conspiratorial wink in return. There was a kinship among those who had done the job, or at least understood its absurdities. Row 6, however, was still pretending not to film. A woman with a phone camouflaged inside a Kindle case kept angling it suspiciously in Sarah's direction.

She ducked through the flight deck door, locking it behind her with a practised hand as the safety lock clicked into place. Captain Eloise Adams, already halfway through the pre-start checklist, glanced over.

"Peanut war?" she asked without looking up.

"Karen in Row 2C. She wants you replaced with a man and is threatening legal action, allergic seizures and regional BBC coverage."

Sarah then grabbed her tablet, which was sat on her seat, and loaded up the Sprint Manifest app, which held details of the passengers, crew, cargo, all for each individual sector that they would be operating that day. The manifest for Cambridge–Beauvais was thankfully short—just 82 passengers, no pets, two mobility-assist requests, and no pre-notified peanut allergy flagged.

One thing she noticed was how, by tapping on a passenger name, she could access the entire Passenger Name Record. The Passenger Name Record (PNR) for 2C lit up with a tap: Mrs. Patricia Winthrope, age 57, Status: Green (no medical flags), SSR: None. No meal requests, no medical assistance, no allergies logged.

The only thing that Sarah noted, which made her chuckle, was that Winthorpe had pre-ordered from the website, on the Buy on Board menu a "Thai Satay Chicken Wrap and a Peanut Butter Smoothie" for the occupant of 2B, a child.

Obviously, a granddaughter, as the child was 6 years old. Sarah stared at the PNR in disbelief.

"You're not going to believe this," she muttered, tilting the screen for Eloise to see.

Eloise squinted. "Is that... the satay wrap?"

"And the peanut butter smoothie." Sarah's voice was flat with disbelief. "For the kid. Same booking."

There was a long silence, broken only by the soft rustle of Eloise flicking to the next checklist item.

"Of course," Eloise said finally, "because what better way to handle a life-threatening allergy than to order airborne allergens for your child and then start a feminist-themed courtroom drama about it in the aisle?"

"I swear we need a new SSR code," Sarah said. "One for drama risk."

Eloise reached for her coffee flask, one of those stainless-steel types designed to survive a nuclear blast. "We could call it KRN1. 'High potential for disruptive entitlement with bonus social media escalation.'"

"Make it gold-tier in the loyalty programme."

They chuckled in tandem, the cockpit temporarily insulated from the absurdity behind the locked door. The soundproofing wasn't perfect, but for now, it was sanctuary. Sarah ran through her half of the checklist; fingers moving over switches and displays as the engines spooled through idle tests. Below them, the apron crew began waving signals and chocking wheels, their Sunday shift as joyless as everyone else's.

Eloise keyed the intercom. "Cabin crew, prepare doors for departure and cross-check."

Eventually the aircraft rolled backwards from its stand in the dull drizzle of a Cambridge morning, nose glinting with that plasticky, too-clean gleam unique to leased A320s given the fast-sponge treatment rather than a proper scrub. Sarah scanned the airport apron—an odd hodgepodge of flight school DA42s, and a lonely refuelling bowser waiting like a loyal dog beside a logbook-stuffed Cessna. Cambridge International wasn't Heathrow. It was barely Luton on a good day. But for today's purposes, it was their launchpad.

With clearance received and pushback complete, Sarah lined up her inputs for engine start. "Starting one," Eloise confirmed, toggling the overhead panel switches with easy grace.

A familiar hum filled the cockpit, followed by the subtle vibrations as the CFM56 engine spun to life on the right. A beat later, engine two followed suit. The aircraft's systems stabilised, and Sarah checked bleed pressures, temperatures, and idle rates.

"All stable," she confirmed. "APU off?"

"Affirm. Transfer complete."

They taxied out slowly, the narrow taxiways of Cambridge demanding low-speed discipline and a keen eye for rogue wildlife or foreign objects—things Sarah had once dismissed as trivial but now regarded with cautious respect after an infamous encounter with a rogue picnic bench at Doncaster during high winds. That bench had become legend in the WhatsApp groups.

"Cambridge Tower, this is Margate Seven One Four One ready for departure, Runway Two Three," Sarah said over the radio, while Eloise, as Captain, was concentrating on observing the instructions of the ground crew and the taxi clearance. A chirpy voice from Tower came back a moment later:

"Margate Seven One Four One, cleared for take-off, Runway Two Three. Wind two-one-zero at six knots."

"Copy, runway 23, wind 210, six knots, Margate 7141," Sarah repeated, confirming that she had received the instructions. She knew the flight, MGT7141, was ready to go.

"Six knots, eh?" Eliose muttered, and Sarah knew that it had changed by 1 knot from when they had arrived less than half an hour ago. But any pilot worth their salt knew that even a single knot could feel like a gust when dealing with airports like Cambridge—where grass verges, microlight turbulence and lazy taxiing from student pilots created a kind of patchwork turbulence of its own.

Eloise steered them onto the runway centreline. "You have control," she said.

"I have control," Sarah replied, easing her grip onto the sidestick as her feet caressed the rudder pedals. Her voice was steady, calm. This part, at least, was sacred—pure, unbothered by drama queens or dairy-free demands.

"Thrust set," Eloise called as the engines roared forward, the airframe surging with power.

"Thrust set, airspeed building… eighty knots."

"Checked."

"V1… rotate."

Sarah pulled gently, and the nose rose, lifting them into the grey British sky. Through the windscreen, the drab East Anglian landscape fell away, giving way to cloud and sky and the pure, clean detachment of the climb.

"Positive rate."

"Gear up."

The gear thunked in, and they powered on through the low layer of drizzle, into that glowing, lemon-silver sunlight that always waited just above the clouds.

Sarah exhaled slowly. "And now… Paris awaits."

* _ * _ * _ *

Cruise altitude was reached in under twenty minutes— Cambridge to Beauvais was barely a hop by jet standards. Still, it gave Sarah a brief window to decompress from the earlier theatrics.

Of course, as they were crossing the Channel, the intercom from the cabin to the flight deck buzzed with the tell-tale double chime of impending mischief.

"Flight deck, forward galley," came Kelsey's dry voice. "Brace for impact. Our Row 2C celebrity has demanded, and you'll love this Sarah, a Snickers."

Sarah snorted a laugh so hard she had to clamp a hand over her mouth to avoid blurting it into the intercom.

Or the Cockpit Voice Recorder.

"She what?"

"You heard me. Snickers," Kelsey replied, each syllable dripping with relish. "Says she needs the sugar. Says the stress of being ignored over a 'life-threatening allergy' has left her feeling faint."

"Tell me you're joking," Eloise said, eyebrows lifting as she thumbed through the METAR for Beauvais on her tablet.

"Sadly not," Kelsey replied. "She's waving cash at Alexis like we're a petrol station. Best thing is that we don't accept cash and there's a contactless pad on the trolley. Oh, and we're out of Coke Zero. Some guy in 18F brought 15 bottles of it."

Sarah reached for the oxygen mask compartment, not to use it, but to rest her forehead lightly against the cold plastic in theatrical disbelief. "This job," she said, not quite to anyone in particular, "is an unending clown parade."

"Legend," Sarah murmured, still grinning as she flipped back to the nav page. "That buys us maybe twenty minutes of peace before she finds something else to be outraged about. I'm betting on the air being too thin, or the sky being too blue."

Eloise made a non-committal sound. "I'll put a fiver on the coffee being 'disrespectfully warm'."

They coasted over the Channel, pale cloud beneath, sunlight above. From this height, the chaos of the cabin felt miles away—both literally and emotionally. Here in the cockpit, all was precision and rhythm: monitoring systems, checking fuel balance, watching the en-route weather patches build up over Normandy.

* - * - * - *

"Good morning, Beauvais Tower, this is Margate Seven One Four One, descending through flight level one-two-zero for ILS approach, Runway Two Seven," Eloise radioed with practiced calm.

The reply came back swiftly, thick with the clipped French formality Sarah had come to associate with this corner of the continent: "Margate Seven One Four One, bonjour, descend and maintain four thousand feet, cleared for ILS approach Runway Two Seven, report established."

"Descending four thousand, cleared ILS Two Seven, will report established, Margate Seven One Four One," Sarah replied, hands already dancing over the mode control panel, dialling down their altitude and checking descent rates. The overhead panel bathed in a soft amber glow, announcing the phase transition. They were dropping into it.

Eloise flicked her screen over to the airport diagram. "Usual spaghetti routing, two lefts and a dogleg through the pasture. Looks like one other traffic ahead on short final, Ryanair, maybe?"

Sarah peered at the TCAS screen. "Affirm—FR forty-seven thirty, already on approach. We'll tuck in behind. No delays."

"Surprisingly civilised for a Sunday at Beauvais."

"Let's not jinx it," Sarah said, just as the seatbelt sign pinged and the cabin crew chimed in.

A moment later, the cockpit intercom buzzed again.

"Flight deck, forward galley," came Kelsey's voice once more. "Mrs Winthorpe would like to log a formal complaint. Apparently, the 'Snickers' she received was 'a fun size', which she considers demeaning. Also, she believes she is entitled to a hot towel."

Sarah blinked, and for a moment, truly struggled to process that last bit. "Hot towel? Is she aware she's on a low-cost carrier and not the QE2?"

Eloise gave a slow, theatrical blink, her hand pausing mid-flick over the approach checklist. "I suppose next she'll be demanding a glass of Chablis and a piano recital."

"Don't tempt fate," Sarah muttered, toggling the intercom. "Thanks Kelsey, tell her that hot towels are only offered on our Gulfstream service and only if she's travelling with a diplomatic passport."

"Copy that," Kelsey replied, audibly stifling a laugh. "Alexis is trying to pacify her with a wet wipe heated against the coffee pot. Improvised spa treatment, Sprinter style."

Sarah covered her mouth again, biting back laughter. "If this gets any more ridiculous, I'm going to need hazard pay."

"Welcome to Sunday service in Europe," Eloise muttered, hand poised over the localiser knob. "Right, only 3 more short sectors today and then we're done for the day."

Sarah chuckled, as she knew that the next sector, a Beauvais to Luton, Luton to Dublin and then Dublin to Manston, where Sarah would be taking her required day of time off was a textbook case of "short sectors, long day"—the kind of roster that looked innocent on paper but turned into a marathon once you factored in turnaround faff, catering misloads, and the occasional airborne melodrama.

The fact that it was only day 4 of Sprint's full operations, and that she was one of the few directly employed, not employed via a Maltese agency or a Lithuanian temp contract, meant that she at least had some protection when it came to shifts, fatigue reports, and filing the dreaded ASRs—Air Safety Reports—that were already stacking up across the company intranet like unpaid bills.

Eloise, on the other hand, was self-employed via a Maltese agency that specialised in supplying temporary contract flight crew across Europe, and like many others, she was living flight to flight—hoping that Sprint's ambitious expansion wouldn't collapse under the weight of its own bureaucracy before summer. Her tax situation, she had once remarked, required a spreadsheet, three passports, and a small candlelit shrine to St. Jude, patron saint of lost causes.

Sarah snapped back to focus as Eloise called out, "Localiser alive… glide slope captured."

"Three greens, flaps three," Sarah confirmed, watching as the runway centreline came into view, cutting a long grey line across the verdant patchwork of French farmland. "Speed checks… gear down."

The familiar thunk of the undercarriage deploying beneath them was oddly comforting—reliable, tactile, physical. A known quantity in a job that seemed to defy predictability with every passing week.

"Cabin crew, seats for landing," Eloise called on the PA, and a moment later, the cockpit chime confirmed they were secured. Kelsey and Alexis, no doubt, had wrangled every errant tray table, convinced Mrs Winthrope to stop performing mock fainting spells, and possibly administered a spiritual cleansing of the peanut zone with an Evian spritzer and the leftover scent of lavender sanitiser.

Sarah handled the final approach with quiet focus. The crosswind was mild, and despite the light chop through 1,500 feet, she maintained a stable descent. Eloise kept a hand poised just in case, but she knew Sarah had it under control. The runway lights blinked up at them as the threshold raced closer.

"Approach stable," Eloise said.

"Runway in sight," Sarah replied, easing the aircraft into a gentle flare as the ground rushed up to meet them.

"Minimums… continue."

With a practised touch, Sarah settled the aircraft onto the tarmac, the main gear kissing down with a smoothness that would have made her old RAF instructors proud. A soft puff of tyre smoke, a slight deceleration, and they were grounded once more on French soil.

"Speed brakes up, reversers normal," Eloise confirmed.

"Decel… seventy knots… manual braking."

The aircraft slowed gracefully as they rolled past the turn-off, and Eloise took the controls. Sarah exhaled quietly, adrenaline receding.

"Well done," Eloise murmured. "Didn't jostle a single fun-size Snickers."

Sarah snorted. "Let's hope that earns me an upgrade to regular-sized sarcasm."

As they taxied toward the stand, the crew began their usual post-landing rituals. Ground staff in high-vis vests waited by the marshaller's batons, guiding them in with slow, ceremonial gestures as though welcoming a returning monarch—or perhaps just another low-cost minion.

The engines powered down, and the cockpit filled with the subtle click of systems shifting to ground mode. The air grew still, filled with the faint hum of avionics and the rising chatter of passengers.

"Shall we open the door and release the kraken?" Eloise asked, voice dry.

"Why not? Maybe she'll review us on TripAdvisor," Sarah replied, flicking the PA switch. "Cabin crew, doors may be disarmed."

A minute later, the forward door hissed open with a whoosh of cold French air, and Sarah was the first to rise, slipping into the cabin before any passengers could mistake the cockpit for an extension of customer service. Alexis, smiling with the patient exhaustion of someone who had once broken up a hen party brawl with a stale baguette, was already unstrapping herself.

"2C?" Sarah asked.

Alexis tilted her head. "She's packing up her Kindle and telling the child—her granddaughter, apparently—that she might be going to court soon. Kid's asking if she means court as in tennis."

"Adorable," Sarah muttered. "Just get them off the aircraft without violence, please."

The disembarkation proceeded with the usual low-level chaos: people standing before the seatbelt sign went off, bags being pulled down like weapons, one old man refusing to move because he believed the apron bus was a "security trap". Through it all, Winthorpe remained a slow-moving hurricane of grievances, muttering about reviews on TripAdvisor and promising an "exposé" in the Mail.

Eventually, the aircraft was emptied, cleaned by a harried local team with industrial wipes and no PPE, and prepped for the short hop back to Luton. Sarah sat in the cockpit again, sipping what remained of her lukewarm flask coffee.

"That," she said, "was the most English flight to France I've ever flown."

Eloise grunted. "And we've got three more legs today. You ready for Luton?"

"As ready as I'll ever be. Let's go annoy some more people with our chromosomes and our failure to provide hot towels."

They shared a quiet laugh.

Outside, the drizzle returned, tapping softly against the windscreen.

Inside, systems blinked awake, and the aircraft prepared for its next absurd adventure through European skies.

And somewhere in the Beauvais arrivals hall, a pink twinset with a vendetta was already composing her first email to BBC Radio Kent.

****

CHAPTER 5 – Olympians & French ATC

Sunday 10th April 2022

"And we're live from Paris Beauvais, where French Olympic Women's Keirin Champion Victoria Gethin is making an announcement," Sarah could hear a Manic Radio newsreader say as she strolled through the terminal during a three-hour break, having completed the third run on former Avion Express LY-NVY between the UK and the French low-cost hub. It was surprising, Sarah knew, that an Olympic Champion, especially one who had been the rank outsider in the Keirin at Tokyo 2020, was doing it not at the French Olympic Headquarters or Paris Charles de Gaulle, but at Beauvais—an airport more famous for Ryanair herds and vending machine croissants than for medal ceremonies. Sarah would have smiled, but she was too tired to summon the effort. Instead, she watched a cluster of high-vis jackets and television mics huddled by a Team GB banner.

"What's happening?" she asked Francois Leveque, the Check-in Supervisor for Sprint at the French terminal, whose expression alternated between mild panic and that peculiar French insouciance that suggested even an airport evacuation would simply be another item on the day's agenda. Francois looked up from his mobile, the corners of his mouth twitching in what Sarah recognised as a suppressed smirk.

"Ah, Mademoiselle Marsh, you are not up to date with the spectacle?" he replied, shuffling a stack of boarding cards with practised indifference. "Victoria Gethin is here. Some sort of... défection."

Sarah blinked, the word lingering in the air like an unexpected headwind. "Défection? She's defecting? To where, exactly—Ryanair?"

Francois gave the classic Gallic shrug that communicated volumes—disbelief, amusement, and a complete lack of further information. "Who knows, Mademoiselle? The journalists say she is not happy with Team France, that she plans to race for Great Britain. Her père is English, and her mère is French, so she has dual nationality. She won gold for France in Tokyo, but apparently, the politics is all too much. She says Team GB gives her 'the opportunity to ride, not to play games'."

Francois' tone implied both cynicism and admiration; Sarah detected, beneath the dry French wit, a touch of pride that even a supposed traitor had managed to make headlines at Beauvais.

"It's all very dramatic," he continued, lowering his voice conspiratorially as a pair of British sports correspondents barrelled past, "but here at Beauvais, drama is all we ever get. That, and cheap Ryanair flights to Edinburgh."

Sarah grinned. "I suppose there's a press scrum for the first Luton connection as well, then?"

Francois snorted, finally allowing himself a smirk. "Non, for that, just disgruntled passengers and missing croissants."

Sarah let herself drift, feet heavy, eyes gritty with fatigue, into the rhythm of the terminal—a rhythm made up of rolling flight announcements, metallic tannoys in three languages, the constant clatter of wheelie bags, the scent of instant coffee, and the unique, sticky-sweet fug of disinfectant layered over old pastry. She'd been a First Officer for just shy of a few months, but airports felt much the same on either side of the flight deck door: a place where time was elastic, and sleep was always slightly out of reach.

Sarah allowed herself a slow exhale, letting the noise of the terminal swirl around her as she took in the carnival around Victoria Gethin's impromptu press conference. There were two cameramen adjusting lenses as if awaiting a Papal resignation, three police officers in ill-fitting uniforms hovering nearby for no apparent reason, and a scrawny airport PR manager waving a lanyard like a semaphore flag in case someone questioned their authority. Overhead, an automated voice mangled both French and English in ways that would have made her old French teacher cry.

A gaggle of airport cleaning staff—mostly North African, mostly invisible to the British press—stood leaning on their mops, watching with detached amusement. They were the uncredited audience for every drama Beauvais had to offer, more attuned than any journalist to the nuances of celebrity and outrage.

Victoria Gethin, the day's headline act, was stepping up to the microphone now. Cameras flashed, and Sarah watched as the athlete adjusted her jacket, the sleeves emblazoned with "Equipe de France" on one side and

"Team GB" on the other—a sartorial conflict that captured the essence of her predicament. Her accent, when she spoke, was pure Parisian with a razor-thin trace of London—a blend that would drive tabloids mad.

"I have decided," Victoria announced, "that my future is with Team GB. I thank France for everything, but I am British as well as French, and I ride to win, not to play politics. I hope you respect my choice."

A ripple went through the crowd—half applause, half indignant gasps, the rest simply murmurs of boredom or confusion. Behind the journalists, a British holidaymaker with a bright red sunburn asked his wife, "Is she the one what does the running or the cycling?" His wife, distracted by her phone, grunted noncommittally.

Sarah found herself wondering what it would feel like to defect, to step so decisively out of one world and into another. For all the chaos of her current career—Sprint Air, Sprinter, British contracts, Lithuanian aircraft—she was still fundamentally the same person, doing the same job in a slightly different uniform. Victoria, by contrast, had just detonated her entire public life. It took courage, or desperation. Or both.

Sarah felt a sudden jolt of sympathy for the cyclist. Airports, she reflected, were the world's natural crossroads, places where people left behind one identity and tried on another, if only for a weekend away in the sun. No wonder so many dramas played out here.

Her stomach growled, reminding her that the last thing she'd eaten was a croissant of dubious provenance somewhere between Cambridge and Beauvais, washed down with a cardboard cup of Nescafé. She scanned the terminal for food and was rewarded only by the distant sight of a "Paul" bakery concession, already besieged by passengers from two delayed Ryanair flights. She considered braving the queue, but the memory of the breakfast service on board—the satay wraps, the peanut butter smoothies, the grim array of vacuum-packed pastries—made her hesitate.

Instead, she wandered towards the staff canteen, a misnomer if ever there was one. Hidden beyond a door marked "PRIVATE—AEROPORT STAFF ONLY," it was little more than a linoleum-floored box with a coffee machine that worked sporadically and a pair of battered vending machines that dispensed Mars bars at random intervals.

Inside, she found Kelsey and Alexis, both slumped over mugs of something that might once have aspired to be coffee. Kelsey looked up, her ponytail limp and eyes puffy.

"Victoria bloody Gethin, eh?" Kelsey said, with a grin. "Only at Beauvais. Next week: Boris Johnson opens a Pret in Arrivals."

Alexis snorted. "He'd try to cut the ribbon with garden shears and end up in the wrong terminal."

Sarah dropped into a chair. "Do we get hazard pay for sharing a break room with Olympic defectors?"

Kelsey rolled her eyes. "Only if you can fit it on an ASR. Imagine—'Crew Fatigue: Caused by excessive exposure to medal winners and French television.'"

"You know, Manic was here reporting," Sarah said, pulling out her phone. "That social media guy, Ianto Hamilton, does the London Vibes patch."

Alexis perked up a little, her interest piqued. "Ianto Hamilton? The bloke with the accent so posh it makes LBC presenters sound like taxi drivers?"

"That's the one," Sarah replied, flicking through Twitter, where #VictoriaGethin was already trending somewhere between #BeauvaisDrama and #PeanutGate. "He's doing a live piece by the doors—something about 'modern sporting migrations and the aeronautical crossroads of Europe.'" She managed to deliver the last phrase in her best pseudo-BBC voice, drawing a snort of laughter from Kelsey.

Kelsey rolled her eyes. "Only in aviation could you have that and still spend your lunch break hiding from vending machine failure."

The staff canteen, like every hidden pocket of every airport, was both a haven and a kind of cage—where crews retreated to eat in peace but rarely managed it. The television, fixed permanently on BFM TV, flickered above the battered coffee machine, now mutely relaying a replay of Victoria Gethin's announcement, this time with French subtitles that butchered both 'Keirin' and 'défection'.

Sarah stared at her own reflection in the vending machine's glass. She looked tired, older than her years, with eyes that seemed to carry the collective exhaustion of every crew member from the past week. The air was heavy with the chemical tang of cleaning sprays, fresh croissant, and the lingering scent of burnt espresso.

She drew her flight bag closer with her foot. "Three hours until turn, and we're back to Luton. I'd kill for something resembling real food."

Alexis gestured at the ancient microwave. "Only thing you'll get here is last week's lasagne and a coffee so strong it might double as de-icer."

Sarah laughed, but it was a dry, knackered sound. "You know, there are moments when I wonder what on earth possessed me to leave PanEuro for this. There again, I was only a glorified cabin crew member, and my best friend got groped. At least she slapped the culprit so hard he fell into the aisle. Not that the company backed her up—just put her on 'development monitoring' for 'inappropriate self-defence'. Here at least, you know where you stand: somewhere between bankruptcy and a Ryanair gate."

Kelsey smiled wanly, rubbing her eyes. "Oh, that JFK that diverted to Shannon back in June? Roger Hargreaves? He sounds like a right prick. At least here, the 'management' can't actually be bothered to sit in the crew room, let alone make you feel guilty for doing the job. I swear, if I hear one more of them talk about 'corporate synergy' and 'flying the flag', I might just put a hole in the wall with the nearest trolley."

"Yeah, well, at least we don't have to hear some underpaid PR intern's version of the 'company family mantra' every week," Sarah responded, her voice laced with tired sarcasm. "But we all know that 'family' only goes one way around here. You take a holiday, and suddenly you're 'not committed enough to the mission.'" She shuddered. "Can you imagine trying to explain to my old crew at PanEuro that I'm flying from Beauvais to Luton for a company that can't even get a decent cup of coffee to save its life?"

Alexis took a long sip from her mug and stared at Sarah; eyes narrowed in mock seriousness. "Don't knock it till you've flown it, Marsh. Where else can you have such... dramatic mornings and still make your mandatory coffee breaks, eh? I mean, sure, it's all paper-thin, but sometimes, I reckon that's just part of the charm." She paused for a beat, clearly enjoying the bitter irony of the situation. "And hey, every time we land in Luton, it's like a homecoming. Except there's no welcome, and everyone's too tired to be excited. But that's probably why we get the big bucks, right?"

Sarah raised her eyebrow, half smiling at the jab. "Absolutely, the glamour of it all." She sat back, tapping the side of her cup absently. "Still, sometimes I wonder what I'm doing here. I mean, what's the endgame, really? If I'd stayed at PanEuro, I'd still be doing my job without all this... side hustle of moral confusion." Her gaze wandered to the screen above, where the image of Victoria Gethin was still looping, now framed by the very ridiculous '#PeanutGate' hashtag. It all felt so strange, disconnected, like watching the world through a filthy window.

Kelsey followed her gaze, a weary chuckle escaping her lips. "I'm with you there, but you know what they say... 'Better to be in the circus than to watch it from the sidelines.'"

"Yeah," Sarah replied with a long sigh, her eyes glazing over for a moment. "Maybe. It's just hard to get used to it, is all."

Before Alexis could offer another word of wisdom—if one could call it that—Kelsey shifted topics, gesturing toward Sarah's phone. "So, Ianto Hamilton's covering this? He's usually more into the 'glamour shots of cancelled flights' scene. That's a bit of a switch for him."

Sarah shrugged, leaning forward to set her phone down. "I suppose. There again, he must have flew from Luton with Ryanair to get here as he wasn't on our flight."

Sarah's feet were beginning to ache, the weariness from a morning's work already threading itself into the lines of her face. Yet, the world of aviation wasn't one to let its participants rest for long. The commotion in the terminal, laced with the echoes of chatter and the low hum of various flight announcements, barely registered as Sarah shuffled towards the staff canteen. It had been a strange few hours. Between the drama of Victoria Gethin's sudden decision to switch nationalities, the omnipresent circus of low-cost aviation, and the ongoing comedy of errors that was Sprint Air, Sarah was beginning to wonder if she'd ever again experience a day where she could simply take off without the weight of the world pressing down on her shoulders.

The journey to the canteen was uneventful, the fluorescent lighting of the terminal casting a sterile glow over the rows of plastic chairs and generic signage. She passed the usual crowd of travel-worn souls, the ones whose faces were becoming more familiar to her than her own. Airport employees in varying uniforms, each focused on the task at hand. The familiar world of trolleys being pushed, luggage being checked, and the eternal wait for the next announcement to signal a potential delay or cancellation.

As she pushed open the staff room door, the musty air and low chatter greeted her, and the dull buzz of the television hanging in the corner provided the backdrop to the usual crew break. Inside, Kelsey and Alexis were already seated, their tired faces illuminated by the flickering TV as they sipped from mugs that seemed to have long since surpassed their usefulness as containers for caffeine.

"That Victoria Gethin thing's going viral, isn't it?" Kelsey's voice broke the stillness, her tone flat but tinged with amusement.

"Only at Beauvais," Sarah replied, slumping into the chair across from her. "You'd think she'd be announcing it from Paris Charles de Gaulle, not here."

Alexis snorted as she pushed her mug aside. "Yeah, well, she's making headlines now, so I guess Beauvais will get its moment of fame."

Sarah leaned back, her gaze drifting back to the TV, which had now moved to a clip of Gethin making her official announcement in front of the throng of journalists. The image flashed across the screen, a collage of athleticism, politics, and media frenzy all stitched together in one brief moment. Gethin's speech was composed, but her words cut through the air like a blade. "I am British as well as French, and I ride to win, not to play politics." Sarah couldn't help but wonder, not for the first time, what it would feel like to throw everything away and shift allegiances. To simply step away from one identity and embrace a new one. For a moment, the thought seemed almost intoxicating—imagine, if only for a second, being able to throw the weight of your past into the wind and start afresh.

Kelsey interrupted Sarah's musings. "No one here is really buying it, though, are they? I mean, it's all well and good saying that, but Team GB's not exactly a fresh start for her either. It's just as political as Team France, if not more. D'you think she's shagging someone on Team GB and someone at Team France knows?"

Sarah grinned, grateful for Kelsey's irreverence, but even Alexis winced slightly, rubbing her temples as if she might erase the image. "Please, Kels, don't. I haven't eaten in twelve hours and now you've put me right off last week's lasagne."

Kelsey shrugged, her usual smirk in place. "Don't blame me. I'm just saying—these things are always about more than medals and tracksuits. You reckon anyone actually chooses their country for the fun of it? I'd choose whoever had the best coffee in the Olympic village. If it was Italy, I'd be singing the anthem before sunrise."

Sarah toyed with the teabag string dangling from her mug, watching the pale brown swirl of weak tea. "If only it were that simple. I'd swap airlines for a working espresso machine, let alone a gold medal." She glanced at the TV again, where the talking heads were now dissecting Gethin's every syllable, picking over the bones of her career for hints of discontent. "But you're right, Kels. There's always more going on. Nobody defects from comfort."

Alexis lifted her mug. "To defecting from comfort, then. May we all be brave enough—or mad enough—one day." The three of them clinked their battered ceramic mugs together, the toast faint and hollow in the half-empty canteen.

For a long moment, silence fell—a rare thing for any crew room, but one born not from awkwardness but exhaustion. Each of them stared at the peeling paint on the walls, the battered lockers, the castoff jumpers draped over the backs of mismatched chairs. It was, in its own tired way, a home.

Of course, the next thing Sarah knew, the Sprint Staff app came up with a notification affecting the next three legs.

"MGT341, RAT341 and RAT7342, BVA-LTN, LTN-BVA and BVA-MSE CANCELLED due to Industrial Action at BVA ATC."

Sarah stared at the notification on her phone, blinking several times to be sure she was reading it correctly. Cancelled. Three flights, all her work for the rest of the day, erased with a single impersonal push notification. No explanation, no apology, no attempt at euphemism—just those four words, so final, so mundane, so perfectly in keeping with the tone of modern low-cost aviation.

Kelsey's phone chimed a second after, the alert sounding far more cheerful than the news it carried. She squinted at the screen. "You have got to be kidding me."

Alexis let out a groan so deep it seemed to rattle the table. "Bloody typical. Is it ATC on strike or have they just nipped out for a smoke and forgotten to come back?"

Sarah offered a thin, bitter smile. "French ATC, Kels. Always on strike, always at lunch, or both at once. I bet there's a bloke with a placard and a baguette holding up the entire sector right now."

Kelsey rolled her eyes. "And I was just about to psyche myself up for a 28-minute sector to Luton, three loops through customs, and a sandwich that tastes of existential despair. This is what I get for not using my last standby to Majorca."

Alexis shook her head and flopped back in her seat, fingers drumming against her mug. "Well, that's the day knackered. What now? We could hang about until they call us with a new roster, or go join the endless scrum at Paul and drown our sorrows in pain au chocolat."

Sarah weighed the options, then shrugged. "Let's see what Ops want us to do. It'll be the usual—'Standby at the hotel, please monitor your app for updates'—then three hours of radio silence, followed by a frantic call at 4am to say 'quick, back to the airport, we've found a slot to nowhere'."

Kelsey shot her a sideways glance, a glint of humour in her eyes despite her exhaustion. "You reckon we'll get night stopped in Beauvais? I bet the crew hotel's got shower curtains older than Victoria Gethin's cycling career."

"It'd be an upgrade from the crew digs in Luton," Alexis replied dryly. "There's mushrooms growing in the bathroom at the Ibis Budget. And not the edible sort."

A silence settled as the reality sank in. The three women, dressed in the uniform of weary modern aviators— practical shoes, crumpled shirts, regulation navy jumpers—sat huddled around a table cluttered with empty coffee sachets and a single, unopened packet of speculoos biscuits.

Sarah's phone buzzed again. This time it was a message from Sprint Crew Scheduling, blandly formal:

URGENT: All Sprint Air crew currently at BVA to report to Gate 9 at 1400 for further briefing. Please remain contactable and in uniform.

She read the message aloud, and Alexis snorted. "Further briefing. That's code for 'We have no clue what's going on and want you to look professional while we figure it out.'"

Kelsey stuffed her phone back in her pocket. "Might as well go. Beats hiding in here when the cleaning staff are looking at us like we're next on the rota."

They gathered their things, grimly efficient, each lost in their own thoughts. Sarah's flight bag felt heavier than it had that morning, the weight of delay, uncertainty, and the prospect of another endless briefing adding to the burden of emergency checklists and a day-old banana she'd meant to eat and forgotten about.

Out in the main terminal, Beauvais was its usual cacophony: children screeching, announcements blaring, the endless shuffle of passengers who'd arrived too early, too late, or simply too lost to care. In the corner, Victoria Gethin was still being swarmed by journalists, her face already a meme on Twitter, her accent dissected by bored interns on YouTube.

The walk to Gate 9 was a slow procession through a forest of trolley bags and confused holidaymakers. The gate itself was roped off, a makeshift barrier of crowd-control tape and a plastic sign in bad English: "STAFF ONLY. CREW MEETING."

Sarah recognised a few faces from other flights—Sprint crews, a handful formerly of Avion Express, even a pair of ex-Thomas Cook pilots who now worked as contract FOs for Sprinter. They all wore the same mask of forced patience and private exasperation.

"Seems ATC decided as soon as Gethin made her announcement, they were going on strike nationwide over the usual pay and conditions," muttered a familiar voice. Sarah glanced over to see Hayley Northcott, her friend and an Easyjet First Officer, approaching. "One of the ATC controllers mentioned it on the radio as I just come into land about a minute ago."

Hayley's presence was always something of a tonic to Sarah, her voice pitched in that particular register of aviation banter that floated above exhaustion and cut straight to the reality of the situation. She stood there now, the orange piping of her easyJet uniform marking her out like a highlighter against the navy shades of Sprint, Sprinter, and whoever else had been roped into the low-cost parade at Beauvais that day.

Hayley looked her up and down, then gave an elaborate wink. "Bit lively for a Sunday, Marsh. Did you see the scrum out there? You'd think Gethin was defecting to Ryanair. Actually, scratch that. You'd need a minor war to make Beauvais this busy otherwise."

Sarah let a tired smile slip. "I keep waiting for Ryanair to claim her as a 'celebrity guest captain' and charge the press for priority boarding. Still, I'd take a cycling gold medallist over another stag do in fancy dress any day."

Hayley grinned. "If O'Leary hears you, he'll have her flogging scratchcards and posing with the cabin crew by Thursday. I see the French are keeping to tradition—ATC strikes on a Sunday, right on the hour."

A cluster of cabin crew in various uniforms loitered by the tape, some leaning against the window staring out at the grey tarmac, others flicking through phones for updates, memes, or a moment of levity in the doomscroll. On the apron, Sarah caught sight of LY-NVY, still wearing the faint blue lines from its Avion Express days, parked up beside a SmartLynx A321 and a battered Ryanair 737. All the aircraft looked equally abandoned, as though they too had just received the cancellation notification and decided, in solidarity, not to move an inch.

A man in a too-bright Sprint tabard—one of the French ground supervisors, whose English was always formal but whose eyes told a different story—stepped forward to shoo a stray passenger away from the crew huddle. "S'il vous plaît, this area is for crew only," he said, his tone weary but polite.

The passenger, a middle-aged Englishman in a Hawaiian shirt, simply nodded and retreated, dragging a bag that made a noise somewhere between a squeak and a sob. Sarah watched him go with a pang of empathy; not for the first time, she wondered if the line between passenger and crew wasn't so much one of uniform, but of expectation.

Gate 9 was rapidly filling with more uniformed bodies— some familiar, others new, their faces caught in the strange limbo between resignation and faint hope. Sarah drifted over to the window, peering out through streaks of spring rain at the static lines of aircraft, the empty apron.

A shout drew her attention—a stocky man with a balding pate and the weathered look of a career dispatcher was waving a clipboard in the air. "Sprint, Sprinter, and all agency crew, this way please!" he called, voice barely carrying over the babble of anxious conversation. "Ops will brief in five minutes."

Sarah fell in with the stream, her ID lanyard cold against her neck. The crew shuffled forward, all quiet professionalism on the outside, but inside every heartbeat with a familiar cocktail of frustration and uncertainty. She exchanged nods with a couple of other FOs—one Polish, one Romanian—who she'd worked with on the Vilnius rotation the month before.

Hayley sidled up beside her, flashing a sideways grin. "If this takes longer than twenty minutes, I'm nicking the biscuits from the crew room. Fair warning."

Sarah was about to reply when the dispatcher raised his voice again. "Ladies and gentlemen, apologies for the confusion. As you may have heard, due to industrial action by ATC, all flights in and out of Beauvais are suspended until further notice. Sprint Air is in contact with Paris Ops, but at the moment, we don't have a confirmed timeline for resumption."

A groan rippled through the assembled crowd. Kelsey, lurking just behind Sarah, muttered, "Could have told us that in the app. Save us all the walk."

The dispatcher pressed on, "You will remain on standby. Hotels are being arranged for crew night stops if the suspension continues. Please do not leave the airport until instructed by your operator. Any crew needing to speak to scheduling, come see me after the briefing."

He paused, scanning the sea of tired faces, then added, almost apologetically, "If there are any dietary needs, or anyone needs medication, please let us know—staff canteen will remain open for crew. Sorry for the inconvenience."

That, Sarah thought, was the full extent of customer service in low-cost aviation: a half-hearted apology, an open canteen, and an unspoken invitation to get on with it. But there was nothing malicious in it—just a kind of weary acceptance. The system was broken, but it was the system they had.

The crowd dispersed in slow motion. Some gravitated back toward the canteen, others to the terminal windows to phone loved ones or tap out emails to Crew Control. Sarah lingered with Kelsey, Alexis, and Hayley. The four of them found an empty row of seats by a vending machine that seemed to alternate between humming and clattering ominously.

Hayley reached into her flight bag, produced a battered pack of Cards Against Humanity, and tossed it onto the seat. "Right. If we're here for the long haul, we may as well make it interesting. Winner gets the last biscuit."

Kelsey perked up, a spark of mischief returning. "Deal. Loser has to ask Ops for actual coffee, using only French."

Alexis looked scandalised. "That's cruel. Even my A-level French isn't up to that."

But Sarah found herself smiling for the first time in hours. For all the grind and grindstone, there was a camaraderie in these moments—unspoken, defiant, utterly irrepressible. Even in a beige departure lounge, with the threat of a night in a two-star hotel looming, they found something like joy.

****

CHAPTER 6 – Manston Madness
Tuesday 12th April 2022

The terminal at Manston Airport was chaos, Sarah knew as she walked through the staff car park into the staff entrance, as, looking on BBC News, Gatwick's baggage handlers were on a sudden wildcat strike and so easyJet had diverted several services to Manston instead. And not just easyJet either. Ryanair had made a few tactical swaps to use their quietest base for inbound aircraft, and even Wizz Air had a single A321neo routed in from Budapest to avoid the snarled-up handling chaos in London.

Sarah stepped through the biometric staff gate, her ID badge lagging behind her weary face as the turnstile bleeped a green light. Walking to the portacabin where Ops, and Luke Rainsford, the local manager of Operations, was supposed to be based, she already heard voices raised.

Someone was shouting. Loudly.

"Which morainic moron parked a bloody 737 Max on stand D when RAT4264 was due to arrive there? Now I've got a bloody taxiway blocked, a Hungarian crew out of hours, and an aircraft full of stag parties wanting their money back!"

Luke Rainsford's voice had only one volume when under pressure: volcanic. Sarah pressed the door with her shoulder, to see Luke on the phone to the Tower at Discovery Park, trying to recover an impossible morning into something resembling order. Papers were everywhere—printed load sheets, telex messages, scribbled notes. A battered whiteboard bore a haphazard diagram of stands and registrations, revised so often the old pen marks ghosted beneath every update.

Sarah stood for a moment in the cramped portacabin, her breath catching in the stuffy, caffeine-laden air. She could see the stress lines in Luke's face as he jabbed the air with his pen, eyes flitting between his phone and the window overlooking the chaotic apron. Beyond, low-cost jets in mismatched liveries vied for space, engines spooling, ground crews sprinting, and a strange orchestra of hi-vis vests and fluorescent wands flickered in the chilly April sun.

She coughed politely, drawing his attention. "Morning, Luke. What's the latest disaster?"

He shot her a look that might've curdled milk. "Oh, morning, Sarah. You're on the Sprint Cologne today, right?"

She nodded, setting her flight bag by the kettle that had, she knew, been brought from Argos a week ago. "No, I'm on, according to the app, a Riga with a Captain Franz Bauer. RAT8741. I did check with the guys at Ramsgate, and I've got F-WWDQ?"

F-WWDQ, Sarah knew, was one of the registrations Airbus used to test the A320 family before they delivered the planes to the airlines—a strange, temporary relic that sometimes showed up in the Sprint Air system when a newly leased aircraft hadn't yet been painted or re-registered. For some reason, Sprint liked, where possible, to keep the tail numbers that had been assigned to the planes that they'd brought, be they brand new whitetails, or be they second hand former Allegiant or Tianjin Air frames, as if hanging onto a childhood nickname that never quite fitted, but whose oddness now made the fleet uniquely theirs. F-WWDQ was technically French, but painted in Sprint's navy-blue livery, complete with Sprint logos and interior fit, even though, legally, the registration wasn't meant for commercial ops. Sarah suspected the only reason they could operate under it was through a sleight-of-hand in Sprint Air's convoluted operating certificate—a legal patchwork spanning Lithuanian wet leases, UK-based dispatchers, and a rotating cast of consultants paid to insist it was fine as long as no one looked too hard. She was, technically, flying a plane that had never been delivered to an airline. Yet here she was, about to take off with 180 passengers to Riga.

Luke didn't look convinced. He rubbed his forehead with his thumb and muttered something inaudible.

"Look," he said at last, flicking through a stack of manifests. "The bloody thing was supposed to go on a Dusseldorf run today. But now we've got an EasyJet A320 sitting in its spot, a Wizz A321 blocking pushback on stand C, and Ryanair have decided to park two 737s on taxiway Alpha, which isn't even a proper stand. One of their FO's came in here earlier and asked if he could use our kettle. I told him if he found a working plug socket, he could brew a cup for me too."

Sarah glanced out the window again, watching a Ryanair MAX trundle slowly across the apron, winglets nearly clipping the edge of a makeshift terminal fence. The airfield looked like a forgotten Lego set someone had tried to rebuild from memory, and the sudden influx of jets had pushed it to absurdity.

"I'll take WWDQ if it's good to go," Sarah offered, trying to cut through the madness. "Is the Captain here yet?"

Luke checked the time. "Nope, he's commuting from Luton on a shuttle that we've diverted from Gatwick. It's somewhere in the stack."

Sarah didn't sigh, but she wanted to. It was always somewhere in the stack: aircraft, people, logic, sanity. "Is there a plan, Luke, or are we improvising as we go?"

Luke gave a short, ragged laugh, pinching the bridge of his nose. "If there's a plan, it's hidden behind the pile of crew transfer slips and my sense of humour. Listen—Ops in Vilnius are trying to swap the Riga and Cologne crews, but half the ground staff are on double shifts and our only working GPU is hitched to a Ryanair. If you see a plan out there, Sarah, please draw it on the whiteboard. In permanent ink."

Sarah smiled, not without sympathy. "All right, I'll take the keys to the museum piece and start the walkaround. When Franz appears, tell him I'm down by the nosewheel, hiding from Ryanair FOs."

As she left, Luke's mobile began to ring—again. He mouthed a silent 'help me' as he answered, immediately launching into a diplomatic tirade about stand allocations, while Sarah stepped outside into the brittle morning. The air smelt of jet fuel, coffee dregs, and distant, impatient humanity.

The scene outside was barely contained anarchy. Where once Manston's apron had seen a handful of business jets and occasional charters, today it looked more like a cut-rate airshow gone wrong: easyJet's orange tails mixed with Wizz Air's magenta, Ryanair's blues and Sprint's hastily applied navy, all parked at strange angles as if the ground crew had given up halfway through a game of Tetris.

Sarah pulled her hi-vis jacket tighter, scanning for F-WWDQ. She spotted it immediately: a newly painted A320 still gleaming, though the Sprint logo looked slightly skewed, as if the livery team had given up after a night at the pub. It wore its temporary French registration with a faint air of embarrassment. Some stickers flaked at the corners.

A ground engineer—young, Polish, and already wearing the kind of existential fatigue common in the aviation industry—nodded as she approached.

"Morning," Sarah said. "I'm First Officer Marsh, Sprint Air. This is WWDQ, right?"

The engineer grinned, white teeth bright against his dark stubble. "Ja, WWDQ. They said you would come. Welcome to Manston. It's like Heathrow, but everyone is lost." He gestured at the main gear, where a low loader was slowly reversing, ground crew frantically waving to avoid clipping the adjacent Ryanair.

Sarah crouched by the nosewheel, checking for any obvious damage. "How's she looking?"

"Beautiful," the engineer said, patting the fuselage with a lover's fondness. "Only... you know... she's still learning to be an airline plane."

Sarah checked the logbook, flipping through maintenance stickers and temporary authorisations. Everything seemed in order, at least on paper. She circled the aircraft, glancing up at the winglets—Sprint blue, painted right over the Airbus house colours. If you looked closely, you could still make out the faint ghost of the test registration underneath.

Climbing the stairs, she headed to the cockpit to ensure that two vital documents were there, the folder with the Air Operators Certificates for Sprint's UK and Lithuanian entities, and the insurance documents. Looking through the folder, she noticed that Sprint's insurance was more complicated than a container ship's ballast log—cover notes stapled to cover notes, underwritten by three different Lloyd's syndicates, Omani Sovereign Fund letters and even an Allianz insurance certificate that stated that the plane was covered for public liability for the sum of £10 million in the United Kingdom, and in the European Union the sum of €12 million, "subject to compliance with all applicable national and EASA regulations." Sarah almost laughed. She'd seen smaller paper trails for war crimes tribunals. She set the folders neatly in the jump seat's document tray, brushing a flake of navy paint from the pedestal.

The cockpit, at least, was clean and smelled faintly of new plastics and coffee. The ECAM screen flickered through its startup test. Every surface still carried that slightly greasy sheen from Airbus's factory protective film, and the sidestick had barely lost the moulded grip marks of its last test pilot. Sarah's name was scrawled on the printed journey log beside "F/O," while the captain's box still read "TBC."

From the flight deck windows, she had a grandstand view of the circus outside: the EasyJet A320 still half-parked on the Dusseldorf stand, a rainbow of high-viz jackets playing charades with a Wizz marshaller, and, at the end of taxiway Alpha, a Ryanair 737 with two ground engineers and a flustered dispatcher arguing over a headset. Every now and then, a ground vehicle would dart between them with the bravado of a dodgem at the funfair.

Sarah ran through her preliminary checks, powering up the electrics on APU, reviewing the FMS inputs, and confirming the flight plan on the MCDU. The route to Riga, as loaded by Ops, was as direct as European airspace would allow, but the NOTAMs printed off the dot matrix in the crew room told a different story: Luton and Stansted sectors overloaded, reroutes via the North Sea, weather squalls over the Baltic and to fly over the Nordics, not Kaliningrad, especially since a PanEuro flight the previous year had almost been shot down and Russian airspace was also closed due to the sanctions from the Ukraine-Russo conflict that had started less than 2 months ago. She scrolled through the messages, sighing as the list of restrictions, alternative routings, and obscure acronyms grew longer with each page. Sprint's dispatchers were nothing if not creative, and Sarah couldn't help but marvel at their knack for squeezing a legal route out of airspace more politically fraught than the United Nations Security Council.

Her mind drifted back to her RAF days, to the clarity of military flight plans: objective, hierarchical, obeyed. This—this was commercial aviation in 2022, all half-truths and 'see and avoid' and a thousand little legal fictions papering over the cracks of a broken continent. She checked the fuel slip, scribbled a quick note for Franz, and opened the side window for a breath of the Kentish air. The tang of jet exhaust and wet grass grounded her for a moment.

"Ramsgate 8741, this is Manston Ops, do you copy, over," Luke's voice came over the radio, crackling through the headset left on COM 2. Sarah keyed the mic, letting the discipline of checklists and comms bring her back to the present.

"Manston Ops, Ramsgate 8741, reading you five by five, go ahead."

Luke's reply was delivered with his usual mix of command and despair. "Sarah, status on WWDQ? I've got Handling on my back about slot allocation. Also need to let you know that Captain Bauer has been redeployed. You've got a new Captain now. Ramsgate Ops have assigned Captain Medusa Cole to you."

Sarah froze, her hand resting on the thrust lever. Captain Medusa Cole. Not a name to inspire serenity, if you'd heard the stories. She'd never flown with her, but Medusa's reputation had spread—half-legend, half-warning. Some said she was ex-EasyJet, some said she'd spent years doing charters to Kosovo and Dakar for anyone with an AOC and a chequebook, and all agreed she was the sort of captain who brooked no fools and no nonsense, and who could terrify a dispatcher just by raising an eyebrow over her half-moon glasses.

"Copy that, Manston," Sarah said, as evenly as she could. "ETA for Captain Cole?"

There was a pause. She pictured Luke scanning the chaos outside. "Last I checked she was in a chopper from Cambridge, ETA 2 minutes."

Sarah blinked. Of all the ways a captain could arrive, a helicopter was not one she'd expected. She tried to remember the last time she'd seen a senior line captain dropped into a field operation by rotorcraft and came up blank—unless you counted NATO war games, and those didn't come with Kentish wildflowers and EasyJet A320s blocking the taxiways.

From the cockpit, she could just make out a speck in the sky to the north, descending fast over the broken hedge line at the edge of the airport boundary. In a place more used to the gentle hum of Airbus fleets, the approaching thump-thump-thump of helicopter blades had a cinematic quality: somewhere between a corporate power move and a UN food drop.

Sarah scanned her surroundings, double-checked the aircraft's parking brake, and made her way down the steps to the apron, drawn as much by curiosity as necessity. The ground crew, already spooked by the day's madness, paused to stare as the helicopter, a brand new AW109, swept in, for a moment over the grass verge, and settled with a practiced nonchalance.

The rotors barely slowed, and Sarah watched as Cole kissed the pilot with an intensity that matched the day's surreal energy—an old comrade, or maybe a partner, impossible to tell in the quick, defiant gesture. In a single motion, Captain Medusa Cole, dressed in a tight leather outfit, grabbed her flight bag and ducked beneath the spinning blades, striding across the grass with the unflinching confidence of someone utterly at home in the weirdest corners of commercial aviation.

Cole's arrival was like the punchline to a joke nobody had finished telling. Sarah had heard every story—the time Cole told a Lithuanian CAA inspector to "bugger off and buy a real ruler", the tale of her once physically restraining a drunken stag from opening an overwing exit at 38,000 feet, and the persistent legend that she'd once landed a 737 in Sarajevo with a single reverser, no APU, and four politicians demanding to smoke in the galley. She wore her notoriety like a badge: tight black boots, a battered tan flight bag patched with old IATA tags, and hair cut to a severe, asymmetric wedge, with just enough silver to suggest experience rather than age.

She was through the fence, across the apron, and up the steps before Sarah could say "good morning". A nod. No smile.

"You're Marsh, right?" Cole's voice had the faintest Midlands burr, but sharper at the edges, made for ordering people around small airports and brokering truce with ATC.

"That's me," Sarah replied, meeting her eyes. "FO, RAT8741 to Riga. Aircraft's good, bar the usual Sprint paperwork sudoku. Ramp's chaos—nothing new."

Cole set her bag on the left seat and started her walkaround of the pedestal, not the plane. She flicked the battery switch, scanned the ECAM, and grunted in satisfaction.

"You do the outside?"

Sarah nodded, handing over the walkaround sheet and pointing out a couple of flaking livery stickers. Cole squinted, shrugged, then ran a finger down the logbook entries. "Test reg, French insurance, Baltic destination, and a queue of hungover Ryanair crews trying to steal our GPU. Classic Sprint day out."

She paused, fixing Sarah with that hawkish stare. "You ever flown this airframe?"

"Not this specific one, but I've flown the type, as well as Typhoons, Hawks and a few Cessnas."

Cole's eyebrow twitched—just enough to betray a flicker of recognition at the mention of Typhoons. "RAF girl, are you? Good. Maybe you'll be the right kind of bastard if the old girl throws a tantrum." She tapped the MCDU with a heavy acrylic nail. "And maybe you won't freak out when Riga ATC starts inventing new holding patterns."

Sarah allowed herself a thin smile. "If they don't, I'll start to worry."

Cole's approval, such as it was, came in the form of a grunt and a quick, competent flurry through the rest of the paperwork. Sarah watched as Cole worked: everything done with a coiled, economical energy, like someone who'd spent too many years in cockpits where things didn't work, and every second could matter. She checked the insurance folders, the Sprint AOC printouts, and a pile of company circulars—then tossed them aside with a mutter about "committee brains". At last, satisfied that nothing in the cockpit was about to explode (at least on paper), Cole slumped into the left seat.

"All right, Marsh. Preflight done. Pax aren't even in the terminal yet, and we're already running late." She eyed Sarah, an edge of amusement in her stare. "How's your patience for ops delays?"

Sarah shrugged. "My patience for delays is bottomless, provided the coffee supply holds out."

Cole actually barked a laugh—sharp and short. "Good. Now, the rules are simple. I'm only with Sprint as Jeff Young is a friend and he needed someone with lots of A320 experience as a captain for his flying circus. I'm trusting you to be the Pilot Flying for all the sectors we do today, as I want to ensure that you can actually handle this crate in the real world, not just in a sim. And, more importantly, because I can't stand babying new FOs. We're short of time, short of stands, and I'd rather watch someone learn by doing than listen to another empty briefing. If you cock it up, I'll tell you. If you don't, maybe I'll buy you a drink in Riga."

Sarah nodded, taking the challenge in stride. She reached across to confirm the radios and slip her logbook into the side pocket. "Fine by me, Captain. But if you want me to fly, you get to do the PA announcements. Company rules."

"Deal," Cole replied, with the faintest smirk.

Sarah set about programming the FMS, fingers skimming over the buttons with a familiarity born of necessity. She loaded in the route, mindful of the labyrinthine airway restrictions, and triple-checked the runway allocation. The take-off runway, nominally 28, had already changed twice that morning thanks to a rolling schedule of arriving diversions. She entered the SID, feeling Cole's sharp gaze linger, not quite judging—testing, perhaps, or maybe just ensuring she wasn't about to make a rookie mistake.

Cole was running her own set of checks, systematically flicking switches, testing the oxygen mask with a brisk exhalation. "You loaded the performance figures for Manston?" she asked, not looking up.

Sarah handed over her scribbled notepad, where she'd worked out the take-off speeds with half an eye on the crosswind and a mental calculator for the effect of the standing water at the runway threshold. "Here. Based on a 10 departure, winds variable at fifteen knots, QNH one-zero-one-five, temp nine Celsius, full thrust. Not that it'll matter when ATC change everything on pushback."

Cole grunted her approval and tapped the pad. "Good. If the tower tells you to hold for wildlife, don't be surprised. Yesterday at Glasgow I saw a flock of sheep wander across the grass while Ryanair were lining up." She leaned in, lowering her voice. "This place used to be run like a military outpost. Now it's every low-cost for themselves. You see the way the Wizz boys marshalled themselves in? Pure chaos."

Sarah smiled, feeling a twinge of kinship in their mutual cynicism. "It's not Heathrow, but it's honest work," she replied, echoing a phrase she'd heard from ground crew a hundred times over.

Sarah set about her work with a quiet, professional efficiency, letting Cole's formidable presence become background noise rather than distraction. She confirmed the fuel load, cross-checked it with the uplift slip and the departure ATIS, then tapped through the ECAM's checks, careful not to let the cockpit's strange, still-new silence lull her into missing a step. Outside, the distant whine of an EasyJet A320's APU battled for dominance with a Ryanair engine start, creating an uneasy soundtrack of interrupted normality.

Cole checked her watch. "We're boarding in ten, apparently. Ops says we've got a Lithuanian cabin crew—three of them, fresh in from a Wizz turn this morning. Don't expect much chit-chat. Their English is good, but they're here for overtime, not the career." She thumbed the intercom. "Cabin, this is Captain Cole. When you're aboard, I want a full crew check in the flight deck before pax. If you're late, we go without you."

Sarah arched an eyebrow at Cole's brusqueness but said nothing. The more she watched, the more she realised that Cole's reputation for terror was not sadism—it was armour. In an industry that asked for miracles on ten minutes' notice, kindness had to be rationed.

The first of the crew—a tall, anxious woman with bottle-blonde hair and a battered trolley—ducked into the cockpit, followed by two men in matching Sprint waistcoats, both looking like they'd just come off a Ryanair leg from Kraków. "Morning, Captain. Morning, First Officer. I'm Asta, lead on this sector. This is Dainius and Arturas. Safety check complete. Galley stowage signed off, hot water available, and the forward toilets are, ah, satisfactory." She glanced at Cole for a reaction, received none, and continued. "Boarding will start once the buses have finished their third lap of the apron."

"Welcome," Sarah said, with what she hoped was enough warmth to bridge the cultural chasm. "If you need anything on the tech side, just shout. And if you see any stag parties trying to board with their own mini kegs, send them straight back to security."

Asta grinned—a flash of real humour amid the exhaustion. "No problem. We had four last week try to check in a full suitcase of Jägermeister. Luton took it away. I think the ground staff had a party."

Cole finished her cross-check and handed over a folder. "Safety demo in English and Latvian, please. Expect turbulence over the North Sea, and we may need to hold for a slot. Be firm with anyone who tries to swap seats mid-taxi. Last week, a Ryanair from Warsaw had six go-arounds because some idiot wouldn't sit down."

Asta nodded, efficiently translated for her colleagues, then led them out, boots clicking on the brand-new vinyl flooring. Sarah watched them go, grateful for their professionalism and stamina. So many in this business, she knew as she prepared for departure, were running on nothing but caffeine, muscle memory, and pride.

"But hey, it could be worse," she muttered. "At least we're not Ryanair."

****

CHAPTER 7 – Disruptive Pax
Friday 15th April 2022

"Good morning, ladies and gentlemen, and welcome aboard this Sprinter service to Ibiza. I'm your First Officer, Sarah Marsh, and between Captain Julie Andrews and I, we would like to ensure you have a smooth and comfortable flight today. Flight time will be approximately three hours and fifteen minutes, and we'll be cruising at an altitude of 36,000 feet. Weather in Ibiza is clear skies with a slight breeze, so expect a pleasant arrival. We'll keep you updated on any changes as we progress, and we appreciate your cooperation throughout the flight. Please sit back, relax, and enjoy your journey."

The irony was not lost on Sarah, as their flight, a former Air France Airbus A318, one that had only been in service a week and was still carrying its French tail number, F-GUGC, despite being refurbished and rebranded with Sprint Air's livery, was anything but smooth.

Despite her professionalism, Sarah couldn't help but grimace internally at the unusual chaos surrounding the aircraft's reactivation. The A318, typically a city hopper for short-haul routes, was more accustomed to serving busy routes within the Air France network, not as part of the patchwork fleet Sprint Air was assembling on the fly.

The fact that the route was Coventry to Ibiza, and this was the first flight of the twice weekly route, designed because, while Sprint and Sprinter both used Birmingham Airport in the main, some of the routes in the 2 week old low cost carrier had planned to run from Birmingham had been moved to Coventry instead due to a shortage of slots, the currency that airlines used to gain access to airports.

The further irony that the majority of the manifest were stag and hen parties, a raucous crowd looking to party in Ibiza, wasn't lost on Sarah either. The mix of exuberant energy and the inevitable chaos of a brand-new low-cost airline made for a tricky combination. The smell of cheap cologne, the sound of laughter and loud conversation, and the occasional burst of giggles all created an atmosphere far from the calm professionalism that Sarah would have preferred.

And then there was the name of the Captain she was working with for this flight. Julie Andrews. The fact that she wasn't the film star who played roles like Mary Poppins, but a seasoned veteran of the skies with a no-nonsense attitude, only added another layer of irony to the situation. The humour wasn't lost on Sarah, though she quickly dismissed it with a mental shake of her head. There was no time for idle thoughts; this was Sprint Air, and every flight felt like a delicate balancing act between aviation professionalism and the chaotic reality of running a low-cost airline in its infancy.

"Coventry Tower, this is Margate 1343, requesting permission to taxi for departure," Sarah heard Julie say, as she herself ticked off, on the iPads that Sprint had installed in the A318s, same with the rest of the fleet, despite the A318s having the CRT and not LCD screens, a small concession to the airline's budget-conscious approach.

"Margate 1343, Coventry Tower," came the reply, crackling through the intercom. "Taxi to runway 23L, winds calm, cleared for departure."

Julie nodded and manoeuvred the aircraft, a few of the passengers turning to look at the cockpit as the engines roared to life, sending a slight hum throughout the cabin. The aircraft's nose tilted slightly upward as the plane began its slow journey towards the runway. As they passed through the taxiway, Sarah's mind began to wander again, and she could not help but think about the situation they were in.

"Margate 1343 confirms taxi to runway 23 left, calm winds, over," Sarah read back to the control tower, her voice calm despite the swirling chaos inside her head. She knew that it was normal for a readback of the clearance to be precise, but today, everything felt out of the ordinary.

The fact that there were rumours that the Wizz planners that Sprint had poached were also using Coventry as a raid on the newly created UK Government's Levelling Up agenda was not something she could ignore either. Coventry, once overlooked, now seemed to be emerging as a key piece in the puzzle of post-Brexit airline restructuring, and Sprint Air was right at the centre of it. The irony of starting at Coventry Airport, the underdog of UK aviation, wasn't lost on Sarah either. She couldn't help but think of how much the airline was trying to live up to its promise of affordable travel, despite the baggage of ill-planned fleet rotations and barely functional airports.

She knew that the APU had been disconnected when they had started their engines, as the stands at Coventry were stairs, not jet bridges, due to the former passenger terminal having been demolished when Wizz, in 2008, had abandoned the airport. But Sprint Air, in its drive to be different, had taken it on with a mixture of optimism and desperation, repurposing old equipment and bypassing the usual luxury of larger terminals. To her mind, the irony wasn't just in the location, it was in the very nature of the airline's identity: low-cost, no-frills, and operating on the edge of chaos.

It was then, during the taxiing, that Julie spoke.

"I swear to God, this reminds me of my Flybe days. You know, back when people used to think regional flying was civilised. Right, alternates, what are they?"

Sarah looked at the tablet, even though she knew that there were at least a half a dozen alternates filed automatically by the flight planning system. But Julie was a belt-and-braces captain. "Palma, Barcelona, Alicante," Sarah said, swiping through the METARs. "Palma's got the better weather, but Alicante has more handling staff on call this time of day if we get a medical or disruptive. As for UK airspace, if we need to land, we've got Brum, back here, Luton, Manston, Gatwick, Bournemouth, and even Southend if we want to ruin someone's day."

Julie chuckled under her breath, but Sarah could hear the steely edge in her voice. "Let's hope we don't have to make that call. I'd rather not be landing at Luton with these lot in tow. They'll be giving us a full debrief on every mile after we touch down. But who am I kidding? It'll be like a bloody war zone before we even reach the Isle of Wight. I think that if we need to, we use Brum,

Manston or one of the French alternates. If it's something serious, let's keep it simple."

"Do you think it's worth just keeping the seatbelt sign on instead of turning it off when we reach cruising," Sarah said, her RAF QRA training kicking in. As the secure flight deck door was locked, she knew that no matter how carefully they planned, this flight would present challenges.

Julie looked over at her, the lines of her face tightening. "That might not be a bad idea, Sarah. These passengers are a mix of chaos and control. If they get too rowdy before we've even cleared the airspace, it'll be a nightmare. Let Piotr know that we're going to keep the seatbelt sign on for the first 30 minutes after departure."

Piotr Adamik, the Lead Flight Attendant on the flight, was a seasoned member of the ULCC cabin crew circuits, and he had a reputation for his calm under pressure, especially in the face of disruptive passengers. He was no stranger to difficult flights, having worked on numerous routes for various low-cost carriers, and his knowledge of crowd control was invaluable.

Pressing the button to call through to the cabin, where the jump seats for the crew were, she waited as it was picked up.

"Hello, Piotr here," Sarah heard the Polish accented voice through the intercom. "How can I help, First Officer Marsh?"

"Piotr," Sarah said, trying to sound as calm and collected as possible, "we're keeping the seatbelt sign on for the first

30 minutes after take-off while you do the first buy on board service. We need you to stay alert and keep an eye on the mood in the cabin. If anyone gets rowdy, don't hesitate to let us know. We're trying to avoid any surprises today."

Piotr's voice was a calm, soothing balm amidst the tension Sarah could feel building. "Understood, First Officer. We'll manage, don't worry."

Sarah replaced the intercom handpiece with a deep sigh. She was grateful for Piotr's steadiness, but she knew better than anyone how quickly things could spiral out of control in the cabin. With the sheer number of partygoers on this flight, the odds of a situation erupting were uncomfortably high.

As the aircraft rolled closer to the runway, the noise in the cabin intensified. A group of stag party revellers at the back were already clinking glasses and whooping with laughter, the sound reverberating through the entire cabin. Sarah could feel the weight of their energy, an infectious kind of chaos that was impossible to ignore. The pressure of keeping them calm seemed immense, though she knew the chances of success were slim.

Julie, ever the professional, had a wry smile on her face as she spoke. "It's like herding cats, isn't it? But let's just get these lot airborne first, then we'll see."

Sarah couldn't help but laugh, though it was edged with exhaustion. It was true. Every low-cost flight seemed to bring its own peculiarities, but today was something else. A brand-new aircraft for Sprint Air, an inexperienced crew, and a crowd of passengers whose only goal seemed to be to outdo each other in mischief before they reached Ibiza.

"Coventry Tower, Margate 1343, ready for departure on runway 23L," Julie said, her voice steady, betraying none of the chaos she had been holding at bay.

"Margate 1343, Coventry Tower, cleared for take-off, wind calm, runway 23L," came the response. "Have a good flight."

Sarah glanced out of the window as the runway lights rushed past them. The moment of take-off was always a strange mix of anticipation and trepidation, and today was no different. As the engines powered up and the plane surged forward, Sarah couldn't help but think about how volatile this flight could turn. Once they hit cruising altitude, it would be easier to control the situation, but for now, they were just riding on the edge of chaos.

As the flight passed over the Isle of Wright, Sarah was on the controls, hand flying the initial overland sector before she and Julie would let the autopilot take over for the majority of the flight. The roar of the engines beneath her feet was a steady hum, and for a few moments, Sarah allowed herself to savour the solitude of the flight deck, away from the tumultuous atmosphere in the cabin. She glanced at Julie, who was carefully watching the radar and keeping a sharp eye on the flight's progress.

"Alright, Sarah, your turn to relax for a bit. Autopilot's engaged, and we're on track," Julie said, her voice as calm as always. "But stay sharp. You never know with this lot."

Sarah nodded and stretched her arms before leaning back in her seat. It was a small reprieve, but the few minutes of calm would be short-lived. The thought of the cabin was never far from her mind—those raucous passengers were still waiting to be kept in check. As much as she enjoyed the quiet and peaceful moments up in the air, they were often fleeting when flying with a low-cost carrier full of partygoers heading for Ibiza.

Before she and Julie could do anything else, the buzzer from the intercom, where the Flight Attendants would be, sounded sharply through the flight deck. Sarah's gut instinct tightened. The cabin had been peaceful for all of two minutes, and that had seemed like a luxury they couldn't afford.

"Flight deck," Julie said as she had picked up the intercom. "Go ahead."

"Julie, it's Piotr," came the voice from the cabin. "One of the hens just groped one of my team. It's up to you but I'd think we're best to deplane given the mood down here. She groped Isack's... male parts... multiple times."

Sarah knew that they were still within British airspace, and so could handle the situation in a way that would prevent it from escalating further, but this was not something they had planned for. Disruptive behaviour was a known risk with low-cost carriers, especially when the flight was filled with partygoers, but this was a new level of aggression. It wasn't just rowdiness; it was harassment, and it needed to be dealt with swiftly.

Julie's expression shifted immediately, her usual calm replaced with a hard edge that Sarah recognised all too well. She didn't need to ask for details. Piotr's message had already given them enough of an idea of what was happening, and it was clear this wasn't just a drunken joke or an unfortunate mishap. This was serious.

"Alright, Piotr," Julie said, her tone cool and composed despite the situation. "You've done the right thing by letting us know. Keep a close eye on her, and don't let her near any other crew members. We'll be talking to her as soon as we can. We'll make a call to dispatch and see if we need to make an emergency landing."

The intercom fell silent for a moment, and Sarah could hear the faint hum of the engines as the aircraft levelled out. Her eyes met Julie's, and without a word, both women understood what needed to happen. The situation was volatile, and it wasn't something they could ignore.

Pressing the radio button to transmit to NATS at London Control, Julie's voice was calm but firm as she spoke into the microphone. "London Control, this is Margate 1343. Requesting emergency landing procedure. We have a disruptive passenger onboard who has physically assaulted a crew member. Requesting permission to divert to Bournemouth or Gatwick, over?"

"Margate 1343, London Control," came the immediate reply. "Understood. Emergency landing protocol approved. Standby for rerouting instructions. Maintain current altitude and speed."

Sarah's stomach tightened as she glanced over at Julie. The calm that the Captain exuded was an anchor, but Sarah knew this situation was far from over. They had already been in the air for less than half an hour, and now they were facing the prospect of turning the aircraft around. The looming uncertainty of what would happen once they landed only heightened the tension in Sarah's chest. As much as she longed for calm, she knew she had to be prepared for whatever lay ahead.

"Alright," Julie said after a beat, her voice steady. "Let's keep the mood calm up here. We've got a job to do, and we need to focus. Sarah, go ahead and contact Piotr again. Let him know we've got the approval for a diversion, but make sure the crew's on high alert. We don't want anyone else taking matters into their own hands down there. I'll contact our Dispatch at Bournemouth, just in case they're needed for a swift response. Let's also make sure we keep this under wraps for now. We don't want to escalate it unnecessarily."

"Understood," Sarah replied, her voice steady despite the knot in her stomach. She picked up the intercom handpiece again and called Piotr in the cabin.

"Piotr, it's Sarah," she said quickly, "We've got the go-ahead to divert. We'll be heading for Bournemouth or Gatwick, whichever's closest. You need to keep everyone calm—especially her. I want you to keep her isolated if possible. We'll be there soon."

"Got it," Piotr replied without hesitation. "I'll keep everyone calm. I'll be on it."

Sarah disconnected and sat back in her seat. She knew that, having been a pilot in the RAF for 10 years and, now, since September, initially at Easyjet undergoing line training, and then, since February when Sprint were setting up a civilian First Officer role, she had faced intense training and demanding conditions, but nothing quite like this.

The minutes stretched as Julie held steady on course while Sarah kept one eye on the radar, ready to assist with any last-minute adjustments if needed. The tension inside the cabin was palpable, but it wasn't just about the disruptive passenger anymore. It was about the weight of responsibility—the aircraft, the crew, the passengers, and now, the fallout of a serious situation that had escalated in a flash.

"Margate 1343, this is London Control, you are clear to divert to Gatwick at this time. Please maintain current speed and altitude. Expect vectors for an expedited approach. We will clear the airspace for you. Over."

"London Control, Margate 1343, understood. Heading for Gatwick, thank you," Julie responded crisply, her hands now steady on the yoke. Sarah could feel the adrenaline beginning to shift in the air, thickening the atmosphere between them. They were committed now, not just to dealing with the disruptive passenger, but to handling the whole situation as professionally as possible under the circumstances.

Julie adjusted the heading slightly, keeping her movements fluid, but Sarah knew the tension was mounting in the cabin. The fact that they were diverting had to be communicated soon, but Piotr had already given them the green light. They weren't in the clear yet, but at least they had made the right decision.

"Sarah, keep an eye on the cabin and let me know if anything escalates. I'll handle the airspace change," Julie said, her tone still as calm as ever, a reassuring presence amidst the storm.

Sarah nodded, though she felt the pressure of their job weighing heavily on her. Being in control of the cockpit was one thing, but having to manage the cabin from here, with a group of people clearly not inclined to behave themselves, was another matter entirely. She stood and moved to the intercom, pressing the button again.

"Piotr, it's Sarah. We're diverting to Gatwick. Keep them calm, and let me know if anything changes. We're going to need everyone's cooperation for a smooth landing," she instructed, her voice firm, though she couldn't mask the worry that lingered underneath.

* _ * _ * _ *

As they pulled onto a remote stand, Sarah noticed from out of the right hand side window that a set of stairs, along with a police car and a relief crew were waiting for them on the tarmac. The flashing blue lights cast a cold glow against the mid-morning sky. The tension inside the cabin was suffocating, and Sarah could feel every second dragging out as they slowly approached their final destination.

Julie remained cool, her hands steady on the side sticks, the A318 coming to a stop as the ground controller with the signalling guidance light waved them into position. As the plane rolled to a halt, Sarah took a deep breath, knowing that this was the moment that would determine how things would unfold. The aircraft was securely parked at the stand, and the emergency response was already in place.

A minute later, a voice came over the radio, one of Sprint's local dispatchers, who had plugged his handheld radio into the aircraft's communications system to provide updates directly from the ground.

"Margate 1343, you're on stand and cleared to deboard. Police are awaiting the passenger responsible for the disturbance. You are clear to proceed with the deplaning process at your discretion. Over."

"Understood," Julie replied, her voice calm, though Sarah could tell the weight of the situation was beginning to settle on her. They had successfully diverted, the situation had been contained, but now the real work was just beginning.

Sarah knew that the SOP for Sprint was that on diversions due to an unruly and disruptive passenger was for the cabin crew to be swapped, especially if the situation had escalated to the level of harassment. It was a precautionary measure—one that allowed the new crew to handle the debrief and any potential follow-up without the prior emotional baggage. She expected Piotr and his team would be swapped out, but the reality of dealing with such a situation would still hang over them all.

As Sarah moved back to the cockpit door, she shared a brief look with Julie. The professionalism they both maintained throughout the flight had paid off, but the task ahead was far from over.

"Alright, Sarah," Julie said, breaking the silence. "I'll handle the communications with the ground crew. You go down and check in with Piotr. We need to make sure the cabin is calm and that no one else tries to escalate this."

Sarah nodded, feeling a tight knot form in her chest. The gravity of the situation hadn't fully set in until now, with the aircraft still humming and the passengers visibly unsettled, many now realising that something had happened, even if the details were still hazy.

"Margate 1343, we're going to plug the APU in," the radio interrupted Julie's steady voice, signalling that the emergency response was ready for the next phase. The ramp agents would soon begin the deplaning process, and Sarah knew the final steps of the flight would bring an entirely new set of challenges. The aircraft had landed safely, the immediate threat had been dealt with, but the aftermath was always unpredictable.

"Got it," Julie replied crisply. "Sarah, go ahead. I'll be in contact with dispatch."

Sarah gave a final glance at the quiet but tense cabin before stepping into the aisle. The weight of the decision to divert, the looming uncertainty of how the passenger would be handled, and the concern for her fellow crew members hung heavy on her mind. It was always an unspoken truth that a flight like this—the ones full of chaos and unmanageable passengers—would end up being an unfortunate stain on an airline's reputation if not handled properly.

As she walked towards the galley, Piotr met her halfway down the aisle. His face was calm but his eyes were sharp, reflecting the tension that lingered in the air. He had been around long enough to know the rules—first and foremost, maintain control at all costs. The seasoned cabin crew member did not waste any words, but there was a subtle exchange of understanding between the two of them as she approached.

"Sarah," Piotr said in his usual clipped tone, "Half the pax are already calling for the disruptive passenger to be thrown off. They were even wanting us to do it mid-air. I've told the crew to keep calm, but it's not going to be easy once we start deplaning."

"Right," Sarah replied, feeling her pulse quicken. This was where her training would be tested. The airline's standard operating procedures were clear—if a passenger posed a threat, no matter how minor, the crew had to act swiftly and decisively. But there was always a fine line between maintaining control and risking a full-scale riot. As she started to move towards the rear of the cabin, the growing tension in the air seemed to press against her chest.

As Sarah moved toward the rear of the cabin, she could feel the unmistakable pressure building. The usual hum of the aircraft, that comforting noise of steady flight, was now replaced with the escalating murmur of anxious voices. The hen and stag parties had, for the most part, quietened down, but the atmosphere was thick with unease. Every so often, she heard a muttered complaint or an exchange between the passengers that hinted at the tension brewing beneath the surface.

Piotr had been right; once they started the deplaning process, the situation would change entirely. The excitement of their party atmosphere would shift, and it was clear that many passengers, now realising the severity of what had happened, were starting to shift into a more confrontational mood.

But she also knew that the bounds of acceptable behaviour had already been crossed. The situation wasn't about to get any better until the passenger in question was dealt with, and the process of deplaning was going to be critical in determining how things would unfold from here.

As Sarah moved deeper into the cabin, she saw the rows of passengers who had been mostly focused on their own excitement or inebriation, now turning their attention to the crew. It wasn't an easy environment to manage. Piotr was right about the mob mentality that could quickly escalate, and the last thing Sarah wanted was to turn this into a full-scale incident.

The disruptive passenger, the woman who had caused the trouble by groping one of the male flight attendants, was seated at the back of the plane. She had clearly sobered up somewhat, but the defiance in her posture told Sarah all she needed to know: she wasn't going to leave without a fight. As Sarah approached, she could see the woman scanning the cabin, her eyes darting nervously but still filled with that sense of entitlement that was so often associated with passengers who believed they could get away with anything. She wasn't prepared to go quietly.

Sarah's heart rate increased slightly, but her breathing remained steady. This was the moment she had been trained for—when the passenger's actions had crossed the line, and the response needed to be swift, controlled, and, most importantly, professional.

"Excuse me, miss," Sarah said as she approached the seat, trying to keep her voice neutral but firm. "I need you to gather your things. We're going to deplane you and ask you to leave the aircraft as soon as possible. You've been reported for inappropriate behaviour towards one of the cabin crew, and we will be handing you over to the authorities on the ground."

The woman blinked, her expression a mixture of disbelief and contempt. "What are you talking about? I didn't do anything!" she slurred, her words slightly blurred from the alcohol still running through her system.

Sarah's patience was beginning to wear thin, but she held her composure. "The situation has been reported, and it's being taken very seriously. Please, don't make this more difficult than it needs to be. Gather your things, and come with me."

The woman's eyes narrowed, and she gave Sarah a defiant look. "This is ridiculous! I've paid for my flight, and you're kicking me off like I'm some kind of criminal!"

Sarah took a deep breath, her heart thumping in her chest as she kept her tone even and measured. "You've been reported for inappropriate behaviour, and that's why we're asking you to leave. If you cooperate, this will be over quickly. Please, just gather your things and come with me. The authorities are waiting for you at the gate."

The woman stared at her for a moment, clearly weighing her options. The stubbornness was evident in her eyes, but Sarah had dealt with these situations before. It wasn't uncommon for passengers to go from defensive to contrite, but this one seemed more determined to escalate.

"I'm not going anywhere," the woman spat, her voice growing louder. "You can't just kick me off a flight for having a little fun! This is outrageous!"

Sarah felt a flicker of frustration, but she kept it under control. "I'm asking you to cooperate for your own safety and the safety of the other passengers. You're not in a position to negotiate right now. Police are waiting on the tarmac."

The woman's face reddened as she realised Sarah wasn't backing down. Her defiance wavered for a moment, but her pride had evidently taken hold. "You're not going to get away with this," she muttered under her breath, but Sarah could see the woman was becoming increasingly aware of the situation she was in.

"We'll see," Sarah replied quietly, her voice firm and unwavering. "Let's make this easy on everyone."

For a brief moment, there was a silence between them, the tension palpable. The woman stared at Sarah, sizing her up, but Sarah wasn't going to let her get the upper hand. If she didn't deplane willingly, the entire situation would only spiral further.

With a huff of resignation, the woman stood up, stumbling slightly as she did. She glared at Sarah as she began collecting her things, still muttering under her breath about how unfairly she was being treated. Sarah, for her part, stood her ground, watching the woman closely. As much as she had hoped for a smooth resolution, this wasn't over yet.

"Thank you for your cooperation," Sarah said, her voice steady. She motioned towards the galley, where Piotr was already waiting, his eyes watching the woman with the same quiet intensity Sarah had learned to rely on. It wasn't just the physical act of moving the passenger off the plane—there was a psychological component too, and Piotr knew exactly how to handle it.

As they reached the aisle, the woman's defiance seemed to reignite. She stopped, turned to face the other passengers, and began to shout. "This is ridiculous!" she screamed, her voice cutting through the cabin. "You're just going to let them throw me off? I've paid for this! You all just wait and see. I'll have all of you fired!"

The other passengers, sensing the drama unfolding, began to murmur among themselves. Some stared, others pretended not to notice, but Sarah could feel the weight of the eyes on her. The last thing they needed was for this to escalate further, so she moved quickly, keeping a calm but firm tone.

"Please, keep moving," Sarah said, trying to keep the situation contained. "The sooner you comply, the sooner this will be over."

But the woman wasn't done yet. She shook her head and began backing away, looking for any excuse to prolong the confrontation. "I'm not leaving. You can't make me. This is—"

Before she could finish, Piotr stepped forward, his presence commanding attention without a word. He was a seasoned cabin crew member who had seen his fair share of difficult situations. His quiet authority cut through the woman's protests like a knife through butter.

"Enough," Piotr said, his voice calm yet filled with an undeniable strength. "You're leaving now. If you don't, we'll escalate this, and you'll face serious consequences when we land. The police are waiting for you."

For a moment, there was a flicker of doubt in the woman's eyes, and Sarah took advantage of the brief silence.

"Please, just gather your things," she said one last time, her voice barely above a whisper, yet it carried the weight of the authority she had learned to wield.

The woman hesitated. She shot one last look around the cabin, taking in the faces of the other passengers. The murmurs had stopped, replaced by the heavy silence of expectation. She seemed to realise the futility of her resistance, and with a resigned huff, she slung her bag over her shoulder and began to walk towards the rear of the cabin, her movements stiff and unwilling.

But at least she was complying.

****

CHAPTER 8 – Passengers Who Don't Talk Back
Saturday 16th April 2022

Cargo, Sarah knew, was the best kind of passenger, as they didn't complain, didn't try to open overhead bins while taxiing, didn't threaten crew with TripAdvisor reviews, and—perhaps most importantly—didn't try to disembark before the seatbelt signs went off. They simply sat there in their crates or containers, inert and indifferent, trusting the cockpit to get on with the job. And on a morning like this one, where the April air at East Midlands Airport carried that damp tarmac chill and not much else, Sarah Marsh was grateful for the silence of boxes.

Their assigned aircraft was HA-LPU, an ex-Wizz A320, still in passenger configuration, had, according to the manifest, 4 passengers, two of them aviation enthusiasts and 2 representatives of a Polish firm delivering airfreight contracts for an expanding logistics network in Lower Silesia. The two spotters were already on the apron by the time Sarah and Captain Harper Whiteman, a Canadian pilot who had moved to the UK in 2013, prior to Brexit, arrived at the aircraft steps, eagerly snapping photos of the fuselage, squinting at nose gear strut placards, and arguing—amicably—about engine nacelle variations between the A320ceo and neo.

All of the seats, she knew, was still in the plane, as its normal job was still transporting human cargo to Ibiza, Kraków, and every other ultra-low cost destination Sprint, as a ULCC, was now serving freight routes on behalf of a

Slovakian logistics startup called "TrackStream", one who, according to rumours, was headed by a Slovakian minister's cousin who formerly ran a ski-lift rental firm in Ružomberok and had decided, post-pandemic, that logistics was the future of the republic's GDP.

The company, TrackStream, had no aircraft of its own, no AOC, and no track record—at least in aviation. But it had investors, a flashy logo designed by a Norwegian influencer, and enough contracts with Amazon, DHL, Chinese e-store Shein, and of course, Sprint's partial owner, the Sultanate of Oman, to launch a pan-European distribution arc under the guise of 'strategic synergy'. Sarah didn't need to know the full story. She just needed to get the aircraft safely to Rzeszów.

Harper, as usual, seemed immune to the operational absurdity. She greeted the spotters with a polite nod and a dry, "Don't step on anything sharp," before disappearing up the steps and into the aircraft. Sarah followed, glancing once more at the stark utilitarian silhouette of HA-LPU— freshly painted in Sprinter.eu livery, the Eastern Europe brand that Sprint ran due to the ongoing trademark war between Sprint and SprintAir of Poland, a cargo carrier whose owner once tried to sue Jeff Young personally.

The fact the livery was fully Sprint navy blue, with only some ghosting of the Wizz livery, and had been fully refurbished to ULCC standards inside—grey plastic, basic seats, faint smell of recycled air—only added to the sense of liminality. The aircraft belonged to neither the past nor the future; it was caught somewhere between Nordic whimsy and Slovakian practicality, between Instagram and invoice, operated by crews like Sarah and

Harper who saw the airline not as a calling, but as a profession that paid—sometimes—on time.

Sarah stowed her flight bag in the cockpit, careful not to dislodge the stack of performance printouts or the secret stash of Haribo she and Harper rationed for late-night ferry flights. From the left seat, Harper was already reviewing the weather for the sector ahead, METARs streaming on her phone, her accent softened by years of British exposure but unmistakably Canadian when she muttered, "At least it's not snowing in Poland for once."

"Wind from the west, patchy fog by the time we hit Rzeszów, maybe a bit of low-level turbulence over the Tatras, nothing we haven't done before," Harper summarised, setting her phone down. She glanced sidelong at Sarah. "I can't believe 2 AvGeeks would board our cargo run just for the flight log. Where did they buy again?"

"One has 12 Foxtrot, the exit row, and another 19 Alpha. Our Polish reps are in 1 Alpha and Charlie, and we've got a full crew in the cabin, complete with buy on board and scratchcards," Sarah said, looking at the Sprint Manifest app on the iPad that served as the EFB.

"Wonder if they'll want a hot bacon roll at FL350," Harper muttered, flipping switches with an ease that betrayed the years since her own AvGeek days, if she'd ever truly had them.

Sarah cracked a smile and busied herself with the first round of pre-flight checks, glancing through the scratched Perspex of the cockpit windows at the thin haze lifting off the apron. The apron team were already manoeuvring an orange-coned cart around the nose, and the forward hold yawned open, waiting to swallow the morning's consignment: a dozen steel mesh crates stacked with e-commerce parcels, a pallet of 'urgent' pharmaceuticals, and—somewhat ominously—one crate tagged "Proprietary Electronic Goods: Do Not X-Ray."

That last crate had drawn a bemused eyebrow from the dispatcher, who'd flagged it as a "security seal verified at origin." Sarah, like most pilots, didn't much care what the box contained as long as it didn't go click in mid-flight. "Wonder if it's the next TikTok drone craze or a batch of pirated PlayStations," she mused.

Harper's reply was a philosophical, "Long as it doesn't crawl out and want a window seat."

The loadmaster, Piotr, appeared at the foot of the steps, radio clipped to his Hi-Viz, clipboard tucked under one arm, the epitome of Eastern European efficiency, or at least its performance. He greeted them both with a stiff, "Good morning, captains," in a Polish accent honed by years in EMA's hodgepodge of languages. "Loading complete in fifteen minutes. Only one box has—how you say?—shifting potential. I have braced. Your logbook is in the cabin."

"Thanks, Piotr," Harper said, giving him a thumbs-up as Sarah went to check the manifest against the reality outside. Satisfied, she returned to the cockpit, stowing her jacket and easing into the right seat, flicking through the aircraft's pages of checklists with muscle memory. The comfort of routine, she thought, was the only reliable thing Sprint ever offered.

The rest of the crew trickled aboard in that easy, fractured manner of an early cargo flight. Lead Cabin Crew for the rotation was Olga Ivanovna Petrova, a former Aeroflot flight attendant, the sort who managed the contradictions of low-cost flying with quiet, enduring grace. She poked her head in as Sarah was reviewing fuel figures.

"Cabin ready. The AvGeeks have already taken one hundred photos of the toilet sign and the window demister knob. One of them asked if they could buy a safety card. I told them no, but gave them a spare," Olga said, her face unreadable.

Harper gave a small, amused snort. "Don't let them open the doors for an outside shot."

"I told them if they ask for a cockpit visit on climb-out, I'll feed them to you," Olga said, grinning. "By the way, I've got a full trolley of snacks, so if you want some grub when we get to climbing altitude, let me know."

"Good," Sarah said, up. "We're all loaded then?"

"Almost. The two TrackStream people are on their phones in Row 1, arguing in Polish about delivery rates. I think they're trying to undercut their own driver. And yes, I checked the galley. The hot water works, but the coffee's what you English call 'despair in a cup.'"

"We're used to that," Sarah replied, giving Anya a grin that was only half false. "Thanks."

As Olga disappeared, Harper keyed up the radio, contacting East Midlands ground for push clearance. The familiar, bored voice of East Midlands Apron Control came back, "Ramsgate 442 Zulu, expect push in six, stand by on 121.8." In the distance, a DHL 757 trundled past, yellow livery bright against the April murk.

Sarah took a moment, just breathing, feeling the tension— such as it was—slip away. A cargo run with four passengers was practically a paid holiday in Sprint terms. No stags, no hens, no inflatables or angry families demanding compensation for delays outside her control. Just the hum of the APU, the occasional shunt of a crate, and the low, constant burble of flight deck banter.

Harper, finishing the pushback brief, turned to Sarah, her tone suddenly light. "Wanna make it interesting?"

Sarah raised an eyebrow. "How so?"

"Bet you twenty zloty that the AvGeek in 12F makes a log of every radio frequency we use today."

"Easy win. He's got an antenna stuck to his rucksack. I'll raise you—he'll ask for the registration change log, too."

"What changes? It's still the same Hungarian tail number that has haunted this poor Airbus since 2013. The only difference is now it answers to a Slovakian call sign and a PR company's Instagram feed," Harper replied, feigning horror. "Honestly, I don't know how these kids keep up."

Sarah chuckled, already picturing the excited, slightly nervous young man in 12F, his notepad out, scribbling furiously at every squelch of the radio and click of the PA.

There was a fondness, almost, in watching the next generation of aviation obsessives at work—though, she mused, none of them would ever understand the true romance of a 01:02 crew report for a foggy cargo hop out of the East Midlands. She checked the fuel numbers again, running a fingertip down the printout, more for the feel of the paper than any lack of trust in the figures. The familiar smell of galley coffee drifted forward, blending with the faint, sterile scent of new cabin plastics and tired HEPA filters.

The apron crew reappeared with the thumbs-up for final loading. Piotr, ever the professional, called up, "Cabin secure. Cargo locked. We are good for close."

Sarah gave a confirming nod, reached back, and pressed the door annunciator. The familiar clunk of doors locking, the gentle hiss of the seal, and the subtle change in pressurisation told her all she needed to know: they were now, in the truest sense, sealed in with their quiet, inert charges. No matter what TrackStream's plans or the AvGeeks' excitement, from this moment on, the aeroplane was theirs.

As the doors closed, Sarah sighed. "You're taking this leg, right?" she asked Harper for the purposes of the black box, the Cockpit Voice Recorder, which meant that if in the event of a catastrophe, the official record would show it was Harper in command. Harper, already settled in the left seat, gave her a wry smile and a mock salute.

"Wouldn't miss it for the world. You can handle the radio, Sarah. Keep our fans entertained."

Sarah's hands moved automatically, fingers brushing over the FCU, arming the auto-thrust, confirming the transponder was set to ALT, feeling the familiar, almost meditative rhythm of cockpit preparation as Harper finished the before-start checklist. Their respective flows met, diverged, and met again in the subtle choreography unique to pilots who'd shared more than a few rotations.

Sarah could hear Olga's voice coming over the PA— precise, calm, a slightly Slavic cadence undercutting the Sprint standard script. "Ladies and gentlemen, and those here on company business, welcome aboard this 01:56 Sprint service to Rzeszów from East Midlands Airport, calling at Rzeszów only. This flight is formed of one Airbus A320, so, for your safety, please remain seated until the seatbelt sign is off. Smoking is not permitted, not even in the lavatories, and for our aviation enthusiasts: please, ensure your phones, tablets, computers and other electronic devices are in Airplane Mode or turned off. WiFi is available thanks to Elon Musk's satellite generosity, though we cannot guarantee connection over the Carpathians. Crew will shortly be performing a safety demonstration; please pay attention, as you never know when you'll end up flying the thing yourself. Safety Information is on the headrest of the seat in front of you, apart from the front row where it is in the pockets ahead. I suggest you read them. Thank you, and we wish you a pleasant, uneventful journey—or at least one worth logging."

The last line drew a muffled laugh from the cockpit and, Sarah suspected, a flurry of frantic scribbling in Row 12. Harper looked up, eyes twinkling. "If Olga ever wants to write the PA scripts, I'd let her. That was the most Sprint's sounded like a real airline in months."

Sarah, grinning, toggled the PA for her own contribution. "Cabin crew, arm doors and cross-check."

A click of acknowledgment, a tap of switches, and the aircraft settled into its final moments on stand, the gentle thrum of the APU the only background music. Outside, ground crew scuttled clear, high-vis jackets ghosting through the dawn haze as Piotr flashed a last thumbs-up, then retreated for coffee and warmth.

"Ground, Ramsgate 442 Zulu, request push and start, stand Juliet One Niner, clearance received," Sarah called.

"Ramsgate 442 Zulu, push approved, face west, start at your discretion," came the reply. There was always a comforting laziness to East Midlands' nonchalance—so unlike the clipped panic of Luton or the dry theatre of Stansted. Here, things got done, or they didn't, but nobody let the drama interfere with the movement of freight.

Sarah's hand danced over the overhead, confirming beacon on, packs off, fuel pumps set. Harper's grip on the tiller felt almost lazy as she called, "Brakes released, push commencing." The world outside pivoted, the nose swinging gently to face the rising sun and a landscape waking to a low, cloudy Midlands morning.

Engines spooled in sequence: one, then two, the familiar whine and distant, muted roar resonating through the structure. Sarah watched the gauges, needles in the green, N1 stabilising just below idle. No alarms. No drama. The best sort of start.

As the crew reengaged the checklists, the aircraft came alive. The overheads flickered with ready lights; the FMGS came online, flight plan snaking its digital path from England to Poland with only minor squiggles to avoid military airspace and the ever-present Brexit "special zones." Harper ran her finger down the map, pausing at the waypoints. "One day, I'd like to see a straight line from A to B again. Just once."

Sarah offered her the usual, "Not in our lifetime, unless we're hauling uranium for the UN." Then, over the intercom, "Olga, please check cabin secure for take-off."

The confirmation came, brisk and cheerful. "Cabin ready, cockpit."

A moment's pause as Harper turned to Sarah, a little ceremony of shared anticipation. "You ready?"

"Always. Let's get this show on the road."

Taxiing from stand Juliet One Niner meant a gentle right turn, holding short of the main. The field was quiet at this hour; the DHL 757 ahead was already rolling, leaving behind only rippling heat and the faint scent of kerosene. The two AvGeeks pressed their noses to the windows, phones out to film the line-up onto the runway. Sarah could almost feel their excitement: the sudden hush, the vibration of brakes released, the deepening rumble as Harper nudged the thrust levers forward.

"Cabin crew, seats for take-off," Sarah called, voice steady. Olga's acknowledgment was crisp.

Line-up. The hold short line fell behind. Harper's hands never trembled; she advanced the levers to fifty percent, waited, then pressed the TOGA detent, the A320 responding with a surge. Sarah's right hand hovered near the throttles, her left over the sidestick, watching the speed build with practiced calm.

"Power set."

"Check."

"Speed's alive."

"Checked."

The landscape accelerated past: aprons, hangars, the grey bulk of the air cargo centre. At eighty knots, Harper called, "Checked," and Sarah's eyes flicked to the engine readings, then back to the outside world—runway centreline, the numbers racing towards them, nothing amiss.

"V1." Harper's voice was calm.

"Rotate," she intoned, and Sarah eased the sidestick back, nose lifting to the sky. The aircraft left the ground, gear tucking away, East Midlands shrinking beneath them.

"Positive climb."

"Gear up."

"Gear up, indicating," Sarah echoed, fingers flicking the lever with a satisfying, almost mechanical finality. A thunk reverberated through the airframe as the wheels locked away. Outside, the overcast Midlands sky pressed low and indifferent, slate grey on silver wing, the sort of British morning that made everyone dream of Mallorca and left only pilots and postal workers undaunted.

Harper guided the A320 smoothly through the initial climb. Sarah kept her eye on the speed tape, cross-checked pitch and roll, all the old habits—routine, practiced, yet never quite boring. To her right, she could glimpse flashes of movement in the cabin, the spotter in 12F peering over a camera so large it looked almost illegal. Somewhere behind, Olga would be wrestling the trolley into the galley's aft niche, prepping for the short climb to top-of-descent that was an East Midlands–Rzeszów sector.

At two thousand feet, Harper called for autopilot. "Autopilot one," Sarah confirmed, pressing the button with a muted beep. The aircraft's nose smoothed, the yoke eased, and suddenly there was space for breath—a tiny moment of peace before the demands of a low-cost morning fully returned.

"Climb thrust, climb sequence," Harper announced. Sarah reduced the power levers, then pulled the flaps, and the aircraft shivered—then settled, clean and ready for the open sky. Below, Leicestershire blurred, greenish-brown, fields divided by hedgerows and the odd golden flash of oilseed rape. Somewhere, a tractor laboured through wet grass, utterly ignorant of this aluminium tube now banking gently east.

Sarah allowed herself a moment of satisfaction. Departures with minimal drama were rare these days, but even more precious on a morning like this, with nothing to do but monitor, manage, and—at intervals—marvel at the absurdity of it all. She took a sip from her battered black flask. The coffee was, as always, a muddy disappointment, but at least it was hot.

Harper caught her eye. "Want the radios now? Or are you hoping our spotter will volunteer?"

Sarah grinned, thumbed the radio and called, "East Midlands Departure, Ramsgate four four two Zulu, passing three thousand, climbing FL100."

A crackle of static, then: "Ramsgate four four two Zulu, radar contact. Continue climb FL220. Direct TLA, resume own navigation."

"Direct TLA, climb FL220, four four two Zulu."

The route this morning was an odd one—a relic of pandemic-era airspace closures and the curious fact that TrackStream's contracts were nearly always one step ahead of ATC logic. The flight would cross the North Sea south of Hull, skip across northern Germany, then thread the needle between Czech and Slovakian airspace. Rzeszów, near the Ukrainian border, had become unexpectedly busy since the war, a fact the Polish pair in Row 1 seemed keenly aware of. Sarah wondered whether they'd brought bulletproof vests or just contracts.

As the aircraft climbed, the cityscape gave way to patchwork fields, then to the infinite, featureless grey of the cloud deck. The familiar hiss and whine of pressurisation faded to the background. Harper, satisfied with the climb, sat back, stretching her legs beneath the dash.

"You know," she remarked, glancing at the faded 'Wizz' stencil barely hidden beneath the Sprint livery on the window frame, "I used to do Vancouver to Toronto on cargo in the nineties. DC-8, barely pressurised. Had to brush snow off the ramp ourselves. This is a luxury by comparison."

Sarah sipped her coffee again, watching as the horizon tilted ever so slightly. "Did your cargo ever try to bribe you for a cockpit selfie?"

"Only once, and it was a crate of BC salmon. Honestly, the stories you hear about Russian oligarchs flying their dogs to Paris for grooming—never happened in Canada. We flew what needed to move. And sometimes, yeah, we wondered what was really in the boxes."

"Probably less cocaine in Nottingham, though," Sarah said wryly.

Harper snorted. "Depends on the football results, if you ask me."

Sarah laughed, and the cockpit fell into that companionable silence born of early mornings and long-haul company—a rare, precious thing in Sprint's fractious, ever-rotating roster world. The altimeter wound its lazy spiral upward as the clouds thickened into a seamless, lumpy mattress beneath them. Somewhere below, lorries crawled the A50, unaware of the European commerce rocketing overhead. This was, to Sarah's mind, the true poetry of aviation: not the glamour of tropical layovers or the theatre of celebrity passengers, but the quiet dignity of a well-flown cargo sector, the comfort of checklists, and the strange sense of stewardship that came from moving things unseen yet essential across a continent.

The autopilot flew, the engines hummed, and Sprint's little A320 with its battered Hungarian paperwork and ambiguous livery pressed on through the English gloom.

Cruise brought with it a gentle slackening of tension. Olga ducked into the cockpit, bearing two cups of 'coffee'— quotations audible in her voice as she handed them over. "Only slightly better than last time. But this time, I remembered sugar." She smiled, flashing a packet as if it were contraband. "And the AvGeek wishes to know, can he have a photo of the overhead panel after landing? He promised not to touch."

Harper took her coffee with a grateful sigh. "Only if he promises not to post it on Russian Twitter."

"Which one?" Olga deadpanned. "We have six now." Then, more softly, "First Officer Marsh, if you need, the TrackStream men say they have WiFi codes for Warsaw. I think they want to show off."

Sarah arched an eyebrow, hiding a smirk. "They'll be disappointed; I can barely get WhatsApp to load above Belgium."

Olga grinned, and as she left, Sarah heard her boots clicking their way down the aisle, the faint sound oddly comforting. In a life that seemed to change gate numbers and company policy every month, the little details mattered. The crew, the flow, the mutual understanding that cargo runs were as close as Sprint ever came to a 'quiet' day.

Sarah settled in for the routine of cruise: systems scans, the lazy, automatic monitoring of ECAM and the endless green arc of parameters, a low-key vigilance built of experience. The North Sea slid by beneath them, pewter and unlovely, as they crossed from British to Dutch, then German airspace, the accents on the radio shifting with every handover.

Harper glanced over, sipping her coffee and pulling a face at the taste. "Still," she said, "beats being screamed at for running out of gin and tonic. I can't believe Sprint has only been a proper airline less than 10 days."

* _ * _ * _ *

Cruise gave way to a creeping descent just west of Wrocław, the flight plan snaking south-eastward past the undulating shadows of the Tatras, invisible beneath the soup of cloud. ATC handoffs multiplied, their clipped Polish, Czech, and Slovak phrasing all variations on the same quiet dance: squawk this, descend that, turn here, speed there. The aircraft responded with quiet dignity, the autopilot adjusting imperceptibly, the hum of the avionics blending into background cognition.

In the cabin, the rustling of snack wrappers and the occasional clink of metal-on-plastic punctuated the otherwise museum-like stillness. Olga appeared briefly at the cockpit door, asking, "Any ETA updates?" Harper replied with an offhand, "Ten ahead of schedule," and Olga, nodding, vanished again—evidently, even

TrackStream's Polish contingent hadn't found anything worth arguing about lately.

Sarah peered at the ECAM—no messages, no warnings, fuel nicely balanced, oil temps well within spec. This was, by any measure, what counted as smooth. Unusual for Sprint. Unnatural, even. She wasn't sure she trusted it.

"You ever flown into Rzeszów before?" Harper asked, adjusting a knob on the FCU, dialling the descent to FL150.

"No. To be fair I only got type rated with easyJet on the A320 in Feb and did line training before defecting to Sprint back in March. Before easyJet I was a FA at PanEuro," Sarah said, repressing the memories of the 4 months there, where she, because of being a woman, had been relegated to the cabin, as the Pan Am cosplay airline had had a rule of men in the flight deck and women only in the cabin—a throwback so absurd it barely deserved breath. "Before that I was RAF QRA. 10 years in the RAF, and then left because of Boris and his COVID cutbacks in the Armed Forces. Served in Syria at one stage."

Harper raised her eyebrows in faint admiration, her hands never leaving the FCU. "Blimey. We get all sorts, don't we? There's a joke about the RAF and EasyJet in there somewhere, but I'm too polite and too Canadian to make it before lunch." She grinned sidelong, the lines around her eyes deepening. "Never did QRA myself—closest I got was chasing snowploughs up and down YVR's north runway. But I know what you mean about odd career moves. Pre-Brexit, I'd never have ended up in

Nottingham at 7 a.m. running Polish cargo out of an ex-Wizz bus."

Sarah smiled, a mixture of ruefulness and something like pride. "Honestly, I don't miss the Air Force much, but I do miss the sense that things mattered, you know? That there was a reason for all the faff. But, well—" she swept a hand vaguely at the sky, the cockpit, the steady rumble of the CFM56s "—now it's all e-commerce and TikTok gadgets and the occasional urgent consignment of garden gnomes to Košice."

Harper laughed, letting the moment stretch. The two women fell into companionable silence, watching the green and amber numerals on the MCP wind steadily down, the arc of their descent a gentle parabola toward Poland's southern edge.

As they crossed into Polish airspace, the world below flickered through broken clouds: a patchwork of late-winter fields, muddy rivers swollen by spring melt, the toy-sized roads and towns of Silesia receding beneath their wings. Rzeszów Approach crackled into life, the controller's English clipped but confident.

"Ramsgate four four two Zulu, descend flight level six zero, direct OSKAR, expect ILS runway two seven."

Sarah acknowledged, repeating the instructions back, eyes already scanning the approach chart on her EFB. The airport sat low in the valley, surrounded by forest and, these days, bristling with new hangars and tented military compounds. The Ukrainian border, so close now, lent the whole operation an air of quiet tension.

"I can't believe it's been 2 months since Putin launched the invasion," Harper murmured, voice barely above the hush of the conditioned air, eyes flicking momentarily to the world outside. "Two months and now half of Warsaw's business elite are running ops out of here. My cousin's in Kraków—says you can barely get a decent meal in town for all the foreign journalists and consultants crowding the bars."

Sarah, watching the green line on the ND curve toward OSKAR, felt a twinge of something like guilt, though she wasn't sure why. She nodded, keeping her tone professional, "It's everywhere. Every time we land in Poland, there's more security, more scanners, more guys in hi-vis standing around with nothing in their eyes but boredom and tired fear."

She keyed the radio, reading the next set of instructions from ATC—descend 3,500ft, establish localiser, report ready for approach.

Harper set the spoilers to arm and dialled in the ILS frequency with a practiced flick of the wrist. "Flap 1 at glide," she said, "Let's see if Rzeszów's as smooth as EMA this morning."

Sarah ran her scan: speed checked, gear ready, descent profile normal, nothing but the slight tremble of windshear warning at the edge of the Carpathians. In the cabin, she imagined the AvGeeks already prepping their phones for the approach, eager to catch every nuance of flaps, gear, spoilers, callouts—the whole poetry of the arrival.

She almost envied them their uncomplicated joy.

Olga called forward, "Cabin ready for landing," her voice as crisp as the static in the headset. Sarah could hear the soft clatter of seatbelts and the muted hush that fell over a cabin in descent, even when the cabin only held four souls.

The aircraft, nose down, cut through the ragged bands of early spring cloud, the cityscape of Rzeszów emerging in streaks of muddy green and pale concrete.

"Localiser alive," Sarah called, scanning the PFD, "Glideslope captured. Three greens."

"Check. Flap 2. Gear down."

Harper's tone was steady, the calm at the heart of a storm only she could see.

On final, with the world narrowing to a strip of tarmac flanked by unseasonal mud and the distant geometry of tent cities—humanitarian hubs and hastily-erected military tents—Sarah felt the momentary weight of the world, a sense of significance even as their flight was, by all external measure, routine.

Sprint, she reflected, always ended up at the heart of things by accident. TrackStream's little logo was now just another piece of pan-European logistical infrastructure helping keep the continent stitched together, one planeload of parcels and quiet passengers at a time.

"Approach stable, three reds, one white," Harper called, eyes flicking from the altimeter to the runway threshold, every line of her body relaxed, focused.

Sarah's hands tensed instinctively, ready to call 'Go-around' at the first sign of trouble, but the runway remained serenely empty, the windsock limp.

"Land," Harper intoned, and Sarah's hand hovered over the thrust levers, ready for reversers.

The aircraft touched with a firmness that brooked no nonsense—firm, but not hard, the kind of landing any cargo handler would respect. The nose settled, spoilers sprang, and thrust reversers roared in the cold Polish morning.

"Sixty knots," Harper called.

"Manual braking."

They rolled to a gentle stop as instructed, exiting left at the first high-speed turnoff.

Sarah exhaled, tension bleeding out, her hands relaxing their grip on the sidestick. "Not bad for a Saturday. Welcome to Rzeszów, home of Europe's most underappreciated airspace."

****

CHAPTER 9 – Ladies Night
Sunday 17th April 2022

The Soho district of London hadn't prepared itself for the invasion of several ULCC First Officers all dressed up for a night on the town, the rivalry of various airlines in the ultra-low-cost carriers forgotten as the group of 12 women all emerged from the glittering lobby of the Zedwell, blinking into the almost-midnight lights of Shaftesbury Avenue. If the city was still in the throes of recovery from lockdown malaise, you wouldn't have known it from the way the pavements thrummed with post-theatre crowds and the kind of laughter that only came from groups who'd known each other for years, or at least survived the same line-check.

Sarah led the way, her black jumpsuit sharp against the London chill, sleeves rolled, hair loosely pinned back to signal that tonight she was neither captain nor first officer, just another woman in a borrowed world. A lanyard poked from her clutch bag—habit, not design. Behind her, Hayley Northcott, Chloe Burns from Ryanair, a few Wizz Air, Jet2, and even two from TUI, with a smattering of regional carriers, all moved in a pack with that boisterous, arm-linked energy unique to women who'd spent a thousand hours at FL370 but never together on the ground. Each was clad in their interpretation of "off-duty chic"—Hayley's red lips and silver boots flashing with every confident stride, Chloe in a dress that would never fit in a flight bag, others draped in jackets with airline pins still attached, forgotten, like tiny confessions of what they'd left at the hotel.

The first stop was inevitable: the garish, overpriced cocktail bar with neon flamingos, the one every airline WhatsApp group seemed to mention after a night at the Zedwell. Inside, the air was thick with heat and false humidity, every surface sticky under the pulse of a thousand spilled daiquiris. The barman eyed the arrival of a dozen flight crew—something in the upright carriage and expensive dental work always gave them away— before launching into a well-practised routine of drink recommendations and knowing banter. Chloe set the tone by waving away the menu and ordering a round of espresso martinis "on the company", the joke landing well enough that Wizz Air's Eszter began to retell her story about once being sent to Tirana by mistake, hungover, and landing in a thunderstorm.

"...so, we had a crosswind which could have qualified as a full-on sidewinder, right, and the approach plate's in Cyrillic, and my Captain's halfway through explaining why his ex-wife's a sociopath—"

"—standard," Chloe interrupted, to a chorus of cackles—

"—and ATC comes on and just yells. In Albanian. I tell the Captain that either we either vector off now or he's going to get us both on Albanian YouTube," Eszter finished, rolling her eyes in theatrical exasperation, espresso martini sloshing perilously close to her sleeve. The punchline landed, dissolving the tension of their newness as a group—laughter ricocheting around the neon jungle, heads thrown back, the sort of wild, unfiltered cackle that had become as rare as a sensible FTL rota.

It was, Sarah thought, what she'd needed: the feeling of being slightly unmoored, the taste of too-strong coffee liqueur and the reminder that every woman at the table had a hundred stories, all variations on the same theme—disaster narrowly averted, another airport, another night, the strange solidarity of women who could recite the MEL for an Airbus A320 by heart but still got lost in Soho. She watched as Hayley mimed a Ryanair brace position to explain a particularly harrowing Wizz Air landing at Beauvais, the table dissolving into shrieks, silver boots kicked under the sticky table.

"...nice cock. Pity that German Sprint FO, Detweiler I think his name was, won't shag anyone," one of the Jet2 First Officers interjected, her northern accent cutting through the shrieking laughter. "He's a hunk, but aloof as sin. Swans about like he's the only man who's read the FCOM. Bumped into him yesterday in Tenerife during a FTL reset and he practically ran away from me."

"Maybe he's one of those 'I only date Lufthansa girls' types," someone suggested, and the laughter that followed carried the shared knowledge of the airline world's peculiar little hierarchies—Lufthansa pilots at the top, everyone else playing in their wake, and Sprint FOs somewhere in the middle: respected enough for their flying, but never for their sense of humour.

Suddenly Sarah's phone beeped, and she noticed that it was a WhatsApp message from Max.

Max Detweiler: *Hey, you got any Balearics next week?*

Sarah blinked at the screen, a smile quirking at the edge of her lips—unconscious, involuntary. Max had a way of timing his messages perfectly, as if he had some sixth sense for when she needed pulling out of herself, or maybe just wanted to check in on the chaos she found herself drawn into. She tapped a quick reply, thumbs stumbling only slightly from the espresso martini:

Sarah Marsh: *Only if you fancy Palma and herds of stags. Got a Dublin to Palma on Sunday if you fancy meeting up.*

She hit send, letting the little blue ticks flash up, then pocketed her phone before the next round of stories began. The bar around them pulsed with music and clatter— early-2000s pop drifting into bad reggaeton, thumping against the battered neon walls. It was the sort of place where time slowed, the mirrors sweating, and everything seemed possible for a brief, weightless moment between rosters.

Hayley had swung into a story of her own, arms flying, vodka soda balanced with terrifying confidence. "So, I'm in Berlin, right, and my boyfriend, Theo, who works for PanEuro-"

The ladies all booed, as PanEuro still had its sexist hiring policy where only men were allowed to fly while the women were relegated to the cabin or, worse, the call centre.

"—shut up, I know, I know," Hayley grinned, unashamed, "and hey, he's not like Hargreaves, the dirty bastard, he's supportive of ladies being captains and First Officers, anyway, we were shagging, when a bloody fire alarm goes off, right? Starkers, both of us, had to leg it out into the corridor—he's got nothing on but his boxers, me with my easyJet shirt, no bra, no panties, and 40 Germans, a Lufthansa crew and the world's most terrifying cleaning lady glaring at us like we've committed a war crime—so I'm hiding behind a drinks trolley and Theo's just waving at the Captain of the Lufthansa crew, who gives him the filthiest look and asks, 'Are you aware your companion is, how do you say, auf ganz natürliche Weise ausgestattet?'"

A ripple of scandalised laughter went round the table. Chloe nearly snorted her martini through her nose. Eszter half-collapsed against the backrest, clutching her ribs, and even the usually reserved TUI pair grinned into their mojitos. The Jet2 FO, who everyone now knew only as "Yorkshire Jen," was pounding the table, tears of mirth streaming down her face.

Hayley took a bow—half-spilling vodka soda and entirely unbothered. "Anyway, that was the end of that hotel booking. They moved us to the ibis Styles, which is basically Ryanair but on land."

"And you still shagged him, though," Chloe pointed out.

"Obviously. Anyway, the next morning, my sister texts me to say she's preggers with her latest boyfriend, a Delta First Officer, and he's gone and told his mum she's cabin crew because he doesn't want anyone to know he's dating a woman who actually flies the plane. As if piloting an Airbus is some sort of back-alley hobby!" Hayley's hands flew up again, indignation mingling with delight. "So now my parents think I'm the sensible one. Which is a first."

"Christ, the bar for 'sensible' is subterranean these days," Jen chimed in, wiping her eyes and grinning at Hayley. "You'll be their golden girl as long as you never tell them about Magaluf."

"God, Magaluf," echoed one of the Wizz Air FOs, Anna, with a shudder. "I still get flashbacks whenever I see fluorescent body paint."

The group roared, a warm bubble of shared memory enveloping them. Sarah let herself relax further into the booth, catching snippets of conversation as drinks flowed faster, the barman's interest piqued by the constant orders and the mess of airline ID cards scattered like confetti on the sticky table.

Sarah's phone pinged again, and before she could read the WhatsApp Max had sent her, one of the TUI First Officers snatched it up with the speed of someone used to grabbing flight plans out of printers at 4am. "Who's Max?" she asked, wagging her eyebrows at the name on the lockscreen, holding the phone just out of reach.

"Give it here, Harriet, you nosy cow!" Sarah laughed, lunging, but it was half-hearted—she wasn't really bothered, and the mood was too light to mind a bit of friendly teasing. Harriet, emboldened by a couple of mojitos, was already holding the phone above her head and scrolling through the pictures on the WhatsApp.

"Fuck, its him, that aloof German FO, the one from Sprint! Detweiler! Jesus, Sarah, you bagged the elusive one!" Harriet declared, voice rising loud enough to draw glances from the bar staff, who by now had probably pieced together the source of tonight's aviation invasion. "Have you shagged him yet?"

Sarah knew that she hadn't even gone out on a single date with him, but they had WhatsApped and bumped into each other in the past week that they had known each other, the past week and few days that Sprint had been in service, the past week that felt like a lifetime compressed between sectors, sign-ons, and crash pad evenings. She rolled her eyes, snatching her phone back with a mock glare.

"I have not. It's called talking, Harriet. Some of us like to get to know a bloke before we pounce."

The table exploded with derisive laughter and a chorus of "liar!" and "as if!" from various corners. Someone—Sarah couldn't see who—threw a cocktail stirrer at her, which landed in her clutch bag with a plop. Hayley grinned, waggling her eyebrows.

"Well, let us know when you do. Maybe you'll get the inside track on those Sprint fatigue rules."

"Or just the inside track, full stop," Chloe fired back, raising her glass with wicked glee.

Sarah snorted, unable to suppress the laughter. The drinks had worked their magic; the stories rolled on, one after another, each more ridiculous than the last. A Ryanair FO named Caitlin—Irish, sharp-tongued, and with a wicked glint in her eye—started complaining about Michael O'Leary.

"...he sent a message down the line last month saying we should all smile more on turnarounds. Smile, he says! As if my lips haven't frozen in place from that poxy Stansted wind. And there he is, striding about in his neon jacket like a traffic cone with a Napoleon complex, telling us we should be more like Aer Lingus. If I wanted to work for Aer Lingus, I'd wear green and talk about Guinness, not deal with some buck-toothed stag from Southend vomiting Carling into a sick bag at 7am. You know, I hate the way he makes us structure our employment status through Cyprus, for tax purposes, but God forbid you mention that when HR's in the room. Last time I did, the base manager started sweating like we'd asked him to recite the operating manual for a 737 in Mandarin."

That brought another surge of laughter, with even the Wizz Air crew—who had suffered through more than their fair share of tax dodge contracts—nodding in hard-earned sympathy. The talk turned for a while to bases: which were tolerable, which were cursed, and which ones always seemed to be haunted by the ghosts of managers past.

"Stansted's fine as long as you don't breathe too deeply in the crew room," Anna said. "I swear it smells of despair and two-day-old Greggs."

"At least it's not Luton," Caitlin fired back. "Last week, someone left a sandwich in the fridge for so long it developed its own call sign."

Chloe leaned across the table, dropping her voice conspiratorially. "You ever flown into Perugia at night? They haven't got an ILS, and the approach is like threading a needle in a blackout. We were down to minimums and the Captain's yelling, 'Visual, visual!' and I'm just praying the runway's actually there. Afterwards, the Italians in the tower handed us a bottle of grappa like it was standard SOP."

Yorkshire Jen nodded sagely. "That's the real benefit of these jobs—booze at destination. Last time I went through Kraków, the ground staff gave us a box of pierogi and told us to take the vodka as well. Said it was 'for the nerves'." She mimed knocking one back, the table dissolving into giggles.

Through it all, Sarah felt a kind of electric warmth—not just from the cocktails, though they certainly helped—but from the pure, unlikely camaraderie of it. Here were women who, by all rights, should have been rivals, swapping bases and banter, each carrying their own baggage—broken contracts, ridiculous passengers, harried check-in staff, missed Christmases, failed relationships—but here, none of it really mattered. They were simply out—on the town, for once the party and not the afterthought, the ones laughing loudest.

The night wore on, the cocktails piling up in garish glassware, stories growing more surreal with each round. Somewhere between a round of Sex on the Beach and a tray of questionable tequila shots (procured after Eszter had convinced the bartender they were "off-duty medical professionals"), someone suggested a dance.

"Come on, we're not dead yet!" Hayley cried, brandishing her phone to summon an Uber. "We'll never get in anywhere as a twelve, but I bet Soho's not seen a gaggle like this since Eurovision."

The flight of FOs spilled back onto the street, laughter trailing like confetti. The city's pulse seemed to quicken as they wove their way down Charing Cross Road, heels clacking, boots shining, occasional whoops drawing curious glances from couples and stragglers. Harriet and Anna tried to lead an impromptu conga line, which promptly collapsed outside the next bar, but no one cared. For a few precious hours, London belonged to them.

They queued briefly at a basement club, the sort with black doors and a doorman whose only qualification seemed to be an allergy to fun. Even he, after a wary scan of airline IDs and a long look at the swirl of hairpins and lipstick, relented, waving them in with a smirk. The air inside was thick—cologne, sweat, the tang of spilled gin and the relentless thump of bass. Downstairs, the floor was a slick, neon-lit paradise: half-empty at first, then suddenly packed, strobe lights painting every surface in electric pink.

Sarah found herself pressed between Hayley and Chloe as the music began to work its magic. The initial awkwardness lasted only a song or two—after all, who could stay tense when "Freed from Desire" came blaring from the speakers and Hayley's boots threatened to take out an unsuspecting banker?

For a while, time blurred: the group circled and recircled the dance floor, hands in the air, belting along to songs they hadn't heard sober since their uni days. Chloe's dress glittered under the lights, and even Sarah, who'd always felt slightly self-conscious in crowds, surrendered to the simple joy of movement and noise, the happy anonymity of being just another face in the crowd.

The club, predictably, was filled with the usual mix: sharp-suited city boys, a hen party in matching sashes, a couple of raucous theatre crew still in eyeliner, and—everywhere—the scent of possibility. The airline group drew attention, their collective energy infectious, the kind of confidence only found in women who regularly landed planes in storms.

Sarah caught a few admiring glances—one from a sharply dressed woman who mouthed "flight crew?" with a conspiratorial wink. She grinned back. For once, it was almost fun to be recognised for what she was, instead of what she wasn't.

Halfway through the second hour, Eszter convinced the DJ to play "Toxic"—with the promise of "unlimited jump seats if you make it loud." The group exploded in cheers, turning the floor into their own impromptu runway, with Hayley doing an ill-advised version of a pre-flight safety demo to the beat. Harriet mimed checking a cabin, Anna did the brace position, and Sarah herself—swept up in the joy of it—found herself announcing "Cabin Crew, doors to manual and crosscheck!" just as the bass dropped.

The words echoed, carried on a tide of laughter and drunken applause. For a heartbeat, the past years of exhaustion, dashed hopes, and over-polished company videos melted away. Sarah let herself fall into the music, movements loosened by cheap tequila and the honest affection of the women around her. It was easy, here: no cockpit authority, no shuffling through layers of company policy or quietly fuming over gendered comments from ageing captains. Here she was one of the gang, laughing until her ribs hurt and her feet ached.

The DJ, seeing the impact, transitioned deftly into "Valerie"—the Mark Ronson version, all bounce and brass and sweet, blurry nostalgia. The circle tightened, arms thrown around shoulders, drinks abandoned to the edge of the dancefloor as the group shouted every word. Chloe swirled her skirt and pointed at Hayley—"Well sometimes I go out by myself…"—while Harriet mugged for invisible cabin cameras, and Jen made a show of tapping an imaginary PA mic.

Sarah caught sight of herself in a mirrored panel: cheeks flushed, eyes bright, a strand of hair escaping the neat up-do. For once, she liked what she saw. It was a face that belonged here, not just in the echoing predawn quiet of a deserted jetway or under the unflattering lights of a crew room, but in the fizz and mess of a night out. She mouthed along, not caring if anyone noticed.

Around them, the club filled in. A pair of city boys made a tentative approach but were shrugged off by Caitlin with a flat, "Sorry lads, girls' night." One made a feeble attempt at aviation banter, something about "flying high with you lot tonight," and was rewarded with a rolling of eyes so synchronised it could have been choreographed by Airbus. Chloe patted him on the head, sending him back to his group, and Anna led the group in a mock demonstration of "unruly passenger restraint" with a discarded neon feather boa.

The hours began to stretch and contract, the way they only do on a proper night out in London—songs seemed to loop, then suddenly you realised you hadn't been to the toilet in an hour, and your drink had vanished. Harriet staged an impromptu contest to see who could find the worst club cocktail ("Sambuca and Sprite, why?"), while Jen and Caitlin somehow ended up with a group of Irish rugby fans convinced they were flight dispatchers for Aer Lingus.

Sarah's phone buzzed again—she checked it in a quiet corner of the bar, heart racing in spite of herself. Another message from Max.

Max Detweiler: *Hope you're raising hell. I'd kill for a pint and a proper night out. You lot look like trouble.*

Attached: a grainy selfie, Max in a bleak Stansted hotel room, paper cup of instant coffee, FTL spreadsheet on the screen behind him. The look in his eye was tired but warm, that sideways grin she'd already come to recognise.

She typed a reply, thumbs fumbling slightly:

Sarah Marsh: *Next time you're in London, drinks are on me. I'll show you how it's done.*

She hesitated a moment—then, emboldened by two tequilas and the thrum of the club, added:

Sarah Marsh: *And I don't mean crew room tea either, Detweiler.*

As soon as she sent that, Sarah noticed Caitlin had left the group, and was now snogging someone from a stag party, the person wearing a 'groom' sash and L Plates on his Elvis suit, both of them pressed into a sticky alcove next to the cloakroom. The rest of the group noticed too, bursting into fresh laughter at the tableau. Harriet snapped a surreptitious photo—"blackmail for next Stansted early," she declared, waving her phone—before being swatted away by a watchful bouncer.

Jen shook her head, leaning on Anna's shoulder. "That'll be another WhatsApp scandal by morning. Bet she's snogged a groom on every continent."

Anna snorted, clutching her mojito. "Even Ryanair hasn't expanded that far. Yet."

Sarah grinned, rolling her shoulders, feeling loose and lovely. Someone handed her another drink—lime, sharp, electric—and she drank it gratefully, letting the music and movement blur away the sharp edges that so often haunted the end of a long week. The world was soft here, friendly, the kind of place you could forget about early sign-ons and roster changes and the endless negotiations with sleep.

Hayley drifted over, cheeks flushed, hair wild, catching Sarah's hand. "You all right, Marsh?" she yelled over the music, voice barely audible above the crash of the bass. "You look like you're having a religious experience!"

Sarah laughed, squeezing her friend's hand. "I needed this. All of it."

"Good. You deserve a proper night," Hayley said, bumping her shoulder gently. "Next round's on me. And then we're kidnapping Caitlin before she gets herself uninvited from the wedding."

A ripple of agreement passed through the group. They regrouped near the bar, the twelve of them weaving through a thicket of stag parties, hen dos, the occasional lost tourist and one persistent man in a glittery captain's hat who seemed to think his best chat-up line was "I'll let you fly my jet any time, darling." (He was firmly told where to go by Chloe, who could kill a flirtation with a single eyebrow.)

Drinks refreshed, they formed up in a loose circle by the dancefloor, swaying together as the DJ spun the kind of anthems that needed no explanation. It was a living, breathing thing—the joy, the togetherness, the feeling that for tonight, at least, they were a crew of their own, answerable only to each other.

Somewhere between 2 and 3am, Anna lost a shoe. The Wizz Air pair orchestrated a search party that would have made Heathrow ground staff proud, but the shoe was finally located under a table, alongside a battered clutch bag and a pack of nicotine gum. "Miracles do happen," Jen declared solemnly, returning the shoe to its grateful owner, who swore she'd never dance in heels again (a lie, as everyone knew).

Harriet and Chloe attempted to chat up the DJ— ostensibly to request "anything but ABBA," but really, as it turned out, to blag free drink tokens. They succeeded in neither, but managed to get the group's photo taken by a club photographer who declared it "the most pilots he'd seen in one place since EasyJet's Christmas party." The resulting picture would later circulate in the various airline WhatsApp groups, captioned: "Flight Deck Commandos, Soho Division."

As the night thinned and the club emptied, the mood shifted into that bittersweet territory known only to those who have to check the time not just to see if the tubes are still running, but to calculate how many hours they have left before the first flight out of Gatwick. A few of the group eyed the clock nervously, aware that sign-on for Monday's early sectors was creeping closer by the minute.

"Should we call it?" Chloe suggested, not wanting to be the first to break the spell but feeling the weight of duty settle on her shoulders.

"Never," Caitlin protested, rejoining the group with lipstick smudged and eyes bright. "We'll just sleep in the crew room. Ryanair won't notice the difference."

Hayley giggled. "You do that, and you'll end up being rostered Athens–Manchester–Wroclaw with a 15-minute turn in Kraków. Again."

"Worth it," Caitlin said, but the consensus was clear: it was time to start the slow, shambolic retreat.

They stumbled out into the Soho night, arms linked, voices loud, an untidy, glorious parade. The pavements were sticky with spilled cider, club flyers clinging to shoes, and the late-night breeze cut through silk dresses and cropped jackets. Sarah felt a pang of nostalgia for nights she'd never quite had, a longing for the kind of freedom that was rarely on offer in her line of work.

They split, not with tears but with promises: next layover, next time, next whatever. Chloe and Caitlin headed for a shared Uber to Stansted's cheapest Travelodge. Anna and Eszter set off in search of a night bus to somewhere near Luton. The TUI pair, ever practical, had already booked a minicab that would take them straight to Gatwick's North Terminal, ready for whatever charter flight awaited them at sunrise.

Hayley and Sarah lingered at the corner, shivering, both unwilling to break the moment.

"At least it wasn't our PanEuro days, eh, babes," Sarah said with a grin. "At least we're not in that hell hole, and hey, the worst thing we've got to deal with tonight is a lost shoe and a bit of glitter in the hair. Not some leery old training captain trying to cop a feel on the sim brief."

Hayley rolled her eyes, but there was a fondness there, too—years of shared hotel breakfasts, joint despair over tech logs, and that rare currency of having survived the same disasters. She pulled her jacket tight against the breeze, heels clacking lightly on the uneven pavement. "Give it time, love. You know as well as I do that even in the promised land of ULCC, there's always some relic lurking, waiting to cock up your day with a six-hour taxi to nowhere. But tonight—" she paused, looking around at the thinning crowds, the way the lights of Soho still bled through the early hours, "—tonight, we smashed it."

Sarah grinned, feeling suddenly, simply content. "Yeah, we did."

****

CHAPTER 10 – Dinner Date
Sunday 24th April 2022

The bottles of lipstick on the table were not what Sarah predicted she'd wear.

They sat there in an odd array of colour swatches, as though Sarah was meant to choose something from the selection before her. The shades ranged from deep burgundy to soft pinks and vibrant reds, almost as if they were laid out for a model in a fashion shoot. She glanced up at the mirror on the wall, as though expecting it to tell her something she didn't already know: she was about to spend her first evening off in months with a man she barely knew, at a restaurant she'd never been to, in a city that felt a thousand miles away from the hustle of her usual life.

It was strange to think that she'd been sitting in the crew lounge just a few days ago, discussing potential days off and then suddenly, after an impromptu WhatsApp DM from a certain Max Detweiler, a strange sequence of events had led her agreeing to, as they were both scheduled to be in Majorca, Sarah having been rostered a Dublin to Majorca and Max a Luton to Majorca, a dinner date in the pre-season Balearic sunset glow. It wasn't something Sarah would have typically agreed to, but she found herself in a place that felt both foreign and exciting. She wasn't sure what it was about Max that drew her in, perhaps it was his easy-going attitude or the strange familiarity that seemed to form in their brief exchanges during their time at Sprint Air. Or maybe it was simply the fact that this was her first real chance to escape from the chaos that had defined the last few months of her life, both the training, which for her had been significantly shorter due to the fact she had a RAF background and so knew air traffic control protocols and aircraft systems inside out, and easyJet, the airline she had done the training with, having therefore progressed her quicker than the 24 month program, which had, for her, been compressed from her first joining the Luton based airline in September 2021, nearly 7 months ago, to a mere six months of intense training and cross-training. It felt like a whirlwind that hadn't really stopped until now. This evening, though, she had a rare moment of pause.

Going on dates wasn't something Sarah was a stranger to, as, having been in the RAF, and therefore having had her fair share of social events, she hooked up with various men and women during her years at the service. However, this was different. Max wasn't some fleeting encounter or a consequence of the kind of nightlife her life used to revolve around. There was something more substantial about him, something that had drawn her into agreeing to a dinner date in the first place.

"Nervous?" Hayley Northcott, who was with her boyfriend and PanEuro First Officer, Theo Sullivan, teased as Sarah adjusted her hair in front of the mirror.

The hotel room that Sarah was stopping in, at the BQ Apolo Hotel, one of the more popular for airlines to stay at when transiting through Majorca, was a typical crew accommodation: clean, functional, and completely uninspiring. The room was modestly furnished with a double bed, as most of the crews, from easyJet to Jet2, often stayed solo unless as a married couple. There was a small table by the window, cluttered with the usual hotel welcome packet, two bottles of complimentary water, and now, Sarah's improvised beauty salon. Her suitcase, the same model that most of the other pilots, cabin crew and other airline staff worldwide when travelling, was laid on the bed, uniform hung on the wardrobe door, and her mobile buzzing quietly every now and then on the side table, mostly with crew group messages.

Hayley, she knew, was in the neighbouring room, as she and Theo were having rare time off, the duo being at rival airlines, Hayley a First officer at easyJet and Theo flying for PanEuro. The duo had been passengers on MGT657, the flight that Hayley had flew from Dublin to Majorca earlier that afternoon. Hayley and Theo had jump seated for the leg, as they were both A320 family trained, and, although they were rival airlines to Sprint, still part of the same intricate web of pilots who knew each other by callsign, airbase, or blurry nights in crew hotels. That mutual understanding—of the long hours, the rotating rosters, the shared glances in cockpit doorways—was something Sarah had grown to value.

"I'm not nervous," Sarah replied with the faintest of smirks, dragging the edge of her thumbnail along the rim of a lipstick tube, "just… wondering if I'm going to regret burgundy in an hour when it's smeared on a wine glass."

Hayley laughed. "Go with the rose nude. Safe, classic, like you're not trying too hard. Subtle confidence."

Sarah picked up the recommended shade, held it near her lips, and tilted her head. "Subtle confidence. That's what we're branding this, are we?"

Hayley stepped over and leaned against the desk, arms folded. "You know, I actually think it's great you're going. Remember when Emma tried to hook you up with that creepy passenger on that one PanEuro flight, and you decked her... and then she took him to the front lav on the Charles de Gaulle and shagged him after you rejected him."

Sarah chuckled, rolling her eyes as she applied the lipstick with a practiced touch. "Yeah. It was the day before you decked Captain Hargreaves for touching you up in the galley on the JFK. I still can't believe that PanEuro tried to cover it up, and Toby reported it to the CAA after the union didn't want to get involved. Honestly, if we'd filmed the whole thing, it'd be a Netflix docuseries by now."

Hayley's smile softened as Sarah stood, lipstick applied, smoothing her hands down the front of the dress she'd chosen. It wasn't anything extravagant—simple navy with capped sleeves, hitting mid-thigh, a little more effort than her uniform but nothing that screamed desperate. It was the kind of dress you could wear again and again and still feel good in. She stepped into her low heels, the comfortable kind a pilot kept for wedding invites and hotel bars, and gave herself a final once-over in the mirror.

"You look stunning," Hayley said sincerely. "Max won't know what hit him."

Sarah arched an eyebrow. "Let's hope he's got a decent taste in wine and not some Ryanair-level palate. Anyway, what are you and Theo doing tonight?"

The wink on Hayley's face was mischievous. "Room service, bathrobe cocktails, and a terrible movie we'll pretend to be watching while we fool around. You know, classic romantic pilot behaviour. Oh, I forgot to tell you… he proposed to me the other day."

Sarah blinked, the lipstick wand paused mid-air as the words sank in. "Proposed? Seriously?" Her voice was a mixture of surprise and something softer—something warmer, maybe hope. The idea of Theo, with his constant dry wit and cool-headed professionalism, dropping down on one knee was unexpected, to say the least.

Hayley grinned, her eyes sparkling. "Yep. We were both on Berlin rotations, and I'd pipped his A320 to the threshold on approach to Brandenburg as I was low on FTL. Don't ask, I'd done 4 sectors that day. He accused me of cutting him off in the most civilised ATC-approved way possible, then over currywurst he pulled out this hilariously tiny ring box—must've hidden it in his lanyard or something. Said he figured if I was going to outrank him in the skies, he might as well try to catch up on the ground." She paused, adding more seriously, "I said yes. Of course."

Sarah let out a long, low whistle. "Bloody hell. Congrats, Hales. That's... wow. Kinda makes my lipstick drama feel a bit minor."

"Oh please," Hayley laughed. "You've got more nerves facing a date than flying into Gibraltar with a tailwind. Go knock him dead."

Sarah laughed too, genuinely, and with a nod of thanks, picked up her clutch and left the room. The corridor smelt faintly of over-bleached towels and that weird lemony hotel deodoriser, but it didn't matter. Her heels clicked softly down the hall, and with each step, she felt herself moving just a little further away from the high-strung cadet she had been, and a little closer to... something else.

* _ * _ * _ *

The warm air of the Balearic evening greeted Sarah as she stepped out of the sliding glass doors of the BQ Apolo Hotel. There was still a pinkish hue in the sky, tinged with the faint gold of the setting sun. Palm trees stood as silhouettes against the twilight, and the air carried the light scent of salt and jasmine. The Mediterranean was just a block away, its surf barely audible, and there was a tranquil buzz to the streets—locals walking dogs, tourists meandering, and the occasional bell of a bicycle.

She walked the few streets toward the restaurant Max had suggested—La Torreta del Mar, an old coastal building converted into a rustic-modern dining spot perched just above the Playa de Palma promenade. The kind of place that got a nod in a half-forgotten Time Out article and became a low-key pilot hangout whenever crews had long layovers. It was quiet tonight—April not yet inviting the full-swing summer crowd. Perfect for a date that was already strange enough in its rarity.

As Sarah approached the front terrace, she saw him.

Max Detweiler was leaning casually on the wooden balustrade, looking out toward the sea, hands in his pockets. He was wearing a light grey linen shirt, sleeves rolled up, and navy chinos. His usual cockpit posture— alert, slightly cocky—had relaxed into something more grounded, more present. When he turned and spotted her, his lips curled into a slow smile. It wasn't smug. Just... content.

"You look incredible," he said, standing up straighter and giving a slight, respectful nod.

Sarah returned the smile, albeit with a self-aware smirk. "Not bad yourself. I was worried I might be overdressed, I mean… well, I… the last date I went on was when I was on Baltic Air Policing, back in the day, so and that was a work dinner disguised as something else entirely," Sarah said, stepping onto the terrace and feeling the slight chill of the sea breeze lift her dress fabric briefly. "This feels... different."

Max gave a small laugh, one that seemed genuinely amused rather than self-deprecating. "Different's good. I'm glad it's different. I wasn't sure if you'd actually show up, to be honest. You seem a bit too sharp for the usual pilot banter, and I feared I might bore you with my stories about air traffic delays and the joys of airline catering."

Sarah folded her arms, a playful glint in her eye. "You clearly underestimate the kind of entertainment an airline pilot can find in delayed departures and catering disasters. Anyway, did you hear that PanEuro got fined the other day?"

Max chuckled and motioned toward the table he'd reserved—intimate but not overly romantic, set just back from the promenade where the scent of grilled seafood wafted over in gentle bursts. A candle flickered between two glasses of water, and a small pot of olives rested in the centre, untouched.

"Fined?" he asked, pulling her chair out gallantly. "What for this time? Not enough Brylcreem in the crew hairdo protocol?"

Sarah sat with an amused shake of her head. "No, nothing to do with aesthetics. You know that Captain, Roger Hargreaves, the owe who got slapped by Hayley mid-Atlantic for getting too handsy? Yeah, turns out that little detour to Shannon wasn't just an HR disaster—it's now a CAA casefile. You see, he's still on the books, and... well, the CAA and the Irish Aviation Authority both decided to investigate further after several crew filed separate complaints. Turns out Shannon wasn't a one-off. Hargreaves had a long history of misconduct swept under PanEuro's velvet carpet of nostalgia and cigars-in-the-briefing-room glamour. The fine itself wasn't massive— more of a symbolic public slap—but it's reopened the discussion about their internal disciplinary procedures. Or lack thereof."

Max winced. "Classic PanEuro. Spend a fortune on ashtrays for their First Class lounge, can't be arsed to train their Captains not to be sleazeballs. Still... at least he got slapped. Deserved it."

Sarah nodded, her fingers idly twisting the stem of her water glass. "Hayley's not one to let things slide. And Toby backed her up with the CAA. I'm not sure PanEuro expected that kind of solidarity among the ranks. Especially not from one of their golden boys."

The waiter appeared and began taking orders—grilled turbot for Sarah, seared duck breast for Max. They opted for a bottle of Rioja to share, something neither too showy nor too casual. As the waiter disappeared inside, a silence settled between them. Not uncomfortable, just… paused. A breath.

"So," Max said eventually, leaning forward with his forearms on the table, "how's Sprint treating you? Still surviving the chaos?"

Sarah exhaled with a laugh. "That's generous. 'Surviving' suggests there's an order to the madness. Honestly? Every day's a new roulette wheel. I never know if I'll be flying a Latvian A321 or a Bulgarian A319 with duct-taped seats. And don't even get me started on the roster. I had three sectors in one day with four aircraft swaps last week. And every time someone calls Ops, it's like talking to a drunk octopus with a rotary phone."

Max grinned. "Sounds about right. I had a flight last month where we refuelled in Girona, even though we were meant to be going nowhere near Spain. Crew scheduling thought Girona was a person. Genuinely. We landed and the ground staff didn't even know we were coming."

Sarah covered her mouth to stop the laugh spraying wine across the table. "You're making that up."

"I wish I was." Max swirled his wine thoughtfully. "But the thing is… even with all the nonsense, I still kind of love it. The unpredictability. The weirdness. It's like being in a very badly-written sitcom. Or a Kafka novel. Only the protagonist is always sleep-deprived and vaguely underpaid."

"I know exactly what you mean," Sarah said, her tone softer now. "For all the madness, I don't hate it. I actually feel... awake. Like everything matters in a different way. When I was in the RAF, everything was structured. Predictable, even when it was dangerous. This? This is chaos. But it's mine. It's messy, and it's imperfect, but I'm not hiding in a cockpit pretending the world is black and white anymore."

Max looked at her with a kind of quiet reverence, nodding slowly. "That's the most pilot thing I've ever heard anyone say."

Sarah smiled faintly, brushing a strand of hair behind her ear as the waiter arrived with their mains. The smell of the turbot, rich with lemon and herbs, made her stomach grumble involuntarily. She hadn't realised how hungry she was.

They ate in a silence filled with good food and the occasional glance. The wine flowed gently, not enough to dull the senses, just enough to soften the edges of the day. And as the sun finally slipped beneath the horizon, the lights along the promenade flickered to life, casting warm amber pools onto the cobbled pavement.

"So, what about you?" Sarah asked after a while. "You've been with Sprint how long now?"

"Just shy of six months," Max replied. "Before that, Wizz. And before that, I did a stint in corporate aviation out of Geneva. Charter work. Rich people with unpredictable tantrums and even more unpredictable flight plans. I once had a Saudi prince ask if I could land in a field in Normandy because he wanted to pick wildflowers for a woman he'd just met."

"You're joking."

"I wish. We diverted to Deauville. He sulked for three days and didn't speak to anyone but his personal falconer."

Sarah laughed, shaking her head. "God, I thought military brass were egomaniacs. That's a different level."

"Corporate flying is like being a waiter with wings," Max said dryly. "Sprint's a step up. At least here, when things go wrong, it's due to incompetence, not malice."

Sarah nodded slowly. "That's... a fair distinction."

They lingered over dessert—chocolate mousse for her, lemon tart for him—watching as the quiet of the Majorcan evening deepened. Couples strolled hand in hand past the terrace, the occasional skateboarder gliding by on the sea wall.

"I'm glad you came," Max said at last. "I know it probably took more mental effort than flying a CAT III into Warsaw."

She gave him a look. "You've flown into Warsaw in fog?"

"Three times. Two of them I thought I'd end up married to my First Officer from the adrenaline alone."

Sarah smirked. "Well, I'm not proposing tonight."

Max grinned. "Noted. I'll leave my ring box at home."

There was a moment then, just a moment, where the world seemed to hold its breath. Sarah looked at Max—not just at his easy smile or the relaxed line of his jaw, but something deeper. Something steadier. A man who had seen the madness of the skies and still found room to laugh.

He reached across the table, not suddenly, not presumptuously, just gently, and rested his hand atop hers.

It was warm.

She didn't pull away.

* _ * _ * _ *

They walked back together, the quiet of the street like a comforting cloak. The lights from the hotel glowed ahead, soft yellow through palm fronds swaying gently in the breeze.

"You know," Max said as they reached the lobby entrance, "you don't have to make this awkward tomorrow."

Sarah tilted her head. "How do you mean?"

"Just… if we bump into each other in the lounge. Or in the shuttle to the airport. You don't have to pretend tonight didn't happen."

Sarah glanced sideways, a flicker of amusement sparking in her eyes. "You mean the whole 'awkward dinner date' thing?"

Max shrugged, his grin widening, a faint flush rising to his cheeks under the soft hotel lighting. "Maybe. Or just… you know, whatever this is between us doesn't have to be a one-off." He paused, searching her face for a reaction, then added softly, "We could do this again. No flight deck jargon, no crazy roster talk. Just normal people having a normal evening."

She regarded him for a moment, the quiet confidence in his voice contrasting sharply with her usual self-doubt around people outside of work. Sarah's life had been a series of routines — meticulously planned flights, rigorous checklists, and the constant hum of ATC chatter. But this… this felt different. Like a small island of calm in the perpetual storm.

"Well," she said slowly, "I'll hold you to that. But don't expect me to fall head over heels after one meal."

Max's laugh was warm, easy, genuine. "Fair. I wouldn't want to scare you off just yet."

They stepped inside the lobby, the cool air conditioning brushing against their faces after the gentle warmth outside. The hotel was quieter now, most of the late arrivals having settled in. A reception clerk glanced up briefly and gave a polite nod as they passed.

The lift chimed, doors sliding open smoothly. Sarah pressed the button for her floor. They stepped inside, standing side by side, the silence between them comfortably unforced.

"So," Sarah said, breaking the quiet, "what's next for you? More chaos with Sprint, or dreaming of something else?"

Max's gaze drifted upward, his fingers tapping a light rhythm on the polished panel. "Honestly? I'm not sure. Sprint is... unpredictable, but it's also where I am right now. There's something thrilling about being part of something so messy and new. But yeah, sometimes I wonder what else might be out there. Maybe a bigger airline, maybe something a bit more stable. What about you?"

Sarah shrugged, a wistful smile touching her lips. "I'm just trying to keep my head above water. I like the chaos, like you said, but I also want a place where I'm more than just another face in the cockpit. Somewhere I can really belong."

Max's hand brushed lightly against hers again, this time deliberately. "You'll find it. And when you do, I hope you'll invite me along for dinner."

She laughed, a clear sound that felt good in the quiet lift. The doors opened and they stepped out onto the corridor.

"Goodnight, Max," Sarah said, her voice softer now.

"Goodnight, Sarah. Sleep well."

She turned toward her room, then paused and looked back over her shoulder. Max was already walking away, hands in his pockets, his smile still there.

The night felt full of possibilities.

****

CHAPTER 11 – Passenger Error
Monday 25th April 2022

Sarah knew it would happen. After all, it was a very rare occasion it happened in the airline industry, but when two flights of rival companies, both going to the same destination use the same gate, adjacent remote stands, and depart 5 minutes apart, a passenger boarding the wrong flight was almost inevitable.

Especially when it was a Ryanair flight right next to the Sprinter Airbus A321, both with Irish registrations, the Ryanair being a Boeing 737-MAX-8 that was only a few days in service, unlike the A321neo that was literally its first day of service, having been part of a Vueling cancelled order, one that the Iberian operator had decided, instead of A321s, they would wait for the certifications of the A321XLR.

Because of the incident, both the Ryanair and Sprinter services, both heading to Luton full of stag do parties, were now delayed, as both sets of crews, her and her captain, a Swedish veteran named Ingrid Sjöholm, along with the Ryanair cabin and flight deck crews, were now filling in a ton of paperwork, because the Agencia Estatal de Seguridad Aérea had decided, upon hearing that the Sprint plane had took off with a passenger who was not listed on the manifest, that this constituted a "grave security failure" requiring immediate grounding of both aircraft and a full-scale investigation.

Sarah slumped slightly in the airport offices as she watched the chaos unfold around her on the sun-drenched ramp at Palma de Sarah slumped slightly in the airport offices as she watched the chaos unfold around her on the sun-drenched ramp at Palma de Mallorca Airport. Outside the glass, the stark white and blue fuselage of the Sprinter A321neo, EI-SPT, gleamed in the afternoon sun, its sleek lines contrasting sharply with the adjacent Ryanair 737 MAX, EI-HGE, its new paint still smelling faintly of fresh gloss. Both aircraft were surrounded by a flurry of uniformed officials — some from AESA, others from the airport's security forces, and several frantic ground handlers who were busy reconciling manifests, passenger lists, and the growing pile of incident reports.

Inside, the cramped office smelled of stale coffee and the faint metallic tang of overheated electronics. Sarah rubbed her temples, trying to steady her nerves. She'd known incidents like this were a disaster waiting to happen, especially at Palma, a notorious hotspot for stag parties and holidaymakers prone to distractions and misadventures. But she hadn't expected it the day after she had gone on a dinner date with Max Detweiler, still half-glowing from the serenity of that rare calm evening. Now, less than twenty hours later, she was caught in a bureaucratic and operational thunderstorm, the sort of cascading failure that airports like Palma incubated in their heat, humidity, and human chaos.

There had been too many times lately where things went sideways, but this was a whole new level of absurdity. The passenger — a sunburnt Brit named Callum Brayshaw from Walsall — had arrived at the wrong aircraft door, clutching a Ryanair boarding pass, slightly drunk but still lucid enough to have passed the perfunctory ID check at the bus gate. It hadn't helped that the ground marshal had gestured to the wrong aircraft when shouting "Luton this way!" in three languages. Callum had happily climbed the Sprinter steps, waved cheerfully to the cabin crew, dumped his Duty Free into the overhead bin, and sat in seat 18A — where there happened to be a no-show.

Nobody realised anything was wrong until they were literally had just took off, when the lead flight attendant, a Portuguese woman named Isabel Ferreira, had alerted the flight deck, with Sarah instantly contacting Palma's tower, the standard procedure for a passenger boarded onto the wrong aircraft. The tower had already begun querying Ryanair's gate handling team about a missing passenger, and the dots connected far too quickly for comfort.

Now they were stuck — legally grounded, operationally paralysed, reputationally vulnerable.

The Ryanair Captain, who was typing his statement up on a laptop that balanced precariously on his knees, glanced up briefly at Sarah through the thick glass partition. He was a stocky man with prematurely greying hair and a perpetual look of mild disbelief — the kind that suggested this sort of chaos was not at all what he'd signed up for that morning. His name was Declan Murphy, a seasoned pilot with over fifteen years' experience, mostly flying for Ryanair's low-cost operations across Europe. Despite his best efforts at professionalism, Sarah could see the tension etched into his features.

Looking at her own statement, which was nearing 6,000 words, her RAF training going into play as she had written a highly detailed narrative of events, complete with time stamps, crew interactions, ATC dialogue transcripts, and a post-incident debrief layout that would make a military intelligence officer proud.

"I, Sarah Hannah Marsh of Sprint Air, hereby provide the following detailed account regarding the boarding of an unmanifested passenger on flight MGT8413B from Palma de Mallorca to Luton, on 25 April 2022," she read aloud softly, then returned to typing, fingers steady despite the tension in the room.

The official statement had to be impeccable. Every second accounted for, every interaction noted, to ensure that no finger could be pointed unfairly, but also to shield the airline from potentially catastrophic penalties from AESA and the Spanish authorities. Sprinter, already struggling to build its reputation against established low-cost giants like Ryanair and easyJet, could not afford the fallout of a security breach, however inadvertent.

"I was alerted at 1209 hours by the lead cabin crew, Isabel Ferreira, that a passenger was seated without a matching boarding pass in seat 18A. Immediate checks confirmed that the individual, later identified as Mr Callum Brayshaw, was not listed on our manifest. The discrepancy was promptly reported to the flight deck and Palma Tower, per company and regulatory procedures," Sarah continued, her voice barely above a whisper as she scrolled through her notes.

Scrolling through her typed statement, Sarah noticed that she had already cross-referenced every timeline detail with the official ATC recordings, and the ground staff logs, ensuring nothing was left to chance. Her RAF background, where precision was non-negotiable, was a comfort now amid the creeping dread of the incident's consequences.

Outside, the sun was dipping lower, casting long shadows across the ramp. The ground crew bustled between vehicles and equipment, their movements frantic yet focused. Over the hum of radios and distant conversations, Sarah could hear the occasional Spanish commands and murmured English phrases as the investigation unfolded.

She leaned back in her chair, allowing herself a brief moment to process everything that had happened in the last few hours.

The origins of the mistake were painfully obvious but not so easy to resolve. At Palma, gate assignments were notoriously tight during peak holiday season, with airlines jockeying for the most efficient slots and stand allocations. It was a logistical nightmare made worse by the fact that Sprint and Sprinter, like the other ultra-low cost airlines, would opt, to save money, using bus gates and remote stands rather than contact gates with airbridges. This meant passengers were bussed out to aircraft often parked side by side, sometimes with minimal signage or differentiation between planes beyond a flimsy clipboard and a shouted instruction from a stressed ground agent.

Sarah remembered the scene clearly. The buses had offloaded two stag groups — one loud and shirtless, the other even louder but in matching pink Hawaiian shirts. The noise had been deafening, the confusion absolute. One of the Ryanair stewards had later remarked to her that he'd had to physically block a group of their passengers from wandering up the Sprinter aircraft steps, believing it was theirs. Somehow Callum Brayshaw had slipped through that net. Or, more likely, had barrelled through it with the confidence of a man already two beers past the point of reason.

What worried Sarah most was the timing. They'd boarded within a 15-minute window of Ryanair, both gates had operated nearly simultaneously, and the ground team had only conducted cursory ID checks against boarding cards in the haste of a double dispatch. She hadn't spotted Callum herself — nor had Isabel — but it was clear from CCTV footage now being reviewed by AESA that he had walked briskly, somewhat erratically, up the steps to EI-SPT with no resistance.

That should never have happened. Not on any flight. Not in 2022. Not with all the digital integration, app-based scanning, biometric boarding and data reconciliation protocols that existed. And yet, here they were. Another system failure masked by operational fatigue and human error.

Pressing submit, she knew that next up was an interview with the Guardia Civil, the Spanish aviation police force, whose responsibility it was to determine if the incident constituted a criminal breach of international air transport law. Despite her clarity in the written account, Sarah dreaded the prospect. The Guardia had a reputation for being thorough, humourless, and unbending in their interpretations of even the smallest procedural infringements. And she could already see the plain-clothed officers waiting outside the admin suite, sunglasses perched atop buzz-cut heads, each armed with clipboards and clipped Castellano.

Sarah stood, stretched her stiff limbs, and prepared herself mentally for the inevitable interrogation. The cool fluorescent lights above did little to soothe the growing tension knotting her stomach. She could hear the low murmur of voices from beyond the office door and the occasional scrape of chair legs on the tiled floor. Moments later, two Guardia Civil officers entered, their expression unreadable but their posture rigid with official authority.

"Señorita Marsh," the taller of the two began in clipped English, "we will conduct a formal interview regarding the incident with passenger Callum Brayshaw on Sprinter flight MGT8413B. Please understand the gravity of the situation. This is a serious security breach under Spanish and EU regulations."

Sarah nodded, already steeling herself. "I understand, officers. I will answer your questions fully and accurately."

The interview began with routine clarifications: her role, the flight details, and the chain of events leading up to the flight. Sarah remained calm and methodical, recounting how Isabel Ferreira had discovered the unmanifested passenger only after boarding, and how Palma Tower had been informed immediately. She outlined the breakdown in the ground handling process and the difficulties posed by the adjacent remote stands with simultaneous boarding operations.

One officer, younger and more aggressive, pressed her on why the ground crew had not prevented the passenger from boarding. Sarah explained the chaotic scene, the inadequacy of signage, and the overworked staff juggling multiple gates. "Mistakes happen in these environments," she said, "but the procedures were followed as closely as possible once the issue was detected."

The officers then reviewed her detailed statement, nodding occasionally, but the questions became more pointed. "Was there any suspicion that Mr Brayshaw was intoxicated or attempting to evade controls?" the senior officer asked.

"Yes," Sarah admitted. "He appeared slightly drunk but coherent. He had a valid boarding pass for the Ryanair flight, but he simply went to the wrong aircraft steps."

"Yes," Sarah admitted. "He appeared slightly drunk but coherent. He had a valid boarding pass for the Ryanair flight, but he simply went to the wrong aircraft steps. Our plane has CCTV, so we've confirmed from the footage that there was no malicious intent. He walked up confidently and casually — as if he fully believed he was boarding the correct flight."

The younger Guardia officer exchanged a glance with his colleague, then jotted a few more notes. The tension in the room was coiling tighter with each minute. Sarah remained still, her posture military-straight, not out of arrogance but out of sheer focus. The RAF taught her to hold the line in interrogation, and this wasn't the first time she'd had to explain decisions in a high-stakes environment. But it was different when you were the one potentially liable.

They asked her about the gate agent — who it was, what they'd said, who had given final clearance for dispatch.

"The dispatch clearance was given by the gate supervisor. But again, it was a dual boarding. Two buses. Two sets of passengers. I believe they were using handwritten checklists because of the temporary breakdown in the scanner system at Gate 12."

The older officer grimaced subtly. He scribbled something down — the kind of note you instinctively knew would end up in a report passed around AESA's morning meeting the next day.

"And after you contacted ATC?"

"We followed regulation. ATC acknowledged our call, confirmed the discrepancy with Ryanair's crew, and issued instructions for us to maintain contact. We requested immediate permission to return, but were denied due to active congestion in Palma's arrival sequence. We were told to hold in the stack and then, 40 minutes later, both my flight and MAY067—the Ryanair flight—were officially grounded when we both returned here at Palma."

The officers conferred briefly, then resumed. "So, you remained in a holding pattern for forty minutes before clearance to land?"

"Yes. ATC deemed it less disruptive to have both aircraft return together than to stagger the landings. We were holding over the sea, fuel reserves were sufficient, and the passenger was compliant. No disturbance. He even asked for a ginger ale."

"Did he indicate awareness of his error?"

Sarah hesitated. "Not immediately. Isabel said he seemed confused when she asked to see his boarding pass again after take-off. He assumed she was checking for drink sales. Only after the cross-check with the manifest did the reality sink in. He was embarrassed. Apologetic. Shocked."

The younger officer raised an eyebrow. "And your airline allowed him to remain on board until return?"

"Well, what would you expect us to do? Dip to 100 feet over the Balearic Sea, open the L1 door and throw him out of the plane in the air? We're not the bloody CIA," Sarah said with the fury of a former Typhoon pilot. "With all due respect, its frowned upon to open the doors while in the air and eject a tourist over international waters. The Yanks might do it as a matter of course, but this is Spain, and we abide by Spanish and European laws, not Hollywood scripts."

"Señorita, with all-"

"No, you were going to suggest that I personally act as if it were a rendition flight, kidnapping a confused, slightly inebriated passenger off the wrong plane at altitude," Sarah said, her voice firm but controlled. "That simply isn't how we operate. The passenger was safe, secure, and compliant. We communicated immediately with ATC and followed every protocol from that moment on."

The senior Guardia officer sighed, nodding slowly. "Understood. This situation presents a challenge for enforcement, certainly. We must determine how such a breach was allowed to occur in the first place. The manifest discrepancy is a serious concern for national and EU aviation security."

Sarah felt the weight of the accusation, but she also knew from her experience that procedural lapses in ground handling were rarely the fault of the flight crew. "The responsibility for passenger management lies primarily with ground operations. Our team conducts thorough boarding checks, but in this instance, the ground staff failed to prevent Mr Brayshaw boarding the wrong aircraft."

The officers exchanged notes, and after a brief pause, the younger one asked, "What measures have you and Sprinter Air put in place since to prevent a recurrence?"

Sarah leaned forward, tapping on the digital tablet beside her. "Immediately after the incident, we coordinated with Palma's ground handling services and Sprinter's operations team to improve signage, increase staff briefings on concurrent boarding operations, and implement mandatory dual manifest reconciliation before pushback. We've also recommended better physical separation of aircraft stands during busy periods and enhanced passenger communication through multilingual announcements."

The officers nodded appreciatively, but the senior one added, "Your statement will be part of the preliminary investigation. We may require additional interviews with ground handling supervisors and security personnel."

"I am available at any time to assist," Sarah replied.

They rose, signalling the end of the formal session. "Thank you, Señorita Marsh," the senior officer said. "Please remain available for further inquiries."

As they left, Sarah exhaled slowly, rubbing her temples once again. The adrenaline that had kept her alert now ebbed, leaving a dull ache behind. She glanced back at the statement on her screen, her detailed account of the passenger error now part of an unfolding bureaucratic saga that threatened to overshadow her airline's fledgling reputation.

Outside, the sun was low, bathing the airport apron in a golden glow. The crews were still busy—ground personnel meticulously cross-checking documents, officials taking photographs, and the cabin crew preparing the aircraft for its next flight, once cleared. Sarah knew this day would linger in the airline's logs for weeks, possibly months.

* _ * _ * _ *

Later that day, Sarah walked into the BQ Apolo Hotel, where she had stopped the previous night after her date with Max Detweiler. The hotel lobby was quiet now, a sharp contrast to the bustling airport chaos she'd left behind. A cool breeze from the Mediterranean swept through the glass doors, carrying with it the faint scent of jasmine and sea salt — a fleeting reminder of the calm that had eluded her all morning.

Sarah had been told to stay in Palma for the night by the European Sprinter Operations team, based out of Prague, the Czech Republic, and that her shift, on the Sprint Staff app, for the next day, would be adjusted so she would pick up an early flight that currently had nobody rostered for. She was tired—physically drained from the constant adrenaline spikes and mentally taxed from the unrelenting bureaucracy she faced. The irony was not lost on her: after a rare, peaceful evening out with Max Detweiler, she had been thrust headfirst back into the messy reality of ultra low-cost airline operations.

The hotel lobby was almost serene now, a refuge from the relentless scrutiny of airport authorities and the mechanical cacophony of ramp-side life. She dragged her suitcase behind her, the soft wheels humming quietly over the polished marble floor. Checking in took longer than she expected; the receptionist barely looked up as she handed over her details. The Sprinter crew's last-minute travel arrangements were evidently a common headache.

Up in her modest hotel room, Sarah flicked on the TV, hoping for some mindless distraction, but the Spanish news was dominated by reports of the incident. Journalists had clearly caught wind of the "boarding blunder" and were spinning the narrative with varying degrees of alarmism. "Security breach at Palma de Mallorca Airport," one headline screamed, "Passenger boards wrong plane amid chaos." Another newscaster speculated about lax controls and "the growing dangers of low-cost airlines cutting corners." She switched off the TV, irritation prickling her skin.

This was the kind of media storm that could swallow a small airline whole, or at least dent its precarious reputation. Sprinter was a newcomer, eager to prove itself amid the giants of Europe's skies. Already, passengers had grumbled about confusing gate assignments and the infamous Spanish boarding buses. Now this. A spectacle to cling to, a symbol of operational chaos that could easily be weaponised by competitors.

Sarah knew her airline's survival depended on strict adherence to safety and security protocols, but also on managing perception. For every seat filled on a low-cost flight, there was a risk of a headline or an incident that could spark regulatory backlash, passenger distrust, or worse, a hefty fine.

She sat on the edge of the bed, eyes fixed on the blank wall. The weight of the day settled on her like a physical presence. The interview with the Guardia Civil, the paperwork, the whispered office conversations about "grave security failure," the repeated apologies from Ops teams — it all converged into a single relentless current.

Her phone buzzed softly.

Max Detweiler: *How are you holding up? Heard about the chaos.*

She smiled faintly.

Palma's streets stretched beneath her, golden with late afternoon sunlight, an untroubled scene at odds with her tangled thoughts.

Her thoughts drifted back to the root of the problem —
the airport's layout and boarding processes. Remote
stands, bus gates, double gate assignments, parallel
boarding times, crowds of stag parties — all combined
into a perfect storm of confusion. It was a known
vulnerability, one that Sprinter and the airport authorities
alike needed to address if incidents like this were to be
avoided.

She recalled the first meeting with the ground handling
team that morning, which had been curt and stressful. The
supervisor had admitted the scanners had malfunctioned
just before boarding began, forcing them to revert to
handwritten lists and manual checks. Staff were stretched
thin; the swelling summer season had caught everyone off
guard. The scramble to process thousands of passengers
through crowded terminals and sparse bus fleets was
pushing the limits of both technology and manpower.

And yet, in the midst of this chaos, one passenger had
somehow managed to slip through the cracks — Callum
Brayshaw, a cheerful, hapless Brit who, despite the best
efforts of everyone involved, had ended up on the wrong
aircraft, crossing international boundaries and creating an
incident that would now spiral into regulatory
investigations.

Sarah sighed. The human factor was always the wildcard.
No amount of technology could fully eliminate error,
especially when faced with real-world pressures, fatigued
staff, and passengers eager to reach their destinations,
sometimes in less-than-sober states.

****

CHAPTER 12 – Breaking
Sunday 1st May 2022

The atmosphere around the staff canteen at Düsseldorf, Sarah noticed, when she walked into it off a flight between Edinburgh and Düsseldorf, a Sprinter route that had been launched that exact same day, was tense, and Sarah couldn't put her finger on it.

The fact that there were crews—not just Sprint and Sprinter crews, but Lufthansa, Eurowings, Vueling, British Airways, easyJet and even Tunisair crews—all hardly talking, mainly looking at phones or the television, several crews all clustered near the plasma screen by the main vending machines, suggested something unusual was unfolding. Sarah glanced at the screen as she made her way to the coffee machine. A ticker was scrolling across the bottom of the Deutsche Welle news feed.

BREAKING: London European Airways Flight 341 Crashed in English Channel

Sarah stood frozen, the paper cup trembling slightly in her hand as the coffee overflowed and spilled onto the floor. She barely noticed. On the television, the Deutsche Welle broadcast cut from the live newsroom to shaky video footage taken from a fishing boat—grains of smoke trailing in the grey sky, something metallic glinting on the water. Another cut, this time aerial—coastguard helicopters hovering above what looked like flotsam in the choppy English Channel.

Behind her, conversation had stilled to whispers. Across the canteen, a Lufthansa purser murmured something in

205

German to a younger colleague, who looked pale. Sarah blinked and finished pouring her coffee, trying to process the words on the ticker.

BREAKING: London European Airways Flight 341 Crashed in English Channel. Emergency response underway. Aircraft en route from London Luton to Düsseldorf. 137 souls on board. Early reports say that only 1 crew member on the flight deck.

London European Airways, Sarah knew, was yet another brand new low-cost outfit, and Flight 341 was its inaugural flight. The shock of the news hit the aviation community like a cold gust. A crash on a maiden flight was the kind of catastrophe that sent ripples through every airline's operations room and staff canteen alike. Even here, thousands of miles from London and the Channel, the impact was palpable.

"Germanwings alles noch einmal," a Eurowings First Officer muttered, and the canteen went into an even more eerie hush. Sarah caught the phrase. "Germanwings all over again."

She tried not to dwell on what he meant, but everyone knew. Germanwings 9525, the horrific memory of it, the shadow it had cast over cockpit security and mental health assessments, the way it had changed the industry almost overnight. The idea that Flight 341 might mirror that kind of event… it was too much.

Sarah turned and quietly moved to a nearby table, still clutching her coffee like a lifeline. Around her, the tension crackled, palpable and raw. An easyJet captain put down his phone and muttered, "They've grounded the rest of the LEA fleet. They've got 8 birds, haven't they?"

"Ja, all leased from a Bulgarian ACMI," A Lufthansa Captain said, a known aviation enthusiast, sighing. "Two second hand ex Air Zimbabwe A320s, and the rest on lease from Chinese Nepal Airways. B-SPAD, looking at FlightRadar24, was the tail number. New livery, new crew, new management—everything rushed. You launch with a channel hop and it ends in the sea. It's unthinkable."

Sarah didn't answer. Her thoughts were racing. Not with theories or gossip like the others, but with an instinctive, gut-level dread. She glanced at the timestamp on the news footage. Just under two hours ago. She had been in the sky herself when it happened. Somewhere over the North Sea, heading south towards Düsseldorf, unaware that a catastrophe had unfolded so nearby.

She pulled out her phone and opened the crew WhatsApp group. The Sprint Air one—not the pan-European, cross-border mess of Sprinter's general chat, but the Manston base chat, the one where she and several others who were officially assigned as their home base were in, and noticed that it was flooded with messages.

Sarah scrolled rapidly through the deluge of messages, the blue glow of the screen painting anxious shadows across her face. The Sprint Air Manston base WhatsApp chat, usually reserved for check-in confirmations, moans about rostering changes, and the occasional meme, had transformed into a hive of panicked speculation and half-verified updates.

Neil Costello: *We've been ordered to hold all departures ex MSE and CQF. ATC and EuroControl decision, not Ops.*

Ian Paul: *What about flights heading to Gatwick. I've got a Vilnius to Gatwick run in an hour, and I haven't had any notice of delay yet.*

Julie Andrews: *No word on Gatwick, but Ops just called me off standby for a Łódź run. Said to wait until they confirm the route is even opening. Apparently French ATC might close us down too. Whole corridor's a mess.*

Miles Cooke: *Not confirmed, but heard from ATC mate in Maastricht. They're shutting the Dover sector down to all non-essential traffic. SAR and coastguard priority. All LARS units pinged. VHF on 124.75 went nuts for twenty minutes.*

A chill swept through her. If Maastricht Control—one of the major coordination centres for northern European airspace—was freezing the Dover corridor, it was more than precaution. It meant debris, rescue flights, maybe even some kind of security protocol. She took a shaky sip of the lukewarm coffee. It tasted like ash.

Across the canteen, a British Airways First Officer, with the slick uniform and easy charm that BA crew always seemed to carry like a birthright, spoke aloud without looking up from his phone.

"FlightDeckLeaks saying the CVR shows no mayday, no PAN, nothing. Just radio silence and a nosedive off radar. Dropped five thousand feet in twenty seconds."

"Jesus," muttered someone else. "EASA shouldn't have dropped the regulations so quickly after Germanwings. This feels eerily similar."

Sarah felt the weight of the words settle on her chest. She hadn't even heard of any mayday call or distress signals coming from the flight. Just silence, a sudden, deadly plunge. The thought made her skin crawl.

Around her, the canteen was beginning to fill with more crew members, many having come off other flights, drawn here by the news or simply out of habit. Yet the usual noise, the hubbub of casual conversations and laughter, was replaced by a subdued, almost reverent quiet. It was as if everyone was holding their breath, waiting for more news, for something, anything to explain what had gone wrong.

Sarah pulled her phone from her pocket again and checked the official sources. London European Airways had posted a brief statement on Twitter:

@LEAir: *We confirm that Flight 341 from London Luton to Düsseldorf experienced a fatal accident over the English Channel earlier today. Our thoughts are with the families of all passengers and crew. Emergency services are currently responding. Further details to follow.*

The tweet was curt and clinical, the kind of statement corporate PR teams are trained to issue, but it offered no answers. No comfort. Sarah's heart sank. She knew that the families of the 137 people on board would be waiting desperately for any word.

Sarah's phone buzzed again. This time the Sprint Staff app.

Ops Alert: ⚠ *All crews remain on high-readiness. Do not self-brief. Await rotation instructions from base supervisors. LEA incident ongoing. Media blackout requested where possible. Do not comment on social platforms.*

Sarah lowered her phone slowly, the weight of the Ops alert sinking into her like a cold fist tightening around her lungs. The instruction was unmistakably clear: no self-briefing, no speculation, no social media posts. She knew the drill. These moments were the worst for any flight crew, when the entire operation was frozen in limbo, waiting for direction, wondering if they or their colleagues were safe, or worse, lost.

Her gaze drifted around the canteen again. The gathering crowd was a mixture of faces from multiple airlines, a motley collection of uniforms and languages, but all sharing the same pall of dread. The usually unshakable easy camaraderie among pilots and cabin crew had dissipated. Most clutched their phones, scrolling newsfeeds or refreshing Twitter in hope of some clarity, some semblance of control in the spiralling chaos.

Then a BBC News alert came on her phone

Watch: Moment passenger recorded pilot being alone on downed flight 341.

She tapped through with trembling fingers. A grainy, vertical video filled the screen. The cabin interior was dimly lit, standard for a low-cost, short-haul flight.

Passengers were seated, relaxed, chatting. The perspective shifted to the front of the cabin. The reinforced door to the flight deck was closed, but the First Officer and a flight attendant were chatting while the drinks trolley was locked in place by the galley bulkhead. Then, chillingly, the video zoomed in as a young boy's voice, barely audible, said in German-accented English: "Look, Mama, only one pilot inside."

The video jumped—a brief jolt, a flicker of motion—and then the start of a dive, and the video ending.

The text below the video on the BBC website said "This video was uploaded to Twitter just before London European Airways Flight 341 disappeared from radar. The uploader has not made any posts since."

Sarah's hand tightened around the phone as she set it down on the table with deliberate slowness. The image from the grainy video still danced in her mind—the innocuous start, the young voice, the single pilot visible through the half-reflected cockpit glass, and then... that awful dip. It was barely a second of motion, but every pilot knew the signs. You didn't need to be an engineer or crash investigator to recognise what a dive looked like when it began, and that had all the fingerprints of something deliberate.

She sat down heavily, almost missing the chair behind her. Her Sprint uniform felt tighter, somehow, constricting her shoulders and chest. The canteen, though still full of people, felt cold, like the oxygen had been quietly sucked out.

The fact that the poster hadn't posted any more tweets was the most concerning, as it either meant they were dead along with other passengers, or they were deliberately silenced or scared into silence. The unsettling lack of follow-up chilled Sarah to the bone.

She knew that she was meant to do a sector between Dusseldorf and Alicante next, the early 'European Stag and Hen' express full of German stag parties and sunburnt tourists eager to kick off a weekend of chaos on the Costa Blanca. But right now, that flight felt trivial, almost obscene. How could she focus on the logistics of that when the entire continent was watching and waiting for answers about the plane that had plunged into the sea?

Sarah remained seated, the chatter and clatter of the canteen fading into a dull, oppressive background. Her mind replayed the video clip over and over—the innocent voices, the locked cockpit door, the single pilot seen briefly in the cabin, and then the sudden nosedive. The eerie silence from the flight deck was like a silent scream across the airwaves.

She glanced sideways to a group of Sprinter cabin crew sitting nearby, their faces pale, some trying to mask their shock with feigned busyness, others openly wiping tears from their eyes. They'd heard the news by now—Flight 341, an aircraft that, according to FlightRadar24, was 16 years old and now on its third ...operator, had dropped off the radar without so much as a radio call, and now the aviation world was watching what could become a defining tragedy of the decade. The worst part was the silence. The utter, complete silence from the airline, the authorities, the regulators. It was as if they were all trying to figure out who to blame before saying anything definitive.

Sarah sat motionless, the weight of the unfolding tragedy pressing heavily upon her. The canteen buzzed with hushed conversations, snippets of speculation, and the occasional gasp as new information filtered through. Her coffee, now cold, remained untouched as she stared blankly at the screen of her phone.

The video clip replayed in her mind—the innocent voice of a child pointing out the solitary pilot, the sudden jolt, the abrupt end. It was haunting, a stark reminder of the fragility of life and the immense responsibility borne by those in the cockpit.

The air in the canteen was heavy, almost thick enough to choke on, as Sarah sat still, replaying the grainy footage in her mind. She had flown sectors in foul weather, diverted aircraft with mechanical faults, once even dealt with a disruptive passenger threatening to open a door mid-flight—but this... this was something else. A catastrophe that spoke not of mechanical failure or miscommunication, but of something darker, possibly deliberate, and unutterably tragic.

Across the room, arguments had begun to bubble up—low at first, then louder, carried by the rising fear and speculation. A Wizz Air captain was engaged in a tense exchange with a Vueling purser, the language switching rapidly between English, Spanish, and Hungarian. Sarah only caught fragments:

"...you don't know that it was deliberate—"

"—no ELT beacon for twenty minutes, no squawk, no transponder drop sequence, just straight down, like a damn missile!"

The word "missile" caught more attention than perhaps it should have. A Ryanair pilot, his tabard still wrapped around his waist, stood abruptly from the far corner, shaking his head. "It's not a shootdown. There's no military intercept chatter, no airspace warnings. ATC would've picked up anything. This isn't MH17."

That sent another ripple through the room. The idea that anyone could even draw comparisons to MH17 was itself an escalation of fear, a signal that things were already spiralling beyond what even seasoned crew could mentally process.

Sarah tuned it out. She didn't want theories, didn't need baseless declarations. What she needed—what everyone needed—was clarity. She stood up, slowly, and walked to the vending machine wall, leaning her forehead against the cool glass. A Lufthansa junior crew member next to her, barely out of her teens by the look of her, was visibly trembling. Sarah turned slightly, offering the girl a small, weary smile.

"You okay?" she asked gently.

The girl shook her head. "My sister flies for LEA. She's based at Luton. I don't know what flight she was on today. She... she was scheduled for rotation. Could've swapped into that flight."

Sarah's heart clenched. "Do you want me to help you call someone? Ops, maybe?"

"I've tried," the girl murmured. "They're not answering."

The infrastructure was collapsing beneath the pressure. Sarah's own attempts to call Sprint Ops had gone to voicemail twice. The Slack channels used for internal chat were overloaded, slow to update. Even the usual airline AIMS rostering system was flagging error messages.

She wandered back to her table. Just as she sat down again, her phone vibrated—not with another news alert or group message, but with a direct call. Neil Costello.

She answered immediately.

"Neil?"

"Yeah. You somewhere quiet?"

"No, but I can be." Sarah stood up again and walked down the corridor toward the crew rest area. She stepped into one of the darkened lounges and shut the door behind her. "What's going on?"

Neil exhaled down the line, the sound of exhaustion pouring through. "Everything's going to hell. Airspace over the Channel has been closed to all but SAR and military. They're pulling every available asset from the coast guard, Navy, even French customs."

"Any survivors?" she asked, her voice barely above a whisper.

A pause.

"None confirmed. They've pulled a few bodies, some debris, but nothing resembling a fuselage section. The tail's gone, they think. Just gone."

Sarah swallowed hard. "The footage, the one from inside the cabin…"

"I've seen it," Neil replied grimly. "Everyone has. It's viral already. And the worst part is the silence. No statement from the pilot's union. Nothing from EASA. I think they're scrambling to see if the cockpit door logs survived."

"Was it locked?"

"There's no word on if it was locked," Neil said quietly, the line hissing with background noise—distant chatter, an engine start, maybe. "But a friend of mine works for the AAIB, so I've asked him if he can find out, off the record. Anyway, I'm currently in Orly, about to do a Manston run. Looks like it might be a long night. Or a very long week, Sarah. Nobody's moving fast on this, but I'm guessing everyone's bracing for the worst."

Sarah took a breath, steadying herself against the bleakness of his words. "Keep me posted, Neil. If you hear anything—anything at all—call me back. Even off hours."

"Will do." His voice was resolute despite the exhaustion. "You're flying soon, yeah?"

She nodded, though he couldn't see her. "Düsseldorf to Alicante. Stag and hen special. I'm already struggling to switch gears."

"Yeah," Neil agreed, with a sigh. "This kind of news hits you hard. Feels like a punch to the gut."

"Thanks, Neil. Talk soon."

She ended the call and sank back into the hard plastic chair of the crew lounge. The hollow weight of that reality settled like cold stone in her stomach. Flight 341, a brand-new airline's maiden commercial hop, lost. Without a mayday. Without a whisper on the radios. One pilot seen in the cabin, alone. The implication of that was staggering, and terrifying.

The next hours passed in a strange blur. Outside the windows of the lounge, the usual bustle of the airport hummed quietly, a soft undercurrent of movement and announcements that felt utterly disconnected from the crisis unfolding in every flight deck, every ops centre, every hotel room where crews were stuck waiting for news.

Sarah's thoughts circled. The difference between what she was trained for—handling emergencies, mechanical failures, diversions—and this. This was a nightmare not in any manual, not in any checklist, not in any safety briefing.

* _ * _ * _ *

It was 5pm by the time things started moving, when the BBC News app sounded off with another alert, and the canteen in Düsseldorf—along with countless others across Europe—shifted from a heavy, mournful stillness to a low murmur of renewed tension and hope.

Watch: Chairman of London European Airways to hold press conference amid ongoing investigation into Flight 341 crash.

The television, however, was on Euronews now, and covering the Ukraine-Russia conflict, as the German Chancellor had announced that Germany would be fast-tracking additional military aid to Ukraine in light of new evidence of Russian drone strikes on civilian areas near Kharkiv. The story on Euronews was urgent and weighty, but it couldn't compete with the tension boiling just under the surface in the aviation community. Several of the crew gathered near the television murmured something about changing the channel. A British Airways purser, emboldened, crossed to the wall-mounted remote and flicked over to BBC World.

A new image filled the screen—podium, blue backdrop, and a logo featuring a stylised globe: London European Airways. The camera panned across a small, crowded press room. Sarah felt her heart rate tick up as the coverage cut to a live announcer standing outside a sombre, beige office block in Luton.

"The chairman of London European Airways, Ewan Marsh, is expected to speak in the next few minutes. This will be the first official press conference following the loss of Flight 341 earlier this morning…"

Sarah moved closer, still clutching her phone in one hand, her forgotten coffee in the other. The canteen was silent again, packed with dozens of crew members who had, without planning, found themselves drawn into a communal vigil. The screen flickered as the podium came into clearer focus. Marsh stepped forward—an older man, probably late sixties, with silver hair and a nervous energy that didn't befit someone in his position.

He looked like he hadn't slept. His tie was slightly askew. There was a smudge on his glasses. When he spoke, his voice was quiet, cracked by grief and adrenaline.

"We regret to confirm that London European Airways Flight 341, operated by an Airbus A320-211, registration B-SPAD, crashed into the English Channel approximately twenty kilometres off the coast of Folkestone at 10:42 British Summer Time today. The aircraft was carrying 129 passengers and 8 crew members. At this time, we do not believe there are any survivors."

There was a collective inhale across the canteen, the sound like the wind before a storm. A Lufthansa stewardess gasped. Someone dropped a spoon.

Marsh continued, his voice hollower now.

"We are working closely with the Air Accidents Investigation Branch, the Civil Aviation Authority, EASA, and the relevant maritime and air safety organisations in both the UK and France. Recovery efforts are ongoing. Debris from the aircraft has been located in multiple areas of the Channel. Some human remains have been recovered. Our hearts go out to the families and loved ones of those on board."

He paused, took a breath, and then addressed what had clearly become the elephant in the room.

"There has been speculation in the media and online regarding cockpit occupancy at the time of the crash. We urge restraint in spreading unverified information. However, we can confirm that according to preliminary flight deck data, the captain was the sole crew member present in the cockpit at the time of the incident. The reasons for this are not yet known. The cockpit voice and flight data recorders have been located but not yet recovered. We hope they will provide vital insight."

The murmurs became audible again across the canteen. That was the confirmation—unwanted, chilling—that the industry dreaded. The captain had been alone. Just like Germanwings 9525.

Sarah exhaled slowly, a cold numbness spreading through her chest.

Marsh finished with a subdued plea.

"To all flight crew and aviation professionals watching— we understand the fear and concern this has caused. We urge unity, professionalism, and compassion during what will be a difficult period for us all. We will share more as soon as possible. Thank you."

The feed cut back to the outside reporter, who began summarising the statement, but no one was listening. The impact of Marsh's words had already done their damage.

A BA First Officer nearby ran a hand through his hair. "Bloody hell... this is going to change everything. Again."

"Door protocol's going back to the two-person rule, guaranteed," muttered a Jet2 captain.

"Assuming it ever left," someone else grumbled.

Sarah didn't join the speculation. She was staring at her phone again. Her inbox had five new emails—all from Sprint HQ. One was the updated crew guidance document. One was an official memo about passenger reassurance messaging. Another was a directive to all cabin crew regarding door monitoring procedures.

Sarah knew, however, that things would never be the same again.

****

CHAPTER 13 – Fake News
Monday 2nd May 2022

The morning after the crash was greyer than most, as if the sky itself understood the collective weight of grief pressing down on the European aviation industry. At Düsseldorf International, that grim veil hung low, soaking the concrete aprons and jetways with an unseasonable drizzle that rendered everything slick, muted, subdued.

Sarah Marsh stood at the crew gate near Pier B, her Sprint Air ID hanging limply from her neck and the weight of a roster she hadn't yet decided whether to honour hanging over her like a cloud. She hadn't slept much, and when she had, it was fragmented—haunted by flashes of that passenger video from Flight 341. In her dreams, she was walking down an aisle, trying to get to the cockpit door, trying to shout a warning, only to see the ocean rushing up to meet her through the forward windows.

Now, in the clinical strip-lighting of the airport's early hours, everything felt too bright and too quiet. She wasn't due to fly until mid-morning, a newly scheduled Düsseldorf to Luton, hastily arranged to take advantage of passengers who had booked with London European and were now stranded or scrambling for alternatives.

The flight, which the Sprint Staff app said that LY-SPTA, the only brand new Airbus A320neo in the Sprinter side of the joint fleet, had been assigned. Her second flight, a Luton to Gatwick repositioning flight, with an Airbus A321LR, only recently delivered to Sprint a week earlier, a "whitetail", or plane that had been built for an airline and then cancelled before delivery, still, according to

FlightRadar24 was in all over white with only Sprint fleet names, and its German test registration, D-NEOL. She knew that she'd then be taking that from Gatwick to Rome.

The news had come through the previous night that London European, however, had had their CAA and EASA operating certificates, along with that of the ACMI, the aircraft, crew, maintenance and insurance provider, suspended indefinitely, pending a full investigation.

Unlike Sprint, who used an in-house leasing company in the main, even though most of its fleet was between 4 and 30 years old, and used a MRC, a maintenance responsibility contractor, that was on the Airbus Broughton campus, it was rumoured that the London European aircraft had been maintained by a shadowy third-party out of Moldova—an outfit with a paper trail as porous as a wet napkin. The CAA hadn't named them yet, but ops forums were already alight with theories, all of them grim. Rumour had it that the base check for the A320 involved more duct tape than diagnostics. Someone in the Manston WhatsApp group had posted a grainy screengrab from an airframe spotter's Telegram channel suggesting the aircraft had suffered rudder control irregularities a year earlier, flagged by its previous operator in Nepal.

Sarah rubbed at her eyes with the back of her hand and exhaled. The air at Düsseldorf tasted faintly of rubber and disinfectant. She turned her attention to the airside apron, where a marshaller was guiding in a Sprint-branded A319, N524VA, a former Virgin America and Alaskan Airways A319, its navy fuselage still faintly betraying its previous liveries, passing a Lufthansa A320neo on its stands nearby. The juxtaposition was stark: the aged yet battle-hardened machines of Sprint Air, steady in their workhorse roles, versus the gleaming, state-of-the-art new aircraft of the German flag carrier, gleaming despite the dreary morning.

Her mind flitted uneasily back to the endless discussions on the WhatsApp group overnight, the blizzard of conflicting information, grief, and professional pragmatism that filled the digital airspace just as thickly as the physical fog creeping low across the runway. It was a morbid irony that the chat had started with mundane banter about rostering and late arrivals before spiralling into a collective trauma response.

She checked her watch. Two hours to briefing.

"Guten Morgen, Sarah," a familiar voice said from behind her, soft and worn.

She turned to find Max Detweiler standing there, coffee in hand, a rare smile not quite reaching his eyes. His hi-vis vest was half-zipped, his lanyard clipped to his belt, and a laminated dispatch report curled in one hand like a reluctant newspaper. His usual flippancy was missing, replaced by something heavier, as if he too had spent the night scouring forums, watching video loops, refreshing news alerts.

"Didn't think you'd show," he added quietly, tone sympathetic.

Sarah gave a slight shrug. "Didn't think I would either. What's your schedule today?"

"One of the Euro loops, Orly, Madrid, then a hop to Athens and finishing in... Baku," he said, looking at her like even he couldn't quite believe the routing. "Ah, that's my A320 for Orly being washed", he said, pointing to a Sprinter logoed one. Sarah looked at the registration and saw it was a French registered one, F-WTBF, which was on one of the remote stands being de-iced despite the mild temperature—a symbolic gesture, perhaps, more for show than necessity. Or maybe someone in Ops just didn't trust the airframe not to sweat through the rivets after the past twenty-four hours.

Max took a sip of his coffee and leaned on the barrier beside her. "Feels wrong, doesn't it? The idea of just... going flying. As if nothing's happened."

Sarah nodded slowly. "It does. But then again, when has it ever felt right after something like this?"

He didn't answer. There wasn't a good answer, and both of them knew it. They watched in silence as a baggage loader skidded slightly while towing a cart of red and grey containers, tyres slipping on the rain-slick surface. A ramp supervisor barked at him in German, his arms gesturing wide in exasperation, and the driver waved apologetically without slowing down.

"They're all running on fumes too," Max muttered. "Ops, ground, tower. Nobody had a full night's sleep. Apparently the CVR recording has leaked."

Sarah tensed, turning to Max. "Already?"

He nodded grimly. "Not officially, of course. But someone from the preliminary listening panel leaked a
226

transcript. It's all over the darker corners of PPRuNe. A few aviation bloggers have started quoting snippets too."

She braced herself. "What's in it?"

Max hesitated, his usual sarcasm nowhere to be found. "Nothing. That's the thing. Just routine chatter until about twenty minutes before descent. Then, just before descent... well, two words. Arabic. Allahu Akbar. Name of the Captain has been released too. And... well, Bild has reported that Hamas have claimed responsibility, as well as half a dozen other news outlets. The FO... he was a Londoner, only just passed line check and was due to complete his first full rotation as part of his probationary period. The press is going wild, but the problem is, nobody knows what happened in the cockpit. Not really. It's all theories at this point."

Sarah felt the bile rise in her throat. She closed her eyes for a moment, trying to breathe past the sensation. As a former Flight Lieutenant in the RAF, she had been trained to face intense situations in the air, but this... this was different. The weight of speculation, the uncertainty surrounding the crash, and the sheer horror of the passengers' last moments weighed heavily on her. She could almost feel the heat of the cockpit, the air thick with fear and confusion. The notion that there were still so many unanswered questions gnawed at her.

"That's insane," she murmured, shaking her head. "How can they even claim something like that without any proof?"

Max leaned against the barrier, his eyes distant. "They're desperate for answers, and desperate people will grab at anything, even if it's just a thread. Hamas, the pilot's personal life, terrorism, mechanical failure... It's like throwing spaghetti at a wall. Everything sticks. But, like I said, it's all theories right now. Anyway, did you see the other circular on the Sprint Staff app? The mandatory drink and drug tests that we're now to do every single day?"

Sarah had read the circular, and noted that it was Sprint doing it, not the CAA or EASA. Another aftershock of the crash, designed to reassure the public that Sprint was taking steps to avoid any hint of negligence or scandal. Still, Sarah found the move unsettling. Every pilot, every crew member, would now be subjected to daily tests. It was a gesture of compliance, but it also felt like a public admission that something had gone terribly wrong.

"I saw it," Sarah replied, her voice low. "I mean, it's all about optics, isn't it? They need to show they're in control, but I don't think anyone's fooled. The industry's going to be looking over our shoulder for a long time now."

Max didn't answer immediately. Instead, he sipped his coffee and stared out at the apron, as if seeking some form of solace in the routine of the morning. But everything was off. The usual hum of activity—baggage carts being loaded, planes taxiing—felt muted, weighed down by the collective shock. And beneath it all, the cruel flood of misinformation began to trickle through every crevice.

"Do you think they'll actually find out what happened?" Sarah asked, breaking the silence.

Max finally looked back at her, his brow furrowed. "I'm not sure. I mean, I hope so. But there's so much noise already. Between the press jumping to conclusions and the chaos surrounding the investigation, it could be weeks before we get any real answers. Or longer." He sighed and shifted his weight. "The problem is, once the media latch onto something, it sticks. And they're already running with it. A failed check ride, terrorism, mechanical faults… Every theory under the sun."

Sarah exhaled, her mind spiralling. The video footage. The names of the crew being dragged through the mud, their reputations and personal lives splashed across the front pages of every tabloid. The speculation was toxic, and yet, in a way, it made perfect sense. People needed something to hold onto, some semblance of control in the wake of such an incomprehensible event.

"I just want to know the truth," she said softly, almost to herself.

Max nodded, his expression unreadable. "We all do. But the truth… It's not going to come quickly. And by the time it does, the damage will be done."

* _ * _ * _ *

"Luton Ground, this is Ramsgate 242, ready to taxi," Sarah said.

It was the second flight of her day, the Luton to Gatwick repositioning leg, and Sarah's thoughts were still clouded by the events that had unfolded in the past 24 hours. The calm, robotic voice of the controller on the other end cut through the fog of her mind as she executed the take-off checklist with mechanical precision. The Airbus A321LR, still in its pristine white, no-frills livery, felt like a lifeline of normality amidst the chaos. But even the rumbling of the engines beneath her feet did little to ease the unease gnawing at her gut.

The irony that it was a full flight, a combination of Thameslink's central section deciding to fall over, and an accident near Heathrow on the M25 causing nearly 230 last second bookings, including a certain good looking Mexican Formula 1 driver who Sarah knew drove for Red Bull, Sergio Perez, only added to the surreal nature of the day. It was all just a few more jigsaw pieces, slipping into place amid the background hum of her daily routine, while a darker cloud hung over the aviation community. Sarah found herself wondering what it must be like for the passengers—clueless to the fact that they were stepping into the same airspace where tragedy had unfolded. What were they thinking as they boarded, trusting that the aircraft would carry them safely to their destinations, oblivious to the storm brewing in the world of aviation?

The fact that the flight, like all the others Sprint, Sprinter and other ultra-low cost airlines operated were from remote bus and walkable stands, not the usual terminal gates, only heightened Sarah's sense of isolation. Even as the crew and passengers moved through the airport with its clean, utilitarian spaces, it felt as though they were operating in their own microcosm, disconnected from the global tragedy unfolding outside. The gates and walkways, crowded as they were with commuters, seemed to exist in a parallel reality, where nothing had truly changed. Yet for Sarah, it was hard to ignore the invisible weight of the past twenty-four hours pressing on her chest.

"Ramsgate 242, this is Luton Ground, you are cleared to taxi to runway 26L. Hold short of runway, as you're second behind Easy 2593, over."

Sarah knew what that meant, that she was to hold at the runway threshold until the EasyJet flight, currently in the process of clearing the final turn from the apron, had completed its take-off. The irony that the orange and white plane in front of her was an Airbus A320, and that she was the First Officer on a newer, larger A321LR, seemed like an absurd juxtaposition. It was a fleeting moment, but the comparison lingered in Sarah's thoughts. Here she was, staring at a fellow A320 aircraft, yet feeling the disparity between her own pristine aircraft, and the tragic history that had unfolded just a day before with another A320.

"Taxiing to runway 26L, holding short of runway 26L, Ramsgate 242," Sarah replied automatically, before bringing her attention back to the procedure at hand. It was a distraction, a way to drown out the murmur of her racing thoughts. She couldn't escape the events of yesterday, no matter how hard she tried to bury them beneath the mechanical hum of the aircraft or the sterile buzz of air traffic control.

Looking at the Captain for this flight, an Irishman with the thick accent of Dublin, Sarah could see he was also tense.

"I hope Gatwick don't arse us around," the Irishman, Patrick Connelly, said with a wry grin. His voice, though light, carried an edge, one that Sarah recognised immediately. He was trying to mask his own nerves with banter, just like the rest of them. There was a strange comfort in the shared tension, even if it wasn't exactly the healthiest form of coping.

Sarah glanced over at him. "I think everyone's running on fumes today, Pat. Gatwick can only be as chaotic as they want it to be. Last time I was there was with a baby bus a few weeks ago. Bunch of stag and hens, one of who decided to grope one of the flight attendants just after we left Coventry. Diverted to Gatwick for a swift landing after that one."

"You've had a baby bus?" Patrick laughed, raising an eyebrow in mock disbelief. "You mean the A318, right?"

Sarah nodded, the memory of that flight still vivid in her mind. "Yeah, the A318. Tiny thing. Not a lot of space, but you know what they say—more room for drama." She allowed herself a brief chuckle, a slight release of tension. It was fleeting, but the shared humour, even in this grim moment, was a small reminder of the camaraderie that kept things together in a world that often felt like it was falling apart.

Patrick smiled but didn't reply, his gaze focusing ahead as the EasyJet flight completed its final roll, its engines roaring to life and pulling away from the threshold. As the aircraft accelerated down the runway, Sarah's thoughts briefly wandered to the passengers aboard, just like the ones she had carried earlier, or the ones she would be transporting later. They were all oblivious, continuing with their lives, their plans unchanged. It was maddening, the sense that life went on despite the undercurrent of tragedy that rippled through the industry, unnoticed by most.

"Ramsgate 242, this is Luton Ground, cleared for take-off, wind 270 at 8 knots," the controller's voice crackled over the radio, slicing through the silence like a blade.

"Copy, clear for take-off, wind 270, 8 knots, Ramsgate 242," Sarah confirmed, as she pulled back gently on the thrust levers, sending the Airbus A321LR's engines into a controlled roar. The aircraft began its slow but steady roll down the runway, the vibrations of the engines reverberating through the flight deck, grounding her in the task at hand.

As the aircraft picked up speed, Sarah's gaze briefly flitted over the instruments, confirming everything was running smoothly. The hum of the engines and the familiar rhythm of the climb helped to dull the edge of her thoughts, pushing the events of the previous day into the recesses of her mind. But they were still there, lurking beneath the surface, a constant reminder that she couldn't escape the reality of what had happened. She wasn't sure what was more unsettling—being unable to make sense of the tragedy, or the overwhelming sense that everything was simply carrying on as if nothing had changed.

Patrick's voice broke through the quiet hum of the flight deck as they reached their cruising altitude, and for a moment, Sarah felt a flicker of normalcy.

"I see that GB News has jumped on the band wagon of all the fake news," Patrick said, as Sarah engaged the autopilot for the short hop between Luton and Gatwick, even though technically, the flight was planned as a circle route, encompassing Bristol, Bournemouth and Gatwick airspace, it being planned so the mileage of the flight would qualify it for extended flight hours.

"Fake news?" Sarah asked, raising an eyebrow, her focus briefly shifting from the autopilot controls.

Patrick gave a small sigh, exhaling through his nose. "Yeah, they've already run multiple segments claiming the crash was some sort of terrorist act, and now they're even connecting it to everything else—Brexit, COVID, you name it. If you listen long enough, they'll tell you the whole aviation industry is going down the toilet because of it." He scoffed, clearly frustrated. "It's all about headlines. About clicks. It's disgusting."

Sarah was quiet for a moment, thinking about the flurry of false reports she'd seen through social media overnight. The tabloids had jumped onto the narrative so fast, even before a full investigation had started. She understood the need for news outlets to make a story out of what had happened—people craved closure, explanations for tragedies they couldn't understand—but the recklessness with which certain outlets ran with unfounded claims was alarming. Some of the theories about the crash were not only baseless but inflammatory, designed to stoke fear, not offer clarity.

"Do you think there's any truth to any of it?" she asked, her voice tinged with hesitation. "About the terrorism, I mean. About Hamas?"

Patrick exhaled sharply, rolling his eyes. "I don't know, Sarah. I don't know. What I do know is that the press isn't helping. The whole thing could have been anything—a mechanical failure, something in the cockpit, a missed check, a pilot error. We just don't know. But the media's already latched on to one theory and started running with it."

Sarah leaned back in her seat, her thoughts heavy with the situation. She knew better than most how quickly false information could spiral out of control in the digital age. The narrative being sold wasn't helpful—it was sensational, made to sell, not inform. Her training had taught her to assess situations rationally, to focus on facts, and this was a glaring example of how that could get lost when the world's eyes were on a tragedy.

"I guess," Sarah said slowly, "we'll find out soon enough. But right now, it just feels like everyone's throwing spaghetti at the wall."

"Exactly," Patrick said, adjusting his headset. "And none of its sticking. They're just looking for a scapegoat. Someone to blame." He paused. "I don't think we'll get the whole story for a while. Not until the investigation is done properly."

They were silent for a moment, both contemplating the uncertainty of the situation, as the Airbus continued its smooth journey towards Gatwick.

"I can't help but think," Sarah added softly, "that the longer this drags on, the more it will hurt everyone in the industry. Pilots, ground staff, even passengers. Everyone will be second-guessed. People won't trust us anymore."

Patrick nodded grimly. "Yeah, it's a tough one. Especially when it's something like this. Not just a routine crash, but one where the media's already painted a picture. If the story sticks, it's going to have far-reaching effects."

Sarah nodded, her grip on the yoke tightening slightly as she watched the horizon line stretch out in front of them. "It's going to be a long few weeks, isn't it?"

"Definitely," Patrick replied.

After a brief silence, Sarah shifted slightly in her seat, trying to clear her mind. She was still battling the ghosts of the previous day—the crash, the horror of what had happened, the endless loop of speculation that would never truly explain it all. But for now, there was nothing to do except get to Gatwick, ensure the passengers disembarked, and then head off for her next flight. The rhythm of aviation, she realised, would continue, whether anyone was ready for it or not.

****

CHAPTER 14 – Ads and Reels
Tuesday 3rd May 2022

It had only been less than 48 hours since the London European Airways crash when the advert dropped, a social media blast by Sprint, a four-minute social media and television advert filmed in the MRO that Sprint used at Broughton, an Airbus owned and operated MRO company that Sprint and the French manufacturer had, thanks to the 11% owner of Sprint, the Omani Sovereign Wealth Fund, set up due to the needs of Sprint buying, every day, at least one brand new or second-hand aircraft somewhere in Europe or North Africa.

The advert, showing a former Air China A321 undergoing a D Check while a brand new Airbus A319neo, one that was in Sprint's navy blue livery, fresh from the Hamburg plant, undergoing a B Check, one that was above the absolute minimum, as Sarah knew that Sprint would rather pay for B, C and D Checks ahead of schedule on the aircraft and comply with technical and airworthiness regulations, and thus avoid a AAIB or EASA inquisition, because in the words of Jeff Young, "it may kill our short term funds making the planes safe, but an AAIB investigation can kill the reputation and the AOC.".

Those words, Sarah knew, were ones from an easyJet veteran, someone who knew that the regulators were utterly merciless when it came to safety lapses, and that aviation was built on the brittle scaffolding of reputation. If an airline's name started popping up in those breathless evening news tickers, or, God forbid, the tabloids, because of some avoidable technical cock-up or a procedural foul-up traced back to cost-cutting, the damage would be generational. Sprint's management, for all their calculated brinkmanship and creative contracts, never gambled with airworthiness.

Throughout the ad, which Sarah noticed, was mainly filled with shots filmed on go-pros, mobile phones and handheld DSLRs, there was a studied rawness: not the glossy, soft-focus optimism of the usual airline spot, but something deliberately honest, almost industrial. The only voiceover, that of Jeff Young, cut through the visuals with the sense of his corporate, easyJet, style of calmness, as if he were doing a Stelios impersonation in a London accent, but with none of the bluster. His script was sparse, direct—punctuated by the background sound of torque wrenches, rivet guns, and rolling hangar doors. "At Sprint, we're concerned about one thing and one thing only, and that is you, our travellers," he intoned, over shots of engineers crawling through wheel wells, torque-testing bolts. "Even though some of our planes are pre-loved, we strip each and every one down to the bare metal, and build them up again. Every wire, every rivet, every panel. Doesn't matter if it's come from Chengdu or Cologne, St. Nazaire or Stansted. If it's flying with us, it flies like new. That's our promise."

The video cut—mid-sentence, almost—to shots of engines being hoisted and mounted, technicians hunched over tablets and checklists, a Lithuanian avionics engineer soldering behind a strip-light, close-ups of inspection mirrors poking into places most passengers never even imagined existed. Time-lapse sequences played out as landing gear was dropped and reassembled, fresh paint sprayed onto cowls bearing distant registry codes, now overlaid with Sprint's navy and white stripes.

"We employ former EASA and Air Accident Investigation Branch investigators to make sure that our fleet are compliant, and all of our maintenance technicians are Airbus certified, meaning that unlike a certain Irish carrier, every part that leaves our hangar is signed off, double-checked, and signed off again. And if something's not right, it doesn't fly."

The advert didn't have any music. Instead, the soundtrack was a collage of the hangar's honest noises: air compressors cycling, the distant whine of a hydraulic test, the shuffle of booted feet on metal catwalks, radios chirping in at least four languages. There was a sequence that, to anyone outside aviation, looked almost theatrical: a team of Sprint engineers in hi-vis orange, all gathered around a battered but now spotless Air China cockpit shell, inspecting the FMS as a Lithuanian technician reeled off items in rapid-fire English, checked, ticked, checked again. The voiceover resumed, as if Jeff Young had just been watching quietly, letting the audience draw their own conclusions.

"If you ever wonder why we can get you a seat for less than a train to Birmingham, this is why," he said. The camera cut to stacks of boxed aircraft parts with 'Airbus Original Parts' labelled on the side, then to crates marked in Arabic, French, and Lithuanian, and to engineers stamping paperwork at battered steel desks under posters in half a dozen languages. "It's not magic. It's logistics. It's working with the best, and the best price, but never cutting a corner. Our brand new and pre-loved fleet have inspections that are above the industry minimums, because we don't believe in shortcuts when you're thirty-six thousand feet above the Channel. The industry likes to talk about safety. For us, it's not just talk. It's what we do, every day, in every hangar. Fly safe, fly reassured."

Sarah was sat in the Shannon crew room when the ad aired before the lunchtime news. RTÉ were set to interview Micheal O'Leary, the Ryanair boss, who had, in teasers before the news, been pre-recorded tearing into "the Kentish airline who paint their planes blue and think that makes them Airbus, but in reality, they're just another Frankenstein fleet running around Europe, hoping the paperwork keeps up with the aircraft." O'Leary's trademark smirk filled the little screen above the Shannon crew room's chipped kettle, his sarcasm all but dripping from the monitor.

Sarah almost laughed—she'd lost count of the number of times O'Leary had slagged off Sprint, as even though they had only been running over a month, Sprint had employed several former Ryanair paralegals, lawyers, financial officers and even former compliance officers, the very people who knew exactly how Ryanair danced through the regulatory minefields and, just as often, how close they sometimes came to tripping. That Sprint had lured these people away with promises of more money, less shouting, and, crucially, tax free bonuses via the Sultanate of Oman's offshore payroll schemes, was not lost on anyone with an ounce of industry gossip. Nor was the irony that the very people who'd designed Ryanair's own compliance playbooks were now building an even more labyrinthine structure for Jeff Young's operation, but this time with more European flags on the tail.

Sarah nursed a mug of lukewarm Lyons tea, eyeing the battered TV as the advert faded and the news jingle blared in. Around her, crews in various states of duty time dozed, read their phones, or watched the segment in that detached, half-amused way only airline staff did when management tried to reassure the public. Out on the ramp, a brand new Airbus A321neo, in Sprint livery, apart from a deliberately placed harp on the tail, a yellow relief line in the middle, the tail number, EI-RYAN, and the Sprinter.eu fleet name, the plane that Sarah and the day's Captain, a Dublin born captain named Ciaran O'Shea, would be taking out on the next sector to Porto, was just being fuelled. The soft hissing of the bowser and the distant rattle of catering trolleys were audible even through the window of the staff canteen.

"Sprint are just taking an opportunistic swipe," O'Leary's voice on the television continued, fusing his usual bombast with a twist of incredulity that only those well-practised in media jousting could summon. "They're only in the game because Brussels and London can't agree whose rules matter. You've got a bunch of ex-Ryanair people over there, pretending they're running a flag carrier. It's a flying circus with a spreadsheet for a compass, and the only thing blue about Sprint is how red their balance sheet gets every time they pay an airport bill. Look at their recent advertisement. They strip 30 year old planes down to bare metal and then try to call it new. It's theatre. And don't get me started on 'Airbus certified'— that just means they paid for a course in Toulouse and got a sticker. If the CAA ever turned up unannounced, half those planes would be grounded before lunchtime. Mark my words, you'll see more of them on the news for delays than anything else. The only thing reliable about Sprint is the queue for the complaints desk."

"But Mr O'Leary," the host said, smiling, "An investigation by RTE has shown that Sprint's technicians are actual Airbus employees, and that their compliance processes are not only signed off by the Irish Aviation Authority, but by EASA as well. And I'm sure that viewers will remember that Ryanair have recently ordered the Boeing 737 Max 8, which, in 2019, was grounded worldwide after two fatal crashes."

"I think you mean the 737-8200, not the 737 MAX, and if you check the record, you'll see Ryanair has one of the youngest fleets in Europe," O'Leary cut in, lips curling into a performative grin.

"Ah, but the IAA classes the 737-8200 as the alternate name for the MAX 8," the RTE Aviation correspondent, who was in the news studio as well, interjected, and Sarah knew that someone fact checking O'Leary would mean that the Irish aviation magnate would make the Dublin born broadcaster regret every word. O'Leary's jaw flexed, but he kept the smile on, radiating that peculiar blend of belligerence and charm which only those truly at home in the arena of live television could summon. He leaned forward, elbows on knees, and Sarah could almost imagine the scent of airport lounge coffee and a stack of hastily printed notes in his jacket pocket.

"Well, the public know where the best value is," he said, with an airy wave, "and it isn't with the blue brigade who have to put their planes through a beauty contest just to keep up. We'll leave the adverts to the marketers, and keep the business for the grown-ups. At Ryanair, we do the work, not the PR."

"Well, we have Sprint General Counsel Fernando Costas, live from their Kent headquarters, and Fernando, what does Sprint say to claims it's all theatre?" The camera cut sharply to a thin, olive-skinned man in a crisp blue suit, sitting in a light-flooded, suspiciously neat office adorned with generic modern art and a framed Airbus photo. Fernando Costas looked every inch the corporate operator—calm, prepped, notebook open but untouched, eyes flicking to a screen off-camera that almost certainly displayed live chat messages from his PR and legal teams.

"Oh, yeah, my old Deputy General Counsel," O'Leary said, quiet enough for Sarah to hear it on the broadcast. "Of course they wheel out Fernando for this," O'Leary muttered, but the RTE host was already lobbing her first question across the digital studio link.

Fernando Costas smiled, a half-smile Sarah recognised from his years as a Ryanair courtroom tactician, and he leaned into the camera with just enough humility to disarm the audience. "Look, I can't speak to Mr O'Leary's unique view of the world," he began, pausing for a fractional second as the host smirked, "but I can say this—when Sprint started, our board made one thing very clear: if you want to survive as a new entrant, especially one that's growing as fast as we are, the only thing you cannot buy is reputation. It has to be earned. And you earn that by keeping your promises. That's what the ad is about. We take our aircraft—whether they're fresh out of Hamburg or coming to us via a second life in Asia or the Middle East—and we make them not just safe, but compliant with the highest standards in Europe. Not the minimum. The maximum. We don't do it because we want a pat on the back. We do it because the alternative—an accident, or even the perception of one—would kill the business before it's even off the ground."

He spoke with a fluency and quiet defiance that came from years defending the indefensible in Irish and EU courts. "We have engineers from six nationalities, all with Airbus or national aviation authority sign-off. Our fleet is certified and audited by the IAA, EASA, the UK CAA, and by third-party investigators. We even have former AAIB and BEA inspectors on our payroll, not as a marketing ploy but because they're the best at what they do. Frankly, I think the public deserve the truth about what goes on behind those hangar doors. If that's theatre, it's a theatre with a very strict script."

The host thanked him and cut the line. The news rolled on to the next horror show—delays at Dublin, another French ATC walkout, Ryanair slashing fares again for a Bank Holiday that was bound to end in stampede and chaos. Sarah sipped her tea, the taste now astringent, and set her phone down on the table as her WhatsApp started to fizz with messages from crew she barely knew, all sending links to the advert, screenshots of the Twitter feed already filling up with hot takes and snark, memes of Jeff Young's "no shortcuts" face superimposed over a Soviet-era propaganda poster.

Sarah let the screen fade into a reflection of the crew room behind her. The canteen's battered furniture, the rattle of flight bags being zipped, and the sporadic chorus of laughter or expletives from the corridor outside seemed, for a second, to ground her more than the broadcast ever could. A French cabin supervisor—Juliette, on a Beauvais rotation—wandered in to refill her bottle, glancing at the screen with that particular blend of European bemusement and world-weary irony. She arched an eyebrow at the last flicker of O'Leary's grin.

"Encore la guerre des low-cost?" she said, tone wry.

Sarah smiled faintly and nodded, flicking her gaze back to her phone, now abuzz with notifications. She barely needed to read them to know their content: memes, industry banter, links to aviation forums already dissecting every frame of the ad. Some posts praised Sprint's "raw honesty" for showing the underbelly of maintenance; others, mostly pilots and engineers from the old guard, called it "reassuringly industrial" or, less charitably, "PR with a torque wrench." A few, inevitably, accused Sprint of running an airline on the same principle as a car boot sale: buy cheap, polish, sell.

In a way, Sarah knew, it was theatre, that Sprint had got nearly 300 planes cheap due to the pandemic, and that, as nearly 250 of them were second hand, and 20 to 30 were brand new, albeit ones that were intended for other operators who had, at the last minute, either cancelled or changed their ordered, fully refurbished in Sprint's 'Navy Easy' interiors, the same style that easyJet's new cabins had launched with in 2020—deep blue plastics, matte chrome seatbelt buckles, and faux-leather headrests with printed Sprint 'S' logos on them. The oldest aircraft, the ones that still had a faint whiff of Air China, Tunisair, or Alitalia clinging to their recirculated air, had been through checks that thorough, they were near enough factory fresh in every way that mattered, even if the signs in the back galley still bore faded Mandarin characters.

Sarah's phone buzzed again, this time with a message from Max.

Max Detweiler: *Seen the ad yet? Boss looks about 80% less dead inside than he did after the Hamburg press conference.*

She couldn't help but smile, her reply almost automatic.

Sarah Marsh: *Yeah. Wonder how much they had to pay the Omani fund to keep him upright for four minutes.*

A laughing emoji flashed back almost instantly.

The gallows humour that ran through the ranks of Sprint—born from the union of disparate airline refugees, Brexit exiles, ex-pats, and opportunists—was its own kind of insulation. They laughed at themselves, at the chaos, because the alternative was to give in to the sense of living perpetually at the edge: regulatory, financial, operational. The advert had set the internet alight not because it promised anything new—every airline on earth claimed to be obsessed with safety—but because it was a rare moment of acknowledging that, at Sprint, obsession was the only thing between success and catastrophe.

Max Detweiler: *What's the rest of your day looking like?*

Sarah thumbed out a quick reply, letting her eyes flick towards the window as she did.

Sarah Marsh: *Taking out EI-RYAN to Porto with O'Shea, then an Edinburgh and back to Manston. You?*

The rain had started again, streaking the Shannon tarmac in thin, wavering lines that distorted the blur of taxiing aircraft and made everything outside look a little less solid, a little more temporary. Beyond the glass, the A321neo—today's "EI-RYAN," in full meme-worthy livery—gleamed under the sodium glare, her paintwork just slightly too new to hide the fact that she'd been rushed into service to fill a slot left by a late delivery and the withdrawal of a worn-out ex-Alitalia bird, now languishing in Kaunas for a skin check.

"Ready to go?" Ciaran said, looking at his iPad, and Sarah knew that their flight departure was due in 20 minutes, and they had to start getting ready to begin the pre-flight ritual that—no matter how many hours you logged or how familiar the route—never quite slipped into autopilot.

She nodded to O'Shea, draining the last of her tea and setting the mug on the table as she flicked her phone onto silent. "Aye, let's get the circus rolling," she said, flashing him a lopsided grin that was only half put on for show. Ciaran returned it with one of those unflappable Irish pilot looks: a dash of humour, a soupçon of fatigue, and the unspoken understanding that behind every slick press release and viral ad campaign lay a day's work that could veer from smooth professionalism to the edge of farce with a single Ops message.

Outside, the wind howled as a gust rattled the windows. Sarah slung her flight bag over her shoulder, checked her ID badge, and led the way out of the canteen, O'Shea falling into step behind her as they threaded through the labyrinthine crew corridors. The hum of anticipation, the buzz from the advert and the ever-churning rumour mill, faded into the more familiar soundtrack of boarding announcements, echoing footsteps and the distant drone of ground equipment.

Down on the ramp, the air was sharp with kerosene, and the smell of fresh rain on hot tarmac was oddly comforting. Their walk to EI-RYAN was punctuated by the sight of ground handlers ducking under plastic hoods, catering staff wrestling with shrink-wrapped trolleys, and a solitary engineer in navy Sprint coveralls giving a thumbs-up as he replaced a panel on the nose gear. There was a faint sense of performance in every movement, as though everyone knew that, somewhere, a smartphone camera could turn their ordinary work into the next viral slice of "Sprint Reality TV."

As they climbed the steps into the A321neo, Sarah paused at the top to glance down the length of the fuselage—navy, with that tongue-in-cheek Ryanair-inspired tail and the deliberately on-the-nose "EI-RYAN" registration. She smirked at the sheer audacity of it. It was a challenge, a wink, and a middle finger to O'Leary all in one: You're not the only ones who can play this game.

The cockpit, by contrast, was all business. That peculiar blend of new-car scent and disinfectant, iPads clipped to yokes, system screens cycling through their pre-start symphony, and the slight rattle of the rain against the windscreen. Sarah slid into the right-hand seat, feeling that usual surge of focus settle in. Preflight was all muscle memory: switch by switch, check by check, flows so ingrained that they provided a rhythm, a familiar script no marketing department could ever rewrite.

O'Shea, meanwhile, was already running through the load sheet, tapping notes into his EFB and muttering numbers under his breath. "Full load again," he said, tone resigned but not surprised. "All stag and hen parties going to Porto. God help us if there's a football match on."

Sarah let out a soft laugh. "At least if they're loud, it means they're alive. And it means the press will be focused on drunk Brits abroad, not on us."

They shared the kind of look that only two people, united by a thousand silent crises, could muster: an acknowledgement that flying passengers wasn't just about technical skill, but about managing chaos in all its forms.

The purser, a Polish woman named Justyna, popped her head in. "Boarding in ten. Crew are all accounted for, no missing catering, and all the bins work. Do you want a coffee? Or three?"

"Three would be safer," Sarah said, with a grateful grin.

$* \_ * \_ * \_ *$

Mid way through the cruise segment, Sarah noticed on her phone when she had logged in to the WiFi a new button on the landing page of the passenger Sprint app, a button called SprintReels, which immediately caught her eye. She wasn't usually one for the latest bits of marketing, but a new button on the company's app was always a source of curiosity, if only to see what new corner-cutting or desperate attempt at "engagement" was being foisted on passengers and crews alike. SprintReels, though, was different.

As the page opened, she noticed that there were several shows on there, with titles such as "The Alpha Is My Mate" and "Three Brothers Regret", with garish thumbnails that looked as if they'd been assembled by an intern who'd spent too long on TikTok and not enough on aviation. The names suggested a fever-dream of Chinese vertical soap opera, with some Japanese and Korean romance dramas, and zero English content. Scrolling down, the shows were even more absurd, as if Sprint had licenced several Duanjus, or low-budget romance and fantasy series, bundling them together in the hope that their passengers—marooned on yet another delayed sector to the Mediterranean—might choose distraction over complaint. Beneath each splashy thumbnail was a translation in broken English, usually something like "The Devil President's Gentle Wife" or "If I Don't Marry The Boss, I'll Die".

As she knew that she was the Pilot Flying for this leg, and Ciaran was the Pilot Monitoring, that meant that, for now, she could allow herself the small indulgence of scrolling—so long as the cockpit's steady symphony of autopilot and air traffic control gave her no new dramas to contend with. The sky outside was a sheet of sullen Atlantic grey, cloud tops far below, a few persistent raindrops still streaking the cockpit windows from their turbulent climb out of Shannon. Every so often, the A321's navigation lights flickered in reflected blue off the engine cowling.

Sarah let her thumb drift over the carousel of SprintReels, amusement bleeding into professional curiosity. What did it say about the state of aviation that, while safety was paraded on television like a badge of civic virtue, the true bread and circuses were now piped into the phones of bored passengers and off-duty pilots? Here was a carrier less than six weeks old, whose fleet comprised everything from box-fresh Hamburg Neos to retired birds from Qingdao and Casablanca, but which could, with a straight face, offer passengers a never-ending scroll of melodramatic drama as compensation for the three-hour delay on the tarmac.

There was a strange, irreverent poetry to it all. The airline that boasted of above-minimum checks and Airbus-certified techs was also the airline of "Alpha President's Sweetheart", available in six subtitled languages and with the first few episodes free of charge, while the rest of the series was, it seemed, paid for, a freemium model which meant that passengers were gently nudged to enter their card details mid-flight if the plot, or sheer tedium, compelled them to know what happened next. Sarah couldn't decide if it was a new low for the profession, or a stroke of opportunistic genius. Maybe both.

She scrolled a little further, half-expecting some hidden Easter egg—perhaps a parody video slipped in by one of the more subversive members of the marketing team. Instead, she found nothing but K Dramas and Chinese Duanju spinoffs, a wall of faces in improbable romance, colliding in plotlines that, she suspected, not even the subtitles fully understood. At least the player worked. She flicked off the screen, checked the nav panel, and scanned the overhead, thumb hovering over the fuel page, a quick glance at the engine instruments out of pure habit. The sky, just beyond the nose, was a smudge of pale blue-grey, sun at their back, the kind of light that always made her think of dawn departures from Stansted in another life.

Behind her, through the closed door, the muffled chaos of a stag-heavy cabin was kept at bay. The faintest notes of a karaoke chant had begun to seep through the PA interphone, Justyna's voice riding above it in two languages—firm, precise, already shifting into that maternal register seasoned pursers adopted when confronting packs of Irishmen with more ambition than sense. On the EFB, Sarah scrolled the weather for Porto: showers, light crosswind, an interminable METAR thread that meant little except a busy approach and, likely, a queue for the stand. No diversions, at least, unless the fates of Sprint decided to deliver a dose of vintage chaos.

She let her thoughts drift, as they always did in cruise, to the mechanics behind the scenes—those endless cycles of check and countercheck that the advert had, with its calculated honesty, tried to sell. It wasn't so much a sales pitch as an invocation, an admission that the job of modern aviation was less about glory and more about not screwing up, not getting your name on the wrong page at the wrong time. There was something almost refreshing, she thought, in the flat delivery of Jeff Young's voiceover: no aspirational nonsense about "the spirit of flight" or "dreams above the clouds", just the cold, clattering reality of torque wrenches and checklists, hangar lights and overtime.

And in a way, that was the real truth, the part that mattered when you were skimming above the Bay of Biscay at thirty-six thousand, with a load of singing Scousers and an aircraft whose entire airworthiness could be traced through a chain of initials, audit trails, and a Lithuanian engineer's signature in a hangar logbook.

The aircraft, in the end, didn't care who had painted the tail, who had won the rights to broadcast football on the IFE, or whether the CEO's accent played well in a viral clip. It cared only for the numbers: fuel, pressure, speed, limits. As did she.

****

CHAPTER 15 – An Almaty Trip
Thursday 19th May 2022

Sarah sat in the crew room at Almaty Airport, her back stiff from another early rotation and a seat that offered all the comfort of a picnic bench. The hum of fluorescent lighting buzzed overhead as she stared at the muted television screen mounted in the far corner, which had been looping the same three news items all morning. Number one was the increasingly absurd saga of the French air traffic control strikes, now in their ninth day. Number two, a developing scandal involving the German transport minister and an expenses claim that apparently included "consultancy" for his cousin's schnitzel truck. And third—the one that had gripped every cockpit, cabin, and canteen from Lisbon to Luton—was the still-fresh aftermath of the London European Airways disaster.

The irony, Sarah knew, that she had just done the once a week Košice to Almaty service that Sprinter had set up using an Airbus A321LR that it had only acquired two weeks earlier, and that the routing, via Georgia, Iran and the Caspian, because of the war between Russia and Ukraine and the closure of several FIRs, made it one of the most surreal passenger legs in European low-cost aviation, was not lost on her.

Especially as she had had, on board this run, Noel Phillips, an aviation enthusiast, who was using Sprint and Sprinter to connect with SCAT Airlines, the 'number 2 airline in whole Kazakhstan', a running joke on aviation YouTube, not just because the name was only unfortunate because in Western English slang, but because of its woeful safety record and because the fleet was a grab-bag of retired European jets and ex-Indian aircraft that seemed held together by faith and gaffer tape.

Everyone knew that SCAT, like Pakistan International Airlines, were part of the most ludicrous airlines in the entire industry, not counting the sexist PanEuro or the legal happy Ryanair, Qatar or Sprint's own Fernando Costas.

But still, here she was, sitting in the terminal at Almaty International, sipping something that tasted vaguely like instant coffee laced with chalk, while SCAT crews were busier discussing irrelevant topics like Eurovision results and how many goats had wandered onto the runway last week.

Sarah had just about stopped laughing when she realised that across from her, one of the SCAT first officers was earnestly trying to teach another the lyrics to "Space Man" by Sam Ryder, the British entry to the Eurovision Song Contest that had concluded the previous weekend, where Ukraine had finished first by a landslide, and the UK, in a baffling twist of fate, had come second—a cultural anomaly not seen since the days of Bucks Fizz.

She sipped the bitter drink and glanced around the crew room, her eyes flicking over the polyglot collection of uniforms and faces. There was a kind of camaraderie in this oddball intersection of aviation's B-teams—Kazakh SCAT, Uzbek Air, Belavia, even a few unshaven Belgians from ASL Airlines who looked like they'd slept in the cabin. Everyone was here, at the edge of Europe, trying to run routes that the big players had abandoned or refused to acknowledge.

And over all of it loomed London European Airways Flight 341. Sarah didn't need to be reminded of the number. It had entered the bloodstream of the industry like an embolism. An Airbus A319, with a novice crew on a promotional service—Luton to Düsseldorf, first day of service, all eyes on them—and it had vanished off radar seventeen minutes after take-off. No distress call. No mayday. Just a gradual descent and then sudden impact into the English Channel, a few nautical miles off the Kent coast.

At first, speculation had turned to mechanical failure. Then, when recovery efforts found the cockpit voice recorder and media outlets got wind of early leaks, the true horror emerged: the captain had been alone. The first officer, a twenty-two-year-old recent graduate from a Spanish flight school, had been in the lavatory mere minutes after take-off and top of ascent. What was known was that the captain had closed the flight deck door—and no one else had entered again.

The industry reeled. Comparisons to Germanwings were inevitable, unhelpful, and impossible to ignore. Sprint Air issued a standardised mental health compliance checklist within 36 hours. Every airline followed. Sarah had already done hers—ten questions, none of them subtle. Do you feel depressed? Have you had thoughts of self-harm? Do you feel confident in your ability to perform your role today?

She'd clicked "No" and "Yes" as required. But the system couldn't detect sarcasm. It couldn't detect the weary exhaustion of flying six sectors across four countries on two AOCs with three different sets of uniforms and no bloody layover longer than nine hours.

The screen in the corner switched to breaking news. Sarah's head turned involuntarily.

"LONDON EUROPEAN BROUGHT BY CHINESE NEPAL AIRWAYS. CEO AND BOARD OF LEA TO LEAVE."

Sarah nearly choked on the coffee. Her mouth hung open for a beat before she slowly set the cup down on the cracked plastic table. The scrolling ticker on the bottom of the screen confirmed what the anchor had just blared in a slightly too chipper tone: Chinese Nepal Airways—a subsidiary of China Eastern Airlines, one of the 3 major state-backed aviation giants in Beijing—had reached a full acquisition agreement with the insolvent shell that now comprised London European Airways. The move, according to analysts already quoted on Sky and CNN, would secure the leases of two remaining Airbus A320s from Air Zimbabwe, as well as the 5 remaining Airbus A320s that they had brought from Chinese Nepal before the before the collapse. Those jets—most lessors had expected them to be repossessed by mid-June—were suddenly safe. Or at least, repositioned. The same could not be said for the executive team there.

A handful of contract pilots, Sarah knew, who worked for the same agencies that Ryanair, Wizz, Sprint and easyJet, would no doubt move to Chinese Nepal Airways now that the deal was done, if only for the security and the prospect of regular pay—something increasingly rare in this fractured corner of European aviation.

She rubbed her temples, feeling the weight of the news settle. The acquisition was hardly surprising to those who followed the slow-motion collapse of London European Airways. The airline had been bleeding cash since its launch, its business model a patchwork of overly optimistic assumptions and cheap leases, shored up by desperate marketing stunts that had done little to stem the tide. Chinese Nepal Airways' involvement seemed less a strategic expansion and more a bailout, a quiet rescue of aircraft assets and slots that Beijing didn't want to lose in the increasingly competitive Asian-European market.

Sarah wondered what the new owners would do with the airline's tarnished brand. Would they try to rebrand, perhaps reorient it as a long-haul feeder for China Eastern's burgeoning network? Or would it simply become a cargo operation, quietly shipping goods rather than people across continents?

She wasn't alone in her questions. The chat groups and WhatsApp threads she monitored between sectors were filled with speculation. Some pilots were openly relieved—any stability was better than the current chaos—but others were more cynical, wondering whether the new ownership would mean longer hours, pay cuts, and a relentless push to extract value from a battered workforce.

Behind the news, the reality was raw. For all the corporate machinations on the surface, the loss of Flight 341 was a human tragedy that refused to fade from memory. Investigations continued, but in the meantime, the industry was gripped by a pervasive unease—pilots, cabin crew, ground staff alike questioned their own safety, their own sanity in an environment that demanded so much with so little margin for error.

Sarah glanced at her watch. Soon she'd be boarding MGT7987, the return leg of the Almaty–Košice rotation, was scheduled to push back in just over an hour. Looking over, she saw a Red Wings Airlines Captain looking at her as if daggers were about to fly from her eyeballs. She nodded politely, but the Captain's scowl didn't shift. Red Wings, like SCAT, had its own issues—delayed salaries, crumbling Tupolevs, and the creeping dread of state oversight disguised as operational review.

That, and several of their A321s and A320s had gone missing at the start of March.

Days before the Russian Government had passed a law that permitted the seizure of all foreign-leased aircraft that hadn't yet been flown out of the Russian Federation. A shuffling of paper, paint, and tail numbers later, and now Red Wings claimed to operate jets that had once belonged to Turkish Airlines, Lao Central, and at least two budget European outfits.

Of course, it was little known that some of the A321s were within Europe, and more specifically back, theoretically, with their leasing company, albeit parked in the UK. Not that she could officially say, even though FlightRadar24, if one had a membership, could trace things back to the start of March... or interrogated her personally. Sighing, however, she pushed the Red Wings captain from her thoughts. There was no point in making eye contact again; he clearly wasn't in the mood for diplomacy. In any case, Sarah had spent enough of her career trying to smooth over bruised egos and misdirected nationalism in crew lounges around the continent. The best tactic was always the same: ignore the posturing, drink the coffee—even if it tasted like damp envelope—and get through the day. She checked her flight bag, confirming her documents were still where they should be: licence, medical, passport, and her newest acquisition—yet another reflective armband with "Flight Crew" in Cyrillic. Apparently, that had become necessary when transiting Kazakh security, as a Wizz First Officer two weeks earlier had been detained for two hours after being mistaken for an Albanian arms dealer.

Sarah stood and gave her limbs a slow stretch, feeling the pull of fatigue in her shoulders. The glamour of aviation, she thought bitterly, really was best observed through an Instagram filter. In reality, it was long shifts, questionable food, suspicious toilets, and geopolitics wrapped around a checklist.

The call came over the Tannoy in thickly accented English. "Attention crew Sprint Air flight MGT7987 to Košice, please proceed to Crew Security Gate 4A." She slung her flight bag over her shoulder, adjusted her uniform collar in the scratched mirror near the staff-only door, and headed out.

The walk to the gate was long—Almaty's refurbished international terminal was modern but sprawling, and the crew access paths were illogically signed. She passed through the final passport check, enduring the blank-eyed stare of the border official as he held her passport sideways, upside-down, and then backwards, as though waiting for it to reveal some secret.

At the gate, her aircraft waited—an A321LR, one of another whitetails that Sprint had obtained cheap, their owner, a billionaire named Lord Henry Jenkins, who Sarah had found out was the father of Global Media Deputy Head of Legal, James Jenkins, a litigious executive who was Global's most feared in contract negotiations and one of the industry's most aggressive defenders of intellectual property. Lord Jenkins's investment in these aircraft was reportedly a bet on the long game, banking on continued instability and the cheap availability of leases in the Airbus A320 family, as airlines were slowly ramping up, coming out of the pandemic, with old and new A320 family members being the main currency of short to medium-haul aviation.

The irony that new planes were joining the fleet daily, a mix of second hand and brand new, and the current number of planes, 212 in a month and half, on the books, an increase from the day one launch of 98 was a figure so ludicrous it had become an in-joke within the Sprint flight ops WhatsApp group: "Fleet growth via auction site and diplomatic incident." Yet here it was—an empire of leased jets built on the back of implausibly narrow margins, overworked crews, and legal acrobatics that Fernando Costas proudly called "strategic regulatory symbiosis."

Sarah boarded through the rear airstairs, stepping into the quiet cabin where a few cleaners were finishing up. The interior still bore traces of its former life—bare patches of glue where Lufthansa stickers had been peeled away, cabin signage in German and Spanish still visible behind hastily applied Sprint decals. The seats had been reupholstered in Sprint's acidic navy, but the armrests still bore scars from years of abuse by tourists and pensioners across the continent.

The cockpit was already humming with pre-flight activity. Captain Kyle McDonald looked up from his tablet, giving her a curt nod. Scottish, formerly of airBaltic, and as Sarah recalled, a man of few words and even fewer jokes.

"Fuel load's good," he said, in a tone that made it sound like a veiled threat. "We have 176 pax, 5 infants. No VIPs... well, what counts as VIP anymore. Cabin crew says one of the babies is 'extremely vocal'. I said good— means someone's alive and feeling something."

Sarah stifled a grin, half from weariness, half from appreciation. Gallows humour was standard currency in their line of work. She dropped her flight bag behind the right-hand seat, shrugged off her blazer, and slid into place, logging into the EFB and pulling up the route charts.

"Same routing via TBS and BAK?" she asked, tapping through the flight plan.

"Mostly," Kyle replied. "Modified departure due to the NOTAM around the fuel depot. Routing through NIPLA then direct to LAGOR. ATC said they'd get us above FL360 early to avoid the Iranian corridor congestion."

Sarah nodded, lips tightening at the memory of the last sector's step-climb hell and ATC confusion over the airspace patchwork. She preferred a steady climb and smooth vectoring. But these days, smooth was luxury. The sector over Georgia and Azerbaijan had become a de facto shortcut for half of Asia, and every plane from Emirates to Pegasus seemed to be cramming into it like bargain hunters at a Boxing Day sale.

Kyle checked his watch. "We've got 23 minutes until door close. Cabin crew briefed?"

"Going now," Sarah replied, already rising.

She made her way back down the aisle, mentally switching gears to the safety briefing. The lead flight attendant, a tall Slovak woman named Anka Horváthová, greeted her with a look that mixed exhaustion and mutual respect.

The plane, LY-SPTZ, was still in its brand new-ish condition for an aircraft of its age—having been originally for LATAM, but the pandemic meant that the aircraft had never even entered service. Instead, it had sat idle in Victorville for nearly two years before being swept up in one of Jeff Young's infamous bulk purchases—secured during a 72-hour auction window that also netted Sprint Air four A320neos, two 319s from an ex-Kuwaiti charter operator, and an Airbus A319neo that had been intended for China. The fact that the CEO himself had attended the auction in person—posing, according to rumour, as an Australian sheep farmer—was the kind of thing that, in most industries, would be dismissed as a tall tale. In aviation, it was simply Tuesday.

Anka stepped into the galley, smoothing her hair and fixing Sarah with a look that suggested she'd already dealt with three minor cabin issues and at least one broken lavatory.

"We've got two stag groups in 24B to 28F," she said, skipping pleasantries. "One lot's Slovak, one's British. Both were drinking in the departure lounge. You can imagine."

Sarah winced. "We carrying any spare restraints?"

Anka's eyebrows lifted just a millimetre. "Three kits. And Piotr"—she gestured to the broad-shouldered Polish steward beside her—"used to bounce clubs in Gdańsk. He'll manage."

Once the briefing was complete and the cabin crew scattered to prepare for boarding, Sarah returned to the cockpit. Kyle had already finished his walk-around and was now adjusting the rudder trim, his face impassive as always.

"Boarding just started," he said. "Twenty-two wheelchair requests. Most of them probably fake. I told Ops we're not delaying again."

Sarah smiled. She'd seen the trick before—passengers requesting wheelchair assistance to skip queues, board early, or avoid paying for priority. Then, upon arrival, they would somehow regain miraculous mobility and sprint for the taxi rank.

"They'll walk the moment duty-free comes into view," she muttered.

They ran through the checklists, verifying fuel, hydraulics, and electrical systems. LY-SPTZ's flight deck was pristine, untouched by years of abuse—almost eerie in its cleanliness. A handful of stickers on the breaker panels still bore Spanish instructions, but otherwise it was standard Airbus. Sarah preferred it this way: familiar, reliable, and not some Frankenstein retrofit with Chinese avionics and Hungarian decals, like some of the earlier Sprint jets.

As boarding continued, Sarah glanced through the open flight deck door. A few passengers paused, peeking inside, one even holding up their phone before Anka barked, "No photos," and slammed the door shut behind him.

"You see the London European update?" Kyle asked, as he tapped the engine start data into the MCDU.

Sarah nodded. "Sold to Chinese Nepal. Whole board's gone. They're keeping the airframes."

Kyle didn't respond immediately. Then he said, "Waste of a good airline. The CAA will have a field day."

Sarah agreed. London European had launched with all the bravado of a flagship—crisp livery, ambitious routes, even talks of transatlantic connections from Luton. But beneath the surface, the finances had been built on shifting sand: over-leveraged leases, promotional fares that never turned profit, and a recruitment drive that prized speed over quality.

And now, an airline that had once promised to revolutionise British low-cost flying was little more than a Chinese asset grab.

"They'll run it like a shell," she said. "Maybe paint over the tail, add a panda sticker. Use it to sneak cargo through weird exemptions."

Kyle didn't disagree.

The passengers were mostly boarded now, the staggered Ryanair-style process complete, though there was a minor dispute erupting at Row 23 over overhead bin space. Sarah could hear Piotr's bassy voice booming something that sounded like "Sir, you cannot bring a samovar in your carry-on," followed by a mechanical clunk.

She ran the final briefing. Cabin secure. Fuel confirmed. Take-off performance updated. With a final sweep of the overhead panel, Kyle called for pushback clearance, and within minutes they were rolling slowly away from the stand, past a hodgepodge of aircraft that made Almaty Airport look like the set of a Cold War aviation documentary.

A derelict Tu-154 sat near a half-covered Il-96, their windows sand-blasted and wings drooping like wilted leaves. A trio of Kazakh military transports—Antonov An-12s—rattled in the distance, engines whining. The contrast to their crisp, Airbus-built jet could not have been starker.

"Let's get out before the sandstorm shows up," Kyle muttered.

Sarah chuckled, as she knew it was going to be an interesting flight.

* _ * _ * _ *

Upon arrival at Košice, Sarah knew that she would be doing a short Košice to Bratislava sector, as Sprint and Sprinter's insurance prohibited them basing their planes near to the Ukraine border, because, even though the Russians were concentrated in the east and north from their newest territorial gains, European insurers remained deeply skittish. Underwriters in Zurich and Luxembourg had agreed on one thing—Slovakia east of Poprad was too "proximate to strategic instability."

So, despite Košice being a perfectly functional, civilised city with an airport that could handle the A321, Sprint aircraft were effectively ghosting through, only allowed to drop off and pick up, not dwell.

Of course, to avoid the cardinal sin of ferry flights, Sprint had sold the return leg as a "multi-city special" with onward connection to Bratislava advertised via a bus that didn't exist, only for ticket-holders to be quietly rebooked onto the same aircraft with a new flight number. Technically it was a domestic repositioning flight, but with Slovakia not having a true domestic air market, and given the Slovak Civil Aviation Authority's laissez-faire attitude to Sprint's schedule, the charade continued.

Sarah disembarked briefly at Košice, not bothering to leave the sterile area. The airport was silent, save for a single vending machine whirring in the corner and a disinterested security officer flicking through a Slovak tabloid. Her next leg was scheduled in 50 minutes. The turnaround team, hired contractually through a local outfit that used to clean Wizz Air aircraft, waved half-heartedly as they began preparing LY-SPTZ for boarding again.

She checked her messages. More crew banter. Another update on LEA. Apparently, the CAA had issued a statement, reminding the public that Chinese Nepal Airways would have to re-certify the airline under its UK AOC if it wished to operate flights ex-Luton. Nobody expected that to be a problem. With post-Brexit aviation law in flux, CAA oversight was patchy at best, and Sarah knew that if LEA was back in the air within a month, no one would blink.

Of course, it was well known that the British Government, led by Boris Johnson, a known opportunist with a flair for grand gestures and a famously flexible relationship with facts, would tread lightly on any matter that involved Chinese investment in the aviation sector. It was no secret that the UK was desperately courting foreign capital to prop up its fragile post-Brexit economy. Whether it was a deliberate policy or a convenient side effect of laissez-faire governance, the result was the same: Chinese Nepal Airways would probably get the green light with minimal fuss, so long as the planes stayed in the air and the service resumed.

"Who's doing MGT7988?" another Sprint crew, one that Sarah knew was doing a run to Luton, running a few minutes ahead of the Ryanair flight to Liverpool, an irony in itself as the Ryanair aircraft would be full as opposed to Sprint's partly loaded flight. Sarah turned to the source of the voice—a short, wiry First Officer named Gábor

Kovacs, who she recognised from their Budapest hub. He was halfway through peeling an apple with the in-flight cutlery and looked about as engaged as a commuter on a rainy Monday.

"I am," she replied, stuffing her documents back into her flight bag. "One way, then I'm done."

Gábor whistled low. "You hear the latest? LEA's former safety director's gone off-grid. Word is he's already in Dubai with a second passport. The usual sources say he got a nice payday from the Chinese Nepal deal."

Sarah blinked. "You're kidding."

"Nope," Gábor replied, casually slicing his apple. "Apparently one of the leasing brokers said the CAA were sniffing around his office this morning. Might be scapegoat time. Best to be in a non-extradition zone when that happens."

She let out a long, slow breath. The absurdity of it wasn't surprising. After all, the pattern had become almost routine—new airline launches with fanfare, collapses under pressure, and senior executives vanish with golden parachutes and conveniently timed retirement plans in the Emirates or the Seychelles. It was the aviation version of a reverse magic trick: watch as your money, your credibility, and sometimes your aircraft, disappear.

Sarah's phone buzzed again. Another update from Ops.

MGT7988: minor delay – slot moved to 17:45. Crew remain on standby. Pax to be informed.

Typical. She'd already mentally checked out of the sector, dreaming of her hotel bed in Bratislava, maybe even a shower longer than five minutes and not delivered via a rusting showerhead from a 90s Ibis. Now it was back into limbo.

"Guess we're on Kazakh time now," she muttered.

Gábor smirked. "That's the thing with Sprint. You think you're in Europe, then suddenly it's Central Asia, and somehow you're filing a tech log report in Cyrillic at 3 a.m. while a goat watches."

"Don't remind me," she replied, rubbing her eyes. "Last week in Chișinău, I had to use Google Translate to explain to a ground handler why our APU was leaking oil. He kept thinking I was offering him a sandwich."

The two fell into a companionable silence, the kind that only people used to the trenches of low-cost aviation could enjoy. Around them, other crews moved through the lounge like zombies, shifting between flights, paperwork, caffeine and creeping jetlag.

A group of Austrian Airways crew passed through, looking crisp and fresh-faced in uniforms that screamed order and efficiency. Sarah eyed them with the weariness of someone who no longer even aspired to that level of polish. Somewhere along the line, the glamour had peeled away. She was just here to fly the plane.

"You think they'll actually get LEA flying again?" she asked eventually, nodding toward the muted television still looping headlines.

Gábor shrugged. "If they do, it won't be what it was. Chinese Nepal doesn't care about legacy or brand. They'll slap a logo on it, funnel passengers into Guangzhou or Urumqi, and call it strategic expansion."

****

CHAPTER 16 – Prickly Crewmates on the AvGeek Express
Wednesday 25th May 2022

Of all the flights Sarah had to be on as a First Officer for Sprint, being on a run that wasn't very ULCC like, a route which was, looking at the manifest, full of aviation enthusiasts all heading to Berlin, on a former Alitalia A320, heading out, of all places, of Hawarden Airport, where Airbus UK mainly where Airbus UK mainly handled its wing production, felt like the setup for a fever dream. Sarah leaned against the dispatch desk, arms folded, as the dew-streaked morning clung to the glass of the temporary terminal building. A bored-looking ground agent handed over the final load sheet, nodding silently, as if everyone present knew this was not what Hawarden had been built for.

The irony that it had just been refurbished by Airbus, and that, as it was ILA Berlin weekend, meant that Sprint, instead of running ferry flights to shuttle their bosses and some of the more over-eager investor types to Berlin for ILA, had decided to run a weekend of "everywhere in the UK to Berlin" low cost flights, going as far as to use even Cambridge, Blackpool, Wick and even Anglesey for one off, for the weekend, daily return flights, and sell them to passengers, meaning enthusiasts would descend upon small regional airfields in droves. Sarah glanced through the foggy terminal window at the growing queue outside. Most were men, ranging anywhere from their teens to their sixties, with the odd woman peppered in. A few sported reflective jackets, adorned with embroidered airline logos or obscure defunct airline patches. Cameras hung from their necks like sacred totems. It was AvGeek Christmas. And they were the elves.

The irony that they were due to depart 3 minutes after Airbus's own BelugaXL, one of the one of the giant, whale-faced transporters that looked like a cartoon character come to life—was not lost on Sarah. Nor, she guessed, would it be lost on the queue of aviation die-hards who were huddled around a jacket potato van that, it seemed, had set up camp outside the terminal building, an oxymoron in themselves: vintage in spirit, half-functioning in reality.

"You FO Marsh?" a Ukrainian sounding voice said in clipped English, and Sarah turned, expecting the usual crew greeting or maybe a brusque update from ops, but was instead greeted by a man in his late forties, wearing a Sprint Air Captain uniform, his name badge reading Maksym Pshenychnyi – Captain.

Sarah straightened from the dispatch desk, brushing a stray wisp of hair behind her ear and nodding politely.

"That's me," she replied, her voice crisp with the forced cheerfulness of someone only half-fuelled by her first coffee.

"Captain Pshenychnyi. Noone told me I fly with woman," he said, and Sarah frowned, as she resisted the immediate urge to bristle.

Her smile tightened into something razor-thin and polite. "No one told me I'd be flying with someone who lacked basic social filters," she said smoothly, then added, "but here we are."

Maksym grunted. Not quite an apology, not quite amusement either. He pulled a laminated folder from his flight bag, checked his watch, and gestured vaguely toward the crew room—a temporary portacabin with "Flight Operations" stencilled in courier font on the door.

"I fly MiG-31 with Russian Air Force, then move to Ukraine in 2014. You?"

Sarah frowned, as she was formerly of the RAF, a Quick Response Alert pilot prior to being a stewardess at PanEuro for part of 2021, then doing her civil pilot training at Easyjet, then moving to Sprint after being poached by their operations lead during the startup chaos. The fact that she had 10 years of RAF service prior to leaving during the pandemic, and retraining in the chaotic aftermath of the lockdowns, wasn't something she felt like broadcasting to a man whose conversational tone hovered somewhere between Eastern Bloc nostalgia and chauvinism.

Especially someone who had been in the Russian air force, someone that she had trained to recognise as the enemy, the enemy she had once been ready to intercept in the skies above the Baltic and the Black Sea. Sarah let the thought linger for a moment, then shrugged off the discomfort with a practiced professionalism.

"I flew the Typhoon with the RAF," she replied carefully, her voice neutral, eyes scanning the modest crew room where a small group of Sprint pilots had already gathered. The room smelled faintly of old coffee and printed briefing sheets.

"Pah, Typhoon. Not as good as MiG. President Putin could easily throw Typhoon in in bin," the Russo-Ukrainian said, and Sarah felt the urge to kick him in the shin and walk out. Instead, she smiled sweetly—chillingly—and took the load sheet with a delicate precision that suggested she might just use it to garrotte him.

"Thanks for the insight," she said with the crisp detachment of a woman who'd flown combat sorties over Estonia while some men still argued about whether her lipstick shade affected lift.

Looking over the hastily erected security pods, the UK Border Force officer who had never been to an airport before this week, and sighed.

The fact that the memory of the London European Airways crash a mere few weeks earlier was still in the industry hung heavily in the air, like a low fog that refused to clear. Aviation professionals—especially those caught in the throttle of operations—were feeling the pressure acutely. Sprint Air, the new kid on the block, was no exception. Though the airline projected its cheery low-cost facade, inside, the undercurrents of stress, scrutiny, and vulnerability rippled under every uniform and clipboard.

Sarah watched as the queue of enthusiasts grew longer, some jostling and laughing nervously, clutching boarding passes or spare lenses for their cameras. The mood was a curious mix of celebration and apprehension, a tribe united by passion yet conscious of the risks just beneath the surface.

She leaned back against the dispatch desk again and unfolded the flight release paperwork. The Alitalia ex-aircraft, EI-DSA, still with its Italian tail number and yet it was in full livery, the blue and the stylised S of Sprint, the smaller version, not the Sprinter slightly larger S, used for the Eastern European side to get round trademark issues that Sprint had with a Polish airline who also called themselves Sprint Air.

"I'm going to do the walkaround, so if you want to get off your high horse and forget about being a MiG pilot, maybe we can get this aircraft off the ground without sparking a diplomatic incident," Sarah said, voice level but cool.

Maksym said nothing, merely sniffed and shifted his weight like a man deciding whether a fight was worth the energy. He gave a short nod and sat down to review the weather briefing. Sarah, already collecting her hi-vis and slipping on the navy Sprint Air jacket over her uniform, turned and left the portacabin with swift, efficient steps.

Walking out onto the misty apron, Sarah noticed both the smell of mixture of jet fuel and springtime dew, as well as VP-BWY, an Airbus A320-232 that she, as part of a team with Aviator Capital and some other Sprint pilots, had liberated mere hours before the Russian Government passed laws which would confiscate leased airplanes that were registered to foreign entities and were operating on Russian leases. The journey to Mineralnye Vody Airport and Moscow Domodedovo, where the majority of the planes that they had liberated, some Airbus A321-231s and some Airbus A320-232s, were still in their Red Wings livery.

The 8 Russian planes were mainly at Hawarden for maintenance, as Sprint and Sprinter were slated to take them on their cross-border, operational flights through Europe, though the mood around the apron was tense.

"I see traitors have stolen Russian aircrafts," Maksym's voice echoed behind Sarah as she approached the aircraft, his words sharp with resentment. Sarah stiffened, as she had been the First Officer on board VP-BWY when it had flown into Hawarden two months earlier. Technically Sprint had leased it from its Maltese leasing company, who had leased it from Aviator Capital, but Maksym's words still felt like an accusation, a sharp jab at a wound that hadn't quite healed. She stopped in her tracks, turning slowly to face him. Her heart quickened for just a moment, but her face remained a carefully sculpted mask of calm.

"Yes, we're all traitors to someone," she replied, her voice even, the tension in the air palpable. "Anyway, I'll have you know I've been at the controls of one of those planes, and I've never had any issues with them. The aircraft is safe and fully operational, thank you very much."

Her words lingered in the air, hanging there as she turned back to complete her walkaround. She didn't expect any further comment from Maksym, but the undertones of his remark made it clear that their paths had crossed in ways neither of them could entirely ignore.

The Airbus, though now wrapped in the blue Sprint Air livery, still bore the marks of its previous life—Alitalia's tail design still faintly visible under the fresh coat of paint. It was a temporary fix, but for Sprint, it would suffice. The plane had been one of many snatched from the grasp of uncertainty, its future tied to the uneasy dance of geopolitics that seemed to dictate everything these days.

As she moved along the fuselage, inspecting the aircraft, Sarah couldn't help but feel a pang of nostalgia for the clean, regimented systems of the RAF. A walkaround in the military had been a simple task—one of precision and protocol. Here, amidst the private-sector chaos of Sprint Air, it was a matter of catching every detail, anticipating possible flaws in the rapidly-assembled operation. The uncertainty of the situation had become palpable in the weeks since the airline's operations began in earnest. They were still finding their rhythm, testing the boundaries of what was possible within the constraints of their resources and their desperation for legitimacy in the fast-moving European aviation market.

She completed the walkaround, mentally ticking off each item on her list. Nothing seemed out of place, but that was the nature of the job—always waiting for something to go wrong. Returning to the aircraft's nose, she glanced back toward the terminal building, noting that the crowd had begun to grow restless. With the weather forecast promising more overcast skies, the fog seemed to have stuck to the tarmac like a stubborn reminder of how far they were from the world of aviation's polished glamour.

"Cool, I never thought I'd see G-ZBAF again," the voice of one aviation enthusiast who was walking across the apron, as it seemed that boarding had been called and the first passengers were beginning to filter towards the aircraft. "I knew Red Wings had reregistered it to VP-BER when AerCap had leased to them, but I didn't know it was back in the UK now. I thought Russia had confiscated all Western aircraft. How does it even fly here?"

Sarah knew that they were referring to one of the other A321s that were parked up in the compound that Airbus and the maintenance operator Sprint used to keep its growing fleet compliant with the CAA maintenance requirements.

"They're probably having a C or D check done," another enthusiast said as Sarah walked around to check the engines were free of any foreign object debris. Sprint's rag-tag fleet, though externally branded with a uniform blue livery, was an eclectic patchwork of pre-loved aircraft stitched together through bureaucratic deals and last-minute grabs. She completed her inspection with a practised eye, resisting the urge to correct the enthusiasts theorising about airworthiness protocols—she'd long learned to choose her battles.

Back at the foot of the airstairs, she nodded to the ground crew and made her way up into the cabin. The familiar scent of ageing plastic, recirculated air, and airline coffee greeted her. The interior had been refitted with the standard RECARO Aircraft Seating SL3510 in navy blue trim, the standard interior for both Sprint and Easyjet, the latter being from where the CEO of Sprint had spent most of his career, so she knew that even the most veteran of spotters wouldn't be able to distinguish between a Sprint or EasyJet cabin from just the seats alone. The only real giveaway was the lack of branding. Sprint was so new that some of their aircraft interiors hadn't been rebranded at all—no logos on the seatback covers, no printed safety cards, just hastily laminated emergency instructions tucked into seat pockets and QR codes that led to hastily built mobile websites. Budget startup chic.

As she stepped into the cockpit, the sight of a Windrose Airlines Airbus A321 on final approach to the runway momentarily caught Sarah's eye. She paused, watching it through the side window—a strange hybrid of colour and consequence in the grey North Wales morning. The aircraft's coral and mint livery stood out starkly against the clouds, an almost garish reminder of the post-Soviet sprawl of airlines that now criss-crossed European skies with a kind of reckless optimism.

Sarah knew that the Ukrainian airline had suspended operations following the opening skirmishes of the invasion, yet here it was—another aircraft finding sanctuary or purpose in the uncertain mosaic of post-COVID, post-conflict skies. It was a sight Sarah had grown used to: planes rehomed from bankrupt carriers, or exiled fleets absorbed into opportunistic start-ups like Sprint. Everything felt transient now. Nothing stayed still for long.

As it landed and started rolling along the runway to park, it wasn't carrying Windrose fleet names, but Sprint ones, which confused the enthusiasts further, their muttering now audible even inside the cockpit.

"I see Sprint buy more airplanes. Not as good as Sukhoi Superjets though," the grating voice of Maksym broke into the quiet cockpit air, his tone dripping with disdain.

Sarah didn't bother looking at him. She was too familiar with his jabs — a constant reminder of the tensions simmering just beneath the surface. "Right now, Sukhois aren't exactly winning any popularity contests in Europe," she said coolly, fastening her seatbelt. "And they certainly don't have the same reliability track record as these old A320s."

Maksym snorted, clearly unimpressed, but said no more. He settled into the captain's seat with the kind of gruff authority born from years in a very different aviation culture — one where rules were often suggestions and risk-taking a part of everyday life.

Sarah toggled the overhead panel switches, the hum of the aircraft systems springing to life a comforting routine amidst the chaos of their startup airline's haphazard operations. The A320's cockpit was familiar, even if the backstory of how it had arrived here, one of ITA's former aircraft suddenly repainted and rebranded, felt surreal.

"I fly, you sit there," Maksym then sharply stated, as if, even though as Captain and had rank, he was running an Air Force drill and not a commercial flight with paying passengers on a civilian airliner.

Sarah gave him a long, expressionless look. "We'll be following CRM, thanks. That means Crew Resource Management. We share the workload. You brief, I brief, and we operate together. You know—civil aviation standards."

Maksym grunted again. She suspected it was the only form of punctuation he respected.

As Sarah reviewed the take-off performance figures, she cast a glance over the flight plan and NOTAMs. The route out of Hawarden was a relatively short hop before picking up a northeast heading, skimming east of Manchester airspace, then a dogleg across the North Sea into Germany. A straightforward sector—on paper.

She noted that Berlin's Tegel was no longer operational, and instead their destination was the spanking-new Berlin Brandenburg. It always felt a little soulless to her compared to the decaying grandeur of Tegel, but the enthusiasts in the back probably didn't care. Brandenburg was the future, even if it had opened ten years late.

Maksym seemed content to let her handle the nitty-gritty. That suited Sarah fine—better she manage the setup than have to deal with his Cold War monologues. As they moved into the brief, she took the lead.

"Standard departure from runway 22, SID is the VATON 3X out of Hawarden, transitioning over the North Sea, then direct LAMSO, followed by TOLNA and BER NDB. Landing runway 25L expected. Weather in Berlin is scattered clouds, light winds. Temps cool. Nothing unusual enroute except for some light turbulence over the Dutch coastline and a NOTAM for parachuting near Osnabrück. Any questions?"

Maksym waved a hand dismissively.

"I fly this same SID when fly Antonov to Kazakhstan," he said with a smirk. "Only with more vodka."

Sarah arched an eyebrow. "Well, today we'll stick with water. Just as intoxicating when properly managed."

The cabin crew poked their heads into the flight deck. A young Hungarian woman named Ilona introduced herself as the senior on today's flight, along with a young Polish cabin crew member, Jakub. Both looked slightly overwhelmed, though cheery.

"Cabin ready in about ten," Ilona said brightly. "The spotters are taking pictures of everything. I think one asked if he could photograph the lav."

"Of course they did," Sarah said with a half-smile. "Let us know if anyone tries to take the seat cushions as souvenirs."

As Ilona disappeared to begin the final cabin checks, Sarah turned back to the panel, running through the before-start checklist. The cockpit was comfortingly familiar. Amid the chaos of Sprint Air's hastily expanded network, aircraft nicked from other airlines, and staff poached or dropped in from every conceivable aviation background, the Airbus remained a solid constant.

Pushback was on time, and Sarah let the comforting routine guide her actions as they coordinated with the slightly flustered Hawarden ground controller—who sounded like they were more used to dealing with factory shunts than passenger movements. As the BelugaXL cleared the runway and lumbered into the sky like an airborne Jabba the Hutt, Sprint Air 1413 was cleared to taxi.

The taxiway had all the elegance of a back alley—potholes, seams of grass sprouting in the concrete, and the occasional rogue traffic cone—but Sarah coaxed the aircraft forward with gentle precision.

"Do they let you fly in England without moustache?" Maksym muttered during the taxi out.

Sarah turned slowly. "Do they let you fly in Europe without manners?"

Maksym, for once, said nothing.

* _ * _ * _ *

It was the final approach into Berlin that proved to be the final straw.

The aircraft was lined up on the ILS glide slope, descending smoothly through the low cloud that had settled over Brandenburg. The engines' steady hum was a comforting backdrop to the quiet tension that had been simmering in the cockpit all flight. Sarah sat upright, monitoring the instruments and cross-checking Maksym's inputs. He was competent enough, but his taciturn attitude grated relentlessly, like the scraping of rough fabric on skin.

"Speed stable. Flaps fifteen. Gear down," Sarah announced calmly, her voice steady despite the nagging irritation creeping under her skin. Maksym didn't respond, but she could sense his eyes flicking to her instruments, his jaw tightening as he fought the urge to assert control.

The aircraft shuddered briefly as a gust hit from the right, a reminder that the weather, though improving, still held its unpredictable moods.

"Trim's good. Rate of descent is steady," she added, her tone keeping Maksym anchored to the procedures rather than the politics that clung to his every word.

Suddenly, Maksym leaned over and jabbed a finger at the navigation screen. "This route is wrong," he said, voice low and rough. "We should be going direct to BER, not via TOLNA. In Russia, we would not waste fuel like this."

Sarah's hands tightened on the control column for a moment, then she forced herself to relax. "This is a standard European procedure, Maksym. Air Traffic Control vectors us this way to manage the flow of traffic. If you want direct, you can take it up with the controllers, but meanwhile, we fly the plan as filed."

She watched as Maksym pressed the radio button and spoke into the mic, his tone brusque as he addressed Berlin Approach with a clipped Eastern European cadence. "Sprint Air 9413 request direct BER."

Sarah noticed that, although she had been using the official callsign for the flight, Ramsgate, or RAT, the IATA code that Sprint's UK operations use, RAT 9413, the official flight number for the day, as there was a Polish airline who's callsign was SprintAir, and so the controllers often mixed them up, Maksym's request caused a pause on the frequency.

"This is Berlin Approach, there is no SprintAir flight 9413 on our radar," came the clipped reply from the controller, the accent unmistakably German and formal. "Confirm your callsign."

"Berlin Approach, this is Ramsgate 9413, I'm sorry, the Captain is being a bit difficult," Sarah interjected smoothly into the mic, easing the tension. "Ramsgate 9413 requesting verification on routing via TOLNA."

The controller's voice was curt but clearer now. "Ramsgate 9413, continue as filed. Expect ILS 25L. Winds are calm. Traffic spacing maintained. You have Margate 9874 ahead of you and Ramsgate 9512 behind you. Slow speed to maintain separation. Advise when established on final."

Sarah released the mic and exhaled slowly. Maksym's brow furrowed deeply, his knuckles whitening on the yoke as he digested the controller's instructions.

"That's how we do it," Sarah said quietly, "no shortcuts, no shortcuts in European airspace. It's about spacing, efficiency, and safety—not showing off your flying prowess."

Maksym gave a reluctant nod, but his eyes betrayed a flicker of frustration. "In Russia, controllers understand real flying."

Sarah's lips twitched briefly in a controlled smile. She'd heard this kind of nationalist nostalgia many times before from pilots who couldn't quite shed their old lives. She was already mentally writing her report to Ops about Sarah was already mentally writing her report to Ops about Maksym's insubordination and general attitude. She knew well enough that Sprint's management had

287

neither the patience nor the resources for cockpit conflicts like this. The airline was too new, too fragile, and still scrambling for legitimacy in a crowded market. Every flight had to be flawless—or as close as possible.

As the Airbus settled on the glide slope, the runway lights ahead began to pierce through the mist, their glow a beacon in the dreary morning gloom. The undercarriage thumped solidly into place, accompanied by the usual mechanical clunks and reassuring clicks. Sarah adjusted the thrust levers slightly, maintaining a smooth approach speed.

"Gear down and locked," she called out, her voice professional, masking the simmering frustration she had buried deep beneath years of training and experience. "Speed stable, flaps twenty."

Maksym's eyes flicked over to her instruments again, but he said nothing. Perhaps he knew this wasn't the moment for argument.

A crackle came over the radio, the controller's voice crisp but courteous. "Ramsgate 9413, you are cleared to land runway 25L. Winds calm. Report vacating runway."

"Cleared to land 25L, Ramsgate 9413," Maksym replied, though his tone remained flat.

The runway lights rushed up beneath them, growing from pinpricks to elongated streaks as the aircraft descended steadily. Sarah felt the familiar tug of the Airbus's fly-by-wire system, so different from the raw mechanical feel of the RAF Typhoon she'd once flown, but no less precise.

****

CHAPTER 17 – Schedules Align
Friday 27th May 2022

If one had to admit that laying in bed with a German First Officer at the same airline as you, who you were dating, who was currently muttering in an organised manner, while holding your hips and kissing your neck, pistoning into the soft nape just below your ear, and making you squirt as his fingers were deep in your clitoris, working their magic and making you feel higher than what a chase against a Russian MiG in a Eurofighter could ever deliver—well, you'd probably think your life had peaked. But after the rush faded and the room grew humid with the scent of sex and sweat, and his chest pressed gently into your back, you'd remember what day it was, what city, what time, and how little sleep you'd had. And that, in an hour, you'd be in uniform and watching him butter toast while humming Dvořák, and pretending you were both just ordinary, utterly boring pilots who hadn't nearly been found out by Housekeeping twice already that night.

Sarah could feel Max Detweiler's erection pistoning inside her rear while he was pleasuring her, and she knew that she had told him that as long as he used protection, that she would let him do anything he wanted—at least within the four thin walls of whatever hotel the Sprint Air roster gods saw fit to book them into that night. She'd whispered that in his ear as dawn threatened to burn through the blackout curtains, and Max—always the cheeky pragmatist—had wasted no time. Now, his breath was hot on her shoulder, one strong arm curled under her chest, the other teasing slick patterns over her clitoris, and her body arched helplessly into him.

Sarah tried to stifle her moan. She thought of the knock they'd barely avoided at three in the morning, the startled "Entschuldigung!" from a cleaner who'd caught a glimpse of one bare foot peeking out from the covers and the unmistakable silhouette of two heads, not one, on the pillow. She'd frozen, heart pounding. Max, ever quick, had simply grinned, called out "Morgen!" and squeezed her even tighter.

It was, she supposed, the only upside of this mad existence: stolen moments, odd hours, the constant chance of discovery. She'd never imagined, during her RAF days or her few months in PanEuro's polyester, that her greatest risk wouldn't be an engine fire or an angry controller in Marseille but getting caught in flagrante by a Berlinerin chambermaid, especially as it was ILA Berlin weekend, where every AvGeek and half the world's industry press seemed to be prowling the halls, eager for a whiff of gossip or scandal. For all that, she was no longer sure she cared. If fate—or the Sprint Air scheduling algorithm—had flung her into Max Detweiler's orbit for even a little while, then she'd decided to wring every illicit, laughing drop out of it.

She lay there for a moment after, skin prickling in the cooling air, and tried to fix the feeling in her memory: Max's hand resting idly on her hip, his breath evening out as he pressed a final kiss behind her ear. The bed smelled faintly of his cologne—something woodsy, old-fashioned, that always made her think of cold beers at Düsseldorf and the distant, haunted woods of his Bavarian childhood. She exhaled, savouring the odd, fragile peace.

But the illusion of stillness shattered when her phone, buzzing with the violence only crew rosters and WhatsApp groups could manage, vibrated twice on the bedside table. She groaned, rolling out from under Max, who flopped onto his back, one arm thrown dramatically over his eyes.

"Five more minutes," he murmured in English, his accent curling around the words.

Sarah scoffed, retrieving her phone. "You're such a cliché. Do you realise your report time is at 0510 and mine is 0511, and we're both doing flights between here and the UK all day."

Max peeled himself off the mattress with the unhurried inertia of a man who'd flown short-haul for years and, despite his optimism, knew exactly how little dignity it afforded. "Yeah, and I have as a captain that 'knob' you had the other day. Maksym Pshenychnyi."

Sarah rolled her eyes at the mention of Maksym. Even now, her skin prickled with the remembered tension of that cockpit—the way every checklist became a battlefield, every routine exchange another chance for Maksym to bristle and posture, as if the Airbus was some Cold War gunship and she the enemy within. She'd told Max the story in fractured bursts last night, somewhere between laughter, prosecco, and lazy kisses: how Maksym had ignored standard calls, overridden her briefings, and declared, over the PA in Ukrainian, that "British procedures were a joke." That last bit had stung, if only for the sheer unfairness of it. She'd wanted to defend herself—her RAF training, her decade of flying—

but what could you say to a man who viewed compromise as surrender?

Max, to his credit, hadn't tried to fix it. He'd simply held her tighter and muttered that "at least you get Lowe next. She's nice, if a bit too fond of Stansted. And she's not likely to talk about the glories of the Ukrainian SSR while taxiing at Southend. What is it you've got today? Here to Birmingham, back, then a Metz, Prestwick and back here, right?"

Sarah let her eyes flutter closed again, her hand drifting over the expanse of Max's bare chest, feeling the familiar thrum of his pulse beneath her palm. For a heartbeat, she tried to pretend the day was theirs to waste, that the relentless tick of the roster didn't loom overhead like an ever-hungry clock. Outside, Berlin was waking: trams screeching somewhere down the Spree, the distant rumble of jets clawing skywards from Brandenburg, and the pulse of a city that, for all its history, never really seemed to sleep.

"We've got an hour before we've got to leave, so... fancy a shag in the shower?" Sarah said, as she felt Max's seed in her anal passage, fresh seed that he had left there with careless affection, the evidence of their nocturnal defiance of Sprint Air's code of conduct and, if she was honest, every sensible rule of sleep hygiene before a rostered day. She smirked as she felt his erection withdraw from her, as his hands reached her breasts, the gentle pads of his fingers tracing lazy spirals along her nipples. He grinned, all wolfish charm and morning stubble, before levering himself upright, lifting her five foot 10 frame and slowly, gently, inserting his erection into her sex while holding her like a favoured possession, the six foot 3 German's frame as he carried her into the bathroom, while gently rocking her, the friction as he made love to her while he walked the 10 feet from the window side of the Premier Inn bedroom to the bathroom, somehow both comic and astonishingly intimate.

"You know, Max, you can go faster if you just drop me," Sarah whispered into his ear, half-laughing, her words dissolving in the steam and sudden shower spray as he swung her around and pressed her up against the cheap tile, water splattering across both their faces. She had to clamp a hand to her mouth to keep from giggling too loudly—above the hiss of the shower, even above the distant echo of a departing EasyJet, their laughter and groans felt like the only reality. For a minute, nothing existed but hands, lips, heat, the slow grind of hips, and the impossible closeness of a morning she'd already begun to mourn.

And then he went deeper, and, feeling his erection completely stuffing her, her walls clamping on his cock, she let herself arch and sigh, surrendering to the moment, knowing full well she'd pay for every moan and gasp with fatigue later in the day. But what was life, Sarah mused through the fog of pleasure, if not a series of delicious risks—especially with a body pressed between cracked Premier Inn tiles and a German who whispered filth in her ear in three languages? She grinned, her knuckles white against Max's slippery back as he braced them both, his pace steady and unhurried, like a man savouring every last crumb before the kitchen lights came on.

In the haze of steam and sex, the world shrank to breath and heartbeat, hips and hands, the hot water washing away any lingering guilt about rosters or codes of conduct. Max's fingers slipped into her hair, tugging her head back gently so he could kiss along her jaw, and she had to stifle another laugh—because yes, it was mad, but so was the whole bloody industry. She thought about the pilots she'd known in the RAF, so many of them self-serious and smug, obsessed with checklist precision and combat stories, their nights usually spent alone with porn in soulless hotels. Compared to that, being manhandled in the shower by a German who actually gave a fuck about her orgasm was, frankly, a massive improvement.

"You know, Max, you're better than my ex," Sarah muttered, as she felt the first wave of orgasm rolling through her, electric and inexorable as a thunderstorm over the Alps. The last partner she had, a RAF Flight Lieutenant, back in her Typhoon days, had been a 'fuck and run' type, only caring about his own pleasure, all bark and barely a whimper of actual skill—more of a quick sortie than a sustained dogfight, to borrow the lingo of the trade. But Max, with his slow, deliberate thrusts and unhurried attention, seemed determined to prove that German engineering had more to offer than just efficient airframes and humourless pre-flight briefings. He held her, his body a heat shield pressed against her, as her climax surged and shuddered through every nerve, her vision greying at the edges, her knuckles digging into the hard muscle of his shoulder.

The spray thudded around them, plastering her hair flat, masking the sound of her panting as Max grinned against her neck and bit down, just enough to send a fresh jolt ricocheting down her spine. For a few seconds, Sarah could've sworn the world fell away—just the two of them, their slick bodies grinding together in a strange ballet of defiance and need. When Max finally followed her over the edge, hips spasming as he gasped her name in a tangled mixture of English and Bavarian dialect, Sarah could only laugh, breathless and hoarse, the sound echoing off the tiles as she sagged into his arms.

"Gott, you are going to be the death of me," he muttered, breathlessly, nuzzling her ear with a warmth she suspected he reserved only for these stolen, half-lit hours.

She pressed a kiss to his temple. "If you die, I'm nicking your uniform and flying your leg. Well, except you've got Pshenychnyi as your Captain, and he's the only man in Europe who could make Ryanair look like a staff wellness scheme." She grinned, unable to resist, and saw the corner of Max's mouth flicker in that way she'd come to love: part amusement, part resignation, part utter devotion. For all the exhaustion, the schedules, the relentless sense that the world was never quite under control, she wouldn't have traded this chaos for anything. Not for the stability of a nine-to-five, not for some sterile, Stepford marriage with a nice accountant from Kent. Not even for the calm of solo nights, which she knew too well from years of living for the next roster update.

But the clock was unforgiving. Steam fogged the mirror, droplets racing one another in streaks, and Sarah could hear the distant thunder of suitcases on the corridor carpet—early crew on their way out, maybe a Ryanair team already bickering in Polish, maybe some poor Flybe holdover who still hadn't figured out the purple luggage tags didn't get you priority boarding in the real world. With one final, lingering kiss, Max turned off the shower and stepped out, dragging a towel across his shoulders, passing one to her, both of them grinning like schoolchildren with a secret. It was almost enough to make her believe—almost—that these moments could last.

Twenty minutes later, the spell had broken. Sarah was zipped into her Sprint Air uniform, pale blue blouse and navy trousers, hair pinned tight in a chignon that never quite concealed her natural chaos. Max, already looking irritatingly composed in his captain's stripes, was buttering toast with the solemnity of a priest. He hummed under his breath—Dvořák's "Humoresque," if she wasn't mistaken. The news from the tiny television bolted to the wall babbled away in a mixture of English, German and the peculiar brand of airline Esperanto that only truly desperate hotel staff seemed to master.

"Coffee?" he asked, holding up a tiny paper cup as if it were a sacred relic.

"God, yes. I'll need it. If I have to hear Lowe give one more safety briefing about hand baggage, I'll start throwing people off at 39,000 feet."

He grinned. "She's not that bad."

"She's exactly that bad, and you know it. She's the only woman I've met who could make a Ryanair safety demo sound thrilling." Sarah shot him a look. "You know, if we're caught like this, it'll be the talk of the crew room for a week."

Max shrugged, mouth full of toast. "Let them talk. They're all jealous."

It was an old joke between them. But Sarah couldn't help the flicker of anxiety. Company policy was vague enough—"relationships between crew members should be conducted with discretion and not interfere with duty"—but in the gossipy hothouse of European aviation, everyone knew everything, sooner or later. And in Berlin, during ILA weekend, even the walls seemed to have ears.

She sighed, took the coffee, and let herself lean against him for a long, silent minute. Outside, rain rattled the window, a fine grey drizzle that seemed to leach the colour from the world.

"Go on, First Officer Detweiler," she said, nudging him with her hip. "Time to be responsible."

"Oh, First Officer Marsh," he replied, his hand on her waist as he smoothed a stray thread from her blouse, "I am never responsible. That's why I fly with you." His smile was all mischief, but his eyes softened in the half-light. For a moment, neither of them moved. The silence between them wasn't awkward, but quietly electric—a rare lull in the relentless turbulence of their lives. Sarah finished her coffee, feeling its cheap, acrid warmth thrum through her, banishing the lingering shadows of sleep and sex.

Outside the window, Berlin was already alive, the streets below slick with last night's rain and alive with the spatter of morning traffic. She watched for a moment, seeing a flock of EasyJet crew in blinding orange slouch across

Alexanderplatz, shepherded by a harassed supervisor, and wondered how many of them had woken this morning in someone else's bed.

She turned back to Max, who was fastening his epaulettes with the precise economy of someone who had been putting on uniforms since childhood. She thought again of that first day she'd met him—Düsseldorf, a snarl of delays, everyone irritable and unwashed. He'd handed her a crumpled METAR with a grin and said, "VFR, if you don't mind a little adventure." At the time, she'd just wanted to strangle him. Now, watching him shoulder his flight bag, she felt an unfamiliar warmth curl in her chest.

"Ready?" he asked, reaching for his own battered suitcase. She nodded, stuffing her pass and ID into her jacket pocket, and together they stepped out into the corridor, letting the heavy door snick shut behind them.

The lift was crammed with cabin crew, a pair of bleary-eyed Jet2 pilots, and a catering trolley that wedged itself between Sarah's shin and the door. She tried not to think about the way Max's hand lingered just a little too long on the small of her back, or how the scent of him, soap and something faintly spicy, clung to her uniform like a secret. The Jet2 captain eyed them both with a knowing smirk—one of those looks that suggested he'd seen it all before, probably with worse outcomes. Sarah gave him a blank stare that usually worked on insistent Ryanair gate agents.

"Going anywhere today?" the Jet2 Captain asked Sarah, and she sighed.

"Birmingham, back here, then a Metz, Prestwick and back here," Sarah said, chuckling. "This dolt has a Belfast, back here, a Coventry, a Metz and then a Luton and back here."

"Coventry? Who on earth thought to bring that dead and alive airport back?" The Jet2 captain gave a theatrical shudder, eyes rolling skyward. "I did my type rating in a hangar there in 2004. Place was haunted then."

Sarah grinned, happy to play along. "Now it's just haunted by hen parties and hungover stag dos. I mean when you offer £9.99 to Ibiza, Prague and Kraków, even Lydd Airport would the masses. Hell, we've got AvGeeks paying £249 to get here from Blackpool, Anglesey and even the Isle of Man, just to bag a Berlin ILA landing in a Sprint Air A319neo."

"Wait, Sprint's running from Blackpool now? Christ. When I started, Blackpool was just wind, rust and one old boy in a flat cap yelling at the radar." The Jet2 captain gave a conspiratorial wink to his First Officer, a fresh-faced woman who looked about twelve and clung to her coffee like a life-raft. "Let me guess, they've done a Ryanair and called it Liverpool Blackpool and played up the bars and Pleasure Beach for the stag crowd."

Max, suppressing a grin, piped up. "Yep, and even Broughton has got the Liverpool Chester branding now, if you can believe it. Our CEO keeps pretending that if you add 'Liverpool' to anywhere within 40 miles, you'll trick people into thinking it's an actual city hub rather than some windswept ex-RAF strip next to a sheep farm and a housing estate full of Range Rovers on PCP."

The Jet2 First Officer giggled, covering her mouth as her captain harrumphed in mock outrage. "I trained on the 737 at Blackpool. We did our base training circuits at dusk, wind so strong you could've drifted the thing onto the prom with the wheels up. Place had character, though. Unlike Stansted."

Sarah leaned back against the lift's cold panelling, catching Max's eye. He gave her that sly smile, the one that meant I love this mess, and you know it. Around them, the crew crowd was thickening—snatches of Spanish, Polish, Scouse and some indecipherable banter from a pair of Ryanair cabin crew who were clearly discussing a passenger with an "emotional support ferret." Sarah raised an eyebrow at Max, who just shrugged, as if to say: it's Berlin, it's ILA, anything goes.

The lift doors pinged open onto the Premier Inn's garish lobby. All plastic greenery and too-bright spotlights, the place reeked of burnt coffee, nervous perfume, and the sour tang of airline curry from last night's rota meal. It was the sort of place that prided itself on a "continental breakfast buffet," which in practice meant a basket of crusty rolls, some salami sweating under a heat lamp, and a pot of stewed eggs.

Sarah checked her watch—time to go. She and Max threaded through the crush of crew bags, past the desperate queue at reception (one man demanding his "loyalty points" in perfect French-accented English, as if this would make the printer work), and out into the drizzle of Alexanderplatz. The city was already throbbing with movement: trams snaked through puddles, U-Bahn trains rattled below their feet, and street vendors set up for the day, hawking currywurst and Brezeln to the first waves of bleary-eyed tourists.

She shivered, pulling her blazer tighter. "Not exactly Mallorca weather, is it?"

Max snorted. "At least there's no sand in your underwear. Come on, let's get a taxi before someone spots us and starts the rumour mill."

They ducked into a waiting cab—a battered Skoda with a driver who looked like he'd survived both the Berlin Airlift and at least three rounds of Ryanair's annual Christmas party. He grunted, nodding at their uniforms. "Flughafen, ja?"

"Ja, Terminal 2, bitte, Mitarbeiterparkplatz, danke," Max said, his native German smooth and self-assured, and Sarah settled back, savouring the rare pleasure of letting someone else handle the logistics for a change. The cab slid into traffic, wipers slashing rain from the windscreen in measured, hypnotic sweeps.

Berlin in May was always a city in motion, a place both forward-looking and hopelessly tangled in its past. The avenue outside the Premier Inn was already thick with tour buses, press vans emblazoned with ILA BERLIN logos, and the odd high-viz marshaller slinking through puddles on the hunt for their first coffee. Sarah's gaze drifted across the river of humanity. She wondered, not for the first time, how many of the faces out there belonged to other pilots running on too little sleep and too much caffeine, all wearing the same brittle smile she'd perfected over a decade.

She reached across the cab's back seat, resting her hand on Max's thigh, a silent gesture of camaraderie. He gave her a sidelong glance, the corner of his mouth quirking. For all their banter and bravado, this—the brief contact, the knowledge that, for now, they were in it together— was what steadied her. The taxi bumped over the tram tracks and turned past a newsagent where a familiar aviation magazine—AV Week, she noted with an inward groan—had a Sprint Air tailfin splashed across the cover. The caption promised "Europe's LCC Revolution: Sprint Air vs. the Big Boys," a headline she doubted any of them had actually read past the press release.

* _ * _ * _ *

Berlin Brandenburg Terminal 2 was chaos, the sort of chaos that masqueraded as order: lines snaking through the atrium, suitcases stacked like barricades, and a constant thrum of multi-lingual PA announcements promising the impossible ("Final call for passengers to Cluj-Napoca... Your gate will close in 90 seconds"). The air was thick with the scent of industrial-strength disinfectant, cheap pastries, and a faint undertone of burnt Jet A-1 that drifted in from the apron every time the automatic doors wheezed open.

Sarah and Max joined the crew entrance queue, flashing badges, making small talk with other Sprint Air uniforms they recognised only by fleeting WhatsApp avatars and roster lines. The rhythm of airport life was immutable— shuffle, flash ID, recite base, endure the scrutiny of a security guard who eyed you like you'd smuggled a ferret in your flight bag.

The security line crawled forward, and Sarah's mind began the gentle, familiar churn of pre-flight: flight plan in her inbox, METARs scrolling in her memory, the roster for the day tumbling through her mind like a well-worn setlist. Today was no different, except for the undercurrent of excitement that buzzed through the terminal—ILA Berlin had brought out the usual throng of spotters, bloggers, industry execs and anorak-wearing AvGeeks, all hungry for a story. Somewhere overhead, she knew, Airbus test pilots and Boeing PR teams were mingling, their world only marginally less surreal than her own.

Sarah tried not to let her nerves show as she approached the ID check. It was second nature now: a smile that didn't quite reach her eyes, a flash of her lanyard, a quick "Moin, alles gut?" to the security officer on duty. The guard, a burly Berliner who seemed impervious to the glamour of ILA week, waved her through with only the briefest of glances. Max, behind her, managed to sneak in a wink and an "Auf Wiedersehen" as he passed, eliciting a grunt from the man in the booth.

Beyond the checkpoint, the world contracted and sped up at once. Crew flows diverged by airline, uniforms and lanyards forming invisible battalions; a ripple of recognition, side-eye, and the faint camaraderie of shared misery spread through the crowd. Sarah saw three ex-PanEuro faces in rapid succession, all giving the same "solidarity smile" that meant: surviving Sprint Air, are you? One or two, she knew from previous overnights in Lisbon and knockabout legs to Knock. There was Eloise Adams, now wearing four stripes and the air of someone who'd not only made it through but come out the other side with stories that would curl the hair of any flight safety inspector. She gave Sarah a subtle thumbs-up—code for, "You're still alive, good job."

The crew room was marginally less frenetic, but only because most people had already grabbed their paperwork and run for the gates. The big whiteboard, updated hourly during ILA, listed the day's unusual routings: charter flights for industry groups, ad hoc positioning sectors, even the odd cameo by a "mystery guest" (rumoured to be an ex-Lufthansa CEO on a secret Sprint Air A320, for reasons no one could quite fathom). Sarah stowed her bag, shrugged into her blazer, and made her way to the duty desk for her crew briefing.

Max was close behind, juggling his own pile of printouts. "You good?" he asked in a low voice, and she nodded, still fighting the strange, jittery elation of the morning. It would fade, she knew—it always did, as routine and repetition took over—but for now, it felt like anything was possible. Even happiness, perhaps.

The duty supervisor for the day was a round-faced, razor-sharp woman named Janka, a Slovak who'd managed to claw her way up through the primordial soup of low-cost aviation ground ops. Janka looked up from her iPad, ticking off names and flights with brisk efficiency.

"Marsh, Sarah—Birmingham, then back here, Metz, Prestwick, then Berlin. First Officer. Captain is Lowe, Helen."

Sarah nodded. "Anything to know?"

Janka grinned. "Metz is a zoo. ATC strike, fuel truck delays, lots of VIPs from ILA. But you'll survive. Everyone's nervous, so be nice to the ground crew. Also, you've got two AvGeeks deadheading to Prestwick. Try not to let them into the cockpit."

"I'll do my best," Sarah said, forcing a smile.

Janka's eyes flicked over to Max. "Detweiler, Max— Belfast, then Berlin, Coventry, Metz, Luton, then Berlin again. Captain today, with Pshenychnyi."

Max winced theatrically. "Any tips for handling him?"

Janka shrugged. "Pretend you don't speak English or Ukrainian, just German. He'll leave you alone. Good luck."

****

CHAPTER 18 – Vil′na Ukrayina & Roster Conflicts
Wednesday 1st June 2022

Sarah noticed as she walked onto the apron of M. R. Štefánik Airport Bratislava, the Ukrainian-liveried Airbus A321 that had been causing a stir all morning on social media. UR-WRJ – nicknamed Vil′na Ukrayina, or "Free Ukraine" – gleamed under the clear Slovakian sky, its fuselage a vivid defiance of both design conventions and geopolitics. The aircraft, a Windrose Airlines frame that had joined the Sprint fleet, kept in its Windrose red and mint livery, with Sprint fleet names and a new, special, Ukrainian flag coloured Sprint S on the tail, along with the names of over 1,000 Ukrainians, all of who had lost their lives in, what the press release had said, the first month of the invasion. A digital composite of names, etched in fine decal vinyl, blanketed the tailfin like a war memorial in motion. There was no effort to disguise the symbolism. Sprint had made a point – this wasn't just another wet-lease on the cheap or an aircraft they hadn't got round to repainting. It was a statement of solidarity, bordering on provocation depending on which side of the geopolitical fence you stood.

The fact it still kept its Ukrainian registration, UR-WRJ, was also no accident. Legally speaking, it was operating under lease from Windrose via the leasing company Sprint owned, one that leased only to Sprint and Sprinter, meaning that the aircraft remained officially Ukrainian property, allowing it to fly with UR registration even as it operated within Sprint's wider European network. That nuance mattered – not just for tax or airworthiness paperwork, but symbolically. UR-WRJ was a flying rejection of Russian territorial overreach, a mobile billboard that proclaimed not just survival, but defiance.

Typing the registration into FlightRadar24, Sarah noticed that it was originally a GB Airways aircraft, delivered back in 2002, moving to British Airways, then easyJet, then to Windrose via DonbassAero, an airline that had been quietly dissolved in the years after the Donbas conflict began. That made this aircraft—now branded Vil'na Ukrayina—a relic of every decade's political storm. A Toulouse built Airbus, nurtured in Gatwick hangars and Luton checklists, reborn in Ukrainian defiance. Now it stood shimmering like a phoenix on the Bratislava tarmac, the aviation equivalent of a protest banner caught mid-flight.

Sarah kept walking, her hi-vis flapping in the warm breeze that rolled over the concrete. Even at this distance, she could see the subtle imperfections in the decal work, the minor ripples where heat and curvature made adhesion a challenge. But the names—thousands of them—were perfectly legible.

"Excuse me," a push by someone who clearly wasn't used to airport apron etiquette jolted Sarah from her focus. A young man with a press lanyard and DSLR hanging from his neck brushed past her with little more than a sideways glance. He had that unmistakable blogger-vlogger hybrid look about him – airline-branded baseball cap, trainers too clean to have walked far, and a notebook overflowing with scribbles that looked more like musings than structured notes.

"Sorry, ma'am," he added hastily in American-accented English when he noticed her glare.

Sarah gave him a curt nod, pausing to let a fuelling truck reverse toward a parked Ryanair 737 across the apron. UR-WRJ stood just beyond it, cordoned off with temporary cones and two security officers—one Slovak, one Ukrainian—flanking the portable stairs.

A few aviation influencers hovered nearby, their phones out, voices lowered in reverence or content-creator glee. One of them was live-streaming. Sarah recognised the voice—some Canadian vlogger who'd made a name in the pandemic by flying around ghost airports and "testing" empty terminals for their ambience.

"Ladies and gentlemen, welcome back to the channel. We are at Bratislava M. R. Štefánik, and that," he panned slowly across the apron, "is the most politically charged A321 in Europe right now."

Sarah rolled her eyes and stepped aside to let a catering van trundle past.

She spotted her Captain for the day already walking toward the aircraft. A young Hungarian named László Székely, wearing a Wizz Air uniform, holding a Sprint ID card and an easyJet labelled suitcase, the same brand as most airline staff across the continent. He waved as he approached, grinning in a boyish, if somewhat fatigued, way that betrayed he'd probably flown three sectors the previous day.

Next to Vil'na Ukrayina, however, was a Sprint liveried A320, G-EZGA, which had once worn easyJet colours, as her registration suggested, but now carried Sprint's palette with a slapdash coat of light blue over the fuselage and a nosecone still in easyJet's signature orange. It was one of those transition jobs that made aircraft look half-finished, as though the plane itself was unsure what airline it belonged to.

László caught up with her near the marshaller's stand.

"Morning! Corfu, right?" László asked, already glancing over his shoulder at the tall red-and-mint fuselage of Vil'na Ukrayina.

Sarah nodded. "Unless Ops has had another moment of inspiration overnight."

He chuckled wearily. "Don't give them ideas. I checked the routing before leaving my hotel—rotation's Bratislava to Corfu, a Luton, and then a Knock."

Knock, Sarah knew, was a dig at Ryanair's obsession with secondary airports, specifically Ireland's less well-known regional hub, which Ryanair had often touted as a point of entry for its low-cost operations. It was an airport that made sense for ultra-low cost carriers like Sprint and Ryanair, who could land anywhere a sheep might graze and still claim it was "just an hour from Dublin."

Sarah snorted at the thought and fell in step with László as they approached the stairs that were next to UR-WRJ, "You know, I saw one of these at Hawarden a couple of weeks ago, when I was doing one of the AvGeek runs to Berlin. You know, because ILA was on. Did you do one of those flights?"

László chuckled. "Yes, I was on the Kirkwall A318 run there. Wildest routing I've ever seen outside of a DHL night shift. Had a group of spotters onboard who applauded every flap setting and one who asked for a signed safety card. You'd think we were flying Concorde." He shook his head, amused. "What did you have?"

"Ex-Alitalia A320, EI-DSA," Sarah replied, climbing the first few steps. "Full and standing, a mix of Airbus folks and some AvGeeks. Oh, and a contingent from the Chester Chronicle."

"Chester Chronicle?" László asked.

"They're a Reach PLC paper that does clickbait headlines such as 'Granny Stuck in Berlin After Jet Mix-Up' and 'Local Man's Sandwich Stolen by Stewardess'," Sarah said with a smirk, reaching the top of the boarding stairs. "They do it so their social media pages go viral, and weirdly, it works. They had a photographer onboard snapping away like we were celebrities. The Airbus PR people were mortified."

They reached the forward galley, stepping into the interior of UR-WRJ, which, despite being fitted with the Recaro SL3510 seats that both Sprint and easyJet use, was still in its Windrose colour scheme: salmon-accented panelling and faux-wood laminate details that felt lifted from a late 1990s Black Sea resort hotel. It wasn't ugly, just jarringly nostalgic – and definitely not on-brand for Sprint.

Overhead bins bore remnants of Ukrainian-language safety notices, and a stray "Дякуємо за ваш вибір" sticker—"Thank you for your choice"—remained stuck beside row 12, curling at the edges. The safety cards had been updated to Sprint's standard trilingual format of English, French and Lithuanian, and were stickers, not paper or card, on the back of each of the headrests, the standard ULCC way of used aeroplane safety compliance rules without wasting a gram on weight or wasting a second on passenger curiosity. Sarah brushed her fingers lightly over one of them as she moved toward the cockpit.

"Kakvo pravish v samoleta mi?" a Bulgarian voice shouted, and Sarah turned to see another set of Sprint crew standing in the galley, a First Officer and a Captain, both looking at her in the way one might appraise an unexpected guest. "What are you doing on my aircraft?"

The older of the two men – wiry, sun-leathered skin, hair like steel wool, four stripes – stared at her with equal parts confusion and irritation. The younger one, maybe mid-twenties, carried the defensive posture of someone who was either inexperienced or sick of being thrown between schedules without warning.

"Sorry?" Sarah responded, switching into her neutral tone, letting her British accent do the heavy lifting of diplomacy. "We're crewed for WRJ to Corfu, László Székely and Sarah Marsh. The Sprint Staff app shows us as being allocated to UR-WRJ for the Bratislava–Corfu rotation," Sarah repeated, holding her phone, which had the Sprint Staff and Sprint Fleet apps on the home screen, the two apps being the standard ones that Sprint and Sprinter used for its crew management system. The two pilots in front of her didn't look convinced.

The younger man – his ID badge identified him as First Officer Ivelin Tsvetkov – peered at her phone, then exchanged a look with his Captain. "That's not what we have," he said in heavily accented English, trying not to sound confrontational. "We were told to prep WRJ for this morning's BGY rotation – Bratislava to Bergamo."

László stepped forward, his tone friendly but firm. "There must have been a change overnight. We've got routing and crew briefing confirmed for Corfu. See—" He tapped his own device and pulled up the same information. "WRJ to CFU, turnaround to Luton, then Knock."

The older Captain scowled and pulled out his own phone. He poked at it with a calloused index finger, then blinked. "This… says Bergamo for us. But yours says Corfu."

Sarah looked and noticed the date on the allocation and saw that it was for the same day, however his allocation had been made the previous night and hers that morning. Looking at his ID, Sarah noticed that the name, Ivan Stoichev, and his language spoken flags, Russian, Bulgarian and English, while hers were English, French and German, were an interesting juxtaposition.

"I'll ring Lithuania Ops," László said, as the plane was under, for the internal European legs, the Lithuanian Sprinter operator's licence. "They should have the final say. Someone's got to know what's going on."

He stepped aside to make the call, pulling out his phone with the ease of a man who had been on the receiving end of roster chaos too many times to count. Sarah watched the exchange between the two other pilots with a mixture of professional curiosity and sympathy. Rostering at Sprint had never been an exact science, especially in the current climate of stretched crews, leased aircraft, and political disruptions. That UR-WRJ was part of the fleet was already an unusual arrangement, and this ambiguity in crew allocation was far from unprecedented, but never easy.

Ivan's jaw tightened as he glanced between László's phone and the Sporadic data on his own. He muttered something under his breath in Bulgarian before glancing back at Sarah. "You're certain about your briefing? This kind of confusion... it's not good for safety or for crew morale."

Sarah nodded firmly. "Yes, I'm certain. The app was updated an hour and half ago, so I should have the most recent version. That said, I agree—this is messy. Let's just get clarity before anyone loads a passenger or flips a switch."

László returned, his phone still in hand, brow furrowed as though he'd just been told Bratislava had been annexed by an IT consultant.

"Right, Stoichev, get off my plane. Now," the Hungarian said with the force of a man who'd spent one too many nights defusing operational landmines and was done playing nicely. "Your fucking plane is EZGA. Didn't you read your fucking roster? You're on that one. We've got WRJ for Corfu and beyond. Ops just confirmed it. End of story."

Ivan's eyes narrowed, but the tired set of his mouth revealed he was no stranger to these battles. After a long pause, he shook his head and stepped back, voice low but edged with frustration, "Fine. But this needs sorting properly. No more of this confusion."

The younger First Officer, Ivelin, gave Sarah a look that mixed exhaustion and reluctant acceptance. "Fine," he muttered. "But this is not how we should be working."

László muttered something under his breath in Hungarian, something that sounded like "bloody amateurs," then pushed open the cockpit door and gestured to Sarah. "After you."

Sarah stepped forward and settled into the left seat, the familiar surroundings of the A321 cockpit wrapping around her like a second skin. The seats, controls, and avionics were a patchwork of age and upgrades. The Flight Management System was a recent retrofit, but the overhead panels bore stickers of Ukrainian Cyrillic script alongside English labels—a reminder of the aircraft's complicated heritage.

László climbed in beside her, plugging in his tablet to sync up the latest briefing packs and NOTAMs. The din of ground operations outside the cockpit was muffled by the thick cockpit door and the steady whir of avionics systems powering up.

"Right," László began, flicking through the tablet. "We've got an early pushback for 1025 local. Flight time to Corfu is 2 hours 30 minutes, cruising at FL360. Winds aloft are a bit variable, so expect a few bumps over the

Adriatic. Ops also mentioned possible slot restrictions at Luton on the return leg, but nothing confirmed yet. Diverts for Luton are for Heathrow, Manston, Birmingham, and Stanstead."

Sarah nodded, as she knew that that the usual quartet of UK alternates were becoming increasingly strained as the summer season approached, particularly given the post-Brexit scheduling clashes and staff shortages. She tapped in her personal authentication to the EFB interface, confirming the final route via the planned flight path down over Hungary, Serbia, skimming the Albanian coast and across into Greek airspace before the descent into Corfu.

"Let me guess, for the Corfu alternates, we've got Athens, Thessaloniki, maybe Ioannina?" Sarah asked, already running the calculations in her head.

"Bang on," said László, dragging a finger across his tablet. "Athens as primary. Thessaloniki secondary, and Ioannina if we feel like punishing ourselves."

Sarah gave a dry chuckle. "Been there, Thessaloniki. Damaged Tornado during Shader. Had to land there as RAF Akrotiri didn't want me damaging the runway with their recovery vehicles. They were busy with a fighter incident over Crete. The stuff you end up doing during overseas detachment." She paused, thinking back on the mission, the heat, the urgency. That was a time when things seemed a little simpler in their chaos. In many ways, the skies above Europe had felt more stable back then, before everything had gotten so... unpredictable.

László nodded knowingly, his face betraying a flicker of recognition. "You were military, weren't you?" he asked casually, flipping through the route charts as if he was reading a familiar story.

"Royal Air Force," Sarah confirmed, her voice softening with the memory of old commitments and an unspoken pride. "You could say the sky was my office back then. Still feels the same now, though the office is smaller. You?"

"101st Aviation Brigade, Hungarian Air Force, Transport Aircraft Squadron," he said. "A319s and Falcons 7Xs. Uncle is a General so I didn't exactly get the hardest postings," László added with a self-deprecating smile, tapping the fuel figures into the FMC. "I've been in and out of Kyiv since 2014 more times than I can count, got out before the shelling really picked up. Flew a few evacuations, some VIPs, some less-than-VIPs. Spent enough nights on concrete slabs under canvas to know I prefer a jump seat and galley coffee."

Sarah offered a wry smile. "It's strange how much we'll tolerate in uniform, and how much we complain about a delayed bus to the terminal once we're out of it."

"Too right," László replied, pressing the INIT button and watching as the flight plan loaded across the MCDU screens. "Although, in fairness, military delays never came with Slovak ground handling union rules, French slot prioritisation, or UK border chaos. Talking about the French, did you see the news this morning?"

Sarah arched an eyebrow as she turned slightly in her seat. "No, I've been avoiding headlines today. Let me guess – another ATC strike?"

"Yes, the Northern sectors, including Brest, Lille, and Paris FIRs. They're on 'work to rule' today, with full strike action threatened from next week if their demands over summer rostering aren't met." László's tone was laced with frustration and resignation as he double-checked the contingency routing. "And yes, our Luton return clips their airspace. So, we've got a lovely little dogleg east if it's active by the time we're coming back."

Sarah muttered something under her breath that didn't bear repeating. "It's not even July yet. This season's already becoming a parody of itself."

There was a knock on the cockpit door and a familiar face peeked in—Marta, the Slovak dispatcher they'd both worked with before. Clipboard in hand, she waved brightly.

"Hello Captain Székely, First Officer Marsh. Just confirming pax count is 174 today, full load. Two infants. One wheelchair. A nice load of up sells from the free small cabin baggage. Nearly £4,000 in overhead bags, plus some hold bags. Catering is fully stocked so the galley carts are bursting. Also—Ops says we need to push on time, because we've got a 30-minute taxi slot constraint out of BTS due to ATC sequencing over Hungary," she added with a grimace. "You've got fifteen minutes. Not a second more."

Sarah nodded, giving her a quick thumbs-up. "Thanks, Marta. All checks underway. We'll be ready."

As Marta disappeared back down the aisle, László finished inputting the final weights and figures. "Looks like we're pushing on time if everyone plays nice."

Sarah flicked through the final pre-flight items: bleed air, packs, fuel pumps, beacon. The familiar symphony of systems waking up always grounded her. No matter how chaotic the roster or ambiguous the airspace rules, the aircraft remained constant. Reliable. Honest.

* - * - * - *

"Luton Tower, this is Ramsgate 3228 Charlie... sorry, old habits. I mean Ramsgate 3228... approaching Lambourne inbound. Requesting vectors for the ILS 25," László read aloud as he transmitted the radio call, his tone calm but tight. Sarah monitored the screens closely, fingers brushing along the FCU knobs as she adjusted their descent profile. The radio crackled in response, the clipped voice of ATC confirming their clearance and sequencing them behind a Jet2 Boeing 757 inbound from Tenerife. Nothing out of the ordinary—yet.

But Sarah's focus wasn't entirely on the descent. The return leg from Corfu had been uneventful in the air, but on the ground, it had been a study in controlled chaos. The Greek ground crews had been overstretched, operating in thirty-seven-degree heat, while Sprint's contracted handling team had double-booked pushback slots, which led to a tarmac stand-off that had delayed their departure by almost fifty minutes. They'd barely clawed back twenty of those minutes en route to Luton, thanks to some favourable tailwinds.

"We're going to be tight on duty time," Sarah said, not looking up from the ND as the green line flicked closer toward the LAM hold. "If there's a go-around, we might bust limits."

Before she could say anything else, the dreaded message from Luton's controller on the radio crackled through the headset:

"Ramsgate 322, be advised: slot restriction now in effect due to staff shortages at Border Control. You are number five in sequence for ILS 25. Expect holding at Lambourne for minimum twenty minutes. Will advise."

László let out a breath sharp through his teeth. "There it is."

Sarah clicked off the transmit switch and flicked her eyes toward the fuel page. "We've got twenty-five minutes extra endurance at this weight. It'll get eaten up fast."

"I've already got the alternates loaded," László replied, his voice calm but weary. "We'll hold for fifteen and then make the call."

Sarah nodded. "I'll notify cabin. Passengers will start asking why we're spiralling over London."

She pressed the PA button. "Ladies and gentlemen, this is your First Officer speaking. We've been instructed to hold near Luton for a short time due to sequencing delays on the ground. We'll update you as soon as we have further information. For now, please stay seated with your seatbelts fastened. We thank you for your patience."

She clicked off, and with a look at László, added, "You'd think June would be quieter. But this? It's not even peak yet."

The holding pattern became a slow aerial ballet above southeast England; their Airbus tracing loops through fragmented cloud layers. Below, Sarah could see the arterial veins of the M25 crawling with summer traffic. Somewhere down there, the same passengers who'd now be watching the seatbelt sign with anxiety would be stuck in customs queues an hour from now, if they were lucky.

Fifteen minutes passed. Then twenty.

"ATC update," came László's voice. "Another ten minutes at least. That'll bust our fuel buffer."

Sarah was already ahead. "Birmingham's clear. Manston's one of our bases, so we've got preferred handling and crew buses," Sarah said, her voice flat with professionalism. "I'd vote for Manston. Luton might clear us eventually, but the clock's ticking."

László nodded, his fingers already flipping through the alternate procedures on the EFB. "Agreed. Manston's quiet, and they're better at managing Sprint than Luton right now. Let me get the clearance."

He keyed the mic. "Luton Radar, Ramsgate 3228 Charlie requesting alternate diversion to Manston due duty time and minimum fuel constraints."

A beat. Then the crackle of weary acknowledgment. "Ramsgate 3228 Charlie, understood. Cleared to Manston direct via Detling. Maintain FL070. Contact London Control 128.1. Good day."

László repeated the clearance back, dialled in the new frequency, and switched. Sarah adjusted the MCDU for the new destination, pushing the modified routing through the system with practised ease.

"Manston it is," she muttered, watching the ND update. "I'll get onto Ops, László, while you finish the route checklists. Hopefully they've got a spare crew for the Knock leg. If not... well, it means that Ryanair has won todays battle on the Knock leg."

****

CHAPTER 19 – Another Welsh Visit
Wednesday 15th June 2022

Hawarden Airport, or Liverpool Chester now as Sprint were calling it in their booking engine, was the same as Sarah last remembered it, the Airbus assembly sheds glinting under a rare slice of North Welsh sun, the whole airfield alive with the distant whine of rivet guns and the low, slow taxi of Belugas as they shuttled wings across Europe. Out front, in the sparse glass and steel terminal, the signage was still a mishmash of Clwyd and Deeside Airparks logos from the nineties, the Sprint Air branding newly plastered in a half-hearted way over old Perspex stands. It was, for all the airline's pretence at rebranding, still Hawarden to anyone with a memory.

Sarah Marsh rolled her tiny hard-shell case through the automatic doors, breathing in the subtle tang of jet A-1 that drifted from the apron, mingling with the faint sweetness of grass and the more pungent waft from the sandwich stand by security. There was something quietly optimistic about the place: a regional airport that had survived the post-COVID massacre of Britain's smaller fields, largely thanks to its proximity to Airbus and its new life as a 'pop-up' for Sprint's ever more ambitious Euro-network.

She paused in the echoey check-in hall, watching as a ragtag collection of passengers—mostly burly men in hi-vis with lunchboxes, some young families with pushchairs, a handful of obvious AvGeeks with camera bags and airline-branded hoodies—queued at the Sprint desks. It was the usual ballet of low-cost chaos: lost bookings, missing baggage labels, the whine of an elderly printer refusing to spit out a boarding pass for a Scandinavian name with too many vowels.

Lane Carlton was on duty at check-in, flanked by Lucy King and a new starter who looked too nervous to speak above a whisper. Lane caught Sarah's eye as she approached, offering a dry, conspiratorial smile— aviation's universal greeting for 'yes, this is absurd, but at least we're in it together.'

"Guten Morgen, First Officer Marsh," Lane said, handing over a freshly printed boarding card. "Or should that be Guten Tag? They've been insisting we brush up on our German for this lot. Some kind of corporate charm offensive."

Sarah knew why, as today, Airbus A321XLR, aircraft MSN 11000, or tail number F-WXLR, was due to do its maiden test flight, the demonstrator that Airbus had built of the ultra-long range variant of the A321, a type Sprint had several, albeit second hand, classic engine ones, as well as brand new and formerly white-tailed neo and LR, Long Range, variants, but never the true XLR. This trip, though dressed as a routine Sprint Air 'Liverpool Chester to Hamburg' rotation, was really an industry junket for Airbus, press, and of course the aviation enthusiasts who had never been to the private airport of the Airbus delivery centre in Finkenwerder, Hamburg. It was the kind of event that happened perhaps twice in a career, if you were lucky or well-connected: a ferry flight masquerading as a commercial one, a rare chance to blend the boundaries between operational normality and industry theatre.

Lane flicked her gaze to Sarah's uniform with mock scrutiny. "You realise the CEO's on this one, right? Not that I'm suggesting you ironed your shirt twice, but I did overhear our esteemed Head of PR, Frankie Mendes, chatting to Ellie Tran from Global Aviation Today. Apparently we're meant to look 'aspirational, competent, and relatable for Gen Z.' Whatever that means. I'm sure if you smile and don't swear at anyone, you'll be fine."

Sarah grinned, accepting the boarding card and bending conspiratorially towards Lane. "If I survive the Instagram crowd and don't spill coffee down myself, I'll consider that a win."

Behind her, a faint commotion by the escalator signalled the arrival of a familiar face: Jeff Young, Sprint Air's CEO, flanked by COO Martina Isleworth, formerly of Wizz Air, CFO Aoife Harrison, formerly of Ryanair, Head of Legal Fernando Costas, formerly of Ryanair, and Head of Fleet Compliance Jennifer Nolan, a former AAIB Senior Investigator who had made her reputation dissecting the sort of operational scandals that usually got other people sacked. The group looked simultaneously over-prepared and utterly at sea, weighed down by lanyards, MacBooks, and the sort of cabin bags that screamed 'exec who never really unpacks.'

Jeff clocked Sarah and Lane at the desk and offered a too-bright, slightly harried smile, the kind he reserved for staff he genuinely liked or press he needed to charm. Martina trailed, phone glued to her ear, dispatching staccato Polish into the ether; Aoife hovered with the cautious presence of someone who had spent her Ryanair years expecting catastrophe; Fernando was already quietly reading the terms and conditions of something—possibly the sandwich stand's allergy policy; Jennifer scanned the boarding area, taking mental notes with the cold precision of a flight data recorder.

A small huddle of journalists—Ellie Tran among them—followed, carrying press lanyards and the slightly hunted look of people who'd had to take the 05:32 from Euston.

Sarah thanked Lane and headed through security, her mind already beginning to compartmentalise: the press, the CEO, the special event and, beneath it all, the routine professionalism of getting a full load safely to Hamburg. She checked her roster app again, confirming her Captain for the day—Ivan Stoichev, who she had last seen in Bratislava when she and László Székely had been assigned to Windrose liveried UR-WRJ, an A321 tribute aircraft named *Vil′na Ukrayina* ('Free Ukraine'), which featured the names of over 1,000 Ukrainians killed in the early stages of the 2022 invasion by Russa.

Security at Hawarden was a sleepy affair. The staff, still in badged-up Deeside uniforms, waved Sarah through with little more than a nod, too busy discussing whether the Beluga was due back before or after lunch to bother with the usual rigmarole. She cleared the airside door, suitcase trailing, and found herself blinking in the pale sunlight of the April morning.

Out on the tarmac, the aircraft gleamed—a brand new Airbus A319neo, one of 5 that Sprint had had delivered, G-WIZZ, its Sprint navy blue being confined to the front, with the Wizz Air pink at the rear and Wizz blue on the tail, with a fresh decal saying "Wizz? Nah, we're cheaper!". The plane had been washed to a mirror shine, and Sarah could see the reflection of the Airbus delivery centre in the curvature of the nose. The boarding steps were already in place, ground crew in high-vis shuttling around with the faintly harried precision that only comes with the threat of visiting C-suite execs.

Sarah paused for a moment at the bottom of the steps, savouring the odd glamour of it all—her own reflection framed by the paintwork's jarring mash-up of corporate identities, a local airport repurposed as a global stage. For a second, she imagined what it must look like to the AvGeeks crowding the fence line, phones raised in anticipation. She offered a small, private wave before stepping up, her shoes ringing crisply against the metal.

The familiar scent of new aircraft—fresh plastic, faint leather, a whisper of jet fuel—greeted her as she entered the forward galley. The cabin was still in semi-delivery trim: sleek new Recaro seats with Sprint-branded antimacassars, USB ports gleaming, and the sort of stillness that comes before a full boarding. Kelsey Norton, today's lead cabin crew, was already present, bent over a clipboard and reviewing the day's seating plan with Alexis, her number two, who was folding Sprint Air safety cards into every pocket.

"Morning, Sarah. You're in early for once," Kelsey said, voice pitched low for privacy, eyes flicking between Sarah and the looming presence of Jeff Young in the background, mid-brief with a suited Airbus representative.

"Had to check Lane hadn't run off with my coffee voucher," Sarah replied, stowing her case and running a hand over her hair, smoothing it with the automatic gesture of a woman who had seen herself on too many passenger TikToks. "Is Ivan here yet?"

"No, he's not. Did you see the decals on the side of this thing?" Kelsey said, and Sarah knew that her colleague was no doubt thinking about the ludicrous branding—half Wizz, half Sprint, all budget bravado. For a brief second, they grinned at the absurdity of it, united in a silent understanding that the airline industry, for all its pretensions to seriousness, was often little more than high-stakes improvisational theatre.

Sarah made her way down the narrow aisle, her shoes whispering on the brand-new carpet. The AvGeeks would love the smell of fresh plastic and the faint, lingering odour of glues not quite cured. The safety cards were so crisp they might as well have come off the printer that morning, the cabin still free of the usual scuffs and tears that passenger service would inevitably bring. She gave Alexis a nod, checked the PA for familiar settings, and found her seat at the front, beside the still-empty left-hand Captain's side.

She took a few moments to ground herself, breathing in the slow anticipation of a day that would inevitably teeter between spectacle and routine. This wasn't a typical day in the cockpit, but it was still a day to fly.

Sighing, Sarah heard the sound of steps coming up the stairs, and she knew who it was.

The arrival of Ivan Stoichev was unmistakable—a tall, broad-shouldered Bulgarian with an ex-military air, his hair clipped short and his walk purposeful. He entered the flight deck with a smile that was more a twitch of the lips than anything warm.

"Good morning," he said in his dry, precise English. "You have coffee?"

She grinned. "Only if you want to make me late for departure. You know how these PR flights go. I hear we're expecting half of Twitter on board."

Ivan rolled his eyes in a display of Eastern European resignation. "Journalists, executives. All usual suspects. The only thing missing is flock of goats."

They ran through their preliminary checks in companionable silence, falling into the old rhythm of a crew who have flown together enough times to require little in the way of unnecessary conversation. The aircraft, for all its newness, performed as expected, systems flicking green, paperwork crisp and unmarred.

"Right, let's do the briefing," Sarah said, reminding herself of the last time she had been here, with the prickly Maksym Pshenychnyi, the former MiG pilot with the Russian Air Force who had told her that he was in charge and that she had to sit there and he would fly, even though CRM dictated that the crew worked as equals. Today, at least, Ivan was old-school, but he was no tyrant. If anything, he treated the job as a shared craft—one to be survived with competence, black humour, and an unspoken understanding of how arbitrary command could be.

She called the cabin crew forward. Kelsey came up, flanked by Alexis and the third member, Jakub, a quietly efficient Czech who had transferred from easyJet. All of them wore that blend of cheerful readiness and slight wariness reserved for flights loaded with execs and press.

"Alright, quick one," Sarah began. "Today's not a normal service. We've got press, the brass, Airbus UK bosses, and a load of AvGeeks," she said, looking at the Sprint Manifest app on the EFB, which contained details of all the passengers, complete with PR notes about allergies, dietary requests, and the preferred angles of certain Instagrammers. "You know the drill. If anything goes wrong, keep it quiet, keep it moving, and let us know immediately. Now, there's a note that Jeff is paying food and drink for all, to the value of £5,000, and that you guys in the cabin are to ring it up on the EPOS and then send it to PR for a reimbursement claim, but frankly, don't get carried away with the Champagne. The last thing we need is another headline about 'budget airline blows five grand on cheese platters'. Just keep the show running, yeah?"

Kelsey smirked, glancing at Alexis and Jakub with an arch eyebrow. "We'll try not to bankrupt the company. Anything else?"

Sarah shook her head, feeling the soft charge of anticipation settling in her stomach—the sense that everything was about to begin, that today would be both spectacle and scrutiny. "Just keep an eye out for any of the journos trying to wander up front. Airbus are bringing an engineering rep onboard, they'll want to do their own walkaround, so don't be surprised if you see someone poking under the seats. Any cabin questions, come find us, but let's keep the flight deck clear unless there's a proper reason. We're wheels up at 08:20, so boarding will start in about ten. Routing wise, we've got a special route, stopping off in Toulouse and then following one of the BelugaXLs from there to Finkenwerder. Air Traffic have got us sequenced between two Belugas—bit of theatre for the spotters.

*_*_*_*

From the cockpit windows, Sarah watched as the world assembled: on the ramp, a small army of high-vis Airbus engineers and Sprint ground staff, brandishing clipboards and radios, conducted their own ballet beneath the wings. Across the fence, the AvGeeks had gathered in greater numbers, pressed tight to the chain link, long lenses and battered DSLRs rising like a forest. In the distance, the pale whale-shape of a Beluga taxied, impossibly slow and grand, a reminder of Hawarden's odd place in the wider world.

"Remind me why we agreed to this," Ivan muttered, running his eyes over the load sheet. "Seventy per cent capacity, half of them journos, all expecting canapés and free WiFi."

Sarah suppressed a laugh, focusing on the tablet propped by her side. "Because Jeff loves a good photo op, and Airbus love showing off their shiny toys. Anyway, at least we're not on a 5am out of Luton to nowhere."

Ivan nodded, eyes sharpening with the old, familiar focus. "Let's see if the shiny toy wants to play ball, then."

They moved through the checklists—cold and dark to fully powered, the aircraft's systems glowing green in the soft light. Sarah felt the click of memory, the old calm that came with ordered preparation: checklists recited, flows rehearsed, every switch and display as it should be.

"Right, the plan is I'm PF and you're PM for this leg, and then for the flight from Finkenwerder to Luton to get back onto the normal schedule," Ivan stated, and Sarah nodded, as she knew that she had indeed been slated to be the pilot monitoring the outbound and flying the inbound. Ivan was thorough as ever, flicking through his own paper checklist, unconcerned by the slightly archaic look when compared to Sarah's pristine EFB, with its glowing apps and notifications from the Sprint Staff group chat pinging quietly away. There was, Sarah thought, something almost reassuring in Ivan's methods—an echo of the time when aviation still had room for human quirks.

As the cabin filled with the muted roar of boarding, punctuated by the clatter of roller cases and the chatter of voices both local and international, Sarah peered through the windscreen at the orderly chaos. The press contingent, marked out by their lanyards and relentless air of observation, clustered by the forward steps, peppering the Sprint PR handler with questions about WiFi, photo ops, and whether they'd be getting cockpit access for that all-important "flight deck selfie." The execs came last, shepherded by Frankie Mendes with the air of someone trying to herd wet cats, their faces set in a blend of anticipation and that peculiar executive anxiety: the sense

334

that something—anything—might go wrong, and that someone would have to answer for it on the Monday morning call.

As the cabin filled with the muted roar of boarding, punctuated by the clatter of roller cases and the chatter of voices both local and international, Sarah peered through the windscreen at the orderly chaos. The press contingent, marked out by their lanyards and relentless air of observation, clustered by the forward steps, peppering the Sprint PR handler with questions about WiFi, photo ops, and whether they'd be getting cockpit access for that all-important "flight deck selfie." The execs came last, shepherded by Frankie Mendes with the air of someone trying to herd wet cats, their faces set in a blend of anticipation and that peculiar executive anxiety: the sense that something—anything—might go wrong, and that someone would have to answer for it on the Monday morning call.

Sarah let her gaze drift to the left, out over the apron to where the Beluga was now stationary, its immense nose upturned, the inside lit by hangar lamps and shadows moving—wings being loaded for a journey across Europe. For a second, she imagined what it would be like to crew one of those: all bulk, all purpose, none of the sleek glamour of the neo but every bit the workhorse of a continent. She resolved, as she often did, to ask one of the Beluga pilots for coffee if she ever had the chance. But for now, there was a job to do—one foot in the theatre of spectacle, the other planted firmly in the routines that made every safe flight possible.

She tuned back into the present as Kelsey pinged the flight interphone: "Cabin ready, first boarding groups coming on. Got an Airbus engineer at L1 asking if he can do the walkaround with Ivan before we get started. He's got a badge."

"Fine by me," Ivan said, already half out of his seat. "You want to join, or shall I leave you with the circus?"

Sarah flashed a wry grin. "I'll guard the bridge. Give me a shout if he tries to steal the pitot covers."

Ivan left, his tall frame disappearing through the galley with the quiet confidence of someone who had performed preflights in everything from 737s to ancient Tu-154s. Sarah settled in, scanning the stream of passengers—press, engineers, execs, and the ever-present AvGeeks. The energy was restless, fizzing with the expectation of something more than just a Wednesday morning out of North Wales.

"Any chance I can have a look inside?" Sarah heard, and she looked from her right hand seat to see a man standing in the doorway, dressed in a high vis jacket with Airbus badging and a Welsh twang. "The name's Pete Granger, and I'm a shift lead for the wing team here at Airbus UK. It was my team who were responsible for this baby's final fit and finish. I grew up five minutes from here and never thought I'd see one of my own bits of work end up on a 319neo. These are as rare as hens teeth, I mean, compared to your A320s and A321s that come through the MRO side here."

Sarah chuckled, as she knew that Sprint's maintenance operations were based here, and that, as Sprint ran the flights in passenger mode out of Hawarden, the ground staff and Airbus engineers often doubled up on roles— one minute marshalling aircraft, the next troubleshooting a minor maintenance snag on a day-old delivery jet. There was something endearingly parochial about it all: a global operation fuelled by the pride of a small, stubborn patch of North Wales.

"Of course you can, Pete. Take a seat—at least until the rest of the circus moves in," Sarah replied, gesturing to the jump seat. "You don't often get to fly on your own handiwork, do you?"

He chuckled. "I'm a bit of an AvGeek to be fair, done nearly a million miles in the air on everything from Yaks to a B-29 Superfortress, and even the Westray to Papa Westray hop in the Shetlands. This flight, ironically, takes me to 1 million miles, if we're going via Toulouse."

Sarah smiled genuinely—she liked the ones who knew their trivia but could laugh at themselves, and there was a warmth in Pete's manner that transcended the usual British reserve. "One million miles, on a bird you helped build. That's a story for the pub if I've ever heard one."

Pete beamed, evidently pleased. "I might even buy the first round myself—if we ever get to Hamburg."

The cockpit settled into a companionable hush, punctuated by the distant shuffling and staccato announcements of boarding. Sarah could hear Kelsey managing the forward galley with her usual brisk competence, shepherding execs and press into seats, fielding questions about WiFi codes and whether the crew would "pose for a TikTok." The energy was half feverish, half childlike—a rare day for everyone, even the regulars.

Ivan reappeared after a few minutes, followed by a slender, balding Airbus engineer with a polite German accent, his badge clipped at a sharp angle, already regaling Ivan with details of fuel trim tanks and the paint thickness on the composite winglets. The two engineers—one British, one German—shook hands in the galley, trading proud statistics and the sort of technical banter that Sarah found oddly soothing. She watched, bemused, as Pete offered the man a hand and promptly began a discussion about spar bolts and the quirks of the A319neo's high-lift devices.

"Right, change of plan," the German said, an Airbus executive. "Your boss has agreed for you to do some formation flying with WXLR at Hamburg when it takes off, as apparently, First Officer Marsh, you were a Typhoon pilot, Ja?"

Sarah blinked in surprise, momentarily off-guard. "That's right—RAF, before the great pivot to budget aviation," she replied, half-awkward, half-proud. It was the sort of thing that usually got a raised eyebrow or, more likely, a knowing smirk among the AvGeek crowd—another military pilot lost to the relentless logic of the passenger schedule. But the Airbus engineer, whose name tag read "Heinrich Albers, Lead Flight Test," only nodded with faint satisfaction.

"Sehr gut. Once you've landed at Hamburg, one of our test pilots will board and give you further instructions. The plan is for you and Ivan to take the controls out of Hamburg Finkenwerder and join WXLR for some gentle manoeuvres over the North Sea—just a demonstration for the press and some photographers. You will have the right seat for the departure; our pilot will be left seat for that leg, and we'll swap again on the way home. It is all cleared, all coordinated. The DLR will be monitoring. We expect only professionalism, you understand?"

Sarah nodded, feeling an electric crackle of anticipation. The idea of flying in formation with the very latest A321XLR, as a former Typhoon pilot, was both a bizarre privilege and a sharp reminder of everything aviation could be, when freed from the treadmill of scheduled service. She shot Ivan a sideways look, only to find him giving her a quick, rare grin—he, too, knew what this meant. This was something to tell at reunions. Or, at the very least, in the WhatsApp group.

The last of the passengers boarded, the cabin doors swung shut, and Hawarden Tower crackled to life in Sarah's headset: "Margate 9974, information Lima, push approved, and—nice to have you with us today, ma'am." There was an undertone of local pride, barely disguised. She could almost see Lane at the gate, mug of builder's tea in hand, grinning from the sidelines.

Ivan ran the before-start checklist with crisp economy, his style a studied calm in contrast to Sarah's barely-contained energy. They negotiated the dance of pushback and engine start, the Leap engines spooling with a soft, newness that suggested barely a hundred cycles.

The flight deck, meanwhile, became an island of quiet certainty: press chattered in the back, execs furrowed brows over emails and PR schedules, but up front it was just the ritual of airmanship, the smell of new carpet and the feel of a yoke that had not yet known trouble.

Sarah's hands moved over the familiar-yet-foreign panels, the air of a cockpit not yet worn in, its switches almost crisp in their resistance. As the ground crew unplugged the headset and gave the thumbs-up, Ivan released the brake, and the A319neo eased away from its stand with a mechanical grace that belied its hybrid paint job. Outside, the AvGeeks pressed tight to the fence caught every moment: cameras lifted, eager faces reflected in a dozen windscreens.

"Hawarden Ground, Margate 9974, push complete, ready for taxi, QNH one zero one three," Sarah called, the radio crackling slightly with the accent of the local controller— one of those small touches that reminded her she was home, even if only briefly.

"Margate 9974, taxi holding point Alpha Two via Bravo, take-off when ready, Hawarden Ground over," the controller responded, his cadence warm with the pride of a regional field made suddenly centre stage. Sarah acknowledged, slotting her finger lightly on the tiller, nudging the nose left towards the parallel taxiway. The aircraft rolled forward, new tyres whispering over concrete patched and repatched by generations of Airbus fitters.

The ramp scenery was aviation at its most surreal: a forest of Airbus tailfins, containers full of wings and pylons, and the giddy press scrum taking photos through every available pane. On her right, Sarah caught Pete Granger in the jump seat still beaming, texting with the speed of a man announcing his childhood dreams in real-time to an audience of WhatsApp groups and, perhaps, his mum. In the mirrors, high-vis vests darted between cones and engine inlets, the choreography rehearsed, the mood lightly electric.

Ivan's hand hovered on the thrust levers, the two of them now working in polished synchrony. Flaps 1 set, trim checked, flight controls full and free. The before-take-off checklist ran like water, every item checked against a landscape both familiar and not.

The cabin PA pinged. Kelsey's voice, strong and professional: "Cabin crew, seats for take-off please."

Sarah caught the brief reflection of Jeff Young in the forward galley, phone already out for a LinkedIn selfie with the Airbus execs behind him. She smiled inwardly; it would be all over the intranet before they'd even reached the Irish Sea.

"Ready?" Ivan asked, one eyebrow raised, his accent lending the question a crisp edge.

Sarah gave a thumbs-up. "Ready when you are, Captain."

Ivan pressed the transmit button. "Tower, Margate 9974, ready for departure Alpha Two."

"Hawarden Tower, Margate 9974, cleared for take-off runway two-two, wind one eight zero at seven knots. Safe trip to Hamburg—and show 'em how we do it in North Wales."

"Cleared for take-off two-two, Margate 9974. Thanks, Tower."

Sarah settled back, hands poised on her side stick. Ivan eased the thrust levers forward, the LEAP engines waking with a subdued, expensive roar. The acceleration pressed Sarah into her seat, the crisp scent of new cockpit plastics rising, the ground spooling past in a patchwork of green and runway grey.

At V1, Ivan's hand slid away; at Vr, Sarah called the rotate, feeling the nose lift, the wings flex and bite into the morning air. The A319neo sprang skywards, their flight arching up over the Dee, across the skeletons of bridges and the old river, flanked by the lumpy hills of Clwyd. On climb-out, the airport shrank below, but she could just see the AvGeeks waving, ant-sized but vivid.

And she loved her job.

****

CHAPTER 20 – The Regulators News
Thursday 16th June 2022

It was the day that everyone was waiting for in the airline industry, the day that the results of the investigations of London European Airways Flight 341 would finally be made public. Even before sunrise, the anticipation felt like a charge in the air: at every airport, in every crew room, WhatsApp group, and pilots' forum, the only topic was the official word from the Air Accidents Investigation Branch, and the European Union Aviation Safety Agency's parallel report.

The fact it was hindered because of the Chinese government's demands, China Nepal Airways trying, and failing due to the CAA blocking the transaction, to buy London European, and that a new airline, Planestation, had instead brought the Air Operators Certificate was only fuelling speculation. Planestation, a ragtag outfit allegedly backed by a YouTuber and Love Island influencer with more brand deals than Boeing orders, had swept in to acquire what was left of the crumpled LEA empire—minus the wreckage and reputational damage. The industry was aghast, not merely at the deal itself, but at the sheer audacity of it.

Sitting in the Muscat Airport crew room, having drawn the lucky chance to be the first Sprint Airbus A321LR flight, MGT7121, between Paris-Beauvais Airport and the Omani desert capital, Sarah noticed that she was the only female First Officer, let alone pilot, in the entire Muscat crew lounge. The air conditioning hummed like an aircraft APU, and the walls, painted a stark shade of white, glared back at her under the artificial light. The other pilots, mostly men in varying shades of navy epaulettes and sun-creased foreheads, were glued to their phones. A group of three Emirati captains were whispering in Arabic near the espresso machine, while a Wizz Air pair in magenta shirts stood transfixed in front of the muted CNN loop on the mounted television.

Sarah leaned back in the vinyl chair, her tablet open on her lap, displaying the EASA press conference timer in one corner, and the AAIB feed in the other. Even though they weren't due to start for another thirty-five minutes, she found herself checking both every few seconds. She didn't need to. The WhatsApp chatter, a mix of Ryanair, Wizz, easyJet, Vueling, Eurowings, Sprint and Jet2 Captains and First Officers were already deafening.

Sarah Marsh: *Anyone else see Planestation's livery reveal? It's like a Poundland knockoff of JetBlue and Monarch had a baby.*

Max Detweiler: *Lol I saw it on Twitter while in the air earlier. The reg is 9H-BBY. They're literally flying clickbait.*

Anka Horváthová: *We're all doomed. I swear I saw a Gucci logo on the tailfin.*

Sarah Marsh: *At least it's not another Ryanair clone.*

Julie Andrews: *Worse. It's Ryanair with a ring light and merch store.*

Miles Cooke: *Press conference countdown now on Sky as well. 28 mins. Anyone watching?*

Hayley Northcott: *I'm stuck on Liverpool to Luton and Luton to Belfast loops all afternoon.*

Sarah Marsh: *I'm due off Muscat to Athens in an hour, so I might be able to catch the first half hour. How's Riyadh, Max?*

Sarah knew that her boyfriend was doing, all week, Germany, Britain and France to Saudi runs, as it was Hajj upcoming, the Muslim pilgrimage season, and Sprint had been routing its flights via Muscat, as, due to a technicality they had agreed for the Hajj season, the connecting flights in Oman to Saudi were being ran as Oman Air flights but with Sprint staff, the Airbus A321LR being the leased core. Most of the passengers didn't know or care. They were going to Mecca, and the safety briefing was in English, German or French for the Europe to Oman sector, and Arabic for the Oman to Saudi sector.

Max Detweiler: *Got 4 hours until the flight back to Muscat. It's a sausage fest here, as all the Oman Air crew are men and I think I just got side-eyed for sipping coffee without three sugars.*

Sarah noticed one of the Vueling Captains was typing, and she instinctively tilted her head forward, as though it might make the message appear faster.

Eduardo Ruiz: *Mate, the livery looks like it was designed in Canva by someone on a sugar crash. It's literally bubble-gum pink and teal stripes. Someone make it stop.*

The group chat flooded with laughing emojis and groans. Someone pasted a low-res image of the livery, showing a wide-body mock-up draped in branding that looked more suited to a cosmetics startup than a scheduled airline. The font was modern but unreadable at speed; the tail logo appeared to be a stylised wing, or maybe a flamingo, depending on the angle.

Sarah snorted quietly, the image of the Planestation livery now burned into her retinas like a migraine aura. She closed her eyes for a moment, leaning her head back against the cold, unforgiving wall behind her. The anticipation in the room was like static electricity— nobody could sit still. Everyone was waiting, for the truth, for justice, or for the scandal to worsen. Maybe all three.

Her smartwatch buzzed gently. Max again.

Max Detweiler: *Just overheard one of the Saudia guys say that PanEuro has the right idea, only allowing men on the flight deck. Almost punched the schweinehund.*

Sarah's mouth tightened into a line, jaw clenching for a moment. She glanced up from the message and instinctively scanned the room again—no sign of Max, of course, but the thought of him stuck in Riyadh with that kind of casual, baked-in chauvinism made her blood simmer. PanEuro's regressive gender politics were already a bitter enough pill, as she had been a Stewardess, not flight attendant, but a Stewardess—lipsticked, girdled, and micromanaged—before finally breaking free to sit in the cockpit where she belonged. And still, the industry tried to remind her that her seat was conditional.

Eduardo Ruiz: *What do you mean?*

Hayley Northcott: *I was at PanEuro and their owners, a bunch of Lords and Rothschilds & Co, wanted to bring back BOAC and Pan Am glamour with people like me looking like flight attendants from the 60s, all girdle and grin. They said it was about "the customer experience." I called it what it was—marketing misogyny. I was a rated A320 pilot and ended up handing out hot towels in heels. @Sarah Marsh was there at the same time as me.*

Sarah read Hayley's reply, her thumb hovering over the keyboard for a moment. The bitter truth in those words, however casually typed, tugged at something raw. She could still picture the exact way her PanEuro blazer pinched at the shoulder seams, how her hair had to be styled into one of three "approved looks", and how Rosemary Havers used to walk through the crew line-ups like she was appraising dolls on a shelf. She quickly typed her response.

Sarah Marsh: *Never forget the time I got pulled up for not reapplying lipstick after landing in Oslo. "Your face is the brand," she said. I wanted to ask if a flare in my face would also be the brand in an emergency.*

A chorus of crying-laughing emojis and shocked faces exploded in the thread. The solidarity—crude, funny, dry—was its own kind of balm. But just as Sarah was beginning to feel the warmth of camaraderie under the fluorescent chill of Muscat's crew room, the AAIB feed updated.

LIVE: Press Conference begins in 20:00

Sarah's pulse jumped slightly at the notice, her eyes flitting to the countdown clock now ticking steadily in the corner of her tablet screen. Twenty minutes. It felt absurd that the culmination of months of investigation, speculation, grief, and grotesque media circus would be ushered in by such a bland countdown. She glanced up again—the room had collectively clocked the update. A kind of synchronised breath passed through the pilots, a subtle straightening of backs, the universal language of "It's happening."

Even the espresso machine, long gurgling and groaning in the background like a senile pensioner, had gone quiet. One of the Emirati captains flicked the CNN screen volume up from mute to a whispering hum, just enough to fill the silence without being intrusive.

Max Detweiler: *Your face is the brand. God, they should've stitched that onto the life vests at PanEuro.*

Eduardo Ruiz: *I didn't know you Krauts had opinions on British airlines.*

Max Detweiler: *Woah, Eduardo, my partner suffered at that prehistoric cesspit. She's a top rate FO now. I'm allowed a few jabs.*

Sarah smiled faintly at Max's defence, but her heart wasn't really in it. The clock was ticking, literally and metaphorically. Nineteen minutes.

Her captain for the Paris–Muscat–Athens–Berlin rotation—a soft-spoken Greek man named Nikos Stavropoulos—entered the room carrying a clutch of papers and a tin of mints. He raised an eyebrow when he spotted her in the corner.

"Marsh. You seen it?" he asked, gesturing with the tin.

"Press conference starts in just under twenty," she said, nodding at the tablet. "Both EASA and AAIB. Going to be a long morning."

Nikos popped a mint, then glanced around the lounge. "You'd think they were showing the World Cup Final in here. Honestly."

Sarah shrugged. "In our world, this is the World Cup Final. Except with more fatalities and worse refereeing."

He chuckled softly, and pulled a chair beside her. "You expecting anything conclusive?"

Sarah hesitated. "I'm expecting... a diplomatic disaster, honestly. They've had the CVR and FDR for weeks. The data's not what's taken the time. It's the blame. I mean, the name of the captain leaked two weeks ago. The thing that gets me is nobody has debunked the rumours that the Captain shouted "Allahu Akbar" before the nosedive. Either it's true and they're scared of the fallout, or it's not and they've lost control of the narrative. I mean, an Arabic name, allegations of claims by Hamas taking responsibility, a single pilot alone on the flight deck, and a media circus with more spin than a Ryanair landing—someone, somewhere, is going to get roasted alive in that press room. It's just a matter of who."

Nikos nodded, thoughtful, his gaze flicking up at the wall-mounted TV as a Sky News ticker scrolled below a photo of the lost LEA jet. "Funny how it's always the industry that pays, not the headline chasers or the suits. What gets me is that the Chinese attempt of buying out London European is the only reason this circus has dragged on so long. If this were an old-fashioned British or German outfit, it would have been a week, maybe two. Instead, we've had four different flag states, six lawyers, and that influencer crowd sniffing around the wreck like it's a photo opportunity."

Sarah gave a mirthless chuckle. "I know. The families must be crawling up the walls. All this time, and no proper closure. Just a new headline every time someone leaks a memo or finds a stray winglet off the coast of Calais."

Nikos nodded. He unscrewed the cap on a small plastic water bottle, glancing at the clock. "Eighteen minutes. What do you reckon they'll actually say?"

"Probably everything except what we need," Sarah replied, tone dry. "They'll tell us what the plane was doing, how many seconds the dive lasted, maybe read out a transcript that'll make the tabloids cream themselves for a week. But what actually happened in that cockpit? My money's on them dodging it until the criminal inquiry is done. Which, conveniently, will be 'ongoing' until no one's paying attention anymore."

Nikos' shoulders rose and fell in a motion that was somewhere between a shrug and a sigh, the world-weary gesture of a man who'd flown through more investigations and PR maelstroms than he cared to count. "And yet, here we are, ready to hear the experts tell us what we already know, or tell us nothing at all."

A ripple passed through the crew lounge as the doors swung open, admitting a pair of Oman Air pilots just off a long-haul from Bangkok, their uniforms immaculate but their faces drawn. They took seats without speaking, setting their own tablets on the low table between them. Sarah realised with a pang that every set of eyes in the room—Emirati, Greek, Spanish, British, German, Polish, a smattering of Asian crews—were now united in a rare communion: waiting for news that would cut across all boundaries of flag, language or uniform.

She checked the WhatsApp group. New messages were piling up. Julie Andrews, one of Sprint's female captains, had just written:

Julie Andrews: I'll bet you 20 euros the words "systemic failures" are used before the first five minutes are up.

Miles Cooke: *I'll take that. I think they'll use "regrettable sequence of events" first.*

Anka Horváthová: *Losers buy drinks next layover in Budapest.*

Sarah grinned despite herself, shaking her head. The banter was both a shield and a release valve. But beneath it lay the same brittle anticipation. She typed a quick reply, promising a drink regardless of the outcome, and glanced back at her own screen.

LIVE: Press Conference begins in 15:00

She took a breath, rolling her shoulders to relieve some of the tension that had pooled there over the past half hour. Nikos tapped his foot, drumming an irregular tattoo on the linoleum floor. The faint aroma of burnt espresso mingled with the sharp tang of disinfectant and air con, a scent now indelibly linked to hours spent in transit lounges.

"I remember after Germanwings," Nikos said quietly. "I was on a layover in Vienna. The look in everyone's eyes, not just the crew but the ground staff, passengers—even the cleaners. Like they were all waiting for the other shoe to drop. This feels the same, but…" He trailed off.

Sarah nodded. "It's worse, because we're all aware now that nothing—absolutely nothing—stops the headlines from getting ahead of the facts. And we've had social media turn every passenger into an investigator. It's exhausting."

She glanced again at the TV. Now Sky was running a package of archival footage: images of the lost LEA A320-211 at Luton, families at arrivals with their faces blurred, crash boats bobbing on grey water. The ticker at the bottom ran.

AAIB & EASA JOINT REPORT EXPECTED. INDUSTRY BRACES FOR FALLOUT.

* _ * _ * _ *

"Well, that was anti-climactic," Sarah said, as Nikos engaged the autopilot. They had just departed Muscat, thirty-eight thousand feet above the burnt ochre and slate-blue Arabian Peninsula, heading west for Athens, and the AAIB press conference had concluded with all the drama of a leaking kettle. Sarah was left staring at her tablet as the live stream faded out, the familiar blue-on-white insignia replaced by a scrolling feed of "Expert analysis" that already felt hollow and repetitive.

Nikos sat back in his seat and gave a low whistle, eyes not leaving the horizon. "At least they confirmed one thing, that it was one man, working alone, and that Hamas and other terror organisations were not involved, but that the "Allahu Akbar" call was what was said on the cockpit voice recorder, and that prior to it, the translation of his speech when the First Officer left the cockpit, was a prayer to Allah for forgiveness and that he intended to end his own life, and that of those on board."

Sarah let out a shaky breath, finally able to exhale something she'd held since the first whispers of the cockpit recording began. The engine's quiet hum and the reassurance of cruise altitude were the only constants left in a world that seemed to have shifted on its axis.

"That's it, then," she said softly, the press conference words replaying in her mind—cold, official, parsed by lawyers, but impossible to blunt. "They said it straight. Suicide by pilot. The same as Germanwings, nearly to the bloody letter. He locked the door, waited for the First Officer to step out, set the descent, said his piece to God, and pushed the nose down. Everything else is noise. You know, I'm glad Sprint, even before we started 2 months ago, insisted on 2 people at all times in the flight deck. We all thought it was overkill, a bit of EASA box-ticking, but... I don't know, Nikos. Today it feels like the only thing that makes sense."

Nikos didn't reply at first, just flicked a glance at the engine gauges, then back out at the clear blue above the

Gulf. The air in the flight deck felt oddly heavy, like something invisible was pressing in on them from all sides. Only the hum of the recircs and the distant crackle of ATC kept it from being total silence.

He said, quietly, "I was just thinking about the families. I mean, it's only been a month and half since the incident, and I've never seen EASA and AAIB leave more questions: how did a man with a brand new airline, new job, pass all the checks and interviews and end up flying an Airbus into the sea? No sign, no warning, no Mayday. Just… faith and despair, I suppose."

Sarah felt a rush of anger, old and sharp, jabbing at her like a needle under the fingernail. "Faith had nothing to do with it. That's what will drive the press now, mark my words. It's not 'pilot mental health' anymore. It's 'radicalisation', 'terror in the cockpit', 'prayers before disaster'. They won't see a human being, they'll see a headline. The fact is, it was a man at the end of his rope, and the rest is window dressing."

Nikos took a moment to respond, clearly weighing his words. "Yes. But the industry will take a hit for it. They'll tighten everything again. Every cockpit door, every background check, every last second of the day. And the families…" He shrugged. "Nothing brings them back."

"I wouldn't be surprised if Air Crash Investigation or Seconds From Disaster have already written the episode for National Geographic," Sarah said quietly, trying to push down the acidic bitterness rising in her throat. She glanced out over the endless blue, where the horizon shimmered in the midday haze. "They'll have CGI, fake voices, probably cast someone who's never been on a flight deck to play the Captain. Cutaways of anxious loved ones in arrivals halls. Maybe even a slow-motion coffee spill. But nothing that actually helps."

Nikos gave a snort that was as much fatigue as humour. "It's always the same template. The narration never changes: 'How could this happen? Was it preventable? Could it happen again?' As if anyone in this job would ever answer 'yes' and mean it."

Sarah tapped her finger absently on the tablet, her eyes flicking over the first draft of the EASA summary as it hit the newswires. Already, the newsfeeds were filling up: BBC, Sky, Reuters, all pushing the same statement out in slightly different fonts. The same quotes, the same careful language.

"We find that the actions of the Captain, operating alone on the flight deck, were deliberate and premeditated. No evidence of external interference, technical malfunction, or crew dispute has been found. The Captain expressed personal distress, alluded to his faith, and used the aircraft as a means to end his life. Recommendations are made for strengthened cockpit access policies, further mental health screening, and a review of operator oversight for new market entrants."

Sarah's stomach tightened. "They never learn," she muttered. "Or maybe they do, and just don't know how to stop this from happening again. We all get another form to fill, another psych consult, another audit from someone who's never flown more than a jump seat. But the problem—the actual human problem—never gets solved. Only shuffled around."

Nikos was silent, letting the hum of the autopilot and the steady tick of the master caution silence between them. At last, he spoke, his tone gentle but brittle: "We can only do what we can, Sarah. We fly. We look out for each other. We watch our own six. And if something feels wrong, we speak up."

Sarah nodded, but the reassurance rang hollow. Her phone buzzed, the WhatsApp group exploding as the first press clippings began to circulate.

Julie Andrews: *Called it. "Systemic failures" and "regrettable sequence of events" in the first two minutes. Miles, you're buying the first round in Budapest.*

Miles Cooke: *They're saying the airline's HR had 'no reasonable suspicion' the Captain was struggling. No red flags. He passed all his checks. Everyone's blaming 'pressure of launch' and 'market uncertainty'. How do you even measure that?*

Eduardo Ruiz: *Our union just issued a statement: 'All flight crew are reminded to utilise peer support channels if feeling stressed, pressured, or otherwise unfit to fly. We support the recommendations of the AAIB and EASA in prioritising mental health and cockpit security'.*

Sarah thumbed out a quick reply, the words almost automatic.

Sarah Marsh: *At least we've all still got jobs, for now. Anyone else notice Planestation just quietly posted an ad* *for new Captains? I'll bet my old PanEuro girdle* that they're sifting through CVs as we speak.

A flurry of reactions—laughing emojis, a thumbs up from Hayley, the odd sarcastic gif. Underneath, though, everyone was in the same stunned place: hearts heavy, heads spinning, hands still on throttles and checklists, because there was no time to stop and process—not in aviation, not in 2022.

Nikos broke the silence, voice softer now. "You know, when I started flying, it was supposed to be a passport to the world. Adventure, freedom, all that. But it's mostly just waiting for regulators to drop another hammer."

Sarah shrugged. "At least the view's still decent. That's about all they can't take away with a committee."

They let the quiet settle, the aircraft eating up the miles to Athens. Every so often, Sarah's mind replayed the now-inevitable media storm—commentators dissecting the Captain's background, the airline's corporate culture, the meaning of every offhanded remark and personnel record. She wondered whether any of it would lead to real change, or if it would just become another layer of defensive bureaucracy for future pilots to trip over.

Suddenly a notification on the Sprint Staff app came up.

Ops Alert: ⚠ *All crews scheduled to operate in and out of German, French, UK, or Irish airspace: please ensure strict compliance with updated cockpit access protocols as per EASA directive. Two-person rule in force at all times on the flight deck. Crew scheduling will contact you regarding any required operational changes or*

357

additional staff. Brief all cabin crew. Any questions to be directed to your base supervisor. Further updates to follow.

Sarah stared at the notification, its bland corporate tone belying the tremor it sent through every airline group chat from Luton to Larnaca. It was official, then—the reactive swing of the regulatory pendulum, carving new lines through rotas and SOPs. She could already imagine the next month: last-minute roster changes, delays for 'crew availability', whispered complaints in airport Starbucks queues, all while management pointed to compliance as both shield and cudgel.

She thumbed a reply into the internal Sprint WhatsApp group, half-distracted.

Sarah Marsh: And so it begins. Wonder how long before the tabloids start shrieking about "dangerous foreigners" and "woke airlines".

Max Detweiler: *They already have. Bild just ran a headline: "Faith or Failure? Inside the Mind of a Disaster Pilot". About as subtle as a Ryanair boarding call.*

Julie Andrews: *Meanwhile, Planestation's influencer-CEO just posted a TikTok saying "safety is our number one priority" from the back of a G-Wagon at Luton Signature. The circus has no intermission.*

Sarah let the banter flow past her, the black humour a kind of ambient white noise. She reached up to the overhead panel, adjusted the cockpit temperature a notch, and let her eyes rest on the endless Mediterranean blue ahead.

Somewhere below, a line of ships stretched from Suez up towards Crete, their wakes crisp against the water. In another life, she'd have found it beautiful.

But the world was different now. Everyone was a potential story, everyone a candidate for scrutiny. It didn't matter that she'd passed psychometric testing, annual checks, endless interviews. The next tragedy might just be waiting for the perfect storm.

She glanced at Nikos, who was quietly updating the flight log. He caught her look and gave a weary, knowing smile. "We get through today, Marsh. That's all any of us can do."

She nodded. "And hope the industry gets it right for once. Not just paperwork and panic."

* _ * _ * _ *

Athens airport shimmered under a dry, relentless sun as Sarah and Nikos taxied their A321LR to a remote stand. It was mid-afternoon by the time they shut down the engines and handed over the aircraft to a Greek Sprint relief crew, the cockpit still humming with residual heat and the sharp tang of aviation fuel drifting through the open hatch. Sarah peeled off her headset and flexed her jaw, only now realising how tight her muscles had become through the entire flight. She shot a glance at Nikos, who was unstrapping with the practiced efficiency of someone who'd spent decades climbing in and out of flight decks.

"Coffee?" he offered, voice hoarse but kind.

"Only if it's not whatever's in the crew room vending machine," she replied, forcing a smile as she gathered up her bag and logbook.

As they stepped onto the tarmac, the blast of Athenian summer hit them square in the face, making Sarah blink. The ground handler, a wiry man with a two-day stubble and a battered high-vis vest, gave them a polite nod before waving a marshaller's baton at a distant follow-me car. Around them, the stand was alive with the chaos of a midday rotation: baggage carts rattling, catering trucks reversing with shrill alarms, and the slow, circling ballet of ground staff in their patchwork of Sprint and local contractor uniforms.

They crossed to the shuttle bus, the familiar ritual of transition between world and world: airside to terminal, pilot to just another body moving through the heat. The bus was already crowded with crew—Sprint, Aegean, Ryanair—a riot of accents and postures, but every face wore the same look: tired, and wary, and just a little bit lost.

Sarah found a seat and checked her phone. The 'All Airlines' WhatsApp groups had detonated again.

Hayley Northcott: *Gatwick security just briefed all crew: "no media comments, no opinions, no nothing." Our briefing rooms look like a police station. Everyone's jumpy.*

Julie Andrews: *Just had our safety manager in Budapest say if we even so much as look at a journalist, we're off the next four flights. Said with a straight face. Never seen* *the place so tense—half the Lufthansa lot look like they're waiting for someone to be frogmarched out by the Polizei.*

Eduardo Ruiz: *Vueling has issued a memo saying no cockpit visits, no flight deck jump seats for off-duty pilots from other airlines "until further notice." A load of Ryanair FOs got sent back to the terminal at El Prat, you should have seen the strops.*

Miles Cooke: *I've got passengers in Manston security demanding to see "the pilot's CV and criminal record" before boarding. The queue behind them lost it, but security just called Rainsford and quietly moved them on.*

Sarah couldn't decide whether to laugh or groan. Every story felt like a new detail in the slow unravelling of the ordinary world of airline operations. The bus jerked to a halt outside Terminal B, and Nikos gave her a faint grin as they joined the stream of high-vis jackets and battered flight cases up the steps into the arrivals hall. The temperature inside was barely cooler than outside, the air thick with body heat and cheap perfume, but the bustle was familiar. It felt—if only for a moment—almost like aviation before all this.

They parted ways at the international crew channel, with Nikos heading off to the canteen, as they had both finished for the day. Sarah paused just before passing through security, catching sight of herself in a fingerprint-smeared mirror. She looked tired. Older. But also, a little surer of herself, if only because, after the endless churn of industry crisis and personal setbacks, she was still standing.

She walked towards the all airline crew room, badge swinging, shoulders set.

Inside, she found Hayley Northcott already slumped on a bench beneath a creaking air conditioner, iPad on her knees, coffee cooling untouched beside her. Sarah knew that her friend and EasyJet First Officer was preparing for her final sector, an Athens to Gatwick, where she'd then finish for the weekend, having done 5 days on the trot, and looked exactly like someone who'd spent the week fielding both press speculation and nervous cabin crew.

Hayley looked up, eyes red-rimmed from tiredness or the relentless blue light of back-to-back news cycles.

"Hey, you ok?" Sarah asked

"Not really," Hayley said, and Sarah could tell that something was about to spill over, the sort of not-really that meant the difference between just another long-haul and the moment you started to unravel. "Theo and I broke up, we had an argument about 10 minutes ago, here in the canteen. Turns out he's been told that if he wants to keep his job at PanEuro, he needs to, quote from his new base manager, 'ditch the easyJet bitch', and he said that he didn't want to, but he... he loves me and he loves flying, and 'PanEuro is still paying slightly more than the ULCC crowd and I need the money right now'. He told me that he still loves me, and that's what hurts the most."

****

CHAPTER 21 – Worries
Friday 17th June 2022

Sarah was feeling worried for her friend, as she lay in her hotel in Athens, having woken up an hour earlier, the hotel room still dim with the gauze of morning light leaking past blackout curtains. The air-con ticked rhythmically overhead, and her crew-issued white duvet was rumpled around her ankles.

The words that Hayley had said yesterday, that her fiancé, Theo, had been pressured to choose between his career at PanEuro and his relationship, haunted Sarah. She couldn't shake the image of Hayley sitting under that rattling air conditioner, her fingers curled around the paper cup of cooling coffee, tears pricking the corners of her eyes but never falling. It wasn't just heartbreak—it was betrayal by an industry they had both clawed their way into, only to be told they didn't belong unless they followed the script.

And then there was her own relationship with Max. That, despite them both being employees of the same airline, that she was theoretically Manston based, and he was Berlin based, being a German national and a freelance contractor tied to Sprint's EU AOC, had begun to strain under the weight of bad rosters, endless operational chaos, and the creeping fear that anything stable in their lives could be revoked by an Ops alert or a reg change.

Sarah sat up slowly, the sheets clinging to her legs as if reluctant to release her. She checked her phone. 06:07. No new messages from Max. She tapped through to the internal crew group—banter, memes, a complaint about vending machine coffee at Beauvais, and an Ops memo about additional post-flight reporting. Nothing personal. She hesitated for a moment, then messaged him:

Sarah Marsh: Morning. Hope Muscat–Berlin was smooth. Missed you last night x

No ticks yet. He was either asleep or still airborne. She dropped the phone on the duvet and swung her legs to the floor. The room was too quiet. A moment later, the kettle clicked on. She hadn't touched the hotel breakfast buffet in three layovers—lukewarm eggs and suspicious sausages had never appealed, but this morning even the thought of a Nescafé stirred with a plastic stick felt like ritual.

Suddenly a ping from the WhatsApp notification sounded. She snatched up the phone faster than she meant to, her heart leaping in that ridiculous way it always did when she thought Max was on the other end.

Max Detweiler: *Sorry, Liebling, I got delayed arriving in Berlin, as Omani ATC decided to stop the plane just as we were taxiing at Muscat. Seemed we had a passenger who was wanted by the Internal Security Service.*

Sarah stared at the message.

Her first instinct was worry—serious delays and ISS involvement weren't exactly routine, even by Sprint's chaotic standards. Her second was a familiar flicker of resentment. Once again, Max had been swept into the absurdity of operational mess beyond their control. Even when they weren't flying together, the job always had its grip on them.

She typed back, fingers quick.

Sarah Marsh: *What? Was it a serious issue? Are you okay?*

The message ticked twice almost immediately. He must have still been holding the phone. A pause. Then the typing bubble appeared.

Max Detweiler: *Ja, fine. The guy had fake docs and they yanked him just as we were entering the runway. Police boarded. Took 2 hours. Cabin crew had to reseat everyone. And of course, the AC was off during the whole thing, so we were baking in uniforms. I'm at the flat now. You?*

Sarah let out a breath she hadn't realised she was holding.

Sarah Marsh: *Athens. Still in the room. Hayley's not okay. It's worse than she said. Theo told her management gave him a "choice." Stay at PanEuro or keep dating her.*

Max Detweiler: *When I see that warmduscher, I'm going to put his clipboard somewhere it'll never pass security.*

Sarah smiled despite herself. The word—warmduscher—was Max's go-to insult for anyone cowardly, overly delicate, or unwilling to take a stand. Literally, it meant "someone who only showers with warm water." In aviation terms, it was someone who never called out bad procedures, never risked rocking the boat—even when the boat was clearly taking on water.

Sarah Marsh: *It's not all on him. He's scared, Max. You know how PanEuro operates. They dangle the glamour and then gut you the minute you step out of line.*

Max Detweiler: *Ja. But threatening someone's job over who they date? That's beyond retro. That's Soviet.*

She thumbed a reply but paused, glancing around her room as if it might offer wisdom. The tick of the air conditioning had become white noise, its rhythm oddly reminiscent of a VOR beacon. She leaned back onto the bed, phone resting on her chest, eyes tracing the cracks in the ceiling paint.

She thought about Hayley again. Her friend's soft Kentish accent cracking at the edges, her long fingers curled tightly around the paper cup. The same Hayley who had flown gliders in cadet school, soloed a Cessna at seventeen, earned her A320 rating just in time to be furloughed mid-pandemic, and had ended up forced into PanEuro's performative, girdled farce of glamour— because it was a job, and jobs were scarce.

Sarah's phone vibrated again.

Max Detweiler: *You're on the rotation that ends at Dundee today, ja?*

Sarah Marsh: *Yeah. Athens to Dusseldorf, DUS to London City of all places, and then LCY to Dundee. Got an A318 for all those. Then tomorrow I start at Aberdeen. You?*

Max Detweiler: *My day ends at Aberdeen, and tomorrow starts at Dundee, so if you fancy it?*

Sarah chuckled, as she knew what Max was proposing, and she smiled, as the schedule gods had done something that she honestly hadn't expected in weeks: given them one night in the same city, without deadheading, delays, or overnight minimum rest blocking the way.

Sarah Marsh: *Sounds suspiciously like fate. Assuming Ops don't reroute you to Reykjavik or something.*

Max Detweiler: *If they do, I'm flying there via Dundee and taking you with me. Do you know what route Theo is doing today?*

Sarah sighed, as she remembered Hayley saying that the Brummie First Officer for PanEuro was returning on the 0712 PanEuro service to Manston, then a Dubai from Manston. She knew that Hayley had told her he was being put on the longer runs that PanEuro did for the next week, mainly from the Kentish airport or Birmingham.

Sarah Marsh: *Think he's doing Manston–Dubai on the A321LR. Hayley said he's getting stitched with all the ultra-long duties to keep him out of their new use of Gatwick. Keep him away from her, basically.*

Max Detweiler: *That's not crew planning. That's emotional manipulation with an IATA code.*

Sarah didn't respond straight away. She rolled off the bed, dragging the hotel-provided robe around her as she padded over to the kettle. The ancient plastic machine wheezed as it worked, and the little complimentary sachet of instant coffee seemed more medicinal than appetising. Still, she stirred the granules in with practised indifference and wandered back to sit on the bed, mug in hand.

The thing was, Max was right. About Theo. About PanEuro. About all of it. The rot in the industry wasn't in the mechanics or the aircraft or even the training. It was in the culture—this quiet, consistent erosion of dignity and autonomy masked with words like "service excellence" and "brand alignment."

She tapped out another message.

Sarah Marsh: *Hayley said he still loves her. Told her that. But that he needs the job more than the fight. That she's strong enough for both of them.*

Max Detweiler: *That's not love. That's cowardice dressed up as practicality.*

Sarah Marsh: *I'm worried about her. I mean, I know Hales is a strong woman. Hell, she showed Hargreaves who he really was at 38,000 feet. But even the strongest people crack when the hits just keep coming. First, they take your cockpit, then your voice, then your dignity— until all you're left with is a smile that doesn't reach your eyes and a role that was never yours to begin with.*

She stared at the screen for a moment, her thumb hovering. Then she added:

Sarah Marsh: *She doesn't deserve this. None of us do.*

Max didn't reply immediately. The pause stretched long enough that Sarah assumed he'd gone to sleep, finally crashed out after the ordeal in Muscat. She didn't blame him. The weight of the last twenty-four hours was still pushing down on her chest like unvented cabin pressure.

Outside the window, Athens was beginning to stir. A haze hung low over the distant skyline, the kind of sun-baked shimmer that blurred everything like bad reception. Somewhere, a scooter buzzed past, and she heard a distant dog bark. The real world, annoyingly persistent.

Max Detweiler: *You know, my sister is a relationship counsellor. If Hayley is fine with it, I could get her to call or text. Sometimes it's easier with a stranger, no? Especially one who doesn't work for an airline, and knows when not to give a 'company line'.*

Sarah smiled, grateful for Max's practical streak. She knew Hayley would almost certainly refuse—Hayley was stubborn, proud, and allergic to being pitied—but it was still the right kind of offer. And it made Sarah feel a little less alone in the gloom.

Sarah Marsh: *I'll ask her, thanks. Means a lot. You get some sleep. I'll message when I'm through Dusseldorf.*

She set the phone on the pillow and closed her eyes for a moment, letting the white noise of the air conditioning fill the room. But her mind refused to settle. Instead, she was replaying the last twenty-four hours on a loop: the buzz of phones, the blunt force trauma of the AAIB report, the flat, professional voice of the EASA spokesperson on her tablet. The ache of a friend's heartbreak, and the sour taste of how little control any of them had over their own fates.

But the worry for Hayley's mental health, especially the day after the results of the preliminary investigations of London European Airways Flight practicalities of her own day—the logistics of getting through Greek security with a mountain of paperwork, the dance of uniforms in the lobby, the ever-present risk of another operational hiccup—she kept circling back to Hayley. Had she even made it out of Athens last night? Was she sleeping at all, or simply turning things over in her head, spiralling as so many pilots and ex-pilots did after yet another blow from an industry that refused to let them simply be?

She took her coffee to the window and parted the blackout curtains an inch. Athens, hazy with June heat, was already alive: cars honking on the distant avenues, the first coaches pulling up for a transfer of Norwegian or Ryanair holidaymakers. Out beyond the rooftops, a haze blurred the horizon where the city gave way to the sea, and somewhere, above it all, was the invisible web of departures and arrivals, slots and slots missed, that defined her world. She pressed her forehead to the glass, letting the cool seeping from the pane ground her.

She checked her phone again—still nothing from Hayley. Sarah considered calling, then thought better of it. Hayley would reach out when she was ready. For now, the best thing was to keep moving. The rituals of airline life, as artificial as they could be, offered at least a kind of comfort: checklists, lanyards, ID cards, all the small affirmations that you still belonged somewhere, even if it was only in the purgatory of another day's flying.

She dressed quickly, her Sprint uniform hanging in a neat arc on the back of the bathroom door. It still felt surreal—hers, but not hers. The cut was too straight, the synthetic fabric unyielding against the sticky air. She fixed her hair in the mirror, thinking briefly of her and Hayley's old stewardess look: the endless panicked checks for flyaway,

370

the three "approved" styles, the endless tyranny of "face as brand". It felt like a different world now, but Sarah knew it wasn't really over—not for Hayley, not for any of the women still in those uniforms.

She checked out of her room just after 07:00, the lobby thick with the smell of burnt filter coffee and a fresh consignment of stressed easyJet cabin crew waiting for their shuttle. She saw no sign of Hayley, which was both a relief and a worry. Outside, the heat hit her like a wave, and she was glad of the sunglasses tucked into her flight bag.

"Mind if I jump on board?" Sarah asked, as Sprint, like Wizz and Ryanair, had their crews use Ubers or local taxis outside selected airports unless rostered to be bussed directly. The van parked outside was half-full already, an older Aegean First Officer climbing in as she approached.

The driver, a middle-aged man in a yellow hi-vis that had clearly seen too many Athens summers, gave her a nod. "Sprinter, yes? Going to Elefthérios Venizélos?"

"Yup," she replied, swinging her flight bag into the back and clambering into the middle row, wedging herself next to a Bulgarian Sprint cabin crew member she vaguely recognised from a shared Budapest layover a month earlier.

The ride to the airport was spent in silence, apart from the occasional beep of WhatsApp and the soft hiss of the driver's radio playing bouzouki music. Sarah stared out at the blur of concrete apartment blocks and tethered satellite dishes as they passed, the smell of warmed vinyl from the van's interior taking her back to hundreds of similar mornings: cities that always felt too big when you were too tired, hotels that blurred into each other, and the long mental runway required just to feel awake enough to speak to ground handlers.

Her phone buzzed again—this time from the Sprint Staff app.

Sprint Ops Alert 07:14: *Athens–Dusseldorf, MGT034, now gate B14. Aircraft N592EL. Slight delay due ATC slot. Crew briefing to begin 07:45.*

Googling the aircraft tail number, she noticed that it, and some of its siblings, had been owned by Aerovías del Continente Americano, and had spent three years in store at Pinal County Airpark prior to Sprint rescuing it at a discount. It was still half-wrapped in peeling blue tape, the navy blue Sprint livery overpainted with a hurried hand, betraying its past life with ghosted lettering and the faded outline of a condor's wing on the forward fuselage. Sarah shook her head—no one in management seemed to care that half the fleet still looked like it had been put together in a hurry during a monsoon. But, as every Sprint crew member said with a wry smile, "if it flies and the toilets flush, it'll do."

The van wound its way around the tangled traffic of the airport perimeter, swinging past a long queue of buses spewing German and British tourists onto the kerb. Sarah clambered out, pulling her flight bag after her, and made her way across the baking tarmac towards Crew Security. She clocked in with a quick beep of her ID badge, the security guard barely glancing at her before waving her through, eyes on the tiny television showing early morning football highlights.

Inside the crew room, a clutch of Sprint and Ryanair pilots were already gathered, uniforms at various stages of disarray, coffee cups in hand, their voices low and tired. Sarah spotted her Captain for the day, a softly spoken Dutchman named Koen Verstappen, reviewing the NOTAMs on his iPad. He glanced up as she entered, gave her a gentle smile, and gestured for her to join him.

"Morning, Sarah," he said. "Have you seen the refurb that they've done on 592? Looks less Avianca and more easyJet but our navy blue."

Sarah gave a quiet chuckle, settling into the chair beside him and pulling out her own tablet. "I saw. Someone in paint shop must've been told 'do your best with what we've got'. The condor on the nose is still visible under the Sprint logo. Looks like the bird's just had a midlife crisis and changed airlines."

Koen smiled, a warm, paternal expression that Sarah had come to appreciate over the past few rotations they'd flown together. He was a good Captain—calm, unflappable, the sort who could land in a storm and still have time to compliment the cabin crew's announcement. She'd taken to thinking of him as "Captain Decaf"— steady, mellow, and unlikely to get anyone jittery.

"ATC slot's holding us until 08:20," he said, sliding a weather briefing her way. "North German low pressure is bottling the airways. Dusseldorf's already showing sector delays, and they've bumped a couple of Lufthansa heavies into holding before us."

Sarah scanned the sheet. Standard summer mess—too much air traffic, not enough airspace, and every second airline trying to make up for two years of pandemic losses in one frantic quarter. The METAR showed patchy cloud and crosswinds in DUS, but nothing exciting.

"I'll get the load sheet once we're airside," she said, flipping to the crew manifest on her tablet. "It's mostly German package tourists today. A few PRMs and one UMNR—young girl flying solo to meet her grandparents in Neuss."

Koen nodded. "Good. Always makes the flight feel more human. I'll check on her once we're boarding."

Sarah smiled faintly. He always did that—checked in on unaccompanied minors personally, offered parents an extra moment of reassurance, took that extra thirty seconds in the chaos of the turnaround to remember there were lives involved, not just seat counts. It was rare. It mattered.

They sat in silence for a few moments, tablets glowing on the desk, the low murmur of other crews building behind them. Outside, the heat shimmered on the apron, and she could just make out the silhouette of 592EL baking in the sun, its A320 shape a familiar silhouette now distorted by its messy repaint.

Koen broke the silence.

"I heard about London European. The report."

Sarah gave a short nod. "Yeah. Everyone has. It's... a lot. No one really knows what to say."

Koen exhaled through his nose. "We're all thinking the same things. 'Could it happen here?' 'Would I spot it?' And then... you try not to think about it."

"Yeah," Sarah murmured, tracing a fingernail across a dent in the desk. "And the problem is that it doesn't go away. The whispers, the rumours, the next tabloid angle. It just... lingers. Like smoke after a fire."

Koen didn't say anything to that. He didn't need to. The truth hung in the air like jet fuel on a humid ramp—unmistakable and cloying.

Their gate call came a moment later: B14 ready for crew boarding. They gathered their gear and made the slow walk down the polished corridor, past vending machines blinking with half-working LED screens and faded Ryanair safety posters. Sarah fell into step with Koen, her flight bag rattling behind her.

"Did you ever fly with anyone you thought might... do something like that?" she asked suddenly, her voice low.

Koen glanced sideways at her. "No. But I've flown with a lot of people who were barely holding it together. Fatigue. Divorce. Money stress. Most of the time, they're just... surviving. You can smell it, sometimes. Like fear. But it's not always visible. That's the thing."

Sarah nodded slowly, absorbing the words.

At the gate, they were met by the rest of the crew—an enthusiastic young Irish purser named Keira, a Polish flight attendant called Jakub who'd previously flown with Enter Air, and a Greek junior named Lydia on only her third week. They were a decent bunch. Keira gave a bright if slightly too-loud hello and began reeling off special meals and seat maps. Jakub checked the galley equipment list with the glazed expression of a man already mentally halfway to his next layover. Lydia hovered behind him like a nervous intern at a high-stakes surgery.

"Apparently this baby bus has only come out of Broughton last week, and has the 'refurbished inside' smell of freshly installed seats. It did a RAT9767 from Broughton to here yesterday with 20 pax, all AvGeeks," Keira remarked as they headed to the walkway, as their stand was a remote one, despite being a standard gate.

They stepped onto the sweltering apron, the concrete already radiating heat through their soles, and made their way to the waiting A320. Even at a distance, Sarah could make out the patched-over logos and hasty painting. She felt a momentary surge of affection for the battered airframe, a sort of kinship: both of them showing signs of too many transitions, too much covering up and moving on.

The walkaround was already underway; a Greek ground engineer was pacing under the starboard wing, clipboard in hand, occasionally stopping to prod a panel or squint up at a static port. Koen did a full circuit, murmuring to himself as he checked for oil leaks, bird strikes, anything that would delay the already sluggish morning. Sarah, meanwhile, ducked up the rear airstairs to stow her bag and check the cabin.

Inside, the refurbishment was basically the 2-2 seats took out of the cabin and replaced with 3-3 standard, all-economy rows, the Recaro SL3510 slimline seats still smelling faintly of plastic and glue. The irony, Sarah knew, that they were brand new seats, the same as easyJet's standard seat, but where the orange on the headrests should have been, there was the Sprint and Sprinter navy blue.

"Looks like someone's gone full IKEA with the refit," she muttered, trailing her fingers along the edge of a seat.

"You know what I love about AvGeeks on fresh metal?" came Koen's voice from behind her as he stepped into the forward galley, "They'll notice the tiniest screw out of place, but you could put the wings on backwards and as long as you call it a 'retrofit' they'd still write a blog post about it. I've just checked the electronic paperwork for this, and it's just come out of a C check at Broughton, but the engineer says half the galley panels are still the original Colombian spec—so if the coffee tastes of Bogotá, we'll know why."

"Coffee or the other famous export from Colombia?" Sarah quipped, grinning as she peeked into the galley trolley, half-expecting to find a brick of something better suited to a Netflix docu-series than an in-flight service. "Either way, it'll keep the crew awake."

Koen smirked. "Let's hope it's just the coffee. Last thing we need is a 'discovery' on final approach. Would ruin the on-time stats, even for Sprint."

Keira, overhearing, giggled nervously. "If we get raided on arrival, I'm hiding behind the AvGeeks. They'll livestream the whole thing before anyone even opens a Customs door."

The crew finished their checks, and Sarah found herself, as always, doing a quick, private sweep of the flight deck. She ran her hands over the familiar panels, letting the reassuring tap of switches and the slight give of the throttles ground her. A new plane—new to them, anyway—always had a different feel, and this one was no different: the screens were slightly less scuffed, the FCU buttons a tad stiffer, the scent of fresh plastic mixing with faint, ingrained sweat of thousands of past sectors.

As boarding was called, Sarah left her bag by the jump seat and helped Koen finish up the last bits of paperwork. Keira was at the front, greeting the early boarders—one, sure enough, an AvGeek in a full Lufthansa retro T-shirt, camera at the ready, excitedly quizzing her about the aircraft's tail number and previous operator. She handled it with the patience of someone who knew how to channel enthusiasm into manageable energy.

Boarding was brisk, even with the inevitable German holidaymakers hefting cases twice the size of the overheads. Sarah stood by the L1 door, helping the slow movers and watching for anything out of the ordinary—a habit from years of flying, sharpened further by the undercurrent of anxiety following the London European tragedy.

As the last passengers took their seats, Sarah nodded to Keira. "Looks like a full house. Any dramas?"

"Just one passenger moaning about the seat pitch—says he's flown first on Turkish and expects the same. I gave him a free bottle of water and a copy of Sprint's inflight magazine. He'll live."

Sarah smirked. "That's more than most airlines give for 'inconvenience'. We're spoiling them."

They finished the final checks—doors armed, crosschecked, PA made. Koen ran the briefing with the same unhurried calm he always brought to the role.

"Today's flight to Dusseldorf should be smooth. There's some patchy weather on descent, but nothing to worry about. Sarah, you're pilot flying; I'll handle radios out of Athens."

Sarah nodded, appreciating the trust. The slow taxi to the active gave her a few precious moments to take it all in: the whine of the engines, the shifting light across the fields beyond the airport, the gentle hush that fell as the cabin settled into the lull before take-off. She found it comforting, this liminal space between ground and sky.

****

CHAPTER 22 – Rail Strikes? Nah, Sprint Extras
Tuesday 21st June 2022

The queues at Gatwick Airport, Sarah noticed, as she arrived for the first flight of her day, a whole day of the same rotations, Gatwick to Luton, was all the way to the car parks, the coach station, the rail station and even into the low concrete bowels of the multi-storey, past the echoing stairwells and the sticky tarmac where staff buses offloaded another crop of shift workers. It was, she thought, a particularly British species of chaos, full of silent frustration and threadbare patience, the collective resignation that made even the most spectacular infrastructural collapse resemble a queue for a sale at John Lewis.

The reason?

The National Union of Rail, Maritime and Transport Workers strike had called a national walkout, shuttering the main arteries of Britain's commuter system. From Glasgow to Portsmouth, trains were thin on the ground, station concourses were either deserted or swamped with the desperate and the lost, and all across the South East, those who usually drifted in by rail now flooded the roads, motorways choked by dawn, and every airport became a temporary encampment for those who'd calculated that flying—even to somewhere as uninspiring as Luton— might get them at least halfway to where they needed to be.

Sprint, in their infinite wisdom, had introduced half hourly flights between every neighbouring UK airport, from flights between Glasgow and Edinburgh, Manchester and Leeds, Liverpool and Manchester, as well as the usual Gatwick to Luton shuttles it ran to balance fleets and allow line training for new First Officers it was onboarding daily from across Europe and beyond. The Sprint extras—these strange, slightly absurd domestic legs—had been advertised as "Britain's Fastest Rail Replacement," which Sarah thought was pushing it. She watched as Sprint's signature crowd, a mixture of weary commuters, aviation geeks, and the odd hopeful business traveller, mingled among the usual Gatwick masses: families, hen parties, lost Americans, clusters of unsupervised children with bags twice their size.

In the staff channel, the jokes had started hours before: memes of Dash-8s in place of Southern Electrics, doctored timetables with A320s slotted between Thameslink services, and screenshots of real passengers gamely asking ground staff, "Where's the ticket barrier for the Luton express?" The mood was both desperate and oddly gleeful. The railwaymen's walkout had become aviation's windfall.

Sarah tapped her lanyard on the scanner, stepped through the staff gate, and braced herself for the first of 8 round trips, all between Gatwick and Luton, the first one leaving the blocks at 03:04, three hours before the scheduled first "real" departure of the day. The night air inside the terminal was dense with too much oxygen, the sort of artificial air that made your nose itch and your brain slightly foggy. It was, she thought, an odd hour to be awake, let alone preparing to fly a brand new Airbus

A319neo up and down M1's air corridor, like a glorified bus driver with wings. She stifled a yawn, feeling the lack of sleep right in the sockets of her eyes, and wondered—not for the first time—why she had ever left the far more predictable world of risking being shot down by Russian MiGs or stopping a Sukhoi from entering the UK's airspace, for a career where the main threat was now being trampled by hen parties wielding inflatable genitalia and staff who'd been awake since before the first coffee shop had even switched its machines on.

Sarah moved with professional purpose, weaving through the crew security lane, nodding at the guards who barely looked up from their phones, and greeting the uniformed Sprint staff gathered by the airside Costa, all clutching paper cups and red-eyed from the 2am start. Her Captain for the first two legs, a Swiss Captain named Lukas Egger, had the unmistakable air of someone who'd been operational since before breakfast was invented, his uniform so crisp it looked bulletproof, eyes pale as arctic glass above a surgical mask. He gave her the faintest nod—a gesture somewhere between fatigue and Swiss neutrality—and she fell in beside him as they walked the length of the South Terminal, past still-shuttered duty-free shops and cleaning staff performing their dawn ballet of bin-bag changes and industrial mopping.

The pre-flight briefing was mercifully short. Lukas, reviewing the manifest on his tablet, noted the first two flights were "full—full in the way only Brits travelling in adversity can fill an aeroplane." Cabin crew, three strong for the A319, included Lucy—one of Sprint's finest at handling stag parties with an iron fist and an arch smile. She was already fielding questions from a pair of off-duty rail workers in high-vis, both clutching printed tickets bearing railway branding, blinking with the bewildered hope that maybe, just maybe, someone would honour them on a flight.

"Will we be offering the 'replacement bus service' today, or just the usual?" Lucy deadpanned, as Sarah scanned the load sheet.

"If the coffee machine's still working, it'll be more than Thameslink managed," Lukas replied, the faintest flicker of a smile beneath his mask.

They moved out to the aircraft, G-EASY, Sprint's parody of the easyJet livery with the Sprint navy blue replacing the white, and the easyJet orange carrying Sprint's fleet names. On the L1 door was a cartoon of Stelios Haji-Ioannou counting money and a speech bubble saying "Easy? No, SleazyJet" coming from beneath his painted grin.

Suddenly Sarah heard footsteps behind her—hurried, hard-soled, and punctuated by the unmistakable jangle of keys on a lanyard. She turned just in time to see easyJet's Base Manager steaming, the face furious, and Sarah knew instantly what it was.

The livery of G-EASY, a plane which she had flew in on RAT013 the previous night from Broughton, where it had, at 12pm, been released from Sprint's MRO following a pre-delivery B Check, a form of aircraft check that is thorough enough to require most of a day, but not so invasive as to strip the interior. The irony it was one of 5 Airbus A319neos, as the plan was a block time of 30 minutes, and 36 minutes turn around, to allow for padding and recovery in case of inevitable, incremental delays—this fact alone would have been enough to get any airline manager's blood up, even before the branding wars started.

"Marsh! Whose idea was this?" The easyJet Base Manager's accent was somewhere between Croydon and fury, as he jabbed a finger at the plane's comic artwork. He looked like he wanted to summon all the gods of Civil Aviation Authority and turn them loose on Sprint.

Sarah tried her most neutral smile. "It was like this when we got it. Came straight from Broughton—Ops said it's above my pay grade."

Lukas, ever the diplomat, interposed himself. "It's all in the spirit of competition, I'm sure. Shall we… board, Sarah?" His tone implied, with subtle Swiss menace, that any further discussion would be about as productive as arguing with ATC during a French strike.

The Base Manager grumbled but, realising he'd get more sympathy from an automated check-in kiosk, stomped off. The aircraft, still gleaming from last night's polishing, was already being surrounded by rampers loading bags and herds of passengers forming a restless, shuffling pen at Gate 14. Sarah glanced at the aircraft's odd blend of Sprint and easyJet branding and, not for the first time, marvelled at the oddity of post-pandemic British aviation.

With paperwork signed, they stepped into the chilly hush of the jet bridge, oxygen and anticipation mixing with a waft of industrial cleanser and coffee from Lucy's galley prep. Boarding began—a procession of early-morning faces, puffy-eyed, dogged, carrying bags, commuter backpacks, laptop cases, and, in one notable instance, a full box of Krispy Kreme doughnuts balanced precariously atop a suitcase. Lucy managed the flow with near-military precision, offering wry encouragement to the less confident and reining in the overeager.

At 02:49, with a full load aboard, every seat taken by holidaymakers who want to get to Luton, Sarah made her pre-departure checks, the cockpit alive with screens and the low hum of ground power. The FMS was programmed for the shortest legal hop: climb to FL120, cruise for all of twelve minutes, and then descend straight back in for Luton. The route itself had become a meme among pilots—the "Faster Than Thameslink Shuffle"—and Sarah found herself repeating the rhythms of set-up by rote. Weather at both ends was VFR but with a risk of early-morning mist, and the NOTAMs scrolled endlessly, a litany of minor runway works, taxiway closures, and, at Luton, a temporary coffee shortage in Crew Room 2.

Lukas ran through the checklist with her, precise and quietly reassuring. As they requested pushback, Sarah glanced out at the surreal dawn: a horizon painted orange by sodium lights and the high, rolling banks of queuing passengers, like a flood waiting for a breach in the dam.

"Gatwick Delivery, this is Ramsgate Niner Zero Zero One, stand 113, ready to depart from stand to the taxiway for Luton," Lukas called, and the familiar ballet of ground-to-tower began.

As they were parked on a remote stand, and the taxiway was in front, Sarah knew that there would be no need for a tug, as the A319neo was primed for self-manoeuvring, one of the small mercies of an early rotation. She released the parking brake as the marshaller signalled clear, and eased the throttles forward just enough to bring the aircraft crawling off stand, the familiar hum and vibration thrumming through the airframe. The morning was already stirring to life—Ramp Control barked clipped instructions over the radio, baggage tugs weaved between refuelling trucks and bleary-eyed ground crew, and above it all, the silver hulls of long-haul aircraft gleamed, haloed by the first hints of a midsummer sunrise.

G-EASY rumbled toward Alpha taxiway. Lukas handled radio, his clipped English betraying a hint of Germanic rigidity, and Sarah followed the centreline lights with the ease of muscle memory, counting the rhythm of every sway, every imperfection in the tarmac—a pilot's sixth sense, honed over years and thousands of take-offs from various airports, and in Sarah's case, RAF stations.

The passengers, no doubt, were too tired or too British to notice the liminality of this moment: wedged between the tiredness of rail chaos and the incongruity of flying to Luton before sunrise, a journey that, by rights, should have been a train ride of Wi-Fi dead zones and broken air conditioning. Instead, they found themselves inside a nearly silent, climate-controlled Airbus cabin, barely awake, the subtle theatre of safety demonstration unfolding in English and Polish and, for reasons only known to Sprint's compliance team, occasionally in Dutch.

The irony that they were the only flight taking off due to the noise abatement restrictions at this hour was not lost on Sarah. Gatwick, normally silent before 6am save for the odd cargo 777 or delayed long-haul, now played host to a singularly British farce: a near-full A319neo packed with commuters desperate enough to substitute aluminium for iron rails, all made possible by a national strike that had paralysed the country's ground transport but turned the skies into a lifeline for the marooned.

"Want to hand fly the cruise phase, Marsh?" Lukas asked as she taxied short of runway 08R, G-EASY's nose poised at the holding point, floodlights glaring white across the wingtips and the distant fence-line shimmer of the motorway. Sarah grinned—a silent thanks for the trust, a relic of her RAF days when 'keeping your hand in' wasn't just a nicety but a necessity.

"Only if you're sure?" Sarah said, knowing that the autopilot would only be on for a few minutes.

Lukas gave a dry little nod. "It's your sector. Take us to Luton as if you're late for a scramble."

Sarah smiled at the memory—scrambles over the North Sea, in a world so sharply defined by risk and reward, and now, this odd form of civilian service, flying commuters between airports so close together that most passengers would spend longer waiting at baggage claim than actually airborne. Still, a flight was a flight, and professionalism was the only thing that separated the absurd from the dangerous.

The radio squawked. Gatwick Tower, clipped and businesslike: "Ramsgate Niner Zero Zero One, line up and wait, runway zero eight right."

Lukas acknowledged, and Sarah guided the A319neo onto the centreline, the big engines whisper-quiet at idle, nosewheel gently bouncing over the faint ridges left by a million previous rotations. She let her eyes roam across the familiar litany of flight displays—the PFD, the ND, engine gauges all green—and out past the nose, where the runway stretched out into the wan blue haze of pre-dawn. Behind, the terminal was a muted beehive, and ahead, the freedom of a slot with nobody else queuing. A rare moment of clear airspace over London.

"Cabin ready, Lucy?" she called, voice light. Lucy's reply came over the intercom—cool, unruffled. "Cabin secure, ready for departure. Good luck, drivers. See you in Luton."

Sarah grinned, feeling her energy finally catch up with the situation. Lukas's hand flicked over the panel, arming the auto-thrust, and she wrapped her left hand around the sidestick, right hand steady on the thrust levers.

"Ramsgate Nine Zero Zero One, cleared for take-off, zero eight right. Winds calm, good luck up there."

Sarah advanced the levers to flex, feeling the familiar surge of acceleration. "Thrust set," she confirmed, keeping the jet on the line as the numbers flicked past—50 knots, then 100, then the satisfying rumble as rotation speed approached.

"V1… Rotate."

She eased back on the sidestick, the aircraft's nose rising obediently into the thinning darkness. For a moment, there was only the sound of air and speed and the quick, perfunctory clatter of the undercarriage retracting. Beneath them, the runway fell away and the lights of Gatwick, the endless ribbons of motorway, and the clustered queues seemed already distant.

The climb was brief—a lazy arc northwards, rising above the fog-bound suburbs of Crawley and Redhill, then over the M25, where headlights shimmered in endless, frozen traffic jams. Sarah kept the hand-flying crisp, feeling out every tremor in the controls, remembering for a moment the freedom of a Typhoon in reheat, but modulating it for the stately, reassuring inertia of a commercial jet. Lukas, calm and precise, handled the comms, reading out the climb instructions, fielding the smooth, businesslike handover to London Control.

"Direct DVR, maintain flight level one two zero. Expect descent in two minutes."

Sarah looked over at him, grinned. "That was the world's shortest climb."

He gave her a look of weary amusement. "If only the Swiss Alps were this flat, eh?"

* _ * _ * _ *

By time Sarah got to her final sector, it was just after 1pm, and the flight from Luton was completely full and crewed by a new shift—as she was now on G-BRDY, an Airbus A321LR in a parody livery of Virgin Atlantic, with a cartoon of Richard Branson dressed as the Scarlet Lady.

Lukas had gone on to do a Euro loop, as he was now line training a junior First Officer on the Amsterdam rotation, but the Gatwick–Luton shuttle, however, showed no sign of losing its manic edge. Sarah's captain for the second half of the shift, a Aberdonian named Fraser Maclean, had joined her for the previous one and half loops, and he was set to go on his break when they arrived at Gatwick on this final sector of her day.

The irony, Sarah knew, of the Sprint navy blue body with a Virgin Red tail, the Sprint name in the Virgin logo style as if it were a parody tribute act, was not lost on any of the ground staff, least of all the Virgin Atlantic dispatcher at Gatwick who'd taken a selfie with the aircraft on stand and then spent most of the turnaround making increasingly facetious suggestions for slogans Sprint could paint on the next delivery.

She listened as the final load of passengers bunched and squeezed their way up both sets of air stairs, both at the L1 and L2 doors, the cabin with a mingled fug of perfume, deodorant, and that particular odour of tired, slightly damp British commuters who'd already spent too long in a queue. The last passengers, a family with an enormous folding buggy and a weary grandmother, shuffled in as Paul Ryan, the Lead Flight Attendant for this flight, ticked them off with brisk efficiency.

"Luton Tower, this is Ramsgate Niner Four Zero Eight," Sarah said as she was, for this leg, the pilot monitoring, and therefore responsible for the radio and the checklists, while Fraser took the role of pilot flying. Their rapport had settled into that low-burn camaraderie typical of professionals working on minimal sleep and surplus adrenaline. Fraser, a man of few words but infinite patience, flicked switches with quiet certainty, calling for each checklist item with the studied calm of someone who'd once flown out of Aberdeen in snow squalls and lived to find humour in London's chaos. "We will be ready for departure in zero eight minutes, over."

As the stand, like every other one Sprint used, was a remote stand, a bus stand, she knew that passengers had already been shuttled out in waves, chivvied along by ground staff who wore that battered, stoical look peculiar to British aviation ground crews on a day of national crisis. Each bus unloaded its allotment, and as soon as the last passenger stepped off, another arrived to take its place, until the apron was alive with the awkward choreography of bag-laden commuters shuffling towards their airborne 'rail replacement'.

Sarah took a moment at the foot of the steps, feeling the weight of the day in her limbs—a cumulative fatigue that was as much psychological as physical. She climbed the narrow metal stairs and entered the forward galley, exchanging a few words with Paul about the passenger mix—mostly commuters and stranded students, one large group of off-duty railway engineers apparently determined to treat the flight as a flying social club. She could already hear the laughter and the clatter of tins; there would be policing to do, but Paul was well-used to herding the unruly, and she trusted him implicitly.

The cockpit was a welcome haven from the clamour. Fraser was already running the preliminary checks, his voice steady as he read from the QRH and double-checked the weather, NOTAMs, and flight plan. The brief for this sector was perfunctory: short hop, fair weather, moderate winds at Gatwick, nothing significant except a mention of "possible traffic congestion" on arrival. The irony of congestion in the air, mirroring the ground gridlock, was not lost on either pilot.

Fraser handed her the printout from the dispatcher. "Turnaround on schedule, load sheet's done. Another full house, naturally. That's a grand total of 196 souls, plus four cabin, two flight. It's like the Edinburgh Fringe, this route."

Sarah raised an eyebrow. "At least nobody's turned up in fancy dress yet."

He grinned, that brief flash of Aberdonian mischief brightening his otherwise austere demeanour. "Wait until the night sectors. I heard there's a hen party who mistook this for the Luton–Palma."

Sarah allowed herself a dry chuckle. "Let's hope they don't try to storm the cockpit looking for the duty-free gin trolley, then."

"Wouldn't be the first time," Fraser replied, settling back in the left-hand seat, eyes flicking between the FMS and the departure clearance scrolling across the ACARS printout. He was the kind of Captain who moved at the pace of calm inevitability, as if every sequence in the cockpit were a note in a larger, invisible symphony of routines, checks, and silent judgments.

With the cabin doors closed, the hum of air conditioning and PA chimes mixed with the muffled banter of the passengers behind. Paul's voice carried through the interphone as he delivered a safety briefing, his tone alternating between officious and sardonic. He concluded, as ever, with a gentle warning about not crowding the forward galley— "especially if you're looking for train connections."

Sarah ran through the before-start checklist, fingers moving with brisk efficiency. She checked the APU bleed, confirmed the hydraulics, and watched the gentle glow of system lights flicker through their paces. Fraser called for pushback, and the ground crew—wiry, sunburnt, battered from hours of shepherding passengers—gave the signal. The A321LR, so recently re-liveried it still gleamed, juddered softly as the tug pulled her clear of the stand.

"Push complete, brakes set," Sarah reported, feeling the familiar swell of anticipation and focus that came before each take-off.

"Engine start sequence, please."

She spooled up the number one, watching the EGT rise, then number two. Each step performed with the ease of a thousand repetitions—yet, she reflected, never quite boring. There was always that faint edge of risk, the knowledge that the systems could surprise you, that aviation, however routine, was never entirely domesticated.

Behind them, Paul's PA crackled again. "Cabin crew, prepare for departure. And yes, we will be flying over Watford. No, you cannot get off there."

The taxi out was a study in patience. Luton, overwhelmed with the chaos of the strike, had stands and taxiways stuffed with aircraft that didn't belong, diversions from Birmingham, Stansted, even the odd regional jet from further afield, all squatting on whatever tarmac could be found. Ground gave them an interminable route via every corner of the airfield, the A321 weaving through a tangle of winglets and tired pilots, every one of them waiting for their own moment to escape the madness.

Fraser, hands steady on the tiller, navigated them with laconic precision. "Suppose we're lucky not to be at Heathrow," he said, more to the cockpit than to Sarah. "I heard they've got aircraft backed up onto the perimeter."

"At least we're moving," Sarah replied, checking the brake temperatures. "If this were King's Cross, we'd still be under the clock, fighting pigeons for a place in the queue."

Their clearance finally came: "Ramsgate Nine Four Zero Eight, line up and wait runway two-six."

Sarah scanned the final items. Flaps set, spoilers armed, trim checked, auto thrust ready. Fraser's hand moved to the thrust levers.

"Ready?"

She nodded, voice steady, betraying only the faintest trace of fatigue. "Ready. Let's get this circus moving."

He advanced the levers smoothly, the A321LR's engines spooling with a muted roar. The aircraft surged forward, heavy with the weight of a full cabin and the day's accumulated weariness, and Sarah felt the subtle ballet of acceleration—weight, thrust, the judder as the main gear left the tarmac.

"Positive climb. Gear up."

The aircraft soared above the sprawling confusion below, leaving behind the tangle of parked jets, coned-off stands, and endless bus convoys. For a few blessed moments, the sky was theirs, the A321LR slicing through clouds as effortlessly as any long-haul flight, even if the total distance to Gatwick was less than a hop over the Channel.

They reached their cruising altitude almost as soon as they had left it, Fraser's hands moving over the autopilot panel, engaging the systems. Sarah stared out at the sunlit patchwork of southeast England, M1 crawling below, lines of lorries and stranded motorists stationary as far as the eye could see. Down there, thousands waited for trains that would not come. Up here, they moved—quickly, surely, and just a little bit smugly.

****

CHAPTER 23 – Heathrow Chaos at 3:15am?

Wednesday 14th July 2022

The Britannia Connect Boeing 737-600, TS-IOM, that was parked on the runway, right opposite the Sprinter liveried Airbus A320neo, G-SPTT, that Sarah was sitting in—the 737's nose wheel ripped off, the runway, 27R, now with a nice hole where the strut had gouged through tarmac and aggregate—looked almost theatrical in the sodium lights. Like an airliner caught mid-faint, its nose had crumpled downward in a slow-motion collapse, fuselage sagging with the grace of a drunken stage actor in a tragic finale.

Sarah exhaled slowly, her headset pushed back onto her curls. It wasn't often you saw a full runway occupancy event like this—especially not at Heathrow. But 2022 had been rewriting aviation rules daily. Sinkholes delaying Sprint's launch from Manston, French ATC strikes, disruptive passengers, even SCAT Airlines trying to cause chaos at Almaty by flying with what looked suspiciously like an expired MEL and a captain who had trouble finding the overhead panel dimmers.

It was, Sarah decided, as if it was if the ITV series Airline, which had chronicled in the late 90s and early 2000s the rise of easyJet and Britannia, had merged with Black Mirror and been handed over to the writers' room from W1A for the reboot. She half expected a drone to drift by the 737's stricken nose, streaming a live TikTok breakdown of Heathrow's most recent descent into chaos, complete with a parody voiceover.

But here it was: 03:15, high summer, and the busiest runway in Britain was closed, thanks to a new Britannia causing chaos, flight BTA034, callsign Britannia 034, from Gibraltar to Heathrow, another new post-COVID ultra-low cost carrier that had, like so many others, appeared overnight and begun bending every rule in the Civil Aviation Authority's book. The fact that their six-hundred-series 737 was Tunisian-registered, as it was wet leased from Tunisair Express, added only a further layer of farce. Sarah could almost feel the collective migraine radiating from Heathrow's airside ops, not to mention the inbound pilots now fruitlessly holding at Lambourne and Ockham, hoping for a slot that would never come.

She glanced at her captain for the shift, a Pakistani born, Bradford resident, Koen Abbas, who was rifling through the NOTAM printouts with an expression that suggested he'd seen this sort of carnage before, though probably not quite so close to home. Koen had the phlegmatic air of someone who'd spent a decade at Pakistan International Airlines, then hopped his way through half a dozen AOCs from Islamabad to Jeddah, before winding up in the maelstrom of British low-cost carriers. He had the gentle stoop of a man accustomed to long hours in bad seats and endless layovers in anonymous airport hotels, and—unlike most captains Sarah had flown with—never felt the need to fill silences with platitudes. Instead, he quietly examined the latest AFTN updates from ATC, eyes flicking from the runways map to his notes, the light of his iPad reflecting back a dozen contradictory instructions from London Control, Eurocontrol, and Sprint Air's own Ops.

"We'll be here a while, Marsh," Koen muttered, folding the NOTAM into a precise rectangle and tucking it away in his flight folder. "That's two hours before they can even get the main runway patched. Maybe longer if they haven't got the aggregate on site. Good news for anyone trying to land at Stansted." He didn't smile, but the corners of his eyes creased with a dry, Yorkshire-inflected humour that cut through the drowsy gloom.

Sarah reached for her cold coffee, glancing at the terminal across the apron, where ghostly blue light shone on the empty jet bridges. The flight, MGT2321 Heathrow to Ibiza, had been one of many sectors of their shift, starting off in Luton, heading to Dresden, Palma, Zurich, Heathrow and the final two legs, Heathrow to Ibiza, then Ibiza to Manston, where they'd finish the day and another crew would take over for the final 4 hours of the planes day.

It was ironic, Sarah knew, that she was doing lates all week, starting at 5 or 6 in the afternoon London time, and not finishing until after dawn the following day—her body clock was a mess, her sleep debt incalculable, and her WhatsApp unread count had long since climbed beyond the point of anxiety. Sprint Air's self-styled "Sprinter" rosters were, like the airline itself, a half-joke, half-threat. "Chasing the dawn across Europe," one of the marketing emails had once boasted. More like running from sleep, Sarah thought grimly, pulling her Hi-Viz a little tighter over her arms in the cockpit chill.

"We're going to have to either go back to the stand and get on the APU," Sarah said, sighing as she watched the fire engines putting a fire out on the number 2 engine of the

737, its fire crews continued to hose down the right-hand engine, steam curling up into the humid July night like wisps from a ruptured kettle. There were smears of retardant on the runway now, pink and white trails curling back from the remains of the Britannia 737's collapsed nose gear, and it gave the whole scene a surreal, over lit feel. A sort of theatrical disaster diorama—if Heathrow had a museum of 'what could go wrong at 3am', this would have been its centrepiece.

Koen leaned back slightly in his seat, glancing across at Sarah again. "APU's probably the only way we'll keep from freezing or baking in here. I mean, we've got a full flight, as what self-respecting stag wouldn't fly at stupid o'clock for £9 and an early arrival into the Med?" he replied, voice a low rumble, rich with both sarcasm and resignation. "I'm going to say that if we're here for a few more hours, then we'll have to call FTL and log a delay for crew rest anyway. We can't take this out and risk a fatigue report; not after that London European thing a couple of months ago. You know, this reminds me of when I was at PIA. Half of our crews were unlicenced, half were asleep, and the other half were technically dead, if you checked their rosters. Do you want to know the true reason why we were banned from the UK and EU?"

Sarah gave a half-smile. "Let me guess. Something to do with your actual number of halves being three?"

Koen's laughter was low and gravelly, like a car starting in winter. "Marsh, you were meant for Sprint. Your sense of humour is wasted anywhere else." He glanced once more at the chaos beyond their windscreen, where the battered 737-600 continued to command the spotlight.

Airside vehicles inched around it, their orange strobes catching in the slicks of foam and oil glistening on the tarmac. Distantly, a Heathrow Ops van bounced along the taxiway, its radio crackling faintly through the cockpit's partially open window. For a moment, the air felt thick with anticipation, a pause in the music before the next discordant note. "The truth is that at PIA, the management knew that some of the pilots had expired or no longer valid licences, but the real sin was that nobody cared until the EU said something about it. We were flying old Boeings into airports where the only NOTAM was 'good luck'—and half the time, someone was repainting the runway numbers while you were on final."

Koen then sighed. "I did a flight as a young First Officer between Islamabad and Skardu in Baltistan. It's a high-altitude airport in the Himalayas where you circle in over the valley, surrounded by snow peaks, and you're relying on rumour more than radar. The joke was, if you could find the runway through the cloud and survive the crosswind, you deserved to keep your licence for another year. We landed once in a sandstorm so thick we used the cabin crew's torch out the window for the taxi, because the landing lights just made it worse. The Captain was... well, let's just say he didn't have a valid medical, but he did have a direct line to a cousin in Islamabad ATC. After we taxied in, the ground crew clapped. Not for us, you understand—for the fact the plane came back at all. Different world."

Sarah snorted, a warm, involuntary laugh rising above the low thrum of cockpit avionics. For all the bureaucracy and endless FTL calculations of British low-cost flying, there was something in Koen's stories—a hint of romance, disaster and gallows humour—that made her grateful for her own relatively mundane career path. Even now, sat in the dim cockpit at Heathrow, chaos unfolding on the runway, she felt oddly at home.

Her mobile vibrated against her knee. WhatsApp—Max, predictably, wide awake on a Manchester stopover, his roster equally masochistic.

Max Detweiler: *Seen Heathrow on FlightRadar? Looks like a spaghetti junction. You stuck in the queue for the world's longest Costa?*

She smiled to herself and tapped back a quick reply.

Sarah Marsh: *More like the set of Casualty, airline edition. Britannia's noseguard's in the next postcode. A little Baby Boeing.*

Koen raised an eyebrow. "Boyfriend?"

"Sort of," she replied. "He's on MAN–TFS–MAN–BER–LCY tonight on one of Sprint's A318s. I don't think he's seen a bed in three days."

"Ah, the A318, weird little bus with the heart of a lorry and the arse of a minibus," Koen supplied, and they both chuckled—a sound oddly muffled in the early-morning hush that pressed against the cockpit glass. Even in a moment of enforced idleness, Heathrow had a sense of theatre, a backdrop for disasters minor and major, farce and farceur. And at 03:15, with the sodium-vapour lights and the fractured reflections on puddled glycol, it all felt a little unreal. "I was on that rotation last week. I prefer the late runs to be fair."

Sarah didn't answer immediately. Instead, she sat back in her seat, feeling the faint hum of G-SPTT's standby electricals through the frame, watching the drama out on 27R with the practiced detachment of the professionally knackered. Somewhere deep in the terminal—an echoing cavern of escalators, vending machines, and security doors—a janitorial team was probably making its first sweep of the night, headphones in, unaware or uncaring of the chaos unfolding yards beyond the glass. The world of passengers and the world of crews overlapped only at check-in and baggage reclaim; here, sealed off from the public, the cockpit felt almost monastic.

Koen busied himself with the overhead, thumbing the APU master switch to ON, the satisfying clunk and muted fan noise a comforting sign of autonomy. There was something oddly grounding about small rituals—fuel checks, ACARS messages, resetting the clock, folding the same NOTAM four different ways. In an industry so dominated by automation and remote instruction, the cockpit was still a space where people, rather than systems, ultimately bore the weight of consequence.

The lights in the cabin flickered, stabilising as the APU came online. Sarah could hear the cabin crew at the forward galley, faint voices over the interphone: Marija, the senior, was running through her own checklist, her English accented by Vilnius and years of cheap coffee.

"Marsh, you want me to brief the pax, or you fancy a go?" Koen asked, flipping open the PA selector. "They'll want to know why we're sat here sweating into the seat cushions at three in the morning."

Sarah shook her head. "You do it. I'll only end up telling them Britannia have put their nose where it doesn't belong."

Koen snorted. "You know, most airlines would kill for your bedside manner." He pressed the PA button and let his voice fill the airframe with calm, practiced clarity. "Ladies and gentlemen, this is your captain speaking from the flight deck. As you may be aware, there's been an incident on the runway involving another aircraft, which means we're unable to depart until the authorities have completed their checks and the runway is cleared. We're working with Heathrow ground staff and our own operations team to keep you updated, and we'll get underway as soon as possible. In the meantime, our crew will begin a Buy on Board drinks service, and we'll keep the air conditioning running so you're comfortable. Thank you for your patience, and we'll update you again in thirty minutes."

He flicked the PA off and grinned. "There. No one can accuse us of underselling the drama."

"Only at Sprint would that be considered a calm night," Sarah replied, stretching. She rolled her head, trying to ease the stiffness out of her neck. It was always these waits—uncertain, indefinite, between duty and rest—when fatigue crept up on you. She considered, not for the first time, that aviation was a profession almost designed to erode circadian rhythm and common sense in equal measure.

"At least the APU can give us some air con," Koen said, and Sarah sighed, seeing that the outside temperature was

16 degrees according to the Met Office, but with the 737 still belching faint smoke as its right engine finally surrendered to the ceaseless attention of the fire crews. The foam was already hardening in the runway's cracks, reflecting the amber lights in ghostly, waxy streaks. A Heathrow tug, gruffly battered, lumbered past G-SPTT's nose, towing a line of cones to mark the latest perimeter of 'do not cross'. Sarah watched as a forlorn marshal, hands on hips, appeared to argue with the Britannia ramp supervisor, both men framed by a backdrop of vapour and blue strobes. It was farce of the highest order—modern aviation distilled to its purest form: precision planning unravelled by a nosewheel and the gods of statistical probability.

Koen was peering at his iPad, running the numbers again. "We're going to blow FTL if this goes past five," he muttered, as if it were a minor administrative bother and not a matter that would have them both grounded by law. "We can push until then, but it'll mean you and I both go out of hours before the return. We might have to call for a hotel at Ibiza, let the next crew ferry the bus home."

Sarah nodded, barely listening. Her mind, dulled by fatigue but sharpened by the kind of ambient tension that only pilots understood, was cycling through possibilities: alternate plans, duty time, how quickly the engineers might patch the tarmac, how Ops would react, and—inevitably—whether any of the passengers would become aggressive if the delay dragged on. She could see their faces in her mind: the boisterous stag groups, the couples desperate for sun, the sleep-deprived family with toddlers already fractious from the late hour.

She keyed her radio. "Heathrow Delivery, Margate 2321. Any update on when we'll get a tow back to stand?"

The answer, when it came, was as clipped as it was expected: "Margate 2321, negative on a tow for the next forty-five at minimum. Airside resources are with the incident on 27R. Remain at holding point Echo Nine. Further as soon as we have it."

Sarah let the radio's static hiss for a few seconds, the words "further as soon as we have it" echoing in her mind like a polite threat. At Heathrow, "forty-five minutes" always meant at least an hour and a half, and even then, only if nobody else had a worse day than you. She thumbed the push-to-talk again, thanked Delivery, and scribbled the time into her log. Koen didn't comment; he was already updating the flight plan, recalculating the fuel figures for a delay that would, inevitably, make the numbers even tighter for Ibiza.

She gazed out at the cartoonish spectacle across the field. The Britannia Connect 737, livery gleaming dully in the sodium wash, looked ever more like an enormous, wounded bird. Its nose, crumpled and abject, almost seemed to point accusingly back at the terminal as if blaming someone—anyone—for its predicament. The fire crew had begun wrapping up, withdrawing hoses and rolling foam-slick boots across the shimmering blacktop. In the background, a low chorus of beeps and idling engines was occasionally punctuated by the distant, tinny sound of a Tannoy in the terminal.

And it was annoying.

Especially as everything was up in the air.

Both literally and figuratively.

* _ * _ * _ *

An hour and half later, the runway was still closed.

The night had begun to pale, a faint indigo rim rising over the distant Thames, but the operational paralysis showed no sign of easing. Sarah had moved through the phases of waiting—practical, hopeful, resigned, slightly hysterical, and, finally, professionally numb. The Buy on Board, which had been loaded at Heathrow, was now nearly depleted, with all of the stock being brought out by passengers, the only items remaining being coffee and, for some weird reason, scotch. The vodka, beer, cider and even the weirdly popular Aperol spritz cans were gone, as if every stag, hen and weary budget traveller aboard had collectively agreed that dawn demanded nothing less than the full British Abroad experience. Somewhere aft of Row 23, an impromptu game of charades had broken out, periodically interrupted by a chorus of groans whenever a PA announcement fizzled into life promising "further information soon".

"Margate 2321, message from Ops," the radio crackled, the line distorted by the faint hiss of too many frequencies competing for space. Sarah clicked transmit, automatically sliding back into her clipped, professional cadence, the lilt of exhaustion giving her voice a brittle clarity. "Margate 2321, go ahead."

The controller's accent was London-neutral, pitched somewhere between harried and apologetic. "Ops advises a replacement crew is en route by road from Luton, however, are delayed due to traffic congestion on the M25. You are going to be towed to a T2 stand where a crew change will be performed. Your duty time will not permit further operation of this sector. You are advised to return to Manston by road. The replacement crew will take the aircraft onwards to Ibiza. Ops requests you brief your passengers accordingly and coordinate with the dispatcher on arrival at stand. We'll update you if anything changes. Apologies for the disruption."

Sarah let the radio handset drop gently against the pedestal, the metal-and-plastic weight making a tiny, tired clunk that sounded much louder than it should have done in the hush of the flight deck. She sat there a moment, drawing a steadying breath, eyes closed, feeling every hour of duty in the ache behind her eyes and the unyielding pressure between her shoulders.

The news was, as so often in this job, simultaneously a relief and a new annoyance. They would not be flying this leg. Their bodies, legally, could not be compelled into the air again tonight—or this morning, as the first hints of grey dawn now admitted. Yet it also meant the exhaustion and anti-climax of a disrupted finish. She felt the odd mixture of gratitude and resentment, the peculiar pilot's resentment that comes not from a love of flying denied, but from a sense of being a pawn in someone else's labyrinthine game. No clean arc to the shift, no clear badge of completion, just an endless handoff—machine, crew, passengers, all traded on a shifting ledger of timesheets, regulations, and other people's schedules.

Koen, characteristically, just nodded once, as if he'd expected nothing else. He exhaled deeply through his nose, slid the iPad away, and ran a hand through hair that was, in the emerging blue light, almost completely silver. "Right," he said, the word heavy with Northern stoicism and the odd comfort of an ending, however imperfect. "I'll let Marija know and get on the horn to the dispatcher. You want to take the PA? Your chance to deliver bad news with style."

Sarah smiled wanly, though her heart wasn't in it. She pressed the button and let the PA system buzz in her ear. "Ladies and gentlemen, it's First Officer Marsh on the flight deck. We've just had an update from both our Operations team and Heathrow ground staff. Due to ongoing delays and flight time regulations for our crew—basically, the law says we can't fly you to Ibiza without a rest period—a new crew are being sent to take the aircraft onwards. We'll shortly be towed to a stand at Terminal Two, where you'll remain on the aircraft. Once the new crew arrive, they'll continue with the flight as soon as possible. We do apologise for the delay and the disruption. We know it's not how any of us wanted to spend the small hours, and your patience is appreciated. Cabin crew will be around with more tea and coffee, and we'll keep you informed."

She released the switch and closed her eyes for a moment, letting the silence fill the cockpit. It was the strangest thing—how the act of making announcements, of giving bad news with as much empathy as you could muster, could almost leach the tension out of your body. You played your part, you shaped the chaos into words, and suddenly it was manageable again, at least for a few minutes.

Koen was already on the interphone, speaking quietly to Marija, who was responding in clipped, unflappable tones. The cabin, Sarah suspected, would be a rising sea of complaints, moans, queries and jokes, and her respect for cabin crew, already considerable, only deepened in moments like this. The art of shepherding 180 humans through the limbo of a terminal-bound delay, at 05:00 and short on gin and tonic, was surely worthy of its own mention in the Queen's Honours list.

She took a sip of the lukewarm coffee still at her elbow, grimacing as it struck her tongue with that peculiar bitterness of airport brew left to stew on the hotplate. The world outside was brightening by imperceptible degrees; the sodium glare was being diluted, the distant terminal buildings taking on their first true colours in months—off-white, patchy concrete, red Jetway paint, all more honest and less theatrical than the nightscape of the past hours.

For a moment, Sarah let her thoughts drift. The whole summer had been one long lesson in contingency. The old certainties of airline schedules, operational plans, crew rotations, were all a memory now, replaced by a daily lottery of delays, technical issues, wild weather, and—here, tonight—spectacular displays of mechanical failure and regulatory improvisation.

In a way, she thought, it was more honest than the supposed 'Golden Age' of flying that PanEuro preached. Here, at least, nobody could pretend the system was perfect. All anyone could do was make the best of what they had: a crew, a machine, a job to do, and the fortitude to see it through.

A faint knock at the door. The chime sounded. Koen flicked the switch, unlocking it, and Marija's head appeared, her dark blonde hair still immaculate after six hours on duty, her eyes as clear and direct as ever. "Ops called?" she asked, in the musical lilt of her native Lithuania, words clipped and to the point. "They are coming soon, yes?"

Sarah nodded. "Replacement crews are on the M25, somewhere between St Albans and purgatory. We're to be towed to T2. You and your team get to deal with the fallout." She managed a smile, though it was heavy with empathy. "Sorry, Marija."

Marija's lips twitched in a smile. "Passengers will complain. They will complain if we land, they will complain if we stay here. At least now we have daylight. No one sleeps in daylight on a stag trip."

Marija then sighed, glancing out the windscreen, her eyes flicking to the battered Britannia 737, still being scrutinised by engineers and airport staff as if it might suddenly leap up and try to taxi away in shame. "I will make more coffee. And I will ration the Scotch. Only British people drink Scotch for breakfast. It will be all gone by 06:00."

Koen chuckled, a sound as gravelly as ever. "Save me a drop, will you, Marija? I'm not proud."

She grinned, and with a nod, retreated to the galley, her presence as solid and comforting as a warm blanket in the dawn chill.

* _ * _ * _ *

Ten hours later, the Air Accident Investigation Branch had already announced the cause of the incident, and, like on the 5th of November 1997, when Virgin Atlantic Flight 024 had run its A340 off the far end of Heathrow's runway, the cause was a classic blend of mechanical failure and poor decision-making.

The AAIB's preliminary bulletin, as Sarah read it in the Birchington flat she had leased, not far, she knew from her friend, Hayley Northcott, and her Broadstairs family home, had made for sobering, if predictable, reading. The nose gear assembly—already suspect thanks to an incomplete maintenance log and a missed Service Bulletin from the Tunisian maintenance provider—had catastrophically failed after the unrestrained end of a brake torque rod became trapped in the keel beam structure within the nose bay.

The sudden collapse under the full weight of the decelerating 737 sent the nosewheel strut shearing sideways and then downwards, punching a dinner-plate-sized hole through the tarmac, instantly grounding the aircraft and causing a slow-motion ballet of sparks and debris, all captured on a dozen mobile phones and, inevitably, livestreamed onto TikTok before most of the Heathrow fire crews had even reached their boots.

The report, briskly written and already being torn to pieces on every pilot WhatsApp and Reddit forum, laid out the facts in the unsparing tone of the technical: "Probable cause—loss of structural integrity in the nose gear due to undetected component failure, exacerbated by deferred maintenance and incomplete documentation from the contracted provider".

`Sarah had read those lines twice, not out of disbelief but with the slightly morbid satisfaction that comes when reality confirms the suspicions of the exhausted and the cynical. "The operator," the bulletin continued, "was in possession of insufficient records to demonstrate compliance with the manufacturer's bulletins. Contributing factors: crew's late report of abnormal vibration on approach, and ineffective last-minute troubleshooting from maintenance."

It was a case study in modern ultra-low-cost aviation—a system stretched so taut by bottom-line economics that even the most basic redundancies became wishful thinking. Britannia Connect would, in the next days, be pilloried by tabloids and aviation blogs alike. A grainy photo of the crumpled nose, backlit by dawn, would run above the fold, just below a headline designed to invoke both outrage and schadenfreude. The reality, as ever, was quieter, sadder, and more routine: poor communication, stretched engineers, a chain of tiny decisions leading, inevitably, to the spectacle on 27R.

But for Sarah, sat now with her legs curled under her on the grey faux-leather sofa, the drama was receding. The adrenaline of the night had been replaced with a leaden weariness—a sensation that went bone-deep and settled behind the eyes like a long-haul hangover. She stared at the blue light filtering through half-closed blinds, the heat of the mid-July afternoon pressing in, and wondered, not for the first time, how anyone could love this job and not go slightly mad.

Suddenly her mobile phone rang and, looking at it, she recognised the number: Max, calling from Berlin, where, according to the latest Sprint Air app notification, his rotation had finally ended in a string of thunderstorms, a temporary diversion, and, for good measure, a suspected lightning strike on short final.

She answered with a grunt, not trusting her voice.

"Sarah?" Max's tone was light, the background noise an indistinct hum of crew-room voices and suitcase wheels on tile. "You alive?"

"Just about." She cradled the phone between her chin and shoulder, staring blearily at the mug on the coffee table— a relic from Gatwick, chipped and adorned with a fading cartoon of a 747. "Did you see the AAIB report?"

He gave a low whistle. "Read it before I got off the bus. What a bloody circus. Heard Britannia's going to try and blame Tunisair. Ops says our 3am stags are now going to Stansted for the next week. All the hen dos are being rebooked via Paris. Apparently, it's an 'opportunity for brand realignment'."

Sarah snorted. "Meaning what? Now we serve wine in paper cups instead of gin in tins?"

"Don't laugh," Max replied. "It'll be wine powder soon, if the bean counters have their way. You look like hell, by the way. I mean that lovingly."

She smiled, the fatigue softening just a touch at the warmth in his voice. "You'd look worse if you'd spent the night breathing in APU exhaust and being yelled at by 180 people who think a nose gear collapse is a conspiracy to ruin their party."

He was quiet a moment. She could almost hear him shifting the phone to his other ear. "You all right, Marsh?"

Sarah considered lying, but fatigue had a way of stripping away the easy half-truths. "Honestly? Knackered. Frustrated. A bit proud we kept it together. And—" she hesitated, surprised at her own candour "—I don't know. There's something about this summer. It's like the whole industry's coming apart at the seams and we're just holding the stitches together with tape and coffee."

Max was silent, and then, in his softest voice: "I get it. You're doing better than most, you know."

Sarah smiled, feeling the tension in her shoulders ease a little. "I'll live. You get any sleep?"

He chuckled. "An hour, if I'm lucky. Got one of those German pensioner groups out of TFS—every one of them wanted to tell me about the war. One old boy gave me a Werther's Original and told me I looked like his nephew. I'll take it as a compliment."

"Take the win," she advised, glancing at her own reflection in the window—a pale, tousled figure with the haunted eyes of the perpetually delayed. "I should try for another hour's kip before I go out for food. Call me if you're routed through London tomorrow?"

"Will do. Marsh?"

"Yeah?"

"Proud of you."

She grinned, a small, private thing. "You too, Detweiler. Get some rest."

The call ended, and Sarah slumped back on the sofa, phone pressed to her chest, feeling the gentle, arrhythmic thud of her heart as if it belonged to someone else.

Sarah's summer was far from over, and so was the story for every Sprint, PanEuro, and Britannia crew across Europe. In aviation, there's always another rotation, another crisis, another morning queue at Crew Room 2. For now, though, the logbook is closed. Tomorrow, someone else will take the controls.

****

Books by Thomas Brant

Broadcasting Boundaries
BROADCASTING BOUNDARIES
BROADCASTING CHAOS
BROADCASTING DISRUPTION

The Wirral Gal
THE WIRRAL GAL... IN SPEKE
THE WIRRAL GAL... NOW A MAM

Fallen
IRELAND IS DOWN

PanEuro
STICK AND LIPSTICK
SPRINTER OF THE SKIES

Standalone Manic Novels
THE BROOKES BABES
THE DAY THE QUEEN DIED
VIXEN
THE MANIC COLLECTIVE CANDIDATE